CW00470903

"Remember the dec

DEAD CITY EXIT

A James Stack Novel

The ultimate race-against-time thriller

They lied to him.
James Stack, ex captain, special forces, is
blackmailed by British SIS into recovering a top-
secret, edge-of-science device abandoned in the
most violent city in North Africa. But he was
tricked. The Topaz device was already in the hands
of hard-line extremists. Stack has just hours to
prevent them using it in a terrible ultimatum
against a major European city.

Mark Wesley

DEAD CITY EXIT

Published by Mark Wesley
Text © Mark Wesley 2019

A word from the author

In this story I have revived an old security department designation known as MI8. Its brief during the second world war was to intercept, locate and close down illicit wireless stations operated either by enemy agents in Great Britain or by other persons under Defence Regulations, 1939. Later, the department was integrated into MI6.

My story entails the deployment of highly secret new technology for similar purposes and so the reinstatement of the old MI8 designation seemed appropriate.

Where do story ideas come from? All writers are asked this question. It's hard to say. For the last two novels, BANGK! and FRACK! *out of thin air* seems to be the answer. However, for DEAD CITY EXIT two sources can be traced. The first, a newspaper story about a covert National Crime Agency unit that had been chased out of Tripoli by the Nawasi Brigade. The second was a report in newspapers and science journals some years ago that intrigued me and suggested a possible conspiracy that would make a juicy story-line.

That's how this yarn begins...

BREAKING NEWS

September 2011

Source: *Scientific American, Daily Telegraph, The Guardian*

An Italian experiment carried out by the Gran Sasso National Laboratory in Italy, studied a beam of neutrinos coming from the CERN high-energy physics laboratory 730 kilometres away near the city of Geneva, Switzerland. They discovered that neutrinos can break the most fundamental rule of modern physics — that they are able to travel faster than the speed of light.

This raised the intriguing possibility of a way to send information back in time, blurring the line between past and present.

Later, in an embarrassing turnaround, the team in Italy found that a cable had not been screwed in correctly, causing what turned out to be a false reading. This avenue of research was abruptly abandoned.

Switzerland: CERN: Meeting Room 7b

' Just sign it.'
The American leaned across the table and nudged the paper another inch towards the Italian scientist.

'This is ten years work. You can't expect me to just walk away from it,' the Italian said.

He sat there, arms folded, refusing to look at the single page document. On either side of him, his fellow scientists were still reeling from the terrible demand that had just been made, their eyes fixed angrily on the two government men opposite.

The younger woman on the Italian's left was struggling to keep calm. She was by nature a passionate person ready to defend her point of view with prickly resolve, but something about the two men facing her, with their icy business-like certainty, made her hold her fire.

'What is in this document?' she asked, her German accent heavy with irritation.

The room became almost silent apart from the breathy hiss from the AC vent above them. Dim winter sunlight splashed a pallid yellow brightness that filtered through the half open Venetian blinds, adding little cheer to the bleak fluorescent lighting. The two officials leaned back in their chairs; their winter coats unbuttoned to reveal similar but not identical dark suits. Their hair differentiated them. One was almost bald with only a horse shoe of black strands remaining. He'd grown a thick moustache to compensate. The other had a full head, blonde, but short, like a buzz cut.

Buzz cut glanced at the man sitting next to him and nodded almost imperceptibly. His balding colleague took a long slow breath and glanced indifferently at his watch as though time was of no importance. He wasted another moment, pretending to appreciate the partially hidden view of the snow-capped mountain landscape way beyond the confines of the research campus.

The Italian blinked first.

'It is already out there,' he said, breaking the silence. 'As soon as we had confirmed our findings, we published in all the journals. I spoke directly to the team in America. Others are involved now.'

'We can't put this back in the box,' the anxious Frenchman on his right said. 'It is like the Manhattan Project, once the bomb went bang the atoms could not be repacked back into the uranium core.' He held his hands out in an appeal. 'This is obvious, no?'

Another short silence followed. Eventually the bald guy spoke with the clipped cadence of an ex-British military officer.

'The document is merely a summary of what we have already told you.' His tone became bored. 'Just sign it and do as you have been instructed. Time is running out.'

The three quantum physicists facing him shifted uncomfortably in their chairs, tempers barely under control. No one made a move towards the treacherous sheet of A4 lying innocently at their elbows.

'I remind you that your careers are at risk. All funding for future projects will be withdrawn,' the British government man said grimly. 'Sign and I guarantee you will become the best funded team at CERN.'

'We are not based here at CERN,' the German said. 'We work at the National Laboratory in Italy.'

'OK, the best funded research team in Italy. But just not for this project.'

Buzz cut broke in with an appeal to reason. 'Look guys, I get it. No one wants to walk away from years of work,' he said looking first at the Brit sitting next to him but then turning to the agitated group across the table. 'But, there could be an opportunity to work with my team in the States... maybe.'

'Or in the UK,' the Brit countered irritably. 'Either way you will post the retraction. It never happened. The results were flawed. Use whatever words you like but kill it. Today!'

The inevitability of their situation began to dawn on the Italian. They were cornered but he wasn't going down without a fight.

'But the findings are correct. There are no flaws in the calculations. We repeated it many times and got the same results. How on earth can an experienced and respected team like ours be expected to simply throw it all away. We cannot justify this.'

'That's right,' the German added. 'But it's not just our reputation. It is the catastrophic loss of irreplaceable knowledge. All the work...'

'We are only at the beginning,' the Frenchman cut in impatiently. 'Who knows where this will take science?'

They all began fighting back noisily. Desperately appealing to reason. A futile last stand against the inevitable. A loud crash silenced them abruptly as the British official slammed his fist down hard on the table.

'Enough! It's over. It ends here, now!' He checked his watch. 'Our people are already at your laboratory in Italy. By now your files will have been sequestered and packed ready for shipment.'

'Shipment? Shipment to where? You are an American and an Englishman. All of us here in this room, we are not your enemies. Why are you stealing our work?' The Italian scientist said, 'What possible use could you make of it? It is all theoretical. Only a scientific principle has been proven.'

'This is correct, no?' the French researcher said. 'You steal our work and we are made to look like fools.'

The American ignored the Frenchman's objections. 'Write the retraction. Say it was a mistake.'

'A mistake!' the Frenchman said, incredulous at the idea.

'OK, not a mistake. An error. Equipment failure.'

'What would you suggest?' the Italian sneered 'The particles were past their sell-by date? Somebody jogged my arm as I entering the results? A wire came loose?'

The others laughed at the absurdity.

'A wire came loose.' the American decided. 'Or maybe a cable wasn't screwed in tightly enough. You tightened it and the results changed on the next test.'

'Use that,' the Brit demanded. 'Write it up. I want to see you post the retraction now. Nobody's fault. Equipment failure. A genuine technical problem. Apologies all round.'

'Let's get it done,' the American said as he stood up and walked around the table to stand behind the three scientists. 'Then we can get out of here and you and your team can move on to the next Nobel Prize-winning project.'

The Brit pulled a pen out of his pocket and rolled it across the table to the Italian.

The American leaned over the scientist's shoulder. 'Just sign it. Then open your laptop and post your retraction to the world-wide scientific community. Tell them Einstein was right after all, nothing can travel faster than light.'

Libya: Five Years Later

You might think it was the suffocating heat that caused the greatest discomfort, but that was to be expected. You learned to live with it. Dust was the biggest problem. Dust and sand. For the average Libyan, or any North African, so what? It's how life was in those desert regions. There are bigger problems. Dust and sand come way down the list.

Right at the top of a 'Top 50 Things That Screw Up Your Day in Libya' TV countdown show, are the countless trouble making militia groups who form the two factions that have divided the country in a devastating civil war that followed the fall of Gaddafi. The ongoing collateral carnage is what puts them at the top of local problems in Tripoli.

It was much the same for other coastal towns like Benghazi and Tobruk where Russia had begun trying to finesse some political elbowroom. But it was even worse for Sirte, a former Islamic State stronghold that was bombed to rubble in a bid to remove them. Some still remain to cause trouble. More are coming back.

Second in the countdown is the ineffectual Government of National Accord that was supposed to run the show in Libya. If they could get agreement from the special interest groups who have carved out regions for themselves across the country, Libya just might stand a chance. Until then, it remains a virtually ungovernable, failed state.

On the other hand, if you are not native to North Africa, the fine, gritty dust and sand goes right to the top of the list of irritations. It gets everywhere.

***

'Got another sat-com from Eight.'

Major Susan Hedgeland wandered through the door that divided their second-floor quarters into two cramped rooms. She read the text from her phone. 'There's been another spike in coms output from our target in Sirte.' She looked up from the satellite phone. 'Looks like 'Chatterbox' has been busy again. They want to know when we're going to be back on-line?'

'Christ's sake, Sue. Tell them we've all gone on holiday and we'll be back in two weeks.'

As one of the two scientists trained for covert operations, Steve Patterson was allowed some slack, though his constant pessimistic griping drove the major crazy. He was working through a gap in the crude box-shaped bed sheet canopy they'd rigged over the table. Just visible through it was the mess of components he was working on, and on the floor, the aluminium flightcase into which the parts were all supposed to be assembled. It was obvious the dust problem was worse this time. Before, they'd had the thing up and running after a day or so. But this was taking longer. Almost a week.

Hedgeland had moved over to the table where an ancient electric fan whirred noisily as it panned slowly back and forth. She offered her face to the meagre air wafting listlessly through its tin blades. It didn't really do much. It just moved the foetid air around for maybe a yard or two while the blades pinged against their wire cage.

She shook her head. Though she was in charge of the operation, the technology was way beyond her understanding of physics. She could lift and carry stuff. Maybe even fix some of the sub-primary circuits but other than that, compared to Patterson, she was just a first grader in a twelfth grade year – outclassed and in the way. She gave up on the fan and wandered over to the window.

'Chris is taking his time,' she murmured as she checked up and down the bustling market in the street below. 'Should've been back by now.'

She scanned the historic quarter of Tripoli's ancient city. To the south, the dazzling vista of white-washed houses and red roofs, separated by alleyways, courtyards and a handful of minarets. In the other direction, a few blocks to the north, the distant blue glint of the Mediterranean Sea was interrupted by the tops of rusting cranes and the occasional bridge of a cargo ship marooned forlornly in the old harbour. Very little was coming in or going out these days, except for the small rubber dinghies crammed to sinking with the tired and desperate escaping the crushing poverty and endless conflicts of the lands to the south. They paid not just with their money, but very often – too often – with their lives, for a chance to reach the promised land; a dangerous sea journey, a hundred miles or so due north.

'This was never going to be ideal, Major.' Patterson had turned away from the cotton canopy, rigged in a vain attempt to protect the strange, laboratory-like collection of parts from the powdery dust. 'We need to be much closer to Sirte.'

The major had heard that complaint so often she ignored it. Sirte was trouble. Only if lives depended on it would they attempt to go in there to get a closer, cleaner contact.

'We've been here for two months now and that bloody thing has functioned on and off for about half that time. The intermittency is increasing. Is it just dust contamination? Or do you think it's a bigger problem with the technology?'

Patterson thought about that for a moment.

'The whole bloody shooting match is still not much more than an experiment. We had it working reliably, but that was in perfect conditions. It's the miniaturisation. Nobody had foreseen how operations in these environments could affect it. This canopy helps a bit, but the dust is like a fine powder. I can clean most of it, but eventually, over time, it's making an already weak contact, weaker. We need to be closer.'

'Well, it could change very quickly If the GNA Army is successful, our target could be forced to retreat south into the desert. That would be significantly further than Sirte and probably even more dangerous.'

'You mean we'd have to move out of this luxury accommodation?' Patterson said casting his eyes around their primitive rooms.

He got up and walked over to the small corner kitchen area and poured himself another cup of coffee, the colour and consistency of crude oil.

'Just get on and fix that bloody...' Hedgeland searched for a word, '...machine.'

As she spoke, Chris Bailey, the third member of the team eased quietly through the front door.

'Right now it's just another failed, over-budget government contract,' he whispered. 'But when the bloody thing works it's called Topaz, remember? Temporal Off-set by Pulsed Asymmetrical Z-bosons? Trips right off the tongue doesn't it? And keep it down, there's a new lot moved in downstairs. They look the ultra-conservative type. They'll be up and down like a whore's drawers five times a day for the call to prayers.'

'That's all we need,' Patterson said, his voice a little quieter. 'Help me get this lot back together. I think I've got most of it.'

'We should look for a new location. We're pushing our luck here.' Hedgeland said.

'I'll get on to it tomorrow.' Bailey suggested. 'I'll talk to Faruk, see what he can find.'

'No, I'll do it,' Hedgeland insisted. 'You two are needed here, covering the target.'

They were all talking in subdued voices now.

'Don't forget major, it still has to be within spitting distance of the main servers of Libya Telecom,' Bailey said. 'If you can get closer than we are now, great, but not further away. We're already at the limits of a functioning stream.'

'But you could make the stream stronger, couldn't you?' Hedgeland reasoned. 'Increase the power?'

'Theoretically, there is some margin. A bit of headroom,' Bailey said. 'But here, in Tripoli, with unreliable servers and old land lines, we could burn out the entire local network. It's best if we don't push it.'

'Anyway, we're getting good results when it works,' Patterson said.

Hedgeland sat morosely on a chair by the window.

'Yes, when it works. So, what shall I tell London?'

'Allow another couple of hours to reassemble. Tell 'em maybe tonight,' Patterson offered thoughtfully. 'Dust willing,' he added.

The low wattage lamp over the table flickered a couple of times, dimmed, over-brightened for a moment, then pinged off leaving the room lit only by the glow of the afternoon light coming through the grimy windows.

Bailey chipped back in cynically.

'Yeah, and while you're looking for another luxury penthouse suite tomorrow, make sure it has some reliable power too.'

***

It was past noon the following day. Hot, damp humidity caused her cloths to cling like shrink wrap. She always felt vulnerable out in the streets of the old city, even in a hijab and her face loosely covered by a scarf. It would only take a curl of blonde hair to give her away.

She tried not to appear furtive and strode purposefully through the busy souk towards the place where she had arranged to meet Faruk. It was just ahead, by the next junction where the narrow thoroughfare she was in crossed an even smaller alley.

When she arrived, she was surprised that Faruk wasn't already there waiting, checking his watch, ready to admonish her for her tardiness and putting him at risk. He had a point. It was a very big risk he was taking in a country where allies switched sides with little conscience, and allegiances were marketable commodities.

He was paid well, but if any of the competing jihadi groups or local militia got wind of his connection as a go-between for the British and other western operatives in western Libya, no amount of money could save him.

She was late, and he wasn't there. That was the point. No matter the risk, he would have waited.

Perhaps he'd been delayed? It had happened once before. She'd been worried then. She found out later he'd been in an accident, nothing major, two cars collide. You can't drive away from the scene of an accident in a street choked with automobiles. Very few were current models. Most were old, North African favourites; Toyotas, Hyundai's, Mercedes, and Fords, all jetting acrid blue smoke out of oil burning engines, their owners blasting their horns impatiently. With no space to manoeuvre in the crowded streets of a city like Tripoli, it was just a two-way procession of battered old cars that had come to a standstill because of you. Money fixed the problem as always, though by then it was too late. A phone call had arranged a new time. But that was it. Just the once.

He was never late.

She turned at the sound of a car approaching from behind. The noisy high revving engine of a Hyundai Avante weaving down the narrow alley at speed. Before it reached her, she was grabbed from behind and pushed towards the oncoming vehicle. She grabbed the arm of her assailant, pushed her hips into his stomach and heaved him not quite over her shoulder, but enough to throw him backside down onto the ground. His head hit the bumper of the car as it came to a halt with doors swinging open. The narrow alley made it difficult for the passenger to squeeze out, but a gun drawn and aimed at her from the driver's side forced her to rethink her next move.

Her gun was hidden underneath the folds of her long robe. There was no way she could reach it in time. She started to raise her arms in fake surrender but turned quickly to escape towards the busy junction. Before she had taken two steps, the guy on the floor had recovered and was trying to grab her feet. She turned and gave him a hard kick to the head. He fell backwards still holding her shoe.

Hedgeland figured that because the guy with the gun hadn't fired, this was what the team had been trained to avoid at all costs - a kidnap attempt. Getting to the busy market street just a few yards away might give her a small, life-saving chance to disappear into the crowd.

She pushed herself hard, like a hundred metre sprinter straining for the finishing tape. Just a couple more steps...

***

The thin rap on the door surprised Patterson and Bailey. They both stopped what they were doing and looked at each other.

'Susan?' Bailey whispered hopefully.

It had been over 24 hours since she had gone missing.

Patterson shrugged a 'maybe'. Bailey got up and quietly crossed the room, trying to smother the metallic snick as he gently eased back the slide mechanism of his Browning semi to load a 9mm round into the chamber. Patterson had turned from the table and sat with his gun ready on his lap. He nodded for Bailey to open the door.

Bailey slowly turned the old brass handle, which squealed just a little as the latch pulled out against the plate. He stood to one side, the wall protecting him as he threw the door open.

'Faruk!'

Or someone who used to look like Faruk. He was in a bad way but tried to speak. Bailey grabbed him as he fell forward. With Faruk's arm over his shoulder to support his weight, Bailey walked him across the room and sat him on a chair.

Patterson had come over to help, shocked at their Libyan friend's condition. He'd been severely beaten. His face bruised and battered. His nose looked broken. One eye closed and bleeding. Blood stains covered his clothes. His body had taken a battering too. He was protecting his chest, which meant some ribs were probably fractured. His voice came in short whispered gasps as he tried to speak.

'What is he trying to say?' Patterson said. 'Get him some water.'

Bailey raised the glass tumbler to Faruk's mouth, but very little water passed through his painfully swollen lips.

Faruk tried to speak, his voice faint and rasping.

'They've taken the major...' He took another painful, shallow breath and tried again as Bailey and Patterson leaned closer.

'They've got Susan.'

***

They had expected Major Hedgeland to be back before dark which gave them several hours to set up and tune the equipment.

They found the target in Sirte as soon as he started using the internet. With each outgoing communication from 'Chatterbox', the MI8 team in the shabby second floor rooms in Tripoli sent a Topaz pulse, in a pre-emptive event that shifted the target signal and the message it contained just a few nanoseconds forward in time, and there it remained – invisible to everyone except the target. To the terrorists hidden in one of the few habitable buildings in the bombed-out town of Sirte, according to the screen on their laptop, the message had been posted. But to the world outside – nothing. Only Patterson and Bailey knew what the contents of the messages were and these they passed on by satellite phone to the MI8 micro-department in London. The strange, time-shifting device had given London a critical edge at last in the inflammatory, propaganda war waged by the many groups that claimed to represent Islamic State.

So intense was their attention as they worked, they hadn't noticed the passage of time. Hedgeland had set out to meet Faruk hours ago. It was dark before they realised she hadn't returned. And another anxious hour before they guessed she was probably in trouble. There'd been no reply from Faruk's cell phone when they had tried calling, though Hedgeland's gave a bleep that could have been an attempt to answer it. Bailey and Patterson took it in turns to check the local streets, one staying behind in case Hedgeland turned up. Again, nothing.

They waited until 8pm local before giving London the news. London wasn't happy.

***

Faruk was laid out on a bed in the other room. He had passed out for a while, but as he regained consciousness, though still weak, he was eager to talk.

It turned out the kidnap was purely mercenary. A western woman was a great prize. Plucked from the streets to be bartered for money. A rogue group within a notorious local militia known as the Nawasi Brigade held her. Faruk was the messenger sent to pass on their terms. This was almost good news. If it had come from Daesh supporting extremists, it would have been a death sentence. Nonetheless, the Nawasi Brigade was made up of many different radical groups, each of whom were dangerous and unpredictable. The mess they'd made of Faruk was part of the message, signalling they were serious and Hedgeland's life was in danger.

'Five hundred thousand dollars,' Faruk said.

'How do they want it paid?' asked Patterson, ignoring the huge figure.

'A bank account,' Faruk whispered. He searched in his clothes for something, then pushed himself painfully up from the bed using his elbow. His hand trembled as he reached out and handed Patterson a cell phone.

'They will call you on this. They will give you an account number. Not a bank. Something different. They said you will have 24 hours to pay.' He fell back onto the bed exhausted. A bubbling breath came from him as his eyes closed and he lost consciousness again.

Patterson turned to Bailey and shook his head slowly.

'Five hundred thousand dollars. Where are we going to get that kind of money and in twenty-four hours?'

He and Bailey walked through into the other room.

'London won't pay a ransom,' Bailey said. 'The major is stuffed.'

Patterson thought about that for a moment and walked to the table where the bed-sheet canopy hung protectively over the aluminium flightcase, now loaded with the reassembled parts. The case was arranged on its side with the lid removed and the controls, such as they were, facing the operator. A wire from the unit led to a laptop on the table next to it and another to a telecoms port on the wall. A mains cable took power from a nearby socket.

Patterson sat on the chair and turned to give the Topaz device his full attention as he considered another possibility.

'You know, Chris, we might be able to do both.'

'Both? Both what?' Bailey said.

'Give them the money – but not give them the money.'

Grand Cayman

The barracuda came out of the water a couple of times, fighting and shimmying before diving back, into the clear Caribbean Sea. It plunged deep to where the water turned as indigo as night. Even so, it couldn't escape. James Stack knew where it was. The fine, fluorocarbon line, humming with the fierce tension of the fight, pointed to it through the white laced wake of the charter boat as it motored steadily ahead.

Safely harnessed into the swivel chair bolted to the stern of the vessel, Stack wound more of the line in after each strenuous pull of the rod, bent now in an impossible whip-shaped curve. With each pull the fish was dragged closer, occasionally becoming visible as a rippling shape just below the waves, its dorsal fins breaking the surface and then diving back down again. Shorter intervals now, and not so deep as more of the line got spooled back onto the reel.

The captain was standing by ready to pull the fish on board with an evil looking long handled fish hook.

Weakened from the effort of the long struggle, the barracuda surfaced just metres from the stern. Stack swivelled the chair ninety degrees, dragging the fish away from the blades of the twin Yamaha outboards.

One last strength-draining heave as he wound the reel to take up the last of the line and the barracuda was finally pulled clear of the water, dangling helpless and exhausted. The occasional defiant flip of its tail showed it still had some fight left.

Stack's arms trembled from the effort of the long fight and quickly weakened now there was no water to support the creature's forty-pound weight. The captain raised the pole ready to stab the fish with the hook but Stack shouted for him to grab hold of it with his hands instead and take some of the weight.

'We'll just pull him in, take a picture and throw him back,' Stack said.

'This is a very aggressive species of fish, Mr Stack,' Captain Samuels shouted to his client, as he grabbed the fish by the gills. 'He may seem quiet now, but he still got a lot o' fight in him. It might be better if I just hook him in. There are plenty more where he come from.'

The twin Yamahas had slowed to a stop causing the charter vessel to wallow freely in the long swell. The barracuda swung with the motion of the boat, occasionally slamming against the side of the vessel with a dull thud. It convulsed and flapped. Still fighting. Still undefeated.

'That's a big sorry fish, nearly a metre and a half I'd say. Those teeth will tear a chunk out o' you if you're not careful, Mr Stack,' Samuels said.

The mate took the other side and they both struggled and heaved as the unwieldy, thrashing creature finally slid over the side, bucking and flapping, onto the wooden deck.

Free of the harness, Stack carefully unhooked the fishing line and between him and the mate, lifted the barracuda up and arranged it in an awkward pose in his arms. This was by far the biggest catch since he'd taken up sea fishing nearly two weeks ago and he wanted a picture to prove it. Something to show a disapproving Summer and a cynical Charlie 'Hollywood' Dawson, his two close friends and associates. Though, to be truthful, the very beautiful Summer Peterson was a little more than an associate and quite a bit more than a friend.

It was just as tricky getting the fish back over the side without lumps being taken out of them. Eventually though, the barracuda fell with a tail beating belly flop back into the warm Caribbean Sea and, with a flash of silver, quickly disappeared into the depths.

Later, as the Luhrs thirty-four foot charter boat pounded the swell back to George Town, Stack and the captain cracked a couple of bottles of ice cold beers together. A toast to the big game trophy captured in high definition on Stack's smartphone.

The picture showed the barracuda being supported between a smiling sea captain in his peaked white cap and orange t-shirt emblazoned with his fishing business logo, and the sun-tanned arms of his six-foot client, James Stack.

In his mid-thirties, Stack wore his dark hair short and unfussy, framing a weather-tanned face that displayed gentle laugh lines when he smiled. A retired army captain who lead a formidable Special Forces squad in Afghanistan, he bore the intelligent but compassionate face of a man who had spent years in command. A fierce determination showed in eyes the colour of dark chocolate. A man who was easy to like and slow to anger. Many had misinterpreted his easy-going charm and found that when pushed to violence it would have been wiser to have walked away.

The smartphone image also revealed that James Stack was beginning to take to this lazy, island life.

***

It had been two weeks since Stack, Charlie and Summer Peterson returned from the UK after the drama of the shale gas sabotage. But, given such a beguiling tropical location, it wasn't hard to see why they had so quickly settled back into the seductive rhythm of Cayman Island life.

The hotels were still busy with late summer vacationers. The warm blue sea that curled lazily onto Seven Mile Beach was in a permanent playful rush hour. Jet ski's buzzed and Wave Runners skipped noisily at high speed across the tops of the ocean swell. Further out, Hobie twin-hulls languished forlornly, their sails limp in the still, humid air, while just yards from the water's edge, canoeists paddled and swimmers splashed.

Away from the water, along the length of the white coral beach, towering modern hotels formed a multi-story barrier to the third world reality of the island.

On the sandy apron in front of them, guests enjoyed ice-cool drinks at tables placed in the shade of palm trees, their giant fronds swaying gently in the brilliant tropical sunlight. And in the background, a constant rhythm of Caribbean music could be heard playing from a bar somewhere further along the beach.

'OK, that's a big fish,' Hollywood said as he dragged his chair closer to the table to get a better look at the image on Stack's smartphone. 'I'll buy you a beer on the strength of that, Jim. Summer? Same again?'

Summer was relaxing contentedly in her chair, enjoying the gentle embrace of the sultry afternoon heat as she drifted in and out of sleep. Her hat was tipped down a little to shade her eyes from the sun that somehow always managed to find a gap through the fat palm leaves. But she had another reason for wanting to appear detached from the conversation at that moment.

'No, I'm fine thanks, Hollywood,' she murmured without opening her eyes.

'You should see this bloody great fish he's pulled out of the water, Summer,' Charlie said. 'Go on Jim, show her that picture.'

'Charlie, I really don't want to see it. The poor bloody creature shouldn't have to suffer that kind of indignity just to be a trophy in a photograph.' Summer was being as principled as ever, and not letting Stack forget it.

'Please yourself.' A man of endless enthusiasm, Charlie turned to the brunette sitting next to him. 'Maddy, take a look,' he said, keen to include the woman he regarded as his girlfriend. 'Bloody great barracuda.'

Madeleine Clark carried her ethics lightly.

'Charlie's right, James, that is one hell of a big catch. What was it, thirty, forty pounds?'

In deference to Summer's principles, Stack chose to make less of it.

'Yes probably.' He quickly changed the subject. 'A beer for me, Charlie.'

Maddy handed the cell phone back to Stack.

'Me too. Not beer. I'll have a chilled white wine this time. Make sure the glass is frosted, Charlie,' she shouted as Charlie wandered barefoot across the hot sand to the straw roofed Tiki bar. While he was away, Stack took the opportunity to talk to Maddy.

'You and Charlie seem to be getting on OK.'

'You sound surprised,' Maddy said.

'No, not surprised. Charlie's a nice guy, but...'

'But what?' Maddy said acidly. There was a challenge in her tone.

Stack paused for a moment and studied Madeleine. She was a forthright mature woman, probably a little older than Charlie and Charlie was a wiry thirty-eight. Barely five-foot-tall, she packed a short fuse that could light fires. In another situation, 'cougar' might be how others would describe her. Confident. Independently wealthy? She seemed to have no shortage of cash. Urbane and metropolitan. She claimed to be in advertising and PR, but as far a Stack could recall, she had not referred to that occupation again since day one.

For some reason that was still not clear to Stack, she was travelling alone but appeared to take no interest in any of the other more likely candidates for companionship that might otherwise have attracted someone like her. He realised as soon as he'd thought it, that he had no way of proving that last point, but she had made a beeline for Charlie from the very beginning and for nearly two weeks now she had stuck to him like glue. No, not just him. To the three of them.

Was that it? Stack wondered. Was she using Charlie as a means – an excuse – to be with the three of them?

It's not unusual for that to happen. People on holiday find themselves stuck with a stranger who they can't seem to shake off. An interesting first couple of days, but soon their conversation starts to thin out and you find yourself looking for ways to avoid them. Very awkward and irritating.

But Madeleine Clark was different. Her interest had been directed at Charlie who, despite his friendship with Stack and Summer, was lonely. Or was he lonely because of Stack and Summer? Their romantic relationship reminded Charlie of his separateness. The awkward 'crowd' in a group of three. A gooseberry, very ripe for picking. As far as Stack knew there hadn't been anyone in his life since the wife he divorced years ago in Scotland.

'But – nothing,' he said to Maddy. 'If you guys are happy, I'm happy.'

Summer was still relaxing in her chair with the hat shading her eyes, but she was listening. Paying attention. She and Stack had had this conversation privately. They both shared the same concerns and doubts about the mysterious Maddy.

And then of course there was the 'call this number' message from Blackstone only a day after they'd arrived back in Grand Cayman. It had put them on the alert. Blackstone – the shadowy figure who moved amongst the upper reaches of the financial institutions of the City of London. A man Stack had yet to meet, but who had both helped and hindered Stack's life with his Machiavellian ability to influence the great and the good to his advantage. Stack had been the beneficiary of Blackstone's manipulative skills, although on the last occasion, he had very nearly ruined him financially. The sale of shares in the drilling company, GeoPower, were finally replenishing his Cayman Island bank account, but it was a very close thing. That unwanted investment got very close to going bust.

Blackstone was an impatient man, used to an instant, unquestioned response to his demands. When Stack finally reached him after tapping out the unique number given in his 'call this number' message, Blackstone was his usual abrupt, pompous self.

'It's been twenty-four hours.' He had said irritably.

'Tough. What do you want?' Stack hadn't been looking forward to making this call. Blackstone's supercilious tone made his skin crawl.

'There may be something you should be concerned about, Stack...'

'I'm listening.'

'A government security department appears to have taken an interest in you. Did you spot anything before you flew out? At Heathrow for instance?'

'No, nothing as far as I can remember. Should I be worried?'

'I don't know. I can't get any further on this. For you to be flagged up though, is cause for concern. They may be tracking you beyond the UK.'

'I appreciate your concern for my welfare, Blackstone. What's in it for you?'

'It's just the milk of human kindness that courses through my veins,' Blackstone said dryly. Then his tone changed. 'You're useful to me. I don't want you out of circulation.'

'Out of circulation? You mean prison?'

'Who knows. Someone has your number and they're looking for you. Keep your eyes open.'

There were no goodbyes. The line just went dead. That was twelve days ago.

***

Later, in the privacy of their hotel apartment, Stack raised the subject of Maddy with Summer.

'Did you hear my conversation with Maddy earlier?'

'Yes, she sounded decidedly tetchy. You know, defensive.'

'Hmm, that's what I thought,' Stack agreed. 'She disappears from time to time. Not to her hotel room. She just wanders off down the beach. But she doesn't seem the type to... you know... to do the aimless stroll down the beach thing. She's much too intense.'

'Well, I'm not complaining. I find her irritating. Charlie is obsessed. But have you noticed how she seems to keep him at arm's length? She's not as interested in Charlie as Charlie is in her.'

Stack gave that some thought before answering. They were outside on the balcony together, leaning against the railing, watching the last bright red fragment of swollen sun sink below the horizon. It dropped behind a bank of cumulus clouds for a moment but reappeared below like the thin, crescent shaped grin of a Cheshire cat, a centimetre above the edge of the world. A rippling mirage, it hovered for a moment, before slipping reluctantly out of sight. In its place grew long brush strokes of deep red water colour hues splashed generously across the turquoise wash of the evening sky.

'So why did she pick Charlie?' Stack pondered.

Summer didn't reply. She wanted to enjoy her selfish moment of solitude with the man she most wanted to be with. A moment that excluded everyone else.

Time passed and the brilliant pin prick of light that was Venus, the evening star, had become visible in the western sky before he spoke again.

'OK,' he decided, 'The next time she wanders off, you keep Charlie distracted. I'm going to follow her. See what she does. Where she goes.'

'James Stack, that curious nature of yours is going to get you into trouble,' Summer teased.

Stack took Summer by the waist, pulled her to him and kissed her.

'Let's see how much trouble my curiosity can get me into right now.' Stack said as he led her back into the air-conditioned luxury of their hotel room.

Maddy

When Stack and Summer sauntered into the restaurant the next morning for a late breakfast, the Charlie and Maddy romance had taken a turn for the worse. Charlie was on his own at the table looking sorry for himself. Summer saw an opportunity for the two old friends to have a much needed conversation - mano e' mano. She excused herself to go to the rest room as Stack slid across the booth to face Charlie.

'So, come on. Let's have it.'

'Oh, it's nothing. I've been stupid,' Charlie said morosely.

Stack waited for him to say more. A waiter came over to the table with a coffee pot and poured two cups. Stack indicated he should fill a third for Summer.

'We seemed to get on, me and Maddy, but the truth is, she hasn't even been to my room. I've had the odd kiss, but it was more like kissing an aunt goodnight.'

'I'm sorry to hear that, Charlie.'

'Yeah, well, last night at the Tiki bar, after you'd left, she was all close and intimate again. But when I suggested we go back to my room - or to hers - she had another of her excuses. I got fed up and told her not to bother. I walked off and left her there. That's it. I mean, I'm not a kid, and let's be honest, neither is she.'

Stack tried to reassure him that maybe he should give it a little more time. But Charlie told him it was over as far as he was concerned, he'd rather go fishing. The next time Stack booked a charter boat, he was going with him.

Summer returned, but sensing the private nature of the moment, said nothing beyond 'Hi' to Charlie. She picked up her coffee cup and took a sip. She and Stack were facing the beach-side window, so they couldn't miss Maddy marching across the sand towards the other hotels. Summer and Stack looked at each other. Stack nodded. Mission on.

He excused himself and headed through the restaurant and out to the beach.

***

The hotels along Grand Cayman's Seven Mile Beach are big eight or nine floor edifices that occupy acres of valuable beachfront real estate, which included the undeveloped spaces in between that provide public access to the beach. To walk past three of them, Stack guessed, was probably a distance of a third of a mile.

He kept himself well back, taking a route close to the hotels, which allowed him the cover of bars, water sport franchise huts and the occasional cluster of palm trees. She didn't appear to be checking for tails and her bright red shirt hanging loose over white shorts made her an easy target to follow.

It was the third hotel along that she made a beeline for, ending up perched on a stool at its beachside bar. She ordered a drink. Looked like water. It didn't take long before she was joined by a tall balding man with just a halo of dark hair. He was an older guy with one of those old-boy military moustaches. He was wearing a flowery Tommy Bahama palm print shirt that hung loose over new jeans and, incongruously, polished black brogues. The whole outfit seemed out of place somehow.

With the fold marks still in the shirt and sharp creases down the jeans, it was almost as though he was wearing an unfamiliar costume. It was clear they knew each other well. There was no formal introduction, they just fell into conversation like brother and sister, or work colleagues. From where Stack was sitting thirty feet away, hiding behind a discarded newspaper he'd picked up from one of the other tables, it didn't look like sunny vacation chit chat. There was a serious nature to it. When tall, bald, military guy showed her something on his smartphone, she examined it with a frown and shook her head. When she spoke, she was giving an opinion.

Stack raised his cell phone and took a couple of pictures as covertly as he could. They were going to be small in the frame but he hoped the high definition would allow him to zoom in for a closer look later.

Over at the bar, the discussion went on for a little longer until eventually she stepped down from the stool and looked around. Stack thought she'd spotted him sitting amongst the other late morning coffee drinkers, even though he had ducked behind the newspaper. Her attention was drawn back to tall, bald guy as he said something to her. It looked like he was giving advice – or a command. She looked at her watch, nodded, turned and headed back up the beach, the way she had come.

***

'You mind if I join you?'

It was early evening and Stack and Charlie were back at the Tiki bar drinking beers, having spent much of the afternoon pulling a series of disappointingly small catches out of the sea from the stern of Captain Samuels' charter boat.

Daylight was ebbing fast. Only a thin dull streak of scarlet remained to hint at the place where sky met sea. The bar sat in a pool of warm tungsten illumination. From the wooden rafters under the thatched roof, a fan wafted refreshing, water vapour-cooled air towards the customers – a welcoming oasis at the end of another hot Caribbean day.

Charlie took a deliberate sip of his beer to avoid saying anything to Maddy. Stack on the other hand tried to be polite and invited her to join them. He had questions and now might be a good time to raise them.

'Look Charlie, I'm sorry about last night,' Maddy said in a manner that from anyone else might have sounded contrite. She turned to Stack to explain.

'I think I upset Charlie last night.'

'Yes, I'd heard, Maddy. Charlie's a grown man. You two can sort it out between you,' Stack said. 'Can I buy you a drink?'

She ordered her usual chilled white wine. Lots of ice. The awkward silence continued between her and Charlie as the waiter prepared it.

'Another busy day at the office?' She joked to Stack.

'Well, funny you should say that, Maddy,' Stack said as he reached into his pocket for his cell phone.

'Charlie and I spent the afternoon fishing.'

Maddy detected a change of tone in Stack's voice.

'I suppose I should ask you what you caught. Anything interesting?'

Stack had the phone open to the image directory and thumbed his way through to the ones taken that morning. He spoke as he searched.

'Not half as interesting as the one I caught this morning.'

He held the phone up with the shot of Maddy and tall bald guy, which he had zoomed into for a close-up. It was unmistakably her.

Maddy was unfazed. She looked closely and nodded slowly.

'So, who's the guy?' Stack asked.

This was the first Charlie had seen of the picture. He had the same question, though for a different reason.

'He's MI6,' Maddy said matter-of-factly.

This wasn't even close to what Stack had been expecting. He was certain tall guy wasn't a boyfriend to challenge Charlie's imagined relationship with Maddy. He suspected it might have been a scam to rip off unsuspecting tourists. If they thought Stack and his friends had wealth, then a long-form con over a couple of weeks could be worth the investment in time.

It was Charlie who responded first after the stunned silence.

'What do you mean MI6? *The* MI6 in that bloody great building on the Thames? Secret spies and all that? James bloody Bond?'

'Even spies have to have holidays, Charlie,' Stack joked. But, having been prewarned, he knew this was the real thing and it was serious.

Madeleine's attitude abruptly changed from frivolous vacationer to all business and in charge.

'Let's go and sit at that table over there, away from the bar,' she said. 'I need your full attention.

Bring your drinks.' She was already leading the way.

No words were spoken as they made their way over and settled into the chairs. The drinks sat discarded on the table. Mouths were dry but nobody was drinking. The mood was sombre. Stack couldn't see any way that this could be good news. This wasn't accidental. They had come looking for them. This was what Blackstone had warned him about a week and a half ago.

MI6 don't waste their time on random targets. A subject of interest had been identified, a plan drawn up and resources allocated.

Given their past activities, particularly concerning their little Bank of England gold bullion enterprise, Stack wasn't surprised that someone had at last come to knock on their door. In a way, he'd been expecting it. But he hadn't been expecting the knock to come from MI6.

'That man, the one in the picture, he's a section head back at Vauxhall Cross, the Secret Intelligence Service in London,' she turned to Charlie. 'That bloody great building on the Thames, as you so accurately put it Charlie. I used to work directly under him. I'm now part of a smaller department. The two are very closely linked. We share resources, and occasionally, operational intelligence.'

'You've told us nothing that matters to us. Why the tour guide?' Stack had recovered and was moving from defence to attack.

From the direction of the hotel Stack saw the familiar slender silhouette of Summer walking towards the Tiki bar. The area of the beach immediately in front of the hotel was decorated with thousands of tiny LEDs in strings that had been stretched above the tables and wrapped endlessly around palm trees. Now darkness had fallen, as the gentle tropical breeze moved the palm fronds, the LEDs twinkled like fireflies. The effect was even more breath-taking as Summer walked into the pool of warm light that spilled from the Tiki hut. She had been in their hotel apartment getting ready for dinner and wore a simple, figure-hugging dress. With her elfin-like blond hair and light skin, tanned by the sun, she was the most beautiful thing Stack had ever seen, just as she was when he first saw her back in London more than a year ago.

She spoke to the barman and he pointed to the table where the three of them sat – in the shadows, away from the light and the interest of others.

As she sat down she noticed Stack's phone with the image still open on it. The image Stack had shown her earlier that day.

'So, you've shown Maddy?' Her chin lifted slightly in Madeleine's direction.

'Yes. You'll never guess what she told us,' Stack tilted his head towards Maddy.

'She's bloody MI6,' Charlie blurted out.

'MI6? The British secret service? A spook?' Summer said, her Canadian accent coming through stronger than usual.

'MI8 actually,' Maddy said. 'A subdivision of MI6. The man with me in the picture is MI6.'

Stack said, 'I didn't think there was a department called MI8.'

Madeleine ignored him and reached for her drink. She held it in her hand for a moment before she took a sip.

'I think you have a question you want to ask me.'

It was a statement offered to all three of them. She put the glass to her lips and drank while she waited for them to reply.

Summer, Hollywood and Stack looked at each other for a moment. Stack spoke first. A simple, one-word interrogation.

'Why?'

Madeleine nodded. 'Why? A good question.'

The coating of frost on her glass had melted in the humid air and left a wet circle on the coaster. She placed her glass back on the table, fastidiously positioning it on the same ring of water.

'You mean of course, why are we interested in you three? In particular, you Captain James Stack?'

'Ex Captain. I'm Retired,' he corrected her. 'I can't imagine why you're interested in us. But I'm sure you're about to tell us,' Stack said in an attempt at urbane disinterest.

'You've had an interesting career, haven't you James?' Madeleine went on to summarise the highlights.

'A captain. No, to be fair, a *decorated* captain in Special Forces with a particularly distinguished record of service in Afghanistan. You left for some reason and ended up in civvy street, working for Metro Metals Futures in the City of London, trading precious metals. That's where it all started to go wrong wasn't it, James?'

Stack said nothing.

'You were a naughty boy and got found with your fingers in the till. What did you get for that? Three? Four years?' You did two. Prison is supposed to rehabilitate you, but you decided bank robbery could be a nice little earner. That's where your old army buddy, sergeant Charlie Dawson here, came in,' she nodded in Charlies direction. 'Yes, we know all about that. The press called it the Hostage Heist. Very clever. We know of three jobs you did. Well, we're pretty confident. They had your MO. The detective on the case thinks so too.'

Charlie reached for his drink and took a long swig.

'And then it all gets really serious,' Madeleine burst out laughing. 'For Christ's sake! The Bank of England! What do you have for balls – plutonium?'

She reached for her white wine again, lifted the glass to toast the three of them and took a drink.

'The extraordinary thing is, you actually pulled it off. I mean, it was a brilliant scheme.'

Stack interrupted her.

'It was just a con. It wasn't supposed to happen. Things got out of hand.'

'You mean you accidently robbed the Bank of England? Come on, it was a beautiful plan put together by a very clever and resourceful man. Detective Chief Inspector Deakins agrees. He's retired now by the way; did you know that? He said you provided evidence that eventually helped convict several of the other perpetrators, and because of that, he kept your names out of the frame. A detail he revealed only to me. He said he'd take that secret to the grave. He was an extremely grateful man. He said you saved his career.'

'They got all the gold bullion back, didn't they?' Charlie added defensively.

'All but one, so I'm told. Who knows where that disappeared to?' Madeleine speculated pointedly.

Charlie had the distinct impression she was accusing him of taking it.

'And then there was the business with the drilling rig in Derbyshire recently. That got pretty ugly. Guns were involved. People were hurt. The police report says you claim to have prevented a massive seismic event when you stopped them fracking. Something about sabotage and a Russian oligarch. They aren't convinced you weren't involved in some way. You have shares, don't you?'

'I had shares. I'm selling them now. And no, I had nothing to do with the Russian.'

Charlie butted in angrily.

'Come on Maddy. If it wasn't for James there would have been a massive disaster. He deserves a bloody medal.'

'A medal!' Madeleine said cynically, 'The official view was that he helped the Russian evade justice.'

'That's outrageous,' Stack said. 'You have no evidence of that.'

'I'm sorry, James, if we choose there to be evidence, evidence there shall be. It's what we do. It's the nature our trade.'

'It's a bloody stitch-up,' Charlie said.

A silence followed as Stack, Summer and Charlie tried to assimilate what she had said and what it could possibly mean for them. A waiter arrived to take orders for drinks. Only Summer wanted something. A gin and tonic.

'Madeleine, you're not here to run through our CV for some kind of This Is Your Life TV special,' Stack said. 'Get to the point.'

'Before I do, and for the purposes of this conversation, we consider Summer to be a victim by collateral association. She can walk away now and return to Canada.'

Summer wasn't sure whether she should be worried or offended.

'What goes for James and Charlie, goes for me,' She said bridling. 'We're a team.'

Stack looked at Summer with even deeper love and respect. She had no need to risk everything by associating herself so closely with his and Charlie's activities.

'Summer, Madeleine's right. I don't know what's coming, but this could be your chance to back away.'

Summer said nothing, but her stubborn streak returned as she shook her head slowly. She was determined to stay, whatever it was that was coming.

Madeleine leaned in and spoke directly to Summer, 'This is your one chance to leave. If you stay, you cross a line and there's no going back.'

Nothing from Summer. She just glared at the SIS agent.

Stack turned to Madeleine and gave a fatalistic, 'get on with it' shrug.

'OK, here it is. We have a problem. And now you have a problem. Let me tell you your problem first. You three will never be able to return to the UK. If you do, you will be arrested and your past will catch up with you in court and finally in prison. That won't be the end of it, because when you've completed your prison term you will be removed from the UK. You won't become one of those celebrated, never-ending cases, defended by human rights lawyers. You'll be out of the country – permanently. Your passports will be stamped *persona non-grata*', which will make you all fugitives in most of the desirable destinations on the planet. We can make that happen. That is what your future holds. Am I making myself clear?'

Madeleine waited for a reaction.

'Perfectly,' Stack said. 'Now tell us why?'

'As I mentioned, we have a problem. It's one that we believe you can solve for us. It's well within your skill set. When you're done, all that bad stuff will go away – permanently.'

There was silence from her audience. Only the gentle surf washing onto the beach twenty metres away could be heard as Maddy reached for her wine and took another sip. Once again, she replaced the glass precisely onto the wet circle on the coaster.

'None of what I'm about to tell you can be repeated, are we clear?'

Another shrug from Stack. 'Get on with it,' he said, deep irritation in his voice.

'We had an MI8 unit working covertly in a foreign territory. It was a highly secret project that was proving to be very successful in undermining the communication and propaganda signals of our target. Our guys were using a unique device to achieve this success. When I say 'unique' this is a very precise use of the word. There isn't another like it. We call it Topaz.

'Of course, our target knew their communications were being compromised, but not *how*. Unfortunately, our problem came from a different and unexpected direction. One of our operatives was taken. It was simply an opportunistic kidnapping in the street in broad daylight by a local gang. They wanted money of course - and a lot of it.

'As you know, we don't pay ransom demands. However, one of our MI8 operatives came up with an idea. He suggested it might be possible, using the unique qualities of Topaz, to pay the ransom and then divert the money back again without the gang realising that they had in fact, not been paid.

It was believed that this 'suspension of reality' in the gang's bank account could be sustained long enough for them to release the hostage. Quite a trick if they could pull it off.'

Summer could see a rather obvious problem.

'Quite a trick! It sounds like a paradox to me. You were trying to create an illusion. To the gang the figure transferred must have been visible in their account, but to the entire banking system, nothing had happened. Surely if they could see it, it must be there in their account?'

'I can't see why they used a bank account that could be traced,' Stack said. 'Why didn't they ask for cash?'

Madeleine gave a short laugh and shook her head.

'Because they didn't ask for a simple money transfer, or cash. They asked for the ransom to be paid in Bitcoins.'

'Digital currency?' Summer said. 'Very clever. It's pretty much untraceable.'

'Well, it seems your people were able to track it,' Stack said, 'And by the way, where did you get your Bitcoins?'

'If you think the Secret Service doesn't have a need to make questionable transactions to dubious people from time to time, then you really don't get what we do,' Madeleine said.

'Anyway, our covert unit successfully pulled that little stunt off and our operative was released. But it backfired. They came looking for the entire MI8 unit, who had just enough time to abandon their position and retreat from the city. It was a close call. They escaped with their lives, but not, unfortunately, with the equipment. It's still sitting in a room somewhere in the city.'

'That's good news, isn't it?' Stack said. 'They got away safely. That's it. Story over.'

'Unfortunately, that isn't it,' Madeleine said. 'We need you to go back in and retrieve the equipment.'

'Equipment!' Charlie said. 'What, radio gear? A computer? Stuff like that?'

'You're not telling us everything, Maddy,' Stack said. 'There's a great big hole in your story or I'm not getting something.'

'When did all this happen?' Charlie asked.

Madeleine looked at her watch. 'Nearly two weeks ago. And before you ask, we did plan to go back in and retrieve the equipment ourselves. We had someone in place waiting to go in, but politics got in the way. They wouldn't let us run the operation.'

'But if this device you're talking about is so vital, surely they wouldn't want it to fall into enemy hands,' Stack said.

Madeleine thought for a moment, considering how much she should reveal.

'The device was a prototype. It uses a faster-than-light discovery that occurs at the very edge of scientific knowledge. But we weren't the only ones working on this kind of thing. The Americans had also been working on something that used the same scientific principle. They had bigger budgets and bigger ambitions, but we got it done ahead of them. We didn't tell them we had a working prototype out in the field.'

'Let me guess,' Stack said. 'Now they've found out and they're pissed off.'

'What our friends in America were trying to do was of an order of magnitude more difficult. We had a much smaller R&D budget, which required us to think...,' Madeleine chose her words carefully,

'Tangentially. To attack the problem from an entirely different angle. We asked ourselves how we could utilise this newly discovered scientific principle speedily and economically. What we came up with you might think was barely worth the effort. The weakest of effects – almost unmeasurable. But, apply it in the right way and a magical thing happened. A conjuring trick. As Summer said – an illusion. Except it isn't an illusion. I don't understand how the thing works. The important thing is that it does.'

'And this effect can make a bank transaction appear on someone's computer screen when the event didn't happen?' Summer asked.

'Oh, the transaction has to happen. The trick is to control *when* it happens,' Maddy said enigmatically. 'The device has one small problem though...' She waited for the inevitable next question.

Charlie said, 'OK, I'll bite, What problem?'

'It won't work from a distance – say, from London. You have to be close to the target, otherwise it has no effect.'

'Wait a minute, where is this equipment anyway,' Stack said.

'Yeah. What country?' Charlie added.

Madeleine threw the lighted match into the box of dynamite and waited for their reaction. 'Libya.'

All three reacted at once, 'Libya!'

Two weeks earlier

Ziya al-Din, commander of Breath of Allah, the jihadi group that formed part of the Nawasi Brigade militia, had finally made contact with Daesh. Or rather, someone on the fringes of Daesh, the terror group more commonly known as Islamic State.

The commander gave the impression that the purpose of Breath of Allah was to glory in the blessings of Muhammed and bring his teachings by sword, bomb and bullet to Christian infidels and other deviant Islamic sects that didn't conform to the true Wahhabi way. In truth the commander was little more than a local gangster looking for profit when the opportunity arose.

This strange box, he believed, was one of those opportunities. A 'blessing' that had fallen into his lap. He was certain that it had great value, but to turn it into hard cash required evidence of its worth. At the moment, all he had been able to achieve was to turn it on and make a pretty violet light.

He had heard that Daesh had attracted people from around the world with many different skills. They would understand its worth. And pay a good price for it.

***

The Breath of Allah had been fooled into releasing the woman. This fact became quickly apparent when the big pay-day number on the computer screen suddenly flicked back to zero. Ziya al-Din ordered his men to find her and bring her back. He would have his revenge.

It had just turned dark but even so, the old city was busy. What light there was came from the occasional street lamp and the scattered lighting from the hundreds of market stalls and shops along Souk al Turk, the ancient market street that ran through much of the old city, north to south, just east of the harbour. They had thrown the blindfolded woman out of a car, close to the place where they had taken her twenty-four hours earlier.

Major Susan Hedgeland had quickly ripped away the cloth covering her eyes and was making her way back to the MI8 base of operations when she noticed two men further down the street, the way she had come. They were pushing aggressively through the crush of people, with the kind of authority only a semi-automatic weapon can bestow. Inspecting nearby faces, then craning to see beyond the crowd, trying to spot something just out of sight, further down the street. The endless crush of noisy stall holders and busy shoppers obstructed their view and frustrated their urgent purpose.

It was obvious they were searching for someone. Somehow, she instinctively knew it was her they were looking for. They were making their intimidating way in her direction but so far, she hadn't been spotted. What had changed their minds, she wondered, unaware of the trick her colleagues had played on her abductors. She wasn't going to stop to ask them.

All across the ancient quarter of Tripoli, the soldiers of Breath of Allah barged through the crowded souks and cluttered alleyways with a belligerent sense of entitlement. Most were on foot, but a few careered at high speed through the narrow streets in battered vehicles. The car that had carried the major had turned around and it too was speeding recklessly back. They knew the labyrinthine neighbourhood well, and hunted her like a pack of wolves, splitting up and pursuing her through the back streets and rat runs, hoping to head her off and corral her into their trap.

At one point, Hedgeland, breathing hard and legs weak from the chase, pressed herself into the deep recess of a doorway, hidden in the darkness, hardly daring to breathe while a pursuer stood with his back just inches away. He looked up and down the narrow street for a sign of their prey. The temptation to reach out, wrap her arm around his throat and take him silently out was almost overwhelming. She tried to control her breathing, which had been coming in exhausted gasps. But seconds later, a shout from one of the others sent him off again.

She realised she was only a couple of blocks away from the rooms now. Her progress was slow as she kept to where the night was at its darkest amongst the winding alleys that ran close to the busy souk. She passed through gardens hidden behind heavy ancient wooden doorways and inched along walls that formed shadowy courtyards. All the time her pursuers drew closer, their footsteps sometimes echoing far away, but more worryingly, clear and perilous in the next street ahead.

She had just managed to find cover behind a stone wall as two rushed by, pausing at a dimly lit junction only yards away. One turned left, but the other walked back into the gloom of the alleyway. He stopped to light a cigarette, the flame of the match throwing a flickering light onto his youthful, bearded face. He drew on the cigarette and the flame grew a little brighter as the cigarette lit. Something made him look up. A ghostly figure illuminated by the match-light, coming out of the darkness towards him. Hedgeland pulled her arm back and slammed the heal of her hand into his forehead as hard as she could. He collapsed instantly, his old revolver clattering noisily to the ground and the cigarette falling from his gaping mouth onto his robe. Hedgeland kicked the burning ember away with her foot and picked up the old pistol. She checked the chamber. It held just a single round.

She was in a side street that joined the busy market a few yards further down and only a couple of doors from her unit's base. From nearby, a muezzin's plaintive call to prayer had begun echoing out. A metallic cry from amplified Tannoy speakers that began repeating itself from one minaret to another across the city. It was Salat al-'isha – evening prayer. Any moment now the street would be filled with the devout heading to their local mosque.

She waited, choosing her moment to blend in with the men who walked in twos and threes down the unlit, uneven, stone paved street. Weaving her way through them, she came at last to the sanctuary of the old sandstone archway that formed the entrance to the medieval block the three MI8 crew called home.

She was as surprised to find Patterson and Bailey coming through the doorway, as they were to see her. The timing was fortunate, because they were just about to head down Souk al Turk to search for her.

'No time to go back up,' Hedgeland told them, her words interrupted by each exhausted breath. 'Something's gone wrong. We have to get out of the city. The militia are looking for me. They're everywhere. If we hang around they'll find our base. Leave everything. We'll come back later if we can.'

Command given, she covered her face and turned to go.

Both Patterson and Bailey hesitated. Bailey, in an attempt to recover their equipment, made a move towards the stairs. Patterson, a timid, by-the-rules guy, pulled him back.

'If the Major says we have to go, we have to go.'

She had already disappeared back into the street and away. Patterson and Bailey followed. The equipment in the rooms on the second floor, reluctantly abandoned.

They'd only gone a few yards, but in the darkness, with the sound of shouting and running feet echoing from all directions and the noises of commerce and music from the busy souk just ahead, it was impossible to tell which way she had gone.

'Look, it'll be safer if we split up,' Bailey said. 'Meet outside the old British embassy at zero-zero hours. That'll give us three and a half hours to locate the major and get to the rendezvous. Faruk can't help us now – we're on our own. If we're unable to get back to recover the equipment, head to Tunisia by whatever means. Good luck!'

***

While some of the jihadi soldiers continued looking for the woman on the streets, others began a hurried search of all the nearby buildings. It didn't take them long. The God-fearing occupants of the apartment below the deserted MI8 base, were happy to tell what they knew of the westerners in the rooms above.

The rooms were empty, but it was clear they had been recently occupied. Clothes and personal effects remained. The place had been abandoned in a hurry, certainly within the last hour or so.

It looked as though three people had been there; the woman they were looking for and two males, just as the traitor, Faruk, had been forced to disclose during the unrelenting beating he had taken. Going through their clothes revealed very little. Anything that could identify them had been removed. A sure sign of CIA or UK Secret Service involvement, probably MI6.

On the table, hidden beneath a canopy made from a bed sheet, was a metal box. Next to it a laptop.

The soldiers waited until the commander arrived to give the place the benefit of his personal attention.

Ziya al-Din stood in the middle of the first room and looked slowly around, the way a detective might when he first enters a crime scene. Two single beds, pushed against the walls, bedding left unmade, a couple of chairs and a table. He then walked the few steps into the second room, taking note of the single bed, two backpacks and clothes, probably belonging to the woman, thrown over the backs of chairs.

He sniffed with contempt, then wandered back into the first room and stared at the table with the canopy suspended above it, now with a flap opened to reveal the flightcase hidden within. This interested him. He wondered about the canopy and why it had been placed there. It didn't do a very good job of hiding the box, maybe that wasn't its purpose. The lid had been removed and the flightcase positioned upright with its controls facing the operator. He noticed the leads running to and from the box.

None of the controls looked familiar. There were no rotatable knobs but coming out of the guts of the machine from behind the aluminium plate were several small diameter stainless steel pipes that had trombone-like sliders. The pipes seemed to pass into strange aluminium valves that had been set into box shaped spaces cut into the control plate. They were protected by a glass cover and sealed with rows of tiny bolts. A small computer screen was mounted to the left and turned ninety degrees like a portrait. Taking up most of the bottom half of the control area was a hinged door with a tiny chrome handle. There were no formal printed manufacturer's labels, just unfathomable words scribbled in marker ink. Nothing to reveal how the strange box worked or a clue as to its purpose.

At a second glance he saw one familiar control – a button. He looked around, eyeing each nervous soldier in turn, sneered, gave a fatalistic shrug, and pressed it.

A low whirring sound increased in tone until it became high pitched like a dentist's drill. Another seemed to do the same, spinning up until it reached a similar note. They both beat together, whining like two tiny jet engines.

It took a while, but gradually he noticed a tingling feeling on his scalp and around his beard. One of his fellow jihadis pointed to his head. He was wearing a Cuban revolutionary cap and the hair that wasn't covered had started to stand up in response to some invisible force. The same was happening to another man standing near the machine. They both gave a short laugh followed by a puzzled look. The tiny computer screen had come alive and line after line of green glowing data was spraying across it. They weren't fancy graphics, just basic computer letters, figures and symbols. The data stopped half way down the screen. Below the last indecipherable line, a curser blinked patiently, awaiting an input from an operator.

Taking hold of one of the trombone sliders he moved it slightly to the left, extending it a little. The numbers changed but not much else happened. Then he noticed through a crack in the small access door a tiny hint of light was being emitted. The door hadn't been closed fully. His curiosity took the bait like a mouse loves cheese. He grabbed the chrome knob and pulled it open. Though the room was lit by a single overhead bulb, its brightness was overwhelmed by the violet brilliance that flooded out from the interior of the strange machine, casting hard shadows of the Breath of Allah soldiers onto the wall behind them. Once again, the commander turned and shrugged at the man standing next to him and opened his hands in an expression of uncomprehending ignorance.

As he stepped forward and closed the small door, extinguishing the exotic light, he noticed the material it had been constructed from and how thick it was. Something about its sturdiness seemed familiar, but he couldn't recall what it was. It would come to him in good time he thought.

He pressed the button again and the strange static effect slowly diminished and the tiny screaming jet noise spun down into silence.

There appeared to be nothing else that could be gained by remaining there, so he ordered his men to take the box and the laptop and anything else they could carry, back to their compound.

In the back of his mind the germ of an idea was forming. If the CIA or MI6 had bothered to bring this strange box all the way to Libya, then it must be important and it must have value. He knew an organisation that might be interested in obtaining western espionage technology. They were dangerous and unpredictable, but he was sure someone connected to the Islamic State movement would pay Ziya al-Din, the commander of Breath of Allah, a great deal for it.

North Africa

The first thing you notice when you step out of a plane in Tunis, the capital of Tunisia - after you've recovered from the oppressive heat - is the taste of dust in your mouth.

Stack, Summer and Charlie were picked up at Carthage International Airport by a VW people carrier and driven the short distance to the British embassy, a modern structure built on the edge of the vast Lac de Tunis to the east of the city centre.

As short as the drive was, it was long enough for the skinny man in a suit a size too big for him, sitting behind the wheel, to give them a summary of the country's recent history. Maybe the suit was too big because it was his larger brother's job and he was just filling in, but by whatever means he came to be sitting behind the wheel, he was keen to boast about Tunisia being the birth-place of the so-called Arab Spring a few years earlier. He was less proud of the murder of thirty-eight tourists who were shot by a lone gunman with a Kalashnikov assault rifle on the beaches of Port El Kantaoui on the coast of the Gulf of Hammamet, 135 kilometres south of the city.

No, the driver explained, that deadly rampage was the work of a madman who himself was shot dead by Tunisia's heroic police, but only after he had enjoyed forty unhindered, bullet-spraying minutes to himself. They hadn't lost a single tourist since then. Now though, holiday makers were flocking back to Tunisia's beautiful beaches, bringing their much-needed foreign currency with them. It was a hell of a sales pitch that the Tunisian Tourist Board could have managed without.

The car was held up momentarily as it passed through the tough security measures that guarded the embassy. Walls, gates, guns and a slalom of concrete obstacles made for a very telling statement about the kind of welcome local extremists would like to offer visitors from the west if they had a chance.

This was North Africa: Morocco, Algeria, Tunisia, Libya and Egypt. The big desert lands of squabbling tribes, ancient rivalries, unforgiving religious sects and fluid political allegiances. A land that reached up to touch the very edge of the Mediterranean coast. It was also a land of big hearted, welcoming people, eager to take their place in the modern world if only history, prejudices and armed religious radicals would allow them. More than anything, they just wanted to get on with their lives.

***

It could have been a discrete lounge in a luxury hotel. Modern, glass-walled, wood-panelled and sumptuous. A low table and leather chairs arranged on a large Persian carpet thrown over a white marble floor. Very cool and efficient.

They had waited patiently in the secretary to the ambassador's anti-room for a little over twenty minutes. Coffee served. Polite apologies offered. Not an unpleasant way to waste time. Stack wasn't counting minutes as he sat in the soft, white leather sofa, relaxed, eyes closed, his shoeless feet resting on the marble and glass table. There was no rush and not much conversation.

Summer had taken to gazing out of the vast floor to ceiling window that faced the lake and, beyond that, the Mediterranean Sea.

Hollywood was studying a large black and white aerial photograph of the embassy that hung on the wall facing a door. A door that he assumed, lead to the inner sanctum of the ambassador's office. The door that had remained stubbornly closed since their arrival and through which they hoped to be summoned at any moment.

'Hey look at this,' he said, pointing to the photograph. 'There's a street called Rue de Lac Windermere. And another one here called Rue Lac Loch Ness. Makes you feel at home doesn't it.'

Nobody responded and the room became quiet again.

Through the double-glazed, toughened glass of the large window, a faint wail of the afternoon call to prayers could be heard, and then another, reminding them of the distinctly foreign nature of the world in which they had arrived. A world of other people and other cultures that existed beyond the westernised bubble of the large modern building.

The British Embassy in Tunisia had become a crowded place since the British Embassy in Libya was forced to close and move to Tunis. Any Brits in Libya needing consular services were on their own.

But then again, in those dangerous post Gaddafi days, any Brits in Libya were most likely there for their own secret reasons and had their own people to take care of them, or, in some extreme circumstances, abandon them. They would be the kind of people that had the resourcefulness to get themselves out of trouble.

And Libya was a whole lot of random, deadly serious and probably insurmountable trouble.

***

It wasn't until the door opened and Paul Kent, the Secretary to the Offices of the Ambassador, entered the room to introduce his boss, that they understood how rare the moment of solitude they had just enjoyed would be from that moment on.

'Let me see if I've got this right,' Kent announced. 'Ambassador Trevallion Caithe–Moore, this is Mr James Stack, Ms Summer Peterson and Mr Charles Dawson.'

'Call me Charlie,' Dawson said as he walked over with outstretched hand.

Stack and Summer also met the ambassador halfway as he crossed the room to greet them.

Another man had entered, and the ambassador invited him over.

'This is Dr Steven Southgate, Ambassador to Libya, currently based, temporarily, we hope, here in Tunis.'

More polite greetings and time filling chit-chat that covered all of nothing in particular, until Ambassador Caithe-Moore checked his watch, apologised that he had other matters to attend to, and left the room.

Steven Southgate, the ambassador to Libya, turned to Paul Kent.

'OK, Paul, when you're ready.'

Kent left the room, leaving Stack, Dawson and Summer waiting for an explanation.

'Yes, well, I'm really just the host,' Southgate said. 'But as this embassy is going to be the *de facto* base for whatever you people are planning to do, there are a few rules I need to explain when the others arrive.'

'Others?' Stack said.

Southgate just offered an inscrutable 'wait and see' lift of his eyebrows.

Stack stuffed his hands in his pockets. Charlie did the same.

By the time the door opened again, another four minutes or so had passed in silence. Of the three people who entered with Paul Kent, only one face was familiar.

'Maddy!' Charlie said flatly without enthusiasm.

'Yes, and a shed load of sand, Hollywood,' Madeleine said dryly. 'But not a beach in sight.'

Summer couldn't hide her irritation at seeing Madeleine again.

'So, who are these people?' she said indicating the other two new comers.

'This is Chris Bailey,' Maddy said. As she spoke Bailey stepped forward to shake hands with Stack and the others.

'Chris was one of the unit based in Tripoli,' Madeleine continued.

She then turned to the third person. A late middle-aged man, going on six-foot tall, bald except for a halo of thinning black hair shot through with silver. His rich black moustache was also losing its lustre to the onset of grey. Stack instantly recognised him as the man Madeleine had met at the bar on the beach back on the island.

He didn't wait for Madeleine, like Bailey, he stepped forward in a pre-emptive introduction.

'Cavanagh, Major, retired.' His manner was that of a senior civil servant marinated in the rarefied company of exclusive gentlemen's clubs and expensive whisky.

'Major William Cavanagh has been involved in Topaz from the beginning – before even MI8 was formed,' Maddy said.

'Before it was a project, to be precise,' Cavanagh interjected. 'I don't know what Madeleine has told you, not too much I hope, but the equipment you are going to retrieve for us is highly specialised. It has a singular purpose.'

'Yes, Maddy gave us the run down,' Stack said.

'Time displacement?' Summer threw the grenade in just for the hell of it.

She got a reaction. Cavanagh had a sudden coughing fit.

'Yes, well. Just go there and bring it back. Time is of the essence,' Cavanagh said without a hint of irony. 'Bailey here will accompany you. He knows the routine. He's a very capable man in a tight spot, as I am assured are you, Stack.'

Chris Bailey stepped forward.

'And who is this?' he said indicating Summer. 'Summer Peterson. I'm with Charlie and James. We're the team that's been invited to enjoy a few sunny days touring Libya,' Summer said.

Bailey turned to Stack.

'She can't go,' he said emphatically. 'Too dangerous.' There was no prejudice in his voice.

'Actually, I'm inclined to agree,' Stack said.

'James!' Summer appealed.

'Here and no further, Summer,' Stack said, his voice carried the authority of the Captain he was trained to be. 'You don't have the experience Charlie and I have. This is familiar territory. We know the culture and we know the dangers. We can't risk you coming along.'

Cavanagh stepped forward and pulled rank.

'A three-man unit. Bailey, Stack and Dawson,' Cavanagh said in his abrupt manner. 'Stack, as a former Captain in Special Forces, and, if your reputation means anything, you will be in command. Ambassador Southgate and the Secretary to the Ambassador, Mr Kent here, will arrange what you need transport wise. Other...' the Major chose his next words carefully in front of Southgate, and Kent, '...shall we say, '*personal protection*' equipment, came with us on the plane out of RAF Northolt this morning. It should have arrived with the embassy's diplomatic consignment by now.'

Cavanagh looked at Ambassador Southgate and nodded, a silent instruction. The Ambassador to Libya understood. He turned to Paul Kent.

'Ah, yes, of course. Paul, can you check to see that the diplomatic bags have arrived and are sent to their quarters?'

The ambassador turned back to the group.

'We have a room set aside that can be used as a base of operations while you're in the country.' He paused for a moment, then his voice took on a solemn tone. 'Before I take you there, let me make myself clear about what we can and cannot do for you as a foreign embassy in Tunisia. It's very simple. We can't be seen to be interfering in the host country's affairs. Nor neighbouring countries for that matter. Diplomats get kicked out for that kind of thing. Friendships in this part of the world are hard won and finely balanced. So, behave! Or at the very least – be discrete.'

He indicated that they should follow him to their temporary base, apologising, as he led them through endless corridors and down stark maintenance stairwells, for the cramped nature of the space he had found for them.

***

'Deniability,' Madeleine said. 'I'm afraid that whatever happens, including everything we have already spoken about or the events that follow in the next few days, nothing can ever be revealed. I want to make it as clear as fresh mountain air that we will not allow knowledge of this to be traced back to London. You're on your own. Simply bring the flightcase back here to this embassy. We will take over at that point.

'If it all pans out, the curse will be lifted and you guys will be able take the next flight to London. Your life can continue as though nothing happened – because nothing will have happened – no evidence will exist that it ever happened, and as far as MI8 and MI6 are concerned, we will have no knowledge of you three or your activities.'

Ambassador Southgate had shown them to a small, windowless caretaker's office at the end of a corridor in the basement. Waiting for them in the room were two bags of equipment including the 'personal protection' items they had been expecting.

Three semiautomatic Smith & Wesson M&P compact hand guns, along with boxes of 9mm ammunition, spare magazines, personal radios, sat nav, a satellite phone and other miscellaneous items had been pulled from the bags and laid out on a small table that, along with the metal chairs, filled the cramped space.

Stack had already taken apart and reassembled his gun. It had the new, out-of-the-box smell of machine oil, gunmetal and polymer. He'd need to fire some rounds to be completely confident. Bailey and Dawson did the same.

All the prep work was done in silence apart from the sharp snick of metal sliding across metal as magazines were filled with 9mm ammo, fifteen at a time.

Bailey double checked the batteries in the radios and satellite phone. And he checked the maps in the sat nav were local and current. Spare batteries were fully charged. Everything was repacked into backpacks.

'I think that just about covers it from the security POV,' Cavanagh said, 'Now, before I leave you to get on with it, is there anything else you need?'

Stack had moved easily into the role of leader.

'Chris? Charlie? Anything?'

'Actually, I have a question.' Summer had her hand up. Cavanagh gave her an upward nod of his head.

'Go ahead.'

'What am I supposed to do while you boys are having all the fun in Tripoli?'

'The most important of roles,' Cavanagh said, 'You will be the axis around which the whole operation will orbit.'

'Don't patronise me, Cavanagh. I'm not a child. I can take care of myself...'

Cavanagh put his hand up to interrupt her.

'I have no time for pleasant little platitudes to charm you into feeling valued. You're here for a reason and you will play a full part in this operation,' Cavanagh said firmly. 'Madeleine and I will be gone by the end of the day. Once this special ops unit is in Libya, it will need a point of contact here in Tunisia. That will be you. You will be the only person who can fix any local problems they encounter. You will not be able to refer to anyone else, particularly anyone in London. Now, are you up for it, or am I mistaken?'

Stack had been listening while he was examining the semiautomatic.

'Don't worry, Major, she'll be perfect,' Stack said, 'But I want a direct line to you, Maddy, in case this turns into a crapfest and we need some big boy's toys.' He was weighing the lightweight pistol doubtfully in his hand as he said it. Maddy snapped a card on the table, penned a number on the back.

Cavanagh checked his watch, took a breath and looked at the people around the table.

'OK, we're going. I will probably never meet you again, so do your job. Bring the flightcase back.'

He got out of the chair and went to the door. Before he opened it, he turned to Stack and spoke a few, final, chilling words.

'Oh yes. The flightcase. It contains some very dangerous material. Don't be tempted to examine it, there's a good chap. Leave the lid closed.'

It was said incidentally, as though by way of an unimportant afterthought. But Stack was certain it carried a critical message, deliberately left to the last moment to avoid questions, or the chance for people to change their minds.

The door closed and Major Willian Cavanagh and Madeleine Clark had gone.

Libya: The sea route

Bulletin from the UK Foreign and Commonwealth Office (FCO).

The FCO continues to advise against all travel to Libya, and for British nationals still in Libya to leave immediately by commercial means. Local security situations are fragile and can quickly deteriorate into intense fighting and clashes without warning.

Terrorists are very likely to carry out attacks in Libya. There remains a high threat throughout the country of terrorist attacks and kidnap against foreigners, including Daesh-affiliated extremists (formerly ISIL) and Al Qaida, as well as armed militias. Daesh and Al Qaida have attacked a number of oil and gas installations and killed or kidnapped workers, including foreign nationals.

Fighting has caused the temporary closure of airports, closed roads and led to the closure of some border crossings. All airports are vulnerable to attack. Tripoli International Airport has been closed since July 2014.

End of bulletin.

***

It took all five men to pull the nets back on board for the second time that day. The catch wasn't much better than before. They would try again in the evening, after they had eaten. After all, patience is a fisherman's great virtue.

Slowly, almost randomly, the fishing boat had made its way across the Gulf of Gabes, stopping every now and then to cast its nets.

The old fishing dhow had motored out of Al Maharas in the south of Tunisia a day and a half ago, just as it had for generations past. But this journey was different. Fishing was secondary to its main purpose. The slow and innocent nature of its progress hid the almost accidental direction they were heading. Ordinarily, the journey of just eighty kilometres, would have taken only a single day's sailing from Al Maharas - if they weren't trying to hide their true destination from the Libyan Navy and coast guard vessels. A destination concealed along the barren Libyan coastline somewhere between Zuwarah and Tripoli.

This was migrant season. The time when thousands of desperate refugees were forced onto cramped, unseaworthy craft and, with little or no knowledge of the sea, left to navigate north, across the treacherous waters of the Mediterranean. The problem was, the dhow crossed the most crowded migration route from Zuwarah, just a few miles to the south. The ancient fishing port was the main staging point from which the people smugglers launched their flotilla of misery.

The sea kept the temperature down a little, but it was still over thirty-six degrees, with barely a breath of wind. Eyes were shielded against the sun's blinding glare on a sea that reached out through the heat haze like an endless sheet of dimpled glass. The men on board had already spotted two of the large inflatable vessels crossing their path a mile or so away and an hour or so apart during the morning. Both were sitting dangerously low in the water, one barely making progress, the other moribund, its engines unable to cope in the heat of the day. Some of those on board were standing up and waving frantically, dangerously rocking the flimsy craft. The people smugglers had sent them on their way in the cynical knowledge that European naval vessels and privately funded rescue ships further out in international waters were waiting to rescue the fortunate few.

As terrible as their plight might be, the dhow's captain kept as far away from the migrant boats as he could. A rescue attempt would overwhelm their own small vessel, and anyway, his passengers were keen to avoid any contact that could cause delay. In particular, they had no desire for any Libyan interest, either government or rebels. This journey was unsanctioned and covert.

**

Summer had set about arranging transport as soon as a plan to get into Tripoli had been crafted. Stack had considered the options; the first took the Coast Road from the Libyan border to Tripoli. It was the obvious route, but it would take them through towns patrolled by rebel militia. They could decant from a car and take a wide perimeter route around each town, then trek across desert terrain for a few kilometres. Not too tough, but it bore the likelihood of accidental encounters that could bring the expedition to an early end. The volunteer driver, a local Tunisian yet to be identified, would then drive the car through the town and pick them up on the other side. The total journey would represent sixty-five kilometres of high-risk exposure.

Stack discounted option one.

He had considered the possibility of posing as oil workers, but even that was a high-risk strategy as western oil personnel in Libya had become handy kidnap-for-cash victims.

There was, however, another route. One that didn't touch Libya until the very last minute but got them close to Tripoli. A sea route. They still needed a driver to get them the rest of the way once they had landed on the coast.

It turned out that one of the embassy's chauffeurs was up for it. The same skinny guy that collected them from the airport earlier that day. His name was Rakim Shadid. He told Summer he was already familiar with the drive into Tripoli. He had family there and made the journey every month or so. By, 'family', as Summer discovered, he meant, 'business'. Smuggling hard-to-get technology like smartphones, iPads and computer parts into the city. Apart from cash, he rarely returned with anything because there wasn't much they had in Libya that anyone in Tunisia wanted and that included trouble. It was a dangerous side-line, but it provided valuable insight, and contacts should they be needed.

Rakim turned out to be doubly useful. A cousin had a fishing boat in Al Maharas. Summer beat out a tough deal. Half now, half when they got back.

The show was on the road. They would start out in the morning.

***

James Stack, Charlie Dawson and Chris Bailey boarded the dhow in Al Maharas and worked their share of duties alongside the crew for the two days it took to reach the Libyan coast.

In anticipation of the mission and to provide some measure of disguise once they arrived in Libya, Stack and Charlie had stopped shaving. By the time they boarded the dhow, Stack bore a visible shadow of dark stubble. Since the onset of puberty, Charlie had been unable to compete with his beard sporting pals. When he tried, all he could manage was patchy clumps of fine fibres. Things hadn't improved over the years, so patchy clumps would have to do. Bailey already had a full beard as a longstanding lifestyle choice since his student days at the University of Cambridge, Department of Physics.

With little else to do during the voyage and to get some relief from the heat of the sun, Stack, Charlie and Bailey took shelter in the crude shack that served as a cabin on the stern of the boat. It had been cobbled together from lengths of old wood, sun-bleached silver. It gave shelter from the weather on three sides but was open to the bow. The roof had been braced with several brine-rotted strips of angle iron and covered in a stiff canvas material that had been tied down to the deck with rope.

The muffled popping of the diesel engine buried in the hull under the deck, had a soothing, hypnotic effect as the old wooden boat made its slow headway, rocking gently in the calm sea. The forward motion, however, produced little in the way of a cooling breeze.

Inevitably, conversation turned to the mission, and most importantly, as far as Stack was concerned, who this new guy, Bailey, was?

Bailey gave Stack the short version which included how he was one of a three-man covert unit in Tripoli. They'd been there for two months. A kidnap and subsequent release of one of them ended with all three extracting from the location, leaving sensitive equipment behind. In other words, nothing to see here.

That didn't do it for Stack.

'And yet, here we are, on a stinking old boat in the middle of the sea heading back to Libya?' Stack said. 'What do you think Charlie? Is it just the catch of the day that smells fishy?'

'You know what I think, boss? If Chris here likes fisherman's tales, you should show him the picture of that bloody great fish you caught the other day.'

Stack laughed.

'Perhaps I should,' Stack turned to Bailey. 'Would you like to see the barracuda I reeled in the other day? It's a big one and I've got a picture to prove it. Maybe you can show me your holiday snaps or pictures of your girlfriend? Anything to avoid telling me the truth about what you were doing in Tripoli.' Stack said. His temper quickening.

'Listen, Bailey. Hollywood and I are old soldiers. We've fought for our lives in some of the worst trouble spots in the Middle East. We knew what we were letting ourselves in for – and why. But this is different. MI6, or is it your mysterious MI8, wanted us in on this game and played hard ball to get our attention. So, here we are. We'll do the job, but we don't want to go in blind. I need to know what to expect and how what happened before, is likely to affect what happens next.'

'It's tricky,' Bailey said hesitantly. 'The Official Secrets Act. No one must know what we were doing in Libya. That's why we have to get the flightcase out. It mustn't fall into the wrong hands.'

'Yes, I've already heard that bit,' Stack said.

There was a pause as he watched some seagulls hovering noisily above the stern, attracted by the activity of one of the Tunisian crew as he tossed the left-over scraps of boiled fish from his cooking pot into the sea. The owners of the boat were a father and his eldest son. While his father sorted the fish, the son was readying the nets, tidying ropes and generally keeping out of the way of the foreigners.

After a while, Stack turned back to Bailey.

'OK. Tell me about the unit. I want to know names, what you were doing in Libya, who the kidnappers were, what happened when they released the hostage, how you got out of Libya and why you left the flightcase behind?'

Bailey answered all the questions in some detail, but Stack felt it was still thin gruel.

'So, the team was led by Major Hedgeland and this other guy, Patterson? He and you operated this device thing? Why did MI8 choose you? These kinds of operations are highly dangerous.'

'I am a scientist. So is Patterson,' Bailey said. 'We're both quantum physicists.'

Stack looked shocked.

'What the hell were a couple of scientists doing in a trouble zone like Libya?'

'We'd both been on the Topaz development team for five years or so. Eventually we had a breakthrough. We got it to do something useful. Then we found a way to miniaturise the components to make it portable. It was all very experimental. The problem was, once the department learned of our achievement, they got all excited and wanted it out in the field and delivering results right away.

There was no way anyone could learn how to operate it without a degree and a lifetime in quantum physics. They decided it would be quicker to give Patterson and me some training and a gun and got us out to Libya asap. I don't recall being asked if I wanted to do that, but as you discovered, they can be hard to refuse.'

'And remind me again,' Stack said. 'What does this thing do?'

'It shifts time forward by a few nanoseconds.'

'You mean it's like the movie Back To The Future?' said Hollywood. 'A bloody time machine?'

'God, no,' Bailey said, alarmed. 'Nothing like that at all. That's what the Americans are up to. Rather unsuccessfully at the moment I gather. We've got a much simpler device that works, but the effect is barely measurable. It's very weak. That's why we can only use it on things that function on extremely low voltages, like the integrated circuits of computers, or servers. We found we could interfere with anything that uses the internet by shifting the moment a message was sent, making it travel ahead of itself by the tiniest slither of time. It's as though we had tuned it out of the present.'

'Like a radio?' Stack said.

'Well, not exactly. It's more like a helix – a loop that never quite gets back to where it started. To the person who sent it, he can see the message displayed on social media as normal. He thinks it's out there. But we have contained it within his own local experience on his laptop or PC. To everyone else in his timeframe, nothing has happened. He clicks send and, as the signal goes out, we shift it forward a few nanoseconds. It doesn't have to be far ahead. We only need to slip it out of the current timeframe. We can keep moving it forward for a while, but eventually the present will catch up with it.

'Imagine a donkey with a stick attached to it, on the end of the stick is a carrot. The donkey walks forward to get the carrot, but the carrot is always the same distance ahead. But in our case only our target can see the carrot, everyone else is back in real time with the donkey, and the carrot is in an invisible future moment. We can only keep it ahead for a little while, until we see that the communication has been successfully delivered. Then we delete it and any attachments. The point is, to the sender, it has to appear as though it has been posted or sent. Technically, though it has been pre-deleted. That is to say, it's deleted *before* everyone else moves forward in time to see it.'

'I'm not sure I've completely got that, but it sounds very clever and, frankly, a bit bloody weird,' Stack said. 'And this thing actually works?'

'Oh yes. We've been able to subvert some critical propaganda posts and commands from the Daesh leadership in Libya. It's had a major effect on their ability to communicate on both the common and the dark web.'

'Why not just delete the message?' Charlie asked. 'Why go to all that futuristic business?'

'Deception,' Bailey said. 'If they believe their activity is uninterrupted, they move on to the next thing. We get advance notice of their intentions before their own people get to hear about it. And no alarm bells ring. It buys us the most valuable thing of all - time.'

'A bit like the codebreakers at Bletchley during the second world war,' Stack said. 'Once they'd cracked the Enigma code, they had to be careful not to alert the enemy by rushing off and warning the Atlantic convoys about the carnage they knew the Germans were planning. That must have been a tough call.'

Charlie had been trying to follow the science. He thought he had it, but something bothered him.

'So, you can only move a little bit into the future. Why not any further, like an hour or a day?'

'In tests we ran it several minutes forward in time, but it doesn't focus well because the miniaturised version of Topaz produces such a weak stream. However, there is another very simple technical reason. It is possible to increase the power of the stream to go further forward in time for longer, but it damages the very internet systems we use to reach our targets, particularly in places like Libya where old servers and land lines are easily damaged by our activity. We found it best to keep it simple. Short temporal distances are fine for what we were doing.'

Stack had other questions, but he was interrupted by worried shouts out on deck. The crew were pointing at something far away, hidden in the distant haze, their eyes squinting against the searing sun. Stack and the others stepped out of the shack to see what the fuss was about. At first it was just a blurry wavering spot on the horizon, but the shape quickly resolved as it drew closer.

It had just turned noon on the second day when the grey shape of the Libyan coastguard cutter materialised like an apparition out of the southern glare. It approached fast, pushing the white spray of a bow wave ahead of it. Then its bow dipped as it slowed to a lazy walking pace and drew alongside, skimming slowly past the old fishing boat just inches from its gunwale. Two or three officers and crew gave a cursory inspection as they peered down from their modern steel vessel to the deck of the ancient wooden dhow passing a couple of feet below them.

The crew had opened the hold so that the fish they'd caught could be seen – and smelled.

Tanned and bearded, from a distance, Stack and Charlie fitted right in as crew members. But hand guns against a heavily armed naval vessel were the kind of odds only a madman would take on. They couldn't out-run them either. Their only chance was to brazen it out as busy deck hands fixing nets, attending to the engine and preparing food for a meal – anything that kept them too busy for scrutiny. Bailey kept out of sight in the hut.

The Tunisians gave the cutter crew a wave of acknowledgement and bowed subserviently. One of the officers gave a stern hint of a wave, like a monarch to the peasants.

Then Stack's heart sank as the older Tunisian seemed to offer the coastguard crew some fish. A crew member jumped down onto the wooden deck and waited while the fisherman scrambled into the hold to find a suitable tribute. Keen not to miss the cutter as it slowly crawled past, the Libyan shouted for the Tunisian to hurry. He looked around while he waited, giving Stack and Charlie the briefest of appraisals. He hadn't spotted Bailey, but he zeroed in on Charlie who sat with his legs dangling into the engine compartment as he fiddled with the fuel injector. The Libyan took a few steps closer and said something. It sounded like a question. Charlie did the only thing he could think of. Although he understood a few words of Arabic, he struggled to understand the Libyan, so he kept his head down and pretended to concentrate hard on what he was doing. At the same time, he nodded and grunted in a noncommittal way that he hoped would imply agreement of some kind. It resulted in a louder more aggressive question from the Libyan who took another step towards him. Charlie was about to try another grunt but was saved by a shout from the old Tunisian whose head had popped back up through the hatch. The sailor held Charlie's gaze for a moment, unsure whether he had time to take the matter further. In different circumstances he would have enjoyed tormenting the pathetic peasant. Instead he turned away from Charlie, to see the old fisherman hefting up one of the biggest of their catches - swordfish.

He made lots of fawning noises about how he was giving him the best fish of the day, but the Libyan seemed unimpressed as he examined it with an ungrateful sneer. His inspection was cut short by anxious shouting from the cutter. The crew were waving and whistling, urging him to hurry. Arms reached out, ready to pull him back on board as the stern began its slow passage past the dhow. He threw the swordfish across and grabbed the outstretched hands. He was hoisted back on board and turned away without a word of thanks to the Tunisians watching from the deck below, his interest already moving on to other things.

As the stern of the cutter passed beyond the dhow and out into the open sea, a sharp, metallic command could be heard from the Tannoy speaker mounted on the bridge superstructure. In response, the cutter's twin engines burst noisily into powerful, deep-throated life.

What had been a mirror calm sea churned into a vortex of sapphire blue water and violent white surf as the propeller blades bit deep, driving the vessel away at high speed.

**

Standing at the stern, Stack balanced against the slow, rocking motion as the dhow puttered slowly onward. He watched the coastguard cutter until it was a mere white speck that disappeared into the shimmering afternoon haze. Then he turned to Bailey standing next to him.

'That was a bit close, and we're not even in Libya yet.'

Hollywood and Bailey nodded in silent agreement.

'So, Chris, where are the other two?' Stack asked.

'Other two?'

'Come on,' Stack said. 'Hedgeland and Patterson. Did they escape with you?'

'I'll be honest with you, James, we think they're both still in Libya. We were on the cell phone with the leader of Breath of Allah as the money transfer happened. They said they were letting her go but we should wait thirty minutes before looking for her. We were literally just going to search when she turned up at the door. She was pretty shaken up as you can imagine. She said soldiers from the militia were searching for her. She didn't know why. Of course, she had no idea about the trick we'd just played on them.

Perhaps we hadn't held the Topaz stream long enough, or maybe they kept the account open longer than we thought they would. Either way, they knew they'd been screwed. I should think they were pretty pissed off. The Major was lucky to have reached our base. She wanted us to leave immediately.' Bailey sketched out what happened next. 'I arrived at the embassy by midnight as planned. Waited for a while. Patterson didn't turn up and neither did the Major, so I made my way to Tunisia. That's it. We haven't heard from Patterson or Major Hedgeland since.'

Stack rubbed the wiry stubble on his chin as he chewed on Bailey's story.

'Do you think one or both have been captured?'

Bailey was looking out at the shimmering sea-scape. He was watching a small dark object slowly traverse the near horizon this side of the heat haze. It was coming from the direction of Zuwarah which was now far behind them to the west. He guessed it was another boat load of human misery.

Bailey exhaled a long breathy sigh as he turned back to Stack.

'One or both? Most likely both, but we've had no demands from Breath of Allah, so nothing can be confirmed.'

'You mentioned this, Breath of Allah,' Stack said. 'Madeleine only spoke about a local street gang who did the kidnapping. If Breath of Allah are part of the local militia in Tripoli, that could be a much bigger deal, especially if they've got both Hedgeland and Patterson.'

Bailey agreed.

'But, as far as I know, MI8 haven't heard from them. They've made no demands.'

Charlie had been listening to the conversation and decided a red line needed to be drawn on what constituted the central purpose of their mission.

'Well, we're only here to get the flightcase back to Tunis,' he said. 'No side issues. No complications. I don't like Libya. I don't want to be in Libya. In and out. That should be the end of it.'

'I agree,' Stack said, smelling the ominous odour of mission creep. 'The flightcase and nothing else.'

Bailey said nothing. He just continued staring out into the wide, blue yonder.

**

The sun had slipped below the horizon several hours earlier. The moon had yet to rise. Five miles out at sea the darkness was total. The running lights of the dhow were off and what light there was came when shielded torches were used. Only the spectacular twinkling sweep of the Milky Way distinguished sky from sea.

They'd been fishing aimlessly during the afternoon and into the early evening, motoring slowly back and forth along a two mile stretch of the coast. It was past eight when they pulled the nets in for the last time and beyond ten when they turned the dhow south towards the long dark stretch of coast between Az-Zawiyah and Janzour, the western most suburb of Tripoli.

Rakim Shadid, their Tunisian driver, considered this to be the safest spot along the coast for the fishermen to drop the three of them off. From there it would be just a ten-kilometre drive into Tripoli.

The pitch blackness was broken only by the blue green glow of bioluminescent plankton that sparkled on the surface of the water like a mirror reflecting the starlit sky above. A shimmering brightness that traced the gentle wake of the boat in a long faint fan behind them, briefly recording the path of their journey before blinking out.

'I think I saw a couple flashes from headlights over there, a bit more to the left,' Charlie said.

'Yeah, I saw them too,' Bailey whispered.

Only by watching as the diffused glow from the distant towns gradually turned into distinct individual lights could they tell how close they were to the coast. As planned, they were coming in closer to Az-Zawiyah than to Janzour, near where the Coastal Road curved in closer to the beach. It was also the place where a small tract of forest cut into the endless rocky coast, reaching right down to the sand by the water's edge.

Stack sent out two quick flashes from his torch. A single flash from the coast came back. Closer this time. The captain of the dhow had already turned the boat a little and the returning signal from the beach was at the dead centre of their course.

With the dhow's engine ticking over in an uneven rhythm of hesitant pops, they were drifting in using the momentum of the boat.

Every now and then they could feel the keel scrape the bottom, but still the old fisherman teased his ancient boat closer. They were going no more than walking pace. Out on the starboard side the fisherman's son paced warily up and down using a long pole to fend the wooden hull away from the rocks as the they entered the shallows.

Another flash of headlights. So close you could almost touch them. And then a forward lurch as the dhow came to an abrupt stop against the sand and settled back a little in enough water to keep it afloat.

Their eyes had got used to the darkness and they were able to distinguish between the darker patch of forest and the bright pin pricks of stars that were abruptly cut off behind the treeline ahead of them.

The three-man Topaz recovery team jumped down into the shallow water a metre or two from the beach and turned to catch their backpacks thrown to them from the dhow. They were joined by a very nervous driver, Rakim, who urged them to hurry. Stack and Charlie threw shielded light from their torches down onto the sand to guide their way up the rock-strewn beach. Ahead was Rakim's old Nissan SUV parked at the end of the dirt track that edged the forest.

As Stack climbed into the front passenger seat, he ran through a mental checklist of what lay ahead. They'd planned to be back at this same spot at the same time the following day. The dhow would be out at sea, watching for two headlight flashes from the beach as before. A window of two hours had been agreed.

Between now and then, all they had to do was avoid any road checks by militia groups on the way into Tripoli. Drive through the city avoiding any further rebel encounters or the curiosity of the GNA army. Recover the flightcase. Then do the same thing in reverse on the way back. How hard could that be?

***

The first problem arrived sooner than expected. They'd just turned left out of the dirt track from the beach onto the Coastal Road; an unrepaired ribbon of potholed tarmac that stretches the full length of the Libyan coast. Strewn with a thin veil of sand, windswept in from the nearby desert like a handful of flour thrown across a bakers table. The highway connects all the main towns west of Tripoli to those in the east, as far as the city of Tobruk. Overhead, dust, high in the atmosphere, had given the newly risen three-quarter moon a reddish hue which bathed the North African landscape in a pale, anaemic light.

Thirty yards ahead on the other side, a beaten-up old canvas-covered army truck was parked three-legged against the hump of sand that bordered the road. Its fourth offside front wheel was missing and the hub raised up on a jack. As they approached they could see two soldiers smoking cigarettes sitting forlornly on the sand bank to the rear of the vehicle, their weapons abandoned on the gravel next to them. Rakim started to pick up speed but a third soldier ran out into the road waving frantically, the light from his torch sketching bright arcs.

'OK guys, keep cool,' Stack said. He turned to Rakim sitting next to him. 'See what he wants and keep us out of it.'

Dawson and Bailey played fast asleep in the back. Stack tried to look bored.

The Nissan pulled up hard, practically touching the soldier who leaped out of the way an inch before the bumper touched the leg of his desert camouflage pants.

The Coastal Road was deserted at this hour. What traffic there was came mostly from the Mellitah oil complex further to the west. Sometimes a gun-mounted pick-up truck from a local militia would journey arrogantly through it. Maybe a private car piled high with goods for sale at a local market struggled along from time to time. Or, occasionally, a truck from an army garrison a hundred kilometres to the east would end up broken-down on a lonely stretch, its occupants seeking help from anyone that passed.

Rakim stepped down onto the road and spoke to the soldier, a sergeant in the GNA army. After a few words they crossed over to the truck. Stack could read the scene. He didn't need subtitles. They had both walked to the front of the vehicle. The corporal was doing lots of finger pointing and head shaking. He was talking excitedly in Arabic. The other two soldiers had managed to drag themselves up from the sand and wandered over to see what was going on. They'd obviously lost a wheel but were unable to fix it. What wasn't clear was what they thought Rakim could do about it.

One of the soldiers, bored with waiting around, sought out fresh company. As he meandered over to the Nissan, Stack murmured a warning to Dawson and Bailey. The response was the subtle metallic click of 9mm rounds going into the chambers of Smith & Wesson semi's hidden under backpacks. From outside they still looked like they were asleep. Maybe the guy would go away. He didn't.

He tapped on the window with the barrel of his rifle. Dawson and Bailey remained comatose. Stack turned to catch the soldier's eye and wave him off. A message he hoped conveyed that he should leave them alone and go back to his friends.

The soldier did turn to go. He even took a couple of steps away. But then he stopped for a moment, sucked on his cigarette, threw it to the ground, turned around and headed back.

This time he put his hand on the door handle and pulled it open. Dawson and Bailey made a passable attempt at appearing to drag themselves out of a deep sleep. They even mimed confusion and surprise in a performance that would have pleased a B movie director.

The soldier asked them something. It had the aggressive tone of stern authority that somehow always sounded the same in any language.

While Charlie was still playing tired and confused, Stack gently opened the passenger door and got out, his 9mm semi cocked and hidden behind his back. He sauntered around the vehicle as though he was merely stretching his legs, heading to where the soldier was standing in the road by the open door. Sensing danger, the soldier took a step back and started to bring his weapon round to bear on the new threat. Charlie was fast. He brought his gun up and out, pointing just inches from the Libyans heart. The distraction was enough for Stack to grab the rifle from of the soldier's grip. As the surprised soldier turned from Charlie to Stack, Charlie stepped out of the car pushing his gun hard into the young conscript's back. Stack threw the rifle into the scrub, raised his finger to his lips and waved his gun. The message was clear. *Silence!*

Across the road, Rakim and the sergeant were still deep in negotiation, but spotting the developing situation over at his beloved SUV, Rakim manoeuvred himself so that his back was to the truck which meant the backs of the two Libyan army soldiers were turned to the Nissan. Even so, something at the corner of his vision had distracted the younger conscript. In the dark and shadowy night beyond the broken-down truck, the sudden brightness of the Nissan's interior light as the door opened made him turn. He raised his rifle just as the three men started walking towards the truck.

Stack knew a few words of Arabic through years spent upsetting the plans of warlords and jihadi extremists in various conflicts out in the remote deserts and mountains of the Middle East. He told the soldier to tell his friend over at the broken-down army vehicle to lower his rifle. At least he hoped that's what he said. A hard push of his Smith & Wesson into the conscript's spine brought forth a machine-gun like stream of high pitched, nervous Arabic chatter. If the anxious tone was supposed to reassure his friend, it had the reverse effect. The soldier raised his rifle higher and shouted something back. By this time the sergeant had been alerted and was pulling his pistol out of its holster as he turned to see what the trouble was. Rakim, alarmed at the sudden dangerous turn of events, stepped back a few steps to get clear of any trouble. With his lucrative smuggling business at risk, this was the very thing he wanted to avoid.

'Please, Mr Stack,' he called out, 'These men only want our help. There is no need for any trouble.'

The sergeant turned to Rakim at the sound of the English words and said something. It didn't sound friendly.

Stack, Charlie and the Libyan conscript had almost crossed the carriageway, but stopped a safe couple of yards back, their guns held out front and centre, a warning to the other soldiers by the truck.

'Drop your weapons,' Stack said in fractured Arabic.

Nothing happened at first until Rakim translated in the local dialect. Stack pushed his gun hard against the young soldier's head, making him tilt it painfully forward. Then Charlie fired a shot in the air. The effect was instant. The rifle and hand gun were thrown down to the crumbling blacktop with the clatter of metal and wood.

'Pick them up, Rakim,' Stack shouted, 'and throw them over there.' He indicated the thin desert scrubland on the other side of the road. Rakim did as he was told.

Stack pushed the young soldier over to join his conscript friend and told them both to climb up into the back of the truck. He indicated with his gun that the sergeant should remain where he was. Charlie saw the soldiers hesitate. He walked over and pushed them both to the rear of the truck, his gun doing most of the intimidation. He frisked them one at a time. There were no other weapons, but he did find and remove the one cell phone they had between them. Once they'd climbed in, Charlie raised the backboard and secured it with the two chain pins. 'Stay!' was his final command before walking back to Stack and the sergeant.

'OK, Rakim. Take this man and put him in the front seat of your car,' Stack said. 'I'll sit in the back with the other guys.'

'We're taking him with us?' Rakim was shocked.

'Yes. He could come in useful.'

Rakim didn't ask any more questions, but Charlie knew what Stack had in mind as he squeezed in next to Bailey.

Tripoli

'You're sure this is the street?' Stack murmured to Bailey, as he checked up and down the Via for signs of any early morning activity.

The moon had glided across the heavens, and now, at two fifteen am, hovered low over the city. By five it will have disappeared below the western horizon and the first stirrings of morning light would arrive to dim the stars, leaving only the brilliance of Venus, the morning star, to guide the sun up from the east.

The local streets appeared deserted and silent except for the occasional bark of stray dogs echoing from somewhere across the city.

'It's just down here on the left,' Bailey whispered as he led them silently past the mud rendered walls and boarded up shop-fronts of the narrow, moon shadowed souk.

***

It had taken just over an hour to get through Janzour and into the western suburbs of Tripoli. Their destination, the Old City, a tiny enclave that clung to the western edge of the Port of Tripoli, lay just two kilometres away.

Unlike the embassy people-carrier that had picked them up from the airport, the back seat of the Nissan was cramped. Chris Bailey had slid across to the driver's side, Dawson in the middle. Stack sat behind the sergeant tapping the back of his head occasionally with the barrel of his pistol, just to remind their new Libyan friend he was there.

So far, not a single road block had interrupted their journey. Though a few kilometres back, a set of concrete barriers had been placed across a dark stretch of road with dangerous disregard for safety. The Nissan's headlights had picked them out of the darkness just in time. They'd slowed almost to a stop expecting an armed guard to step up and challenge them. But the blockade was unguarded apart from two men over on the side of the road sleeping next to an old rusting brazier, its burning embers long since extinguished, much like their enthusiasm for their cause at that time of night. One of the men stirred lazily, pulling his coat further over his head, as the Nissan negotiated its way around the hazards.

It was once they'd passed through Janzour and onto the Gergarish Main Road that they entered the dangerous and disputed territory that heavily armed local militias defended with lethal determination against rival gangs and the GNA Army.

As had been the case for much of their journey, the streets were mostly deserted. The transformation from desert road to inner-city conurbation had been noticeable for the last couple of kilometres. Shops, businesses, commerce of all kinds lined the route. Many were boarded up and abandoned. Others had steel shutters rolled down and locked to prevent looting. Very few had illuminated displays of any kind. Road junctions with traffic lights were rare and the few that had them were often not functioning. It had all the signs of a city on the edge of civil war.

They had to slow down as they approached a junction with just one traffic signal working. It was permanently fixed on red. Nothing came along the road that crossed it, but just ahead the flickering light of two smoky oil drum fires told them their path was blocked. A wooden barrier had been dragged across the road and waiting in front of it were four or five GNA army guards, their weapons raised and ready. One with a torch was already flagging them down and pointing to the exact spot on the road where they should stop.

'I can't see how they could be expecting us,' Charlie said. 'I took the only cell phone they had between them back at the truck.'

'Listen to me,' Stack said in Arabic, as he gave the sergeant another prod with the barrel of his semiautomatic. 'I don't care what words you use, but you will persuade them to let us through without checking ID's.' He turned to Rakim. 'You tell him again. Make sure he understands he'll get shot first if he tries anything stupid.'

They were just slowing to a stop as Rakim finished explaining the rules to the nervous hostage next to him. From the tone of his voice, the sergeant didn't sound confident, so Stack tapped his head again, harder this time, which brought a cry of pain from the man. Message delivered.

Outside, the guard used a winding hand gesture to indicate Rakim should lower his window. He was already doing so anyway. The soldier had his hand out and said something. Stack guessed he was asking for an ID. Two other guards were standing back, but their weapons held ready in an attempt to show they were alert. The other two were further away by the side of the road leaning against a truck, smoking. Curfew kept most Libyans at home. This had been the only vehicle in an hour. Stack could see they were all bored and tired.

In Stack's view, the sergeant had already missed his cue so he gave him a nudge to encourage him to deliver his lines. The nervous sergeant responded by leaning over Rakim towards the open window, making a show of his stripes on his GNA uniform. As a sergeant he out-ranked the corporal and he gave it to him in spades. Lots of noisy authority, just this side of friendly. The corporal stood back, straightened and saluted. Stack was impressed.

The guard shouted something to the others who snapped out of their torpor, took hold of the heavy barrier and dragged it back, making a gap just big enough for Rakim to drive the Nissan through.

In seconds the barrier and the burning oil drums were behind them and disappearing into the night as they headed away at high speed towards the old city.

'What did he tell them, Rakim? He was talking so fast I didn't catch all of it,' Stack said.

'He told them his wife was about to have a child and we were taking him to the hospital because his own car had broken down,' Rakim explained. 'He told them it was an emergency.'

They all laughed at the unlikely story from a man who looked as old as Methuselah. Even the sergeant joined in, until he remembered he was their captive.

'And they went for that?' said Charlie. 'So, what are we going to do with him, boss?'.

'We can't take him all the way,' Bailey said. 'We need to get rid of him asap.'

'What do you think Rakim?' Stack said. 'Drop him off at the next junction?'

'Yes. I don't think we will have any more road blocks so far into the city,' said Rakim, eager to get rid of the GNR soldier. Then, concerned for his own safety. 'It will be safer if I don't take you too close to the house, you can take the back streets. Just a short walk.'

The sergeant was released at a crossroad a kilometre from the last checkpoint. He waited on the corner as the SUV drove away. Rakim checked his rear-view mirror and saw him turn and start walking back the way they had come.

The next stop was just inside the walls of the old city, a few narrow streets from Souk al-Turk. It was agreed that Rakim would wait until they returned. They didn't expect to be long.

**

They had walked to within a street of the abandoned MI8 base. Before they went further, they paused within the shadows of an alley one building shy of their target. Their attempts at stealth were nearly undermined by the loud squeal of a cat as it ran out of the darkness, across the narrow road and up onto a high stone wall opposite, where it sat staring at them resentfully.

'Shit! I nearly had a heart attack,' Charlie said.

'Keep it down,' Stack hissed.

'It's been more than a couple of weeks, Chris. Do you really think the stuff will still be there?' Charlie whispered.

'Why not? The rooms weren't rented. We own them. There's no reason for anyone to check to see if the tenants had trashed the place.' Bailey replied softly.

'So, you have the keys?' Stack said.

Bailey nodded, then pressing himself against the wall, inched towards the corner and took a quick peek up and down the street. Apart from the cat, the Souk al-Turk was deserted. He signalled silently that it was safe to continue. As they arrived at the entrance to the building set in a narrow passageway to the side, Bailey drew an old bronze skeleton key from his pocket. The main door had a simple gate latch, which Bailey thumbed gently to prevent the old iron work from clacking noisily and alerting the other residents to their arrival.

Stack followed as they entered a short hallway that he guessed led to ground floor accommodation and to one side, a set of stone stairs that disappeared up into darkness. Bailey switched on his torch and, with his hand shading the light, led them silently up to the first landing, the one leading to the apartment recently taken by the devout, prayer-going ultra-conservatives.

'Watch the floor boards here,' Bailey whispered. 'Use the edges.'

As he said it, Charlie's foot had already found a noisy plank. He froze for a moment as though he'd stepped on a mine, then tried to ease his foot off. In the stillness of the house the complaining squeak as the board rubbed up against its neighbour sounded clear and obvious. Maybe, if the occupants had heard it, they would think it was just the natural cooling of the building after a hot day. They waited for a moment - the time it took to hold a long breath, before moving stealthily on.

The second flight of stairs was quickly negotiated by torchlight. To the right was the ancient oak door that hid behind it the primary purpose of their mission.

Bailey inserted the key and tried to ease it very gently counter clockwise. The first hint of a possible problem came as he realized the key wouldn't turn because the door wasn't locked. His hand moved to the brass knob and slowly turned it. It had become loose and ill-fitting over time and squealed as it rotated. The door opened with just a tiny creak of protest from its old dry hinges. Without a word all three entered the room. Stack was last and closed the door quietly behind him.

'OK, Chris, you're on,' Stack whispered. 'Show me the flightcase.'

***

Fifteen days earlier, three things happened in quick succession when Ziya al-Bin and his militia arrived back at Breath of Allah's high-walled compound in the Souk al Jum'aa district in the eastern suburbs of Tripoli.

Personal items taken from the flat in the old city were dumped in a cinder-block storeroom next to the main building. But the flightcase was brought directly to the commander's office for him to inspect.

Thirty minutes later the woman they had spent the night chasing was recaptured and brought in.

Fifteen minutes after that, a westerner, probably British, was seized. He too was dragged back to the rebel garrison and thrown into a room with the woman prisoner.

The following morning, the commander ordered the man be brought to him. He was made to sit on an old steel chair with his arms forced painfully around the back and strapped tightly together with plastic ties.

'You are one of the spies from the house on Souk al-Turk.' It wasn't a question. The commander had surprisingly good English. So did Patterson, but he didn't say a word.

'What is your name?'

Patterson could think of no reason to lie, so he told him.

'Have you eaten yet?'

Patterson shook his head.

'Well, I imagine you will start to feel hungry in a few days. Maybe thirsty too?'

Perched on the edge of a table with his arms folded, Ziya al-Din looked at the man sitting forlornly before him. With his arms pulled behind the chair his head was forced unnaturally forward. The commander assumed it must be very uncomfortable. In time it would become painful also.

He had little sympathy for the criminals from the west that had brought about the death of the Colonel and an end to his dictatorship. He had no love for the madman Gaddafi, but his beloved Libya was now torn apart and his own life reduced to impoverishment as a result. As a senior loyalist in Gaddafi's Revolutionary Guard, many looked to him for salvation after the collapse of the regime. They chose to go with him, as the many different political and religious factions coalesced into bitterly divided bands of armed militia. His group was simply trying to defend the district that had been their home for generations. But often, it meant taking the fight to their enemies, or leaving a violent message in a car placed near offices of the Government of National Accord.

Violence; it brought fear and radicalisation. But religion provided the means to control it. Breath of Allah brought both violence and religion and called it redemption.

Ziya al-Din walked over to where the flightcase had been left by the door. He picked it up and took it over to the table, undid the D clips and removed the lid. He plugged the mains cable into a nearby socket then walked over and sat on the edge of the table again, facing Patterson.

'This is a strange thing, no?' the commander said, indicating the flightcase with a nod of his head. 'What is it for?'

Patterson said nothing.

'I have switched it on, but I can't make it do anything. You and your CIA or MI6 friends brought this to my country. Why?'

Patterson looked up awkwardly.

'I have no idea what it is. It's nothing to do with me.'

'Oh, you are here in Tripoli on vacation, yes?' The commander laughed at the notion. 'Are you enjoying our wonderful culture? The explosions? The gunfire? The tourists love it. Please tell me what hotel you're staying at?'

'I didn't say I was a tourist.'

'What are you doing here then?'

'I work for an oil company. I'm supposed to return to London tomorrow.'

Like the others, Steve Patterson had been given a script on what to say he was doing in Libya if asked. But the fake cover was never expected to survive scrutiny under real pressure.

'Well, we'll just have to take you to the airport then,' the commander toyed with him. 'After you tell me the truth. Why is MI6 here in Tripoli and what is that machine?'

'I need to speak to my embassy. You have no right to detain me.'

'The British have run away like frightened dogs. You have no embassy here,' Ziya al-Din sneered.

He got up and turned to the flightcase.

He'd played with it for a while the previous night but hadn't managed to get it to do any more than it had in the room back on Souk al-Turk. Just the same bright violet light which flooded across the room once again when he pulled open the small door on the control surface. The light had felt strangely warm and tingly as it played across his face. And again, it had been accompanied by the high-pitched dentist drill sound and a static charge.

Only when he had switched it off again could he see what was causing the curious illumination. A series of tubes that each led to a single point within the chamber. It was from that tiny point that the light was emitted.

He had also tried to understand the information on the small computer screen, but apart from the changes to the figures as he moved the tubular sliders, he hadn't been able to make any sense of the data it was displaying. He gave up and turned it off.

Now, with the prisoner watching, he pressed the blue button once again and the machine came to life with the familiar low whistles that rose higher until they screamed like tiny ultra-high-speed motors. Patterson was too far away for the static burst to have any effect. When he and Bailey used the machine, they had a wire attached to their wrists to earth the charge. He noticed his interrogators hair had a distinctly prickly look to it.

'I ask you again. What does it do?'

Patterson said nothing.

'I am not a fool. Please do not make this mistake,' the militia leader said. 'Two days ago. When you sent payment to me in return for your woman, I could see the payment on the screen in my account.

It was there. And then after we had released the woman, it was gone. As though it had not been there in the first place. This is not something that is easily done.'

The commander squatted down and looked up into Patterson's face. He spoke quietly, almost reverentially.

'Is this machine capable of doing this? Can it make such a thing happen?'

'I don't know. It's nothing to do with me.' Patterson said.

The commander searched his victim's eyes for a moment, and then came to a decision. He slapped him on the knee like an old friend and stood up again.

'OK. Tell me, what is this light?' The militia leader walked back over to the machine, took hold of the handle to the small door in the control panel.

Patterson watched in alarm.

'No! Don't do that. Don't open it!'

Too late. Ziya al-Din had already yanked it open and the beam spilled onto the ceiling, partially bathing the commander once again in the strange violet light.

Patterson instinctively pushed back into his chair.

'Please close it,' he attempted a calm voice.

For some reason, the quiet voice from the helpless man in the chair sent a small shudder of ice down the militia leader's spine. He didn't sneer or challenge him as he might have done but simply closed the door. The light was immediately dowsed.

He turned back to Patterson and looked at him. The relationship had changed. The man in the chair, tied up and helpless, should have been the one who felt threatened, his interrogator, the one in command; merciless and indifferent. Except now, somewhere deep within his core, Ziya al-Din, for the first time, experienced an unfamiliar sensation. The cold shiver of fear.

He tried to push back against it. To send the irrational thought back down to the dark, hidden recesses of his soul. It was how he controlled his fear in battle and he would do so again now.

He straightened himself, head up and turned to Patterson.

'So, I ask again. What is this light?' His voice full of an uncertain bravado.

Patterson understood that the game was up. It hadn't taken long.

'It is the light that is emitted from an extremely radioactive element when neutrinos are fired into it at very high energy to create a Z-boson stream.'

He wasn't concerned that he had given away any state secrets. To most people quantum physics was mystical witchcraft.

Ziya al-Din, a man of shrewd intelligence, took a moment to assess whether his captive was lying or telling the truth. He decided there was no way of knowing. But more importantly, he still had no idea what the box did.

'This... machine,' he started hesitantly, 'it has something to do with the money transfer. Yes? You will show me how you can do this.'

'Do what?'

'Make credit appear in an account... and then make it as though nothing had happened.'

'That sounds crazy to me,' Patterson bluffed.

The commander gave a brief, derisory snort, nodded his head slowly and began pacing thoughtfully back and forth in front of the table, tapping his lips with his forefinger. He was considering his options. Unfortunately for Patterson he chose the wrong one.

He stopped pacing and turned to his victim again.

'I think you are not going to tell me, are you?' He had that sneer back on his face.

Nothing from Patterson.

'You think you are a brave man, Stephen Patterson. But I wonder how brave you would be if I let my men talk to you. They can be very imaginative. Maybe you would resist for a time, but eventually you would talk, though you would not be much use to me when they had finished.'

The commander squatted down again and peered up into Patterson's eyes as he spoke. His words weren't for Patterson, but for the guard standing behind the chair. It was Arabic but Patterson clearly understood three English words – bring the woman.

The reaction was just as Ziya al-Din had expected and was the reason he chose those English words. Words he knew would give away Patterson's relationship with the woman. The commander nodded and smiled with satisfaction.

After the guard left, the room went silent. The commander said nothing and Patterson had nothing to say. The only sounds were the occasional footsteps, unidentifiable mechanical noises, doors closing and snippets of Arabic conversation that drifted through the window from the compound outside. Random and inconsequential life, as though listening to the background sound effects in a radio drama.

After a short while he heard footsteps echoing from within the corridors of the building. Two, perhaps three people. By the hesitant stagger of their steps and the angry protests of a voice, one was resisting.

The door opened and Susan Hedgeland was dragged in and thrown to the ground. The guards stood back in sneering triumph, semiautomatic weapons levelled at her.

'Major!' Patterson shouted in shock. 'Are you alright? Have they hurt you?'

Hedgeland looked up and noticed Patterson strapped to the chair for the first time. She shook her head.

'I'm OK. Say nothing.'

Ziya al-Din looked on and smiled with pleasure at the plight of his victims. He turned back to Patterson.

'Ah, yes, consequences, Mr Patterson, consequences. You know her very well. I think you will be more helpful now. Don't you?'

***

As helpful as Patterson wanted to be, the machine just wouldn't function.

He'd been put in a room with windows barred and door locked and guarded. In the room with him was a table and a bed. On the table had been placed the flightcase and, on his instruction, the laptop. Both had been connected and powered up, but despite the usual nerve shredding singing of the ultra-high-speed motors, the finely tuned and fragile apparatus just wouldn't work. With all the brutal handling as it was carried through the streets to the compound, and the subsequent carelessness as the commander investigated it, the Topaz device had once again succumbed to the irresistible ingress of its nemesis.

***

In Libya, in the summer, the hot North African wind known as the Sirocco, blows in from the Sahara Desert, lifting clouds of abrasive dust high into the atmosphere. It turns the air thick and scours the throat. This season was particularly bad, sending a plume that travelled far into Northern Europe.

The Sirocco arrived in Tripoli as a humid breeze that flowed through windows, doors and corridors. Penetrating deep into every nook and cranny. Covering everything, including the complex apparatus contained within the aluminium flightcase, in a fine coating of sand coloured powder.

It took all of Patterson's powers of persuasion to convince the commander that the problem was dust and not an attempt at delay. On several occasions Susan Hedgeland had been dragged into the room again and forced to her knees with a pistol to her head. Patterson tried to explain that every time they open the door they made the problem worse and that he needed a canopy like the one they had in the rooms on Souk al-Turk to help keep the dust out of the device.

It was a conversation that happened on regular occasions over the following days. As the delays grew longer, Ziya al-Din's patience grew shorter.

The commander had become unwell. He was beginning to show the early signs of radiation sickness, his face pale, his eyes yellowing and less focused. On one terrible day, when the commander's frustration and illness became unbearable, Susan Hedgeland had been dragged back to Patterson's room again. Lack of food and sleep had weakened her. She was unwashed, her clothes soiled and torn. She stood there bowed forward as a guard pulled her arms painfully behind her and forced up high to an almost unbearable breaking point. She scowled as the commander raged, and, through the pain, winked at Patterson in an attempt to fortify his resistance to Ziya al-Din's cruelty to her. The Topaz device must never be allowed to work and Patterson's courageous delaying tactic must be sustained for as long as possible. Except, Patterson had no courage, nor was he attempting a crafty delaying tactic. The device simply wouldn't work. If he could switch it on now he would, without hesitation. To save Susan Hedgeland's life? Yes. But to save his own also.

***

It had been over a week and he still hadn't managed to clear all of it. Parts were spread out on the table. As each component was cleaned Patterson fitted it carefully back into place. Some items where so finely manufactured he had to use a magnifying glass to be sure. But he was never sure.

There were occasions when he'd finished the delicate cleaning task and reassembled the machine, only to find it still wouldn't function correctly and he had to start over again.

The commander of Breath of Allah was becoming ever more irritated and erratic. But what Patterson did notice as the days went by, and it was getting worse, was the increasing paleness of the commander's skin and the way he used the table for support more. He was weakening. The creeping poisoning from exposure to the radioactive isotope at the core of Topaz was breaking down the mitochondria in his blood cells, causing an irreversible anaemia. It had reached his kidneys and the thyroid gland was fighting a losing battle against the deadly enemy.

As the illness took hold, Ziya al-Din asked Patterson if it had something to do with the device. He knew the answer of course, but he was used to facing an enemy he could see. Where death or injury comes by blade or bullet. This was no way to die. Not by an assailant that sneaks invisibly into your very being by way of a pretty, violet light.

Patterson tried to offer a small measure of reassurance to the commander, drawn from a very dry well of compassion, but he knew it was only a matter of time before the terrorist leader would succumb. His time as commander of Breath of Allah was coming to an end and he would soon be answering to his God - the one whom all violent jihadis claim had sanctioned their terrible deeds.

Double-Cross

'Why am I not surprised,' Stack said. 'It was unrealistic after such a length of time.'

'The place has been ransacked,' Charlie said. 'Except the bed in the other room looks like it's been used recently.'

Bailey was still checking to see what, if anything remained. Not much it seemed. Just the chairs, beds and the table with the canopy swinging above it. The whole place had been scavenged. Even the old fan had gone. His own stuff was missing as well. Of course it was. If you're there looking for stuff to steal, you'd take all you could carry.

'Well, when we left, the flightcase was on the table, the lid off and ready to operate,' Bailey said. 'It's completely useless to anyone. Even someone with a decent science degree.'

'Maybe the material has some value?' Stack ventured. 'Scrap metal? What was inside?'

'You had better hope they haven't dismantled it, James. There's an exotic isotope at the heart of it. A highly dangerous element that you wouldn't want getting into the wrong hands.'

'Define wrong hands?' Stack asked.

'Everybody but us!'

Stack and Charlie had eased themselves into the chairs in the first room. Bailey gave up checking around and came over to sit on the bed. It was still dark outside and the single, naked bulb, hanging in the centre of the room, was giving out a bleak yellow light. Stack wondered how it was possible that a room filled with light could remain so gloomy.

The three of them sat in silence considering their next move. The problem seemed insurmountable. Sometime, over a period of the last twelve days or so, a random thief breaks in and steals everything. The flightcase could be anywhere by now.

He reached for his backpack and removed the satellite phone. Charlie guessed his purpose.

'You giving Summer a bell?'

'Yes. I think I should give her a heads-up. Let her know we're alive - and see if she has any news.'

What he left unsaid was how much he wanted to hear her voice.

***

Back in Tunis, the last few days had been a nightmare of worry for Summer. They had agreed communication would be minimal, but the radio blackout gave her imagination a chance to conjure all kinds of bad things that might have happened to James, and of course, Charlie.

Paul Kent, Secretary to the Offices of the Ambassador in Tunisia, had arranged accommodation for Summer in a hotel not far from the embassy; a modest place, used for the less important embassy guests. Probably two or three stars at most. The UK taxpayer would be pleased at the economy.

The room was small with a separate shower and WC. Most of the living space was taken up by the small double bed. That, and the large, timeworn oak closet with doors that no longer closed properly but creaked like a house of horrors when they were pulled open. At least the room had air conditioning. She was prepared to put up with the clanking starting-up noises as it turned on and off at regular intervals, and the low hum once it got going, but she was grateful for the chilled breeze it blew across the hot, airless room.

Besides worrying about James and Charlie, she'd spent the last few days in nearby Rue de la Mosquée, drinking coffee at a bistro called Café Picadelly, which she assumed was a misspelling of Piccadilly, or, reading the English language newspapers offered at the hotel, or simply watching the chaotic Tunisian day pass by on the bustling street as she waited. There was nothing she could do until she heard from James. And even then, the only thing she wanted to hear was that he was on his way back.

Her sleep had been restless, what with noise from the busy street and music from the popular hotel bar two floors below, so when her cell phone chirruped, it didn't take her long to surface. She awoke to a dark room striped with the multicoloured glow of neon light that spilled through gaps in the drapes from the street below. As her eyes began to focus, the time on the small cell phone screen eventually resolved into the low numbers of very early morning.

She fumbled clumsily at first but eventually found the green button.

'James?' She asked hopefully.

Her familiar sleepy voice, with its easy Canadian drawl made Stack smile, even though the satellite-delivered signal made it sound thin and metallic.

'Hi,' Stack said intimately. He coughed self-consciously, bringing himself back to the reason for the call.

He told her briefly where they were and about the missing flightcase. She was concerned when he mentioned they were going to stay for another day.

But understood it was important to see if they could locate it, and, like Stack, she agreed that was a long shot.

The main thing as far as she was concerned, if he didn't have any local problems, he would be back in a couple of days.

After they'd said their goodbyes, Stack waited until he heard Summer cancel the call her end before he red-buttoned the satellite phone. He turned to Bailey.

'Look, Chris,' he said. 'Why don't you head back to the rendezvous point and keep Rakim company. There's nothing more you can do here. As I told Summer, Charlie and I will hang around and see if we can come up with a plan.'

Bailey nodded agreement.

'I was thinking the same thing. Beyond being more dangerous than helpful with a gun, I can't contribute much tactically.'

'Once you meet up with Rakim, make yourselves scarce for twenty-four hours, then return to the rendezvous point again. One of us will come to give you a heads-up on what the plan is. If we're not there within, say, two hours, bail out and head back to Tunisia.' Stack tried to sound confident. 'You'd better go now, before first prayers.'

Bailey picked up his backpack and wished them luck as he left.

Stack turned to Dawson.

'Let's make use of the cots and get some shuteye for a couple of hours. Maybe I can dream up some kind of plan.'

***

In Sirte, four hundred kilometres east of Tripoli, Ghazi Ibn Wali, the self-appointed leader of the violent insurgent group known as Sayf al Tahrir, ignored the message from Ziya al-Din at first. The extremist militia had formed from the remnants of the defeated Islamic militants to the east. Despite the bitter struggle to maintain a foothold in the war-ravaged Libyan town, there was no shortage of jihadi groups who wanted to shelter under their flag or, more likely, enjoy the reflected glory and terror that came with such an affiliation. There was a difference though. The message from Breath of Allah hadn't specifically asked for a meeting, it merely offered the prospect of some equipment they might be interested in. It didn't mention weaponry, and, as that was what they needed right now, he put it to the back of his mind.

A week later, another messenger came the circuitous route via remote but trusted desert communities. She had travelled with her young son and was returning to re-join her husband in Sirte. She carried with her words from the leader of Breath of Allah and a 'burner' cell phone. These single-use phones were still the preferred method of covert communication despite apps and software that can provide multiple, use-once, numbers.

The words were much as they had been before, but this time had added news of western hostages that could operate the equipment.

He was intrigued. What was it about the equipment that this commander in Tripoli felt he might be interested in? And what did he want in return? This, he thought, would provide the excuse to make the dangerous journey to Tripoli and recover something much more valuable.

Something that had been concealed many years ago. He switched on the cell phone and selected the only number stored in the contacts list.

***

His hands shook. He tried to stop them, but he had no control. Patterson tried to concentrate, but deep in his core he was gripped by a dreadful fear that writhed and twisted, occasionally rising up from his gut, bringing with it a burning acid bile to his throat. Since the arrival of the stranger, the terrible foreboding that curled like a restless snake around every nerve fibre in his body refused to go away.

Looking on from a chair behind him, Ghazi Ibn Wali twisted ragged tufts of his grey flecked beard thoughtfully between his fingers.

He was puzzled. Islam demanded an unquestioning faith. It was a faith he understood. It had been with him all his life. But this abomination being assembled before him. This outrage to nature. He was being asked to believe the unbelievable. Yet, this nervous man working at the table, this scientist, he believed - not in faith, but facts.

Is this not the very definition of heresy? Should men be tampering with things only Allah could know? Fate; what comes to pass has already been written and will only be revealed when Allah wishes it to be. We are surely not allowed to have foreknowledge of those events? Only bad things can spring from such hubris. And yet, this Patterson, with his trembling hands, says it can be so.

After many more similar thoughts, he found at last a means by which he could satisfactorily unpick the knotty theological conundrum. It was simple; if it turns out to be true then surely Allah himself must have allowed it.

Among his men and women followers, Ghazi Ibn Wali had a feared and terrible reputation. A man not known for his forbearance. Today though, he would for once have patience. He would wait a little longer and see this magical thing for himself.

Just as the commander of Breath of Allah had promised, Ghazi Ibn Wali thought, the heroic martyrs of Allah may soon have in their possession an instrument of formidable and game changing potential. *If*, the nervous scientist at the table can make it work. If not, he would simply shoot the fool himself.

He stopped twisting the hairs of his beard and reached down beneath his robes for the holster strapped across his broad chest.

Patterson had managed to complete the fine cleaning of another small component and was just fitting it back into place when his peripheral vision caught the movement of the man behind him. He turned to look and saw him withdraw a pistol from within the folds of his clothing.

The old militia leader smiled and nodded at Patterson, pleased to see the younger man's discomfort at the sight of the gun. He lay the weapon on his lap and went back to slowly stroking his beard. Patterson inwardly shuddered and turned back to his task. From the nape of his neck to the base of his spine, he could feel the Arab's eyes drilling mercilessly into his back.

They had rigged a canopy similar to the one back in the rooms on Souk al-Turk, which had helped to reduce the dust problem a little. He had seen less of the commander recently – not at all in the last forty-eight hours. The last time he was so weak he had to be supported by a fellow rebel. He pushed the soldier away once they had entered the room in an attempt to show authority, but it was clear he wouldn't last much longer. It was on that occasion he had boasted about a deal he had done with Islamic extremists in eastern Libya - the one sitting behind him now. He threatened that the device must work or both he and Hedgeland would be executed. Patterson shuddered again at the thought, as he reached into the canopy. Just two or three tricky parts to assemble and Topaz would be ready to fire up – again. Third time lucky he hoped.

***

After the chill of the night, it was hard to know what wakes you first in the morning, the brightness of the sun or the heat.

Stack rubbed his eyes and looked around. He'd slept better than he thought he would on the creaking iron-frame bed with its thin mattress. Every coil spring, he was sure, must have tattooed his entire body with red circles.

'Ah, you are awake at last.'

At first Stack looked across the room to where Charlie lay, still fast asleep, under a bundle of blankets, and then in the direction of the voice. It took a moment to resolve the image of the man silhouetted against the window by the bright morning glare. He was leaning on the sill and looking out to the market below, a gun hanging casually in his hand, but not pointed at Stack.

Stack's immediate reaction was to reach for his backpack under the bed. He swore at himself for not having his weapon close by.

It didn't seem to bother the man at the window that Stack was about to arm himself. He just kept peering through the dusty glass. After a while, he spoke again, his tone regretful and, despite his middle eastern accent, his English was clear and educated.

'I have always liked this view of the old city. Did you know it was founded by the Phoenicians in the seventh century BC? The Romans controlled it for many centuries after that. They called it Regia Tripolitana – the region of the three cities. Not much remains from those times,' he said wistfully, 'except the odd one or two columns and the Marcus Aurelius Gate, just over there. Everybody has had a piece of it: Vandals, Byzantines, Spanish, Ottomans. The Italians again, and of course, you British.' His voice grew sorrowful as he turned at last to Stack. 'I like how it used to be known, Mermaid of the Mediterranean. Such a pretty name. It is not such a pretty place now. It has become a city of the dead. Perhaps those days will return.'

Stack watched the man. Although he had a pistol in his hand, he didn't seem threatening. They watched each other for what seemed a long time.

'Forgive me for lamenting my beloved city. I used to be a teacher of history, before all this...,' he turned to indicate the city beyond the window, '...came to pass. My name is Faruk.'

He stepped forward and offered his hand. Stack reached for it hesitantly.

'I have been waiting for you,' Faruk revealed.

'Waiting for us?' Charlie said as he threw the blankets off and sat on the edge of the cot. 'How could you be waiting for us?'

'I was told to expect three of you,' Faruk said.

'Well, right now we are two,' Stack's voice was beginning to fill with irritation. 'Who the bloody hell are you and how did you know to expect us?'

'Yes, I was made aware that you may not possess a full understanding of the circumstances.' Faruk said as he walked over and drew a chair towards Stack and sat down.

Away from the bright, backlit glare of the window, Stack could see the man's face more clearly. He was shocked by the scars and the broken nose. They looked like recent injuries. Faruk noticed Stack's reaction to his appearance and instinctively drew his hand up to touch his face.

'It is getting better, I think. My ribs will take longer to heal.' He used one hand to undo some buttons and opened his shirt a little to show the bandages that swathed his chest.

'Good grief!' Charlie said. 'Did you get hit by a bus?'

Faruk gave a grunt of a laugh that brought a flash of pain across his face.

'I would have been grateful to have merely been in a traffic accident, rather than the victim of one of our many violent militia groups.'

He went on to explain his relationship with the MI8 unit and the events that brought their mission to an end.

'I heard them in the street, while I was still laying semi-conscious in bed. Then they were talking to people on the floor below. I knew they would come. I managed to drag myself onto the landing outside.

There is another flight of stairs that go to the roof. That is where I waited until they had gone. When I returned, all the equipment had been taken.'

'And this was when?' Stack thought he knew the answer but Faruk's reply shocked him.

'One. No,' he corrected himself. 'It must be over two weeks ago. I was quite unwell for much of it, so my memory is not very clear.'

'Over two weeks!' Stack repeated.

'Two weeks?' Charlie said. 'Hang on a minute, that can't be right.'

Stack agreed, either Faruk has got his dates wrong or they had been tricked into accepting the mission.

'Faruk, you said you were helping the MI8 team. How?'

'I arranged services that needed local knowledge. Like these rooms. Or, contact with the British embassy in Tunisia, or, if the embassy had things they wished to pass on to them, envelopes or other material. I was, how do you call it? A go in between.'

'A go-between. A local agent,' Stack said. 'I should think that was very risky in this town.'

'There are some very bad people that want to change Libya. To steal our fledgling democracy, our independence – what little we have. I will do all I can to prevent this.'

'And you kept in touch with the embassy?' Stack said.

'Yes. After the equipment was taken, I warned the embassy that Major Hedgeland, Mr Bailey and Mr Patterson might be in danger.'

'So, the embassy knew the equipment had been taken more than two weeks ago?' Stack pressed.

'That is correct,' Faruk confirmed.

'Wait a minute,' Charlie said. 'That bloody woman, Maddy Clark knew all along while she was sunning herself on the beach, that the kit had already gone missing.'

While Charlie was getting wound up about the MI8 revelation, Stack had walked over to the window. He too now gazed out to the ancient whitewashed buildings of the old city. A light haze hung in the air dimming the morning light a little, and further off, sitting like a thin band of smog across the distant southern horizon, a darker cloud threatened.

The question going through Stack's mind was, why had they lied about the equipment? He thought he knew.

'Well of course, there has to be more to it than the equipment, Charlie.'

Stack turned to Faruk and explained that Bailey had made it to safety, though he had returned to Libya with them. 'Do you know what happened to the other two? Are they still in Libya?'

Faruk shook his head slowly. When he spoke, his voice was filled with regret.

'I'm afraid it is not good news.'

'Tell us what you know, Faruk,' Stack said. 'All of it.'

It didn't take long for Faruk to summarise what had happened. A splinter group of the Nawasi Brigade known as Breath of Allah had been the original kidnappers of Hedgeland. They were the ones who took the equipment. And, through a reliable contact, he knew for certain that they had both Hedgeland and Patterson and they were being held at their compound in the east of the city. But worse, Patterson was being coerced into operating the device. The last he heard, and this was the most alarming news, Sayf al Tahrir - *Sword of Liberation,* were now involved.

'Christ! They told us that in all events, the Topaz device mustn't fall into enemy hands, but they already knew that's just what had happened,' Stack tried to control his anger.

'The bastards sent us out here under false pretences,' Charlie said. 'This wasn't simply about picking up the kit and bringing it home.'

'I'm afraid you're right Charlie. They knew that permanent exile from the UK wouldn't be enough of a threat to persuade us to take this job on if we knew the truth. They wanted some expendable saps who could handle a near impossible recovery job. They knew our strengths and our weakness. We were handpicked to sneak into Libya and steal the bloody thing back from one of the most barbaric groups in the Middle East.'

'They have become feared and revered in equal measure,' Faruk said. 'Sayf al Tahrir – Sword of Liberation. Liberation!' he repeated scornfully. 'They don't bring freedom, only chains of medieval ignorance, imprisonment and death.'

Looking across to the compact Smith & Wesson 9mm pistol his old Special Forces boss was holding, Charlie went into full, Sergeant 'Hollywood' Dawson movie mode.

'Captain,' he said with a fatalistic intensity. 'To misquote a well-known blockbuster, we're going to need some bigger guns.'

'Yeah,' Stack noted angrily. 'But the game has just got a whole lot more dangerous. There are hostages. People's lives are at risk, and I need to have a little word in the ear of the person who's to blame,' Stack said as he reached for the satellite phone and punched in the number Madeleine had written on the back of the card.

**

The cell phone was chirruping brightly as Madeleine Clark returned to her office after another Sirocco mission up-date. Like all the other daily briefings since the recovery plan had been set in motion, it produced not much of very little. She picked it up and punched the green button.

'Clark – go ahead.' She could see this was a satellite call. Incoming from Tripoli.

She listened attentively, responding only to confirm she understood. Then made a note of a final set of instructions from the caller.

'OK. Copy that. I'll get back asap.'

She red-buttoned the phone to cancel the call. Then, pausing for a moment to compose herself, she picked up her internal phone handset and punched a number. Only two periodic purring tones passed before it was answered.

'It's Maddy. Just heard from Tripoli. The shit has hit the fan. You got a moment?'

Time Proof

Patterson was aware of it first, but then, he was expecting it. It felt as though his skin was coated in a fizzing energy. He reached over to touch the metal flightcase and the static instantly discharged. Not so for the man sitting behind him. The hair on his head and arms started rising alarmingly. Ghazi Ibn Wali threw a dangerous look towards Patterson. This was not something he understood or expected. Patterson touched the flightcase once again with his right hand and reached across with his left to touch the arm of the Jihadi leader. The static charge grounded instantly with a tiny *snap!* as before.

Patterson's fingers flew across the keyboard of the laptop wired directly into the Topaz machine. Glowing green characters displayed unfathomable instructions in endless sequences on the machine's small display screen. Once again, the tiny, ultra-high-speed electric motors started spinning up inside the box, then they stopped, hesitated and started up again. It took nearly thirty minutes of tiny adjustments and false starts, but eventually he managed to get the pulsed ignition to hold – at last.

Patterson sobbed with relief and his head dipped in silent prayer for a moment. Then he turned to the man in the chair behind him.

'It's working,' he whispered, the long stressful days showing in the dark lines and deeply shadowed eyes of his gaunt face.

The militia leader nodded that he understood it was working, but then he opened his hands, palms up, in a 'show-me-something' gesture.

Patterson thought about that for a moment. How could he prove Topaz was working? There was one obvious way it could be done. The equipment was still tuned into the commander of Breath of Allah's bitcoin account – the last occasion it was used.

'Bring the laptop the commander used when we transferred money into his account. He will know what I mean.'

As little English as Ghazi Ibn Wali knew, he understood what the scientist wanted. He instructed a guard standing by the door to bring it.

Some time passed before the door opened again. The guard entered carrying the laptop and supporting Ziya al-Din, who had weakened further. He was only just mobile. The guard brought a chair over and placed it at the table next to Patterson. The commander sat down slowly and painfully, as though his every sinew was on fire. The radiation poisoning had ravaged his once healthy body, making him look emaciated and pale but his voice, though feeble, was clear.

'I would be very interested to see how you played your trick,' he whispered hoarsely.

Patterson asked him to provide the bitcoin account security number again. The commander scribbled it down on a scrap of paper and slid it along the table to him.

'I need you to dial up the account on your laptop,' Patterson said.

While Ziya al-Din was slowly doing that, Patterson used his own laptop keyboard to adjust the settings on the Topaz control panel and start the complex routine that connected the Topaz stream to the bitcoin account.

Behind them, the Daesh leader looked on with interest, staring first at the Topaz device and the nervous scientist's intense activity, and then at the commander's laptop screen. He wasn't sure what he should expect to see. All he knew was that according to the Breath of Allah commander, by some extraordinary sorcery, time can be moved forward so that the future becomes visible. It is the stuff of science fiction.

He knew of H G Wells and Ray Bradbury and their mind-poisoning western trash. All good Muslims must reject such idolatry. But, he thought, if this device can do what they say, then he can imagine many ways it can be used to make the west pay for their destruction of the caliphate in Iraq and Syria and the recent bombing of their brave warriors in Sirte.

For security and privacy reasons, the Breath of Allah commander used a bitcoin program stored on a USB stick to open his bitcoin wallet. It automatically connected to the internet and was now showing a confusing page of instructions and terms with which the extremist leader, watching from behind, could make little sense. The credit in the bitcoin account didn't seem impressive but he'd heard that bitcoin values had soared in recent months, so the number could be misleading. A curser sat blinking in a box on the bitcoin exchange website, waiting for an input.

Patterson's laptop was showing exactly the same screen, with the same field waiting for a number to be entered.

'Now this is important,' Patterson said. 'I'm not hacking into your account in the usual way. What I'm going to do isn't permanent. I don't have access to the MI6 bitcoin wallet that we used before, so I'm just going to change the value of the bitcoins in your account. It'll look as though you've sold some.'

He reached over to the tubular sliders on the Topaz control panel and began to move one very slightly to the right. Amongst the mess of data on the screen, one line looked familiar. It was the current date and time. In other words – now. The date didn't change, and at first, neither did the time. Then, as he moved the slider, the figures started to advance. Not the hours, minutes, or even the seconds. It was the last digit in a long row of zeros that split the seconds into infinitely smaller fractions that started to climb in microscopic increments.

He stopped it when it had reached the targeted time. Then, using the duplicate of the commander's bitcoin screen that was displayed on his own Topaz laptop, he tapped a number into the exchange field. It was a debit of the exact figure that the account was in credit. He then used the other slider to time-shift the duplicate exchange screen from the Topaz laptop across to Ziya al-Din's laptop. A momentary fuzziness was the only indication that anything had happened. It was impossible to tell that the display on al-Din's laptop had moved just a few nanoseconds into the future.

What had changed though, was the account balance. It had dropped to zero.

As ill as he was, the commander leaned in to make sure his eyes weren't deceiving him and, having satisfied himself that the numbers didn't lie, he turned on Patterson angrily.

'Where has it gone? What have you done with my bitcoins?' he said breathlessly.

Patterson was expecting this.

'Look, here, on my laptop. You can see that your credit hasn't changed.'

The commander leaned painfully over to see for himself. It was true, on Patterson's laptop everything remained as it had been. But was it a conjurer's trick?

'So, which one tells the truth?' he said warily.

'They both do.'

'How can that be so?'

'Because, it is your account in the future that has been changed. It exists less that a second ahead of real time. The Topaz device automatically keeps moving it ahead by this small amount, but it can't keep it there for ever. It's like trying to walk up a down escalator. The gap will grow smaller and very soon the margin of time will disappear altogether as present time catches up. At that point, the figure in the bitcoin wallet on your laptop will return to normal.'

The commander wasn't convinced. The figure that was now missing represented a huge amount of money.

'I'm warning you, Patterson. It will be you and your Major woman who will have no future if this is a trick.' He coughed as an intense wave of nausea washed over him causing him to gag into a blood-stained cloth he held in his other hand. It had been many days since he had consumed anything other than water and the dry wrenching held him in a painful seizure for a moment.

Patterson leaned back in his chair and watched him. Relaxed and confident for the first time after nearly three weeks of captivity.

'Just wait a few moments – please.'

The commander looked up as the nausea passed. On the small Topaz screen, the figures whirled in a blur of speed as it counted down. Eventually, after a few minutes, the numbers clicked back down to zero, and returned to current time. On Ziya al-Din's laptop, without even the clue of a fuzzy glitch, the screen slipped back to the present – or to be more accurate, the present caught up with it and the credit line showed the correct amount again.

The commander nodded with satisfaction and turned to Ghazi Ibn Wali sitting just behind.

'Are you satisfied?' he whispered.

The terrorist leader also nodded. If what he had just seen could be repeated, then yes, he was very satisfied. A deal will be done.

It was the nightmare scenario MI8 had feared. The Topaz device was now in the hands of a violent extremist group.

Ghazi Ibn Wali turned and signalled for a young man dressed in western clothes, who had been seated silently in the back of the room, to come forward.

'Karim, you have seen all this. Tell me what you think,' he asked him.

'It's impressive,' the young man said in a familiar London accent. 'This technology is so far out there. I don't think there are many people on the planet who could understand how this thing works. It's at the extreme edge of quantum physics.'

The leader of the most dangerous Islamic group in Libya nodded that he understood.

'But could you operate it, or will you need the help of this man?' he asked, indicating Patterson with a nod of his head.

'Not off the bat. Maybe, given enough time.' Karim rushed to qualify his remark, 'But I'm the undefeated champion on computer and internet technology, as you know.' What Karim Mahmoud meant was that he was an accomplished hacker and disseminator of the groups extremist ideology.

Ghazi Ibn Wali nodded once again. It was a skill he was acutely aware of and used regularly to advance his jihadi cause.

'Very well. It's good that you remind me because I have a use for those skills of yours now.'

***

After Patterson had been taken to join Major Hedgeland in her cell and the exhausted commander of Breath of Allah had been assisted back to his quarters, the leader of Sword of Liberation, whose single purpose was the establishment of an Islamic caliphate in Libya, was finally alone with his young acolyte, Karim Mahmoud.

The terrorist leader carefully unfolded a time-worn document and handed it to the young man. It was an old, dog-eared sheet that had partially torn along the folds. The young man held it reverentially as though it was some kind of ancient relic and listened as the grey-haired old terrorist explained what he wanted him to do.

***

The young computer expert's fingers danced across his laptop keyboard as he hacked into the shipping logistics system of the Port of Tripoli.

The screen was filled with common English language programming code mixed with Arabic script, in rows upon rows of text that flickered up in an endless stream from the bottom of the page. He paused the script every now and then, to alter a word or character here, a file extension there, or to add his own short variations of code.

Eventually, he sat back, satisfied that he had reached deep into the heart of the remote system. Access was totally within his command. He was proud of his skills and was keen to brag about it to the old, battle-hardened soldier.

'Nothing to it,' Karim Mahmoud said. 'We're in. It belongs to us.'

The old leader didn't have time for the swaggering boastfulness of the young man. He waved a dismissive hand.

'Enough. We have work to do. Get on with it,' he growled.

Mahmoud looked once again at the flimsy paper. It referred to a particular container stored in a warehouse many years ago. He had to search far back to the very earliest listings, when they had first begun digitising their warehouse storage system. The year he was looking for was 2003.

It had been a busy time for the port with much container import and export activity. But the one he was looking for had been kept apart from the commercial business of the warehouse in a section reserved for the private use of high-ranking government officials. This narrowed the search down significantly and he quickly found the container he was looking for. It had been designated on the inventory as 'DO NOT REMOVE GLAR CMMG Await Instructions'.

The GLAR was Government of the Libyan Arab Republic and the CMMG was Colonel Muammar Mohamed Gaddafi. As for the Instructions, after nearly two decades, they were at last about to arrive

Spring 2003: Ace of Hearts

Twenty-one days. A mere blink of an eye. That's all it took to overwhelm Saddam Hussein's Revolutionary Guard and the mass of ordinary conscripts that made up the Iraqi army.

Operation Iraqi Freedom, as the serried ranks of allies ranged against the Iraqis, called their invasion, had a primary mission - to rid the world of an aggressive dictator whom they believed planned Armageddon using Weapons of Mass Destruction.

As clever, wily and vicious as Saddam was, his sons, Uday and Qusay believed they were infinitely more intellectually agile. They'd been protected throughout their lives from any sense of responsibility or accountability. Aggressive and capricious, no one dared oppose them. Of the two, Uday was by far the worse.

Before becoming the Ace of Hearts on the allies' most wanted playing cards list, Uday had the run of Iraq as though it was his own personal fiefdom. A cruel and sadistic monster who raped women at random and killed and tortured without consequence, he called himself Abu Sarhan – The Wolf – and, as Saddam's son, he believed he was above the law. That might have been true, but he wasn't beyond his father's disapproval. He was banished to Switzerland, but caused so much trouble he was eventually thrown out and returned to Iraq. Unchanged and unchallenged.

For some years the allies had been watching Saddam Hussein, whom they believed was secretly building a war chest of nuclear, biological and chemical weapons. These weapons of mass destruction, they believed, would be used in a future war to subjugate neighbouring countries of Iran, Kuwait and Syria. He'd used chemicals before in Iran, murdering hundreds of innocent civilians in a reign of terror during the Iraq-Iran war.

In an attempt to establish himself as the favoured son, Uday secretly carried out a plan that he believed would assist his father's ambition. If successful, he intended to present the horrific fruits of his labour to Saddam in return for a promise of succession as the rightful heir to the Hussein dynasty. Such was his insanity, he believed his delighted father could not refuse.

***

There was to be a meeting at Uday's private palace in the grounds of his father's presidential estate, later described by American troops as a tasteless Arabian Nights fantasy of indoor fountains and erotic murals.

A disgruntled scientist, code name Primrose - an old time Stalinist - had arrived in Iraq that morning. He was full of raging indignation at his country's capitulation to the hated American START treaty. A treaty he believed emasculated his beloved USSR's military might. He came to Uday to do the Devil's business. In exchange for a great deal of US dollars he would guarantee the delivery of a quantity of one of the world's most dangerous radioactive materials - Plutonium-239.

This material, he assured Uday, offered the simplest means by which to produce the crudest of nuclear devices. Merely the threat of such a weapon, he confided, would be as effective as it's activation.

Such was the President's oldest son's deranged excitement at the prospect of being in possession of a nuclear weapon, that, after making the agreement with the Russian, he went on a brutal orgy of torture and rape for three days.

But, despite paying half of the cash price upfront, the promised Plutonium-239 failed to arrive. It took another year and the elimination of several members of the scientist's family before the dangerous radioactive isotope finally entered the country, by which time a great army was being assembled across the border in Kuwait ready for the invasion of Iraq.

Uday had yet to present his 'gift' to his father. But even he, with his messianic delusions, could see that, with the armies of the world waiting just over the horizon, the prospect of inheriting the mantle of President of Iraq was becoming more and more unlikely.

As the chaos of the invasion and its terrible conclusion became inevitable, Hussein family members began their preparations to flee the sinking ship.

Operation Iraqi Freedom was an overwhelming success in removing Saddam Hussein from power and crushing his army and the despised Republican Guard. But it had a more noble purpose: the search for Saddam's weapons of mass destruction.

Teams of specialists with detailed maps of 'proven' locations provided by a network of 'reliable sources' toured facilities in towns and cities and deserts and mountains, unaware that in the whole of Iraq only one small package containing two kilograms of fissile material existed. It wouldn't remain in Iraq for long.

***

Colonel Abu Hussan al-Iraqi sat impatiently on a silk covered couch in the large reception room of Uday Hussein's palace. He had been waiting an hour already. He kept checking his watch. This was madness. He had a battalion of Republican Guards defending a hopeless position near Mosul. If they fell, he would be blamed. Unbelievably, at this critical time, he had been called away, seemingly on a whim by the criminal, Uday. He had no choice. His route had taken him along the dangerous road through Erbil down to Kirkut and across to Tikrit, the home city of the Hussein household.

And so he sat and waited. Bored and frustrated, his eyes followed the activities on the sleazy mural that flowed across the far wall. A godless depiction of carnal depravation. The colonel, a very religious man, was sure Allah will have noticed. Uday Hussein will be called to account in the hereafter, of that he was certain.

The silence was suddenly broken by a voice that brought terror even to his friends.

'Colonel. I have an urgent mission I wish you to undertake for me.' Uday had arrived without apology.

'You have only to ask, Uday.' Colonel Abu Hassan al-Iraqi understood that he was merely a servant whose duty was to obey without question.

Uday was carrying a glass which he refilled from a whisky bottle over by a well-stocked, glass and gold trimmed bar. He walked across and sat on the matching couch opposite the colonel. An expansive white marble table inlaid with black onyx lay between them at shin height.

Uday slouched back imperiously, like a pasha.

'You are one of our most favoured officers and a close friend of our family. But can I trust you, Abu Hussan al-Iraqi?'

'With my life.'

'I hope so,' Uday said threateningly. He paused for a moment to stare at the man facing him. Abu Sarhan - The Wolf, knew how to intimidate.

'I have the most secret of missions for you to undertake, Colonel. Under any circumstances you will not fail, or everything I have been planning will be at risk. I am going to disclose something to you and then you will leave without delay.'

As Uday spoke, the colonel tried to hide his shock upon hearing of the plutonium. But even greater alarm seized him as The Wolf revealed his plan.

Saddam Hussein was not the only tyrant in the middle east. Another equally vicious dictator ruled a land over two thousand miles to the south west. His name - Colonel Muammar Gaddafi.

'You are to take the plutonium to Libya. My friend Colonel Gaddafi is expecting you. He will provide a safe place to store it. You are to remain there and await my arrival.'

Despite his fear of Uday, the colonel had even greater concerns.

'But surely, this plutonium is highly dangerous. Even the particles are deadly to breathe. Are you sure it will be safe? And there is the question of the journey. The Americans are everywhere; no route is safe from their troops.'

'A vehicle awaits outside with two of my most trusted men. It has fuel and provisions.'

'And the plutonium?'

'I am assured it is entirely safe unless processed into a fine powder.' Then he chuckled to himself, 'Or it is made into a bomb.' He looked up to see if the colonel was enjoying the joke. The colonel gave a suitable attempt at merriment at the not so subtle quip - in Uday's company, not to laugh could be fatal.

'However,' Uday continued, 'it has been sealed in a box which has been constructed as part of the vehicle. No search will discover it. Now, quickly, go and change out of your uniform, from now on you are just a civilian trying to escape from Iraq.'

**

Their Toyota Landcruiser had been packed with bags of clothing and personal items. Theatrical props chosen to suggest the hastily gathered possessions of people hurrying to leave their war-ravaged country,

They took the desert route south of Lake Tharthar. The four-wheel drive, off-road abilities became critical when they were forced to divert across the desert floor to avoid road blocks or columns of invading army vehicles. They were stopped twice. Once in a cursory search by American military police. The second time in a more thorough investigation by a suspicious British Army captain searching for snipers who he believed were attempting to sneak behind the allies lines.

Once in Jordan, it was a relatively easy drive to the West Bank where Palestinian leaders of Hezbollah provided safe passage through to Lebanon. From there they boarded a ferry to Cyprus. The next day they boarded another to

Tripoli via Port Augusta in Sicily. Altogether, it had taken them six days.

Despite being a delegation from an important friendly country, authorised and expected, it took another four days to finally meet the capricious dictator, Gaddafi. Until then they had to kick their heels at the local Sheraton Tripoli with the Toyota and its deadly cargo parked in the lower ground floor car park.

Colonel Abu Hassam al-Iraqi entered Gaddafi's large Bedouin tent, which opened into a modest reception area of low couches and scattered carpets. Tea and sweet baklava were served by Gaddafi's female bodyguards, until eventually, he was invited into Gaddafi's inner sanctum.

Gaddafi, wearing his traditional gold coloured robe and North African fez, looked on from an impressive Louis XV chair of gold leaf and pink silk, while his guest was offered a soft bolster to lean against on the carpet covered desert floor. The tent itself was an expanse of silk and printed textile material the colours of sand and palm greens. Chandeliers hung absurdly from the two highest points of the structure.

It was clear from Gaddafi's arrogant tone that he felt the Hussein dynasty in Iraq was coming to an end, unaware that in just seven years he too would go the very same way. Nonetheless, he was happy to provide a suitable storage place for his visitor's deadly material. The very idea of its presence in Libya amused him. An opportunity to tweak the nose of the Americans, perhaps, at some future date.

***

As for Colonel Abu Hassam al-Iraqi, he found Colonel Gaddafi even more distasteful than Saddam Hussein. He had already wasted too much time in this land of the eccentric dictator. Despite the crushing defeat at the hands of the alliance, it was time to return to Iraq, though what the future held for him the fates had yet to reveal.

It turned out to be misery and unemployment for all military men, including officers, particularly any with an allegiance to Saddam Hussein's old Ba'ath Party. Saddam had been found hiding in a hole in the ground and summarily executed. His sons didn't survive, Uday and Qusay were surrounded by American troops at a house in Mosul and were shot dead after a six-hour battle.

Despite advice to the contrary, the Americans had hollowed out the Iraqi administration, leaving a desperate population penniless and without income. A population boiling with resentment, easy pickings for the new charismatic leaders of Islamic State.

Experienced officers from the Revolutionary Guard, desperate for money, joined the group and became the main planners of Islamic State's swift military successes across Iraq and Syria. Most of these officers were not religiously motivated and stood back once the fighting was done. One significant exception was Colonel Abu Hassam al-Iraqi. He saw Islamic State as an appropriate response to correct the decadence of the Hussein years: a holy duty.

He threw off the old military clothes, the old political associations and his old name. From now on he would be known as Ghazi Ibn Wali – *Attacker Campaigning for Allah*. And he would take the sacred jihadi fight to Libya and, if it pleases Mohammad – *peace be upon him* – into the devil's heart of the cursed Kufir.

***

Present Day

By the time the loadmaster in his office at the Port of Tripoli had answered the phone and called up the record for the container in question, everything looked just as it should on the screen in front of him. Approval was given for the immediate removal of the container from the warehouse. Nothing out of the ordinary. Just another day in the office.

Curious at the sight of the large doors opening for the first time in years, several warehouse men stood watching as the heavy mobile reach stacker disappeared into the cavernous storage space. It was gone for less than a minute and returned with the twenty-foot steel box hanging from its jaws, eight feet off the ground. The diesel-powered handler took the box directly to a waiting truck. The driver had the matching documentation and so the container was loaded and driven out of the port and into the city, lost from the warehouse logistics system forever.

Back in the warehouse, two anxious men with clip boards and walkie-talkies ran back and forth among the remaining containers, re-examining the faded writing on the shipping cards fixed to the doors and speaking frantically to the loadmaster in an office somewhere in the main building. It was he who gave permission for the box to be moved.

The load master had received a phone call from a logistics company, or so he believed. He was told a truck would be arriving soon to collect a very specific container. One that had been placed in storage long ago. So long in fact that it had become a forgotten artefact hidden right at the back and far behind the containers deposited later. This container was one of a very few that sat isolated in a section unworked for over a decade. The large sliding doors that gave access to it warned in a bold red, time-faded Arabic script that read from right to left: GLAR: AUTHORISED PERSONNEL ONLY.

Yellow Dust

The radiation poisoning continued to ravage Ziya al-Din. What had once been a fearless, charismatic figure had now been reduced to a feeble ghost of a man in the space of little more than two weeks. After the successful demonstration of the Topaz device, the commander of Breath of Allah had been helped back to his room. But not before the deal was struck. Sick and emasculated, Ziya al-Din's physical power now came through his two loyal guards who stayed close by, silent, committed and deadly. If their guest, the self-appointed jihadi leader from the eastern provinces of the country reneged on the deal, they would deliver their leader's violent response.

Not that Ghazi Ibn Wali had any intention of tricking the commander. The device was much more than he had hoped for – or could have imagined. It was worth every penny. He asked only that in addition, they could remain in the compound a little longer to complete their plans. A request willingly acceded to. No Arab denies hospitality to another.

***

Once it was out of the warehouse, the container was driven back to the Breath of Allah compound. Over fifteen years had passed since the container's doors had been shut, locked and hidden within Colonel Gaddafi's private warehouse. Time at last to take a look at its contents, for the first time since the journey from Tikrit so long ago.

To keep their activity hidden from the prying lenses of American spy satellites, the truck, with the container still loaded, had been parked under a large canvas canopy. They smashed the heavy lock apart and the doors scraped open with a harsh metallic squeal. Two steel ramps were put into position and the Toyota Landcruiser allowed to free-wheel down. Even with tyres that had rotted flat over the intervening years, by the time the heavy SUV hit the sandy ground the momentum was enough to send it ten yards across the compound before it came to a standstill. They pushed it back under the canopy and immediately started work to repair the damage suffered through the many years of neglect.

Two volunteers wrapped in rudimentary protective clothing, began taking apart the steel compartment welded under the rear of the vehicle. They carefully lowered the containment box and placed it on the gravel next to the Toyota. They had drafted in a willing conscript to the cause, who claimed to have a PhD in physics from a local university. His rudimentary knowledge of fissile material, which in truth wasn't much better than many others in the compound, made him the in charge guy when it came to handling the box. It also gave him a healthy respect for its contents. He knelt down and carefully slipped out the rods that held the two sides of the container together. It hinged open like an oyster to reveal the plutonium-239 isotope. It looked like a short length of four-inch diameter lead rod but weighed twice as much.

What immediately concerned him was the large amount of corrosion. When exposed to water vapour, the kind you might find at a sea port, plutonium-239 decomposes to plutonium oxide, a highly toxic yellow dust. Clearly, the containment box wasn't airtight.

They still had nearly half a kilo of plutonium, which could be used to make a simple nuclear device, but now they had an alternative weapon. One that would produce fear and terror in a population. It was simply a matter of scattering the dust into the air. When inhaled, particles of plutonium oxide can cause cancer over time. The perfect threat.

But Ghazi Ibn Wali didn't want to take any chances. He wanted the ultimate weapon. He wanted the plutonium packed together with conventional explosives to create a dirty bomb. A twin threat. The carnage of a powerful explosion followed by the stealthy, creeping poisoning of the scattered plutonium debris.

The plutonium was repacked into the containment box and resealed under the floor of the Toyota. The innocent looking old SUV would be the best chance to get its terrible cargo to their target city.

He called his plan, 'Ghibli', after the wind that carried the troublesome dust to Northern Africa. Elsewhere it is known as - Sirocco.

Extraction

'I was wondering when Stack would get around to making this call,' Major William Cavanagh said. 'We don't want to start a war, but the small arms they're carrying will just get them into more trouble. They need some decent close quarter combat armaments.'

'To be fair, major, they weren't expecting things to go south so quickly,' Madeleine Clark said. 'Looks like they've heard from Faruk and now know the truth. Even so, the good news is that they're still on board. But, if I know James Stack, his priority will be more about rescuing the hostages than retrieving Topaz.' Maddy was eager to get moving. 'So, how soon can we get something to them?'

'We have our usual contacts in the area,' Cavanagh said. 'Put them together with Faruk. He's a resourceful man. He can get the weapons to Stack.'

'And the satellite imagery of the compound, Stack requested?'

'Our people at GCHQ are on it. They're going to send a file to Stack's smartphone. You'd better let him know.'

It was a late summer afternoon in London. A rain shower had just splashed the armoured glass of the office window on the third floor of the Secret Intelligence Service building on the corner of Vauxhall Bridge, a post-modern, dark-green and cream fantasy that was part nineteen twenties art deco architecture, part wedding cake.

'Look, however we get the weapons to them, remember to keep your distance,' Cavanagh said. 'No MI6 finger prints.'

'Or MI8 for that matter,' Maddy reminded him irritably.

'And for heaven's sake, Maddy, his primary job is to recover Topaz. Don't let him forget.'

***

'Faruk should have been back by now.'

Charlie was getting worried. They'd already wasted two days. The plan to recover the hostages and maybe the Topaz device was imprecise and under-equipped. But that wasn't the problem for Charlie. As always, when danger threatened, his old boss, Captain James Stack just seemed to become calmer, almost Zen like. Fatalistic even. But Charlie was different. He got the jitters. Not scared, just hot for the action. Like he'd drunk too much coffee. He didn't like waiting. Once the button was pressed, he wanted to go.

Faruk had given them all the knowledge he had about the Breath of Allah, the main players and the layout of the compound. Not that he'd actually been inside. He'd heard that the commander had succumbed to a mysterious illness and was incapacitated. Faruk didn't know how this would affect the rebel's fighting capacity.

What was certain, according to the latest rumours, they still held the two westerners. But there were also worrying stories about the arrival of someone from Sirte. Word was he was big news amongst Islamic extremists in that part of the world, which would make him, and the Breath of

Allah compound, a bright and shiny target for the CIA.

This last piece of intel was the most worrying. Stack made the assumption that if he and Charlie knew about this then the CIA did too, and they were already prepping for a drone strike. Delay could risk the lives of the captives.

Then some indefinable moment arrived. It seemed no different to any that had passed before. Stack just got up and went to the window. It was night. About 10 pm. The misty, burned orange glow of the half-moon, hovering forty-five degrees above the horizon, offered some reduced but useful light. Stack spoke without turning.

'OK, Charlie. If I were the Americans with a Reaper nearby, fired up ready to hit the compound, tonight would be a good time to do it. It multiplies the risks, but I think we should go now. We can't wait for Faruk to bring the close combat weapons. We'll have to go with what we've got.'

He picked up the satellite phone, redialled the number and punched send. The call was sent twenty-five-thousand miles up to a satellite and back down to a third-floor room in London.

It was answered without delay.

'Stack!' Maddy didn't waste time.

'Have you heard anything from the Americans?' Stack asked.

With all the political sensitivities in the Middle East, spotting a target and immediately eliminating it with a drone strike was out of the question. Approval had to come from the very top. And it took time. Missions had often been abandoned as a result.

'It's still a target. They haven't given us a time,' Maddy said.

'If it was my call, I'd press the button now,' Stack countered. 'Faruk hasn't turned up, so we're going in as we are, just the two of us and the Smith & Wesson's. We can't wait.'

Maddy weighed the options in her cold, calculating, politically savvy mind. A drone strike now would take out the Daesh commander and solve the problem of Topaz being in the wrong hands. But the collateral damage would include Patterson and Hedgeland. She absentmindedly arranged the pens and papers on the table into a fastidiously tidy pattern of right angles and parallels as she considered how that scenario would play out in Downing Street.

Or, she thought, Stack and Dawson could go in, out-gunned and outnumbered, and see what they could do. She couldn't see much coming out of that scenario, but at least she could offer it to her bosses in mitigation for the loss of Patterson and Hedgeland. So, she decided, the special ops first. Get in and out if they can with or without Topaz. Then send in the drone. That could work.

'I'll get on to the CIA. See if they can get Creech Air Force base to hold off for a while. Assume it will be a maximum of one hour. Can you get clear by then?'

'Christ! Maddy. One hour! Make it ninety minutes at least.'

'Can't guarantee it. Assume one hour, max.'

The call ended perfunctorily, without any pleasantries. He picked the phone up again.

One more call. To Summer this time. Just to hear her voice before they set off. When they spoke, he tried to sound positive. But she understood what was at stake. What the risks were.

'One way or the other, we have an hour to do something,' he said.

'Well don't waste time talking to me. Go!'

Summer's words sounded bolder than she felt. What she really wanted to say was, *'Don't go. Why risk it? Let's go home.'*

***

It wasn't much of a plan, but they had run out of time. Chris Bailey had commandeered Rakim Shadid's shabby Nissan for the drive across the city. The roads were unfamiliar, but they guessed they were within a street of the Breath of Allah compound. The sat nav map was unreliable in Tripoli, so they used a simple map reference. 'X' marks the spot.

They parked up and Stack checked the satellite image sent from London once again. The smartphone screen wasn't big and zooming in was fiddly. He couldn't quite get the image of the compound big enough to be useful without outlying imagery showing the approaches to the compound falling off the edge. Still, it was current, probably no more than a few hours old. Better than nothing. From this satellite photograph and Faruk's scratchy intel, a meagre plan had been drawn up.

They had a good idea where Patterson and Hedgeland were being held. A store room in the north east corner of the quadrangle that made up the main buildings had a guard outside, according to the satellite image. A good sign something important was inside. Stack was working on percentages and this came in at a healthy eighty percent of probability as Patterson and

Hedgeland's cell. When they get into the compound, if the guard was still there, that will be target number one. People first – everything else next.

Stack and Dawson exited the car with the semi-automatics tucked into their belts and spare mags of 9mm rounds in the pockets of their gilet's. They scouted around the back streets until they came to a low, narrow wall that butted onto a building. They climbed up and tightrope-walked along its narrow brickwork to the end. A sheer wall faced them but using window ledges and protruding stonework, they managed, with some difficulty, to scale it and roll over onto the roof of the adjacent building. They scampered across two more rooftops, then dropped down to a ledge that placed them just a metre below the top of the compound wall. They peered over. In the corner directly to their right, just as they had hoped, one of the rebel soldiers stood guard near the storeroom. He was armed with a Kalashnikov, slung casually over his shoulder by a strap.

What they hadn't expected was the activity in the middle of the compound. In the satellite imagery, all that was visible was a beige coloured tent-like structure that stood close to the main buildings.

The tent turned out to be a couple of tarpaulins tied to the top of some scaffold poles rigged out in the yard. The other end was secured against the building. Anything they did under its cover would be impossible to see from the sky. They had wondered what lay hidden beneath it.

The area was floodlit and the centre of interest was a truck. It was loaded with a container. Parked behind was a white SUV.

The Toyota looked like it was being made ready for a journey. From the four discarded tyre remnants lying nearby, it looked like new tyres had just been fitted. Bright blue flashes coming from under the car, indicated someone was working with an oxyacetylene torch. Whatever they were doing, Stack guessed they'd almost finished, as tools were already being cleared away.

He checked his watch. They'd wasted twenty-five precious minutes, and they still weren't inside.

***

High above the desert ten miles to the south east of Tripoli and invisible to any observer, the Reaper drone circled like a shark. Its navigation system had locked on to the coordinates with high accuracy and was waiting for the signal to send its payload in for the kill. Despite the low light and dust thickened atmosphere, the forward camera had zoomed in to give the pilot at Creech Airforce base in Nevada, a reasonably good view of the target. On board, the AGM-114 Hellfire missile, with its twenty pounds of high explosive warhead, was being powered up. All they were waiting for was the ground laser to paint the target and a 'Go' call from the boss higher up the chain of command.

***

'Looks like they're prepping a car bomb,' Charlie whispered.

'That's what I was thinking. We can't hang around here any longer. But that activity is a useful distraction, even the guard has moved nearer to get a better look. Maybe we could just drop down into the shadows over there.'

Stack pointed to a recess in the wall to the side of the store room. It was less of a drop if they used its tiled roof, but they'd need to shimmy along the top of the wall to get to it. He looked at his watch again.

'Come on. Go!'

Charlie went first. Stack followed. They kept their profile as low as possible by riding the wall side-saddle, leaning away from the compound, like a trick pony stuntman in a western. It was slow going to cover the fifteen yards. On the ground, the glare from the two floodlights prevented anyone from seeing much beyond the bright area around the vehicles.

Stack and Charlie dropped down one at a time, landing first on the store room roof, then the rest of the way to the ground. A loose tile followed them down, breaking on the stony gravel below with the *ting* of oven baked clay. They crouched deep in the shadow of the recess and waited. Nobody reacted. No urgent cry, running feet or the metallic snick-clack of weapons being cocked. The percussive chatter of the old truck engine turning over lazily and the activity around the Toyota Landcruiser covered the sound of their fall. Six more minutes had passed but they were in.

The guard was just ten feet away from the cinder-block building, his back to them. Stack crept the few steps out from their shaded position, round to the wooden door in the front wall of the structure. Exposed and vulnerable, he tapped on it lightly. Nothing. He tried again, a little louder, watching the guard as he did. With all the noise in the compound, it was unlikely he would have heard anything.

Still nothing from inside. Charlie was standing by ready to jump the guard if he turned. Stack gave the door a louder knock and whispered into a gap between the wooden door planks. 'Major Hedgeland - Patterson!'

Three things happened at once.

Hedgeland responded with a combative '*What!*'

In the middle of the four steps it would take Charlie to reach the guard, his backpack emitted a noisy '*in place and ready*' squawk from the walkie-talkie inside.

The third, and most alarming, the guard turned at the sound and started to raise his rifle.

Charlie leaped forward, grabbed it and yanked the surprised guard towards him. Turning his back, he pushed his arse into the rebel, leaned forward and pulled him over his shoulder in a classic 'smack-down' wrestling move. The guard fell to the floor. Charlie fell on top, slamming his Smith & Wesson down hard on the rebel's head.

At the same time Stack hissed that Charlie should find the key. Charlie fumbled amongst the man's clothes, found the key and threw it over to Stack.

Stack caught it, drove the key in the lock, gave it a turn, put his shoulder to the door and pushed. Before it was fully open, Charlie had dragged the unconscious guard over the few yards of gravel and crossed the threshold, looking back towards the activity under the canvas awning as he did so. All three stumbled unceremoniously into the sanctuary of the cinder-block cell. Stack leaned his back against the door and heaved it shut. The whole thing took no more than a few seconds.

It was dark except for splinters of light that bled through the cracks in the ill-fitting door frame and down through gaps in the titled roof.

There was silence for a moment. Then Major Hedgeland spoke.

'And who the hell are you?'

Stack was trying to see through a slit between the wooden door frame and the stone wall. It was hard to get a clear view, but it didn't look as though they been seen. He spoke as he surveyed the compound outside.

'I'm James Stack, Captain Special Forces retired.' He thumbed over his shoulder towards Charlie. 'That's Sergeant Charlie Dawson SF retired. You'll have to wait until sleeping beauty here wakes for his CV,' he said pointing to the unconscious guard on the floor.

He turned around and scanned the room.

'We're going to try to get you out of here. Where's Patterson?'

'Not here. They took him away an hour or so ago. They've had him working on the Topaz machine for days. Patterson says they have plans. We have no idea what.'

Stack stepped closer to her, concerned at her condition. Even in the half-light he could see she was in a bad way.

'Well, we don't have much time. Can you travel?'

'Don't worry about me.'

Charlie bent down and picked up the guard's Kalashnikov.

'You handled one of these things before?' he asked as he handed it to the major.

'Looks familiar,' she said sarcastically, unclipping the magazine to check how many rounds it had left.

Once again Charlie's backpack squawked.

'Repeat. In place and ready.'

'Oh shit!' Charlie said as he pulled the walkie-talkie out and pressed send.

'Yeah. Got you the first time. Stand by.'

'Copy that. Standing by.'

Hedgeland's ears pricked up, 'That sounded like Chris Bailey.'

'Yeah, it is,' Stack said. 'He's out in the streets beyond the compound. He's part of the plan.'

'So, how do we find Patterson, major?'

'I think I've already found him, boss,' Charlie said as he peered through the gap in the door frame.

Stack came over and found another slit between two weathered boards.

Outside the oxyacetylene work had stopped and the Toyota was being lined up, ready to drive back up the ramps again. Standing off to one side, flanked by two heavily armed guards, was Patterson. Even from a distance he looked washed out and barely able to stand. His fist clasped the handle of a silver box – the Topaz flightcase. It looked heavy. In the other hand he held the straps of a backpack. Someone - probably a senior bad guy, took the case and backpack from Patterson, opened a rear door to the Toyota and placed them on the seat.

Stack and Charlie watched as, after several attempts, they managed to drive the SUV up the steel ramps and into the container. The senior bad guy raised his arm and pressed a button on the key fob, causing the rear brake lights to flash twice. The ramps were discarded, and the container doors closed and secured with a heavy padlock.

Stack raised his cell phone and grabbed a shot of the container. Then he opened an app and typed some figures. He looked up just as Patterson turned to protect himself from a sudden gust of wind-driven sand that blew across the open space of the compound. One of the guards quickly ushered Patterson up into the cab of the truck. Once in, he pulled the cab door closed to keep the worsening weather out.

After a minute or so another younger man walked briskly out of the main building, placed his foot on the steel step and heaved himself up and into the truck beside Patterson. Across the drill ground, a hundred and fifty feet away, the double wooden doors of the main gate were hauled open. The truck revved a couple of times, gears crunched, and it whined and jerked its way across the wide gravel expanse of the yard and out into the city streets beyond.

'Well,' said Charlie as he watched the doors being closed. 'I wonder what that lot are up to?'

Stack looked at his watch.

'No idea, but we have bigger worries incoming soon.'

'What's he talking about?' Hedgeland asked.

'No point in worrying you, major,' Stack said. 'We just need to clear the compound asap.'

'Define, 'asap',' the major asked.

'Less than five minutes! Hand me that walkie-talkie Charlie.'

Charlie dug it out of his backpack and passed it to Stack.

'OK, Chris. Go, go, go.'

Nothing...

Stack pressed send again.

'Chris. Go! NOW!'

Nothing.

'Jesus! Where the hell has he gone?' Charlie said.

Stack pressed the TX button again.

'Chris. Bailey. Come on. Go, Go, GO!'

'Sorry, James. Did you say something. I had some inquisitive kids crawling around the car. They've gone now I think.'

Stack took another breath and bit his tongue.

'Chris?' he said patiently.

'Yes?'

'Go, go, GO!'

'Copy that. Out.'

***

It wasn't much of a business, located in the street next to the compound in a largely unpopulated part of the city that no one drove through anymore. You couldn't make much profit from selling gas in a country that sat on some of the world's largest oil reserves. Still, he turned up every day, switched the pumps on and went inside the filthy office to sit on the ragged oil-stained cushion that still, somehow, managed to ease the discomfort of his painful haemorrhoids. His day was spent reading filthy girly magazines until a customer drove on to the forecourt. Then he'd reluctantly heft his bulky carcass off the threadbare office chair and shamble slowly over to the pumps. There were two - gas and diesel - and they sat in the full glare of the sun with no canopy to provide shade from the heat.

There was a new BP station on the junction a kilometre down the road. He couldn't compete with the price, so business was slow. Before, during the halcyon days of Gaddafi, when there were no rebel brigades or jihadis, business was brisk and he made good money.

His least favourite day was when the fuel tanker arrived. One had arrived today. The gas station's two cavernous steel storage tanks were set above ground, over to the side of the forecourt, next to the wooden office, a sun-bleached shanty construction long in need of a fresh coat of paint. It was less than half the size of a container box.

They wouldn't start pumping gas and diesel into the tanks until he'd paid up-front, and that was the problem – liquidity. The way it went was - he handed over whatever cash he could afford and they pumped fuel to the same value into the big tanks. Usually, it was never as much as he needed. The truth was, his own poverty-stricken customers had the same problem. Hand to mouth, from one end of the food chain to the other.

He used to open early and close late. But these days he kept it simple. Eight hours was enough. And anyway, he was getting older now, much closer to his date with Allah, so he took to going to Salat al-i'sha, the evening prayer, and closed the business by eight.

Tonight, would be no different.

***

Stack checked his watch again. It showed 8:17 pm. The hour was nearly up. He had eased the door open a crack to get a better view across to the compound wall and city beyond. He shook his head impatiently.

'Something should have happened by now... wait a minute.' There was the distinctive, low, *womp* of an explosion that rattled the door and dislodged some roof tiles. 'That was it. OK Charlie, major – stand-by. Any second now.'

In the street that ran alongside the compound where the old gas station was, a secondary, ground shaking explosion sent great plumes of flames and toxic black smoke rising up like an atomic cloud, high into the air. It took a moment for it to register in the compound but, slowly, at first just one or two and then several, until there were sixty or seventy rebel fighters scrambling for the main gate. The call went up for water, buckets, anything they could find to bring the growing conflagration in the street outside, under control. Wind gusts were increasing, blowing flames and throat scouring smoke towards the compound wall. Burning smuts and sparks were already falling dangerously close to store rooms where large amounts of stolen explosive ordnance were held. It wouldn't take much to set it off and turn the whole compound into a smoking crater.

Charlie pulled some old robes out of his backpack and put them on. Stack gave his to Hedgeland. He ripped the dishdasha off of the unconscious guard and pulled it over his jacket.

'OK, this is it. Keep your heads down and join the crowd.'

Not all the jihadi rebels had joined the panic. Two officers stayed back, preferring to let the peasant soldiers do the work. shouting instructions from the safety of the canvas shelter. Small patches of material were already beginning to smoulder dangerously from burning embers that had fallen onto it.

As soldiers ran frantically back and forth across the wide, uneven compound ground, one of the officers, casually drawing on a Marlboro cigarette, took an interest in three he hadn't seen before. They were coming from the direction of the store room. They attracted his attention because nobody should be in that area. He nudged his fellow officer and pointed them out with the cigarette between finger and thumb and a lift of his chin. They both wove their way through the panicking mob to head them off, bringing their weapons up as they drew near.

Stack, Charlie and Hedgeland had made it almost halfway when they spotted the two men coming towards them. One of the officers called out. Not quite a command, more of an enquiry. Not one that should be ignored, but Stack signalled for Charlie and the major to continue. They were almost within the crowd now. Soldiers rushed past shouting for more water and more help. Some tried to tug them towards the fire, pleading for them to hurry. The panic become ever more urgent as flames, fanned by the wind, took hold of nearby buildings in the street outside. The intense heat from the other side of the wall could be felt within the compound now.

Stack's Arabic was unreliable, but, above the noisy pandemonium, he clearly understood the command, 'You. Stop!'

They had no choice. They stopped as the officers finally cut them off, weapons raised. Stack didn't understand what they said next, but one started to circle them, looking them up and down suspiciously. Then the other recognised Major Hedgeland and pushed his gun into her chest and laughed. She tried to brush it away and Charlie shouted a profanity that couldn't be translated into Arabic. Stack stole a quick glance at his watch. There were only seconds left. He looked up as something caught his eye. A flickering red mark on the wall of the building behind the two officers.

'We're out of time Charlie...'

***

The drone had dropped down to fifteen thousand feet and moved to within four miles of the target.

Back at Creech Airforce base, the drone operations commander had heard the request from London. Ninety minutes was a non-starter. With a significant target of interest already overstaying at a known location, he was reluctant to delay any more than sixty minutes, and that was final.

They maintained an eyeball on the location throughout the hour and although a truck was seen leaving the compound, they didn't believe the target was on board. He was more likely to use anonymous transport such as an old private car. Something that wouldn't draw attention. Nothing had left the compound since.

When it came, the 'Go' command started a sequence of operational events that initiated in turn; the Hellfire missile's navigational systems, the explosive payload circuits and the solid-fuel rocket motor.

The pilot had flown the Reaper drone to within twenty-four thousand feet of the target, the maximum range of the 'fire and forget' missile. At over nine hundred miles an hour, Hellfire could cover that distance in two minutes. It had been in the air for twenty seconds when the pilot, watching on his screen back at Creech, saw the sudden plume of fire erupting from the building nearby. He ignored it and waited for the lock-on confirmation when the ground laser painted the target. Lock-on came at seventy seconds into the flight and became intermittent by ninety.

***

Another large explosion shook the compound as the gas station's second fuel tank erupted. Everyone ducked in fear as a wave of hot air blew over the wall. But it was something closer that distracted the rebel officers. The canvas canopy finally burst into flames, endangering the building it was tied to. As the rebel officers glanced away, the major grabbed the barrel of the weapon pressed to her chest and pushed it away. The man holding it staggered back a little, then angrily stepped forward pushing his face into hers, enraged at his humiliation at the hands of this foreign woman. She must be taught a lesson as he pulled the rifle back with both hands ready to sweep it back down hard on her head. He would teach her obedience. He wasn't quick enough. Stack and Charlie were already raising their 9mm Smith & Wesson's. They instinctively shared the two targets and fired double taps, blasting the militia officers, backwards, off their feet.

Another gust of stinging Sirocco wind forced Hedgeland to turn her head away, blinking to clear her eyes as she brought her stolen weapon up to cover the injured soldiers as they went down. But once they hit the ground they didn't move again.

Up on the wall of the building, the red laser target was still flickering. Still guiding the missile in.

'Well, major, no point in hanging around.' Stack's urgent command had an effect like a rabbit at a dog track. Charlie grabbed Hedgeland's arm and hustled her rapidly towards the open door.

Stack was counting the seconds in his head as he ran. If they had ten left, they'd be lucky.

No one paid them any attention as they struggled to force their way through the crowded gateway and out into the narrow street. What set them apart from the panicking crush was the direction of travel. As desperate soldiers of Breath of Allah ran towards the fire, they headed in the opposite direction.

They got as far as the next corner of the compound with its thick wall at their backs when a colossal blast exploded behind them, lifting the very ground they were standing on. It momentarily sucked the oxygen out of the gas station fire and sent a 360-degree pressure wave across the city.

Stack knew they weren't far enough away. They should be dead.

The shock was as powerful as any he'd experienced on the battle field. Windows smashed and the ground shook. Dust and debris were hurled in a great choking column a thousand feet high. But the fat walls of the compound remained standing. A direct hit and the walls would have been blown out and the three of them buried under tonnes of rock.

'Looks like they missed the target,' Stack said as he wiped grit from his eyes. 'Must have been the fire from the petrol station that deflected it.'

Smoke and dust swirled in a cloying fog around them as Charlie, his ears ringing and nose bleeding, shouted.

'I'm surprised anything for a hundred yards is still standing after that.'

Major Hedgeland, supporting herself against the wall was bent over and coughing violently. She only just managing to keep her legs from giving way, as she beat rock dust from her clothes.

'*No point in hanging around,* is that what you said, Stack?' She repeated his words angrily between coughing fits. 'That was a bloody missile strike! And you didn't think I might like to know it was on its way?'

Before she could vent her fury any further, a car screeched to a halt across the road. The passenger window was open. The driver leaned across and called to them.

'Come on guys, quickly, get in.'

'Bailey, aren't you a sight for sore eyes,' Charlie shouted back.

Stack helped Major Hedgeland over to the Nissan and eased her into a rear seat. It turned out Bailey wasn't alone.

'Faruk!' Hedgeland grinned, pleased to see her old friend again.

Charlie had scooted round to the other side and climbed in next to Hedgeland. He gave a look of astonishment to find that Faruk had surfaced and was sitting between them. Stack joined Bailey in the front.

'Where did Faruk come from?'

'Good question, but we've got the weapons you wanted in the back,' Bailey replied.

'They would have been useful about five minutes ago.' Stack turned and gave Faruk a disapproving look.

'I'm sorry. Things got delayed.' Faruk said. 'They dropped me and the weapons off next to the Nissan further down the road. Chris Bailey wasn't there. Then there was an explosion and Chris Bailey came running down the street back to the car. So here I am.'

'I thought you were dead, Faruk,' Hedgeland said.

'Dead? He'll be late for his own funeral,' Charlie joked

'Sorry. What funeral?'

'Doesn't matter, Faruk,' Stack said. 'Come on Bailey let's get out of here.'

Bailey slammed his foot down and the Nissan was gone, racing into the dark streets, away from the burning carnage behind them.

Ocean Trader

The 'broom cupboard' in the cellar of the British Embassy in Tunis didn't appeal to Summer. In the end, Paul Kent, the Secretary to the Offices of the Ambassador allowed her to use the anteroom to his own office when she needed it. Though he would never admit it, he enjoyed seeing such an attractive woman around the embassy, the nearer to him the better. And she was happy to take advantage of his interest in order to enjoy the embassy facilities – far better than the primitive cubical in the basement and the crowded internet cafés in the city.

Yes, she could use her cell phone to make and receive calls and text messages from her hotel, but with little news coming out of Libya, the embassy felt a lot closer to the action if and when it happened. Plus, there was a bonus, she could use the Nespresso coffee machine when she wanted and wrap Paul Kent around her little finger to finesse favours.

Being so distant from Stack and Charlie, she didn't feel as though she was contributing to the plan as much as she would have liked. She understood that Tripoli was hazardous, and that she wasn't skilled in the kind of work that James and Charlie were trained for, but she wasn't afraid to take her share of the risks.

It was early evening. She was trying to make a Latte Macchiato; a final beverage before heading back to the hotel. The Nespresso wasn't so much a coffee machine as a science experiment. It wasn't that it was complicated, she just struggled to stay focussed. Her mind kept wandering across the desert to Tripoli - and James. As a result, they either came out as a strong Americano or an over milky Latte. This one was working out better. Then her cell phone rang.

'It's me.'

'James! Thank God. What happened?'

Through a scratchy, low bit-rate digital signal that sounded like the thin whispers of an early transatlantic wireless call, Stack gave Summer the headlines on the action in Tripoli. He failed to mention they were nearly wiped out by a Hellfire missile. He'd save that worrying sound bite for another time.

'So, you got Major Hedgeland out. How is she?'

'Recovering,' Stack replied. 'We're about to start back now. We'll be rendezvousing with the dhow at Jadda'im later tonight.'

Summer was relieved to hear that, though she knew the route out of Tripoli was treacherous.

There was a short hiatus, each waiting for the other to speak. Then they both spoke at the same time.

'You go,' Summer said, eager to hear James' voice.

'Look, I've got something you can do that's right up your alley. You'll need your passport.'

Summer listened as Stack told her what he had in mind.

***

They had only travelled a few hundred yards from the damaged compound and the blazing gas station when Stack yelled for them to stop. He turned to Faruk sitting in the back.

'Can you get us to the harbour, Faruk?'

'Of course. Turn around and head back. Go left at the junction.'

'Get to it, Chris, and fast,' demanded Stack.

'What have you got in mind, Jim?' Charlie asked as the Nissan took off back the way it had come.

'Where Patterson and that flightcase goes, we go,' Stack said. 'That truck. It's hauling a container. There's a fifty-fifty chance that it's either taking it out of the city across country, or heading to the port. My guess is we should try the port.'

The ancient port was managed by the Government of National Accord - but only just. Others competed to control the facility with violence, making it a dangerous place to be. But the factional infighting affected security. While all eyes were greedily contesting the ownership of the port estate, goods coming in or out got superficial attention. Money was the new unofficial documentation. Enough of it would get someone through the gates and into the quayside freight handling area.

***

The rebranded twenty-foot container complete with fake documentation, had already been transferred from the truck to the deck of a small, rusting coaster. The box had been hidden under a large canvas tarpaulin the crew had just finished tying down.

A pair of corroded steel rails ran parallel to the edge of the quay along which two tall gantry cranes ran. In the past, the cranes would have been hauling hundreds of boxes into and out of the cavernous holds of ocean-going behemoths, but on this evening the only vessel moored along the pier was the tired old freighter almost hidden below the stone quayside.

The wind had picked up again and the abrasive dust that was carried on it thickened the air as the Nissan pulled up alongside the corroded steel wheel of one of the giant cranes. Stack noticed as he watched that there was little other activity. Thirty yards away, the crew on the ship laboured in near darkness, despite the port having a several lighting towers that each held aloft a grid of twelve floodlights. Little or no maintenance meant that only two or three of the sodium lamps were working, throwing a feeble amber light across the coaster.

As the truck reversed out of Stack's field of view, two men could be seen boarding via a wooden gangplank. The vessel, an aging tub called 'Ocean Trader' and no more than a hundred and fifty tonnes, rode low in the water, its mid-section nearly level with the quayside. The container resting on the deck was just over eight feet high, which put the top of it almost level with the windows of the vessel's bridge.

The mooring ropes were thrown from weather-pitted bollards by a solitary dock worker who hung around to watch as the ship prepared to sail. The ancient eight-cylinder engine could be heard turning over with a lazy, rhythmic thump, each cylinder coughing out great clouds of black smoke through the funnel, rising only a few feet into the night sky before a gust caught it, sending it away from the port and out to sea in a long, sooty ribbon that disappeared into the blackness.

A tug was positioning itself ready to nudge ancient tramp out of the safe embrace of the old stone harbour walls, into the dark expanse of the Mediterranean Sea beyond.

From the wheelhouse a bell rang and water began to churn under the power of the slow revving propeller. Engine bearings that should have been replaced decades ago knocked in protest at the workload.

Where the bow met the sea, a small white necklace of wake began to appear as the ship gradually picked up speed. She slowly manoeuvred out into the long swell to become, after an endless passage of time, just a tiny speck of light on the distant, dark horizon.

***

The dockhand had hung around to watch as the ship negotiated its passage through the harbour entrance. Then he turned and started to walk away, his shift over for the night. Stack was curious to know the ship's destination. He asked Faruk to see what the port worker knew.

Faruk got out and intercepted the man just a few yards from the Nissan. Stack couldn't hear, but he could see them talking. The worker waved his arms dismissively. Why should he care? It was of no importance to him. He started to walk away. But Faruk reached into his pocket and brought out a handful of notes. This seemed to get his attention. More talking followed. Faruk nodded and returned to the car. The dockhand walked on past, folding the money into his wallet, his mind already on other things.

'France.'

'France?' Stack repeated. 'It's big place. Any particular port?'

'Marseille.'

'OK, that must be a good eight-hundred miles or so from here. That old rust bucket couldn't do much more that fifteen knots.' Stack pondered the maths for a moment. 'Say, two and a half days, maybe three, if she doesn't break down on the way.'

As Stack spoke, Bailey started the car and they drove back between the steel walls of abandoned containers, past run-down warehouses and rusting handling equipment towards the port gates.

'Marseille? Then what?' Charlie wondered. 'They pick up the container and take it somewhere else?'

'It's a bloody big port. How do we keep an eye on it once it arrives?' Bailey said as the car approached the gates.

The Nissan slowed, but was waved through by an armed security guard whose eyes never left the screen of his smartphone.

'I can think of one way we might be able to keep an eye on it, but we need to get back to the rooms on Souk al-Turk asap,' said Stack. 'I've got to make a call to Tunis. I know someone there who could tail that container, but she needs to catch the first plane to France in the morning.'

The port sat on the edge of the old city where the rooms on Suk al-Turk were. Even so, sirens could still be heard from the emergency services heading towards the blast zone far across town. On the horizon the glow of fires still pulsed with undiminished fury. Their journey back along the Coastal Road would be dangerous. Trigger-fingered rebel fighters and government army patrols would be nervous tonight.

***

Diesel fumes were the overwhelming smell in Ocean Trader's cramped crew quarters. Bad enough on their own, but together with the cooking odours from the open galley and the nausea-inducing sway and roll of the ship, they produced an urgent compulsion to throw up. Patterson rushed back up the slippery steel ladder and out to the open deck. He paused for a moment to breathe the fresh sea air until a gust of wind forced him to take in a lungful of toxic smoke that scoured his throat. He leaned against the gunwale, his head over the side, and threw up.

Karim Mahmoud joined him after a while. He seemed immune to the rolling motion and not particularly sympathetic to Patterson's condition.

'Look at the horizon. I've heard it helps,' he said indifferently.

Patterson looked up and tried to concentrate on the receding lights of Tripoli. It did seem to ease the symptoms.

'Remind me again,' Patterson asked. 'Why the hell have you dragged me on board this bloody ship?'

'Like we told you, mate, where that box of yours goes, you go. Cause me the slightest problem and your major woman gets hurt. Cause a bigger problem and you *and* her get dead.'

On their way to the port, Mahmoud, an eager recruit to the jihadi cause from Peckham, South London, had spoken to Ghazi Ibn Wali by cell phone. They hadn't driven far when they'd heard the gas station explosion, which lit the city horizon behind them. Mahmoud wanted to know what had happened. Even as they spoke the sound of shouting and confusion could be clearly heard in the background.

It turned out the compound was safe despite the fire. And then, while he was on the phone, another enormous explosion. This time Ghazi Ibn Wali wasn't so sure of the source, but his best guess was a drone strike that had missed its target – namely him.

They were still on the line when Mahmoud heard someone talking excitedly to the extremist leader. He waited to see if this had any relevance to the mission. It turned out Major Hedgeland had escaped. This was not good news. Their leverage over Patterson was gone. Except of course, Patterson didn't know, and as long as they kept that news from him, he would still be under their control. Karim Mahmoud took a more cynical view. He believed Patterson was weak and would do anything to save his own life. Still, there was no need to test that theory unless he learned that Hedgeland was no longer their prisoner. Mahmoud was going to make sure that didn't happen.

'So, where are we going?' Patterson quizzed.

'Like I told you before, you don't need to know. Just enjoy your nice Mediterranean cruise, mate.' There was menace in his deceptively chummy south London accent.

Patterson started piecing things together.

'What the hell are you and that old guy from Sirte up to?'

'You're much too nosey, mate. But since you ask, I take care of all the technical stuff for the cause,' he boasted. 'You may think that you and that machine of yours are clever, but I can hack into anything.'

Patterson gave that some thought, and then the penny dropped.

'Had any difficulty posting your precious propaganda recently?'

'What do you mean?' Mahmoud asked.

'You're Chatterbox.'

'What the hell is Chatterbox?'

'You are my friend,' Patterson said triumphantly. 'We've been pre-deleting your propaganda posts. Nothing's been getting through has it? Some hacker!'

Mahmoud sniffed his contempt for Patterson. His anger rising.

'And yet, here you are on my ship. Not so bloody clever are you – you and your precious CIA or MI6. Be patient you miserable Christian Kufir. A new Islamic order is coming.'

He turned to go, but Patterson hadn't finished.

'What's going on with the car? Can't you get a rental when we arrive at wherever it is we're going?'

Mahmoud didn't bother to answer. He just stepped through the rusty bulkhead door and closed it noisily behind him.

Patterson, alone once again, noticed the heaving motion of the ship and remembered his debilitating nausea. He turned to the horizon to seek relief in the distant lights of Tripoli.

Marseille

It was a long-shot. Success depended on one unlikely event. Spotting the container coming out of the gates of the Grande Port Maritime de Marseille.

Summer had managed to grab a seat on a direct flight from Tunis to Paris and then a connecting flight to Marseille. Nearly two days had passed since James told her of his plan and her part in it.

She'd picked up a five-door Peugeot 308 rental from the airport, driven straight to a pre-booked hotel near the seaport, grabbed some coffee and a baguette loaded with cheese and salad, and driven over to the port entrance. This turned out to be not as straightforward as she had hoped, despite checking it out on Google Street View. It took a couple of attempts to enter the approach road. The first time, she missed it completely and drove past.

As the area was all port related commercial and industrial business, there were no cafés or other retail places where she could hang out while she waited. The only option was to park up in one of the visitor's spaces that lined the business frontage just up from the security gates. This would give her a view of any vehicles as they arrived or drove away from the port.

She had a good vantage point. She had coffee and food. With any luck, as a French-speaking Canadian, she could blag the use of the WC from one of the businesses when she needed it. She settled down for the long haul until James and Charlie arrived in a day or so.

***

The Grande Port Maritime de Marseille is several kilometres long. Going south to north it catered for roll-on roll-off freight, general cargo and cruise liners whose passengers were often disappointed to find their view of the historic town of old Marseille hidden by the vast container port just across the water. Further north lay the giant tanks of an oil products business and, beyond that, the private marina of L'Estaque, a northern suburb of Marseille.

It was midnight by the time Ocean Trader had tied up against the piers of one of the smaller and more remote quays in the Bassin National in the central area of the port, not far from the main entrance. The container wouldn't be lifted off until the morning shift began at around 8 am.

The berth where the old coaster had been moored was a small concrete strip that jutted out into the harbour from a rundown area of the main port. It was also the site of a port machinery repairs business. A warehouse filled the central area and the hard-standing around it was littered with forklift trucks, tugs and other handling equipment awaiting repair or simply abandoned to be scavenged for spare parts. It was a grease and oil-stained stretch of concrete that resembled the forecourt of a neglected automotive repair shop.

At the far end, a few containers awaited removal by straddle carriers that would lift them between their spindly legs and drive them to the forwarding apron in another part of the port when the time came for collection by their owners.

Unlike the container port further north, the small quay didn't have gantry cranes to unload boxes. Instead, the port provided large mobile harbour cranes that could be used for specialist heavy lifting services. It was one of these that arrived to remove the container from the deck of Ocean Trader. It was a simple lift for equipment capable of handling over a hundred tonnes. The box was lowered amongst the others on the quay and the crane moved on to the next job elsewhere in the port.

The following day the container doors were unlocked and opened; their activity concealed by the wall of boxes that surrounded it.

A little later, the Toyota was driven out and away. The driver dressed like any other port worker in his yellow hi viz jacket and hard hat. He drove the vehicle across the short bridge that connected the quay to the main port area and followed the road until he came to the car park that served the port management offices. He parked up alongside the other vehicles, locked the door and walked back to the ship. It would be safe there for the time being. With so many employees and visitors coming and going, no one would take an interest in another parked vehicle.

What the car couldn't do was leave the port. It didn't have security badges on the windscreen provided for all port employees, nor did it have the temporary security paperwork that is provided for all visitors to display on their dashboard shelves.

***

When a container is collected from a port, the truck arrives towing an empty flatbed trailer. Empty going in, loaded going out. Summer's attention was on the ones that were leaving. It wasn't the truck so much as the container it carried that she was interested in. She knew from the image James had sent her that it had been painted with the familiar, green, SeaTrack logo. She'd already seen a few of these forty-foot long boxes leave the port, but the one she was interested in was the shorter, twenty-foot version. When she spotted one, she checked the container number written on the side, front and back. James had made a note of this number while in the compound rescuing Hedgeland. Although it might be fake, copied from another container, it was unlikely that the original counterpart bearing this number would be in the Port of Marseille at the same time.

Her plan, if she spotted the container, was a simple one. Photograph it and the truck, and then follow it, keeping tabs until James and Charlie caught up with her.

During the first day, she swapped between sitting in the rented Peugeot and getting out to stretch her legs, walking up and down the short road. Never going quite as far as the gates. She didn't want to draw unnecessary attention. The weather was overcast but warm, so sitting in the car meant leaving the AC on with the motor ticking over. Which meant adding to the already heavily polluted port environment, something she was reluctant to do.

She stayed until eight in the evening, well past the time when the other vehicles parked alongside had left for the day. Traffic leaving the port had dried to a trickle. She figured that the best chance for them to get the container out would be when the port was at its busiest and the trucks were backed up at the gate. The hard-pressed gate security would be dealing with irritable drivers that were falling behind schedule. At the same time, the guards were under pressure from port management to strike a balance between security and the commercial efficiency of the port, waving many trucks through with little or no checks.

It was past three in the afternoon the following day as the heat and boredom began to take its toll. That's when something caught her eye and a neglected thought in the back of her mind was unexpectedly nudged back into life.

She was sitting in the car sipping coffee, trying to stay alert, when, through a gap between the outgoing vehicles, she spotted a car going in the opposite direction, towards the security gate, heading *into* the port. There had been plenty of other cars over the last day or so that hadn't attracted her attention, but this one jogged a memory. White, Toyota, Landcruiser, early 2000 model. It had stopped by the security barrier waiting for authorisation to enter. She grabbed the scrap of paper lying in the well by the hand brake and read the index number written on it. It matched the plate on the car that was now moving forward into the port area.

She wondered how that was possible. The Toyota was supposed to be inside a container that had just arrived from Libya. It made no sense.

***

The driver slowly approaching the security booth was a young French man of Moroccan descent. Emile Tajeb had lived in Marseille for most of his unremarkable life. He had found himself in his late twenties with unfulfilled ambitions and a growing resentment of the low expectations his fellow Frenchmen had of him; shelf-filler, gas station attendant, taxi driver and currently, salesman for an office supply company. His frustration was shared by many of the other young men of a similar age who hung around on street corners with him after prayers at their local mosque.

Although he was French through the nationality of his single mother, by culture, he felt closer to the land of the father who had abandoned him, blaming his mother for bringing shame to his family. Emile Tajeb had developed an itch that needed scratching. His friends spoke of the causes in which they might be prepared to engage. He wanted to be useful too. Amongst the company he kept was the scratcher-in-chief of a very dangerous cause, who could easily find many useful things for someone such as Emile to do.

**

Emile drew level with the security booth and stopped at the barrier. He lowered his window and handed his business card to the guard, telling him he had an appointment with the head of office administration at 3.15. The guard checked down his list of todays approved visitors – the ones with appointments – found Emile's name, and filled out a form which he handed to the driver, telling him to display it clearly on the dashboard shelf so that it could be seen through the windscreen. He touched a button and the barrier was raised.

Emile thanked him and drove off.

It had taken a few persistent phone calls, but with the help of the manager's secretary, with whom he had flirted outrageously, he'd managed to secure an appointment to discuss how his company could provide inexpensive office supplies at prices far below their competitors. He wanted only for them to give him a chance.

He had driven around the boundary road that, according to the signs, would take him to the port offices. He parked his Toyota Landcruiser in the farthest available space in the office parking lot, removed the security pass from the dashboard shelf, placed it in his brief case and went in to the building for his meeting with the office supplies manager.

By the time the meeting was over and he had left the building, it was 3.45 pm and the sun was finally making an appearance through the persistent clouds that had blanketed Marseille over the past few days. The temperature had begun to rise as he climbed into the Landcruiser. He started the engine, switched on the AC and gave the windscreen a quick wipe with the wiper blades to remove the thin coating of sandy dust that had settled on the glass. Satisfied, he put the car into gear and drove out of the parking lot.

He glanced in the rear-view mirror and smiled.

'I am Emile.' He said to the two men sitting behind him as he took the security pass from his brief case and placed it on the dash board shelf.

At the barrier, the guard signalled the white Toyota Landcruiser to stop. Emile opened his window and handed the security pass to the guard. The guard checked the car details and walked to the front of the vehicle to compare the number plate. It was the same as was written on the form. Satisfied, he signalled the driver to move off and his attention quickly moved on to the next vehicle waiting behind.

***

Summer still couldn't figure out how or why an identical car with the same number plate had just entered the port. She had seen it pick up a security pass, which meant it was just visiting and was likely to come back out again within the next couple of hours. So, she waited and watched.

It didn't take long. In just under an hour she saw the very same car returning. The exit security barrier was further back in the port, which meant the car had already been vetted and was following the other traffic out.

Summer watched as it passed and noticed three passengers including the driver. It had arrived with only one. By some kind of devious switch, this was the car from the container, she was certain of it.

She started the motor of the 308 rental and began following the Toyota. There had been no call from James or Charlie since she'd arrived in France. She'd left messages. She autodialled again and let it ring but got nothing. She was so distracted by the repeated attempts to contact Stack she hadn't noticed the Toyota beginning to slow. By then, they were on the main autoroute out of Marseilles and she nearly drove into the back of it as it came to a sudden halt. She swerved wildly, quickly recovered, parked up ahead and waited to see what it would do next. It took less than a minute. The Toyota's left signal flashed, it pulled out and drove past, leaving the original driver, Emile Tajeb, standing on the side of the road. He was making a phone call. Summer guessed he was calling up some transport. She grabbed her smartphone and took a couple of snaps; his picture might be useful.

As she put the car into gear and pulled out on to the highway again, her cell phone rang. It was James. They'd just landed in Paris and he wanted some news.

'Well, James, you'll never guess what I'm following.'

Debrief

'Run that past me again, Bailey,' Cavanagh said. 'You blew up a gas station? In the middle of Tripoli? Who the hell thought that was a good idea?'

'Well, James Stack for one. And frankly, me, for another,' said Bailey.

'I suppose I'm not going to get any disagreement from you Major Hedgeland,' Cavanagh mused sarcastically.

***

It seemed like they were never going to get home, but after a three-and-a-half-hour flight, Chris Bailey and Major Susan Hedgeland had finally placed their feet on UK soil at RAF Northolt, west London. They'd had to wait until a BAE 146 flight, en route from RAF Akrotiri in Cyprus to London, could be diverted to Tunis to pick them up.

Before that, they had to endure a journey back to Tunisia that took the two of them, along with Stack and Dawson, nearly three days. Rakim Shadid and his battered old Nissan left them to make his own way back to Tunisia by road, after dropping them at the rendezvous point with the dhow crew at Jadda'im.

The Coast Road from Tripoli was as dangerous on their return as it was when they'd arrived several nights before – more so – because of the drone strike on Tripoli.

In the confusion, the gas station explosion and Hellfire missile strike had morphed into the same event. A major disaster that was still being brought under control, but had resulted in a local skirmish between opposing rebel groups.

Breath of Allah fighters battling the gas station fire had taken a major loss from the drone strike. The missile hadn't hit its target but exploded amongst the soldiers who had left the compound to bring the fire under control. Then, seeing an opportunity to make a tactical gain from the confusion, they came under fire from former allies in the Nawasi Brigade. They'd had their eyes on the strategically placed compound to expand their area of influence in Tripoli.

Breath of Allah rebels countered the attack and held their ground, but for two days and nights small arms fire could still be heard in the area. Although things settled down, tension remained across the city and other armed groups became alert and protective of their own local power base. This made the journey out of Tripoli extremely risky.

Once again, they travelled at night. Rakim managed to blag his way through the first road block that had been erected where the Second Ring Road joined the Coastal Road on the western edge of the city. By a combination of bluster, reassurance and the happy coincidence of an old trading friend who knew Rakim, plus the inevitable outlay of cash, they managed to slip through. The next hazard wouldn't be so easy.

They had just passed Janzour and were not far from the forest road turn off that led to the beach. The barrier ahead was no more than a couple of small trees cut from the nearby forest and dragged across the road. Even through the sandy dust that whipped in sporadic gusts across the road, it was clearly visible in the reddish gloom of the rising moonlight – and so were the three men manning it with their Kalashnikovs.

Rakim stopped fifty yards ahead of it. Stack and Charlie got out and armed themselves with the Heckler and Koch MP7 close-quarter weapons Faruk had thrown in the back. He hadn't managed to deliver them in time for the rescue at the Breath of Allah compound, but they could be put to use now, to provide the firepower they might need.

A woodland that edged the road on both sides provided perfect cover as Stack and Charlie made their silent way through it towards the roadblock, Stack on one side, Dawson on the other. At the same time the Nissan drove up to the barrier and stopped.

It was a crude plan. If Rakim managed to talk his way through the road block, he'd drive off and wait for Stack and Dawson to catch up farther down the highway. On the other hand, if he couldn't talk his way through and the rebel guards got twitchy, Stack and Charlie would rush out of the trees hard and noisy, firing in the air, but ready to take the rebels out if they put up a fight.

As the two ex-Special Forces soldiers picked their way through the Aleppo pine and wild olive woodland, Rakim once again tried to talk his way through the road block. But the older rebel wasn't buying his story about his two European passengers, Bailey and Hedgeland. Rakim revved the engine a little, easing the clutch and inching forward. Two of the soldiers weren't much older than twenty and full of cocky indignation. Couldn't the driver see they had the full authority of their Kalashnikovs?

They brought their AK47s up and told Rakim to get out. Rakim had a better idea. He kept chatting and stayed in the car.

Angered by his refusal, the rebels began shouting and threatening, raising their weapons, ready to fire. Their authority had been questioned. They had something to prove. Amongst Libyan extremists, reputations were built on the body count one group is prepared to leverage against another. The three occupants would be marched into the forest to become just another notch on their Kalashnikovs, and, when their bodies were discovered, a message to others who might want to challenge their terrorist credentials.

Firing short, threatening bursts into the air, they stepped forward to pull the car doors open and drag their victims out.

Bailey had his hand on his Smith & Wesson pistol and, like Hedgeland, who was still suffering from the brutality of her recent captivity, he was getting very nervous.

'Come on, guys. Anytime now would be good,' he said under his breath.

Rakim had engaged the central locking system. Unable to open the doors, the soldiers started smashing the stocks of their rifles against the windows. The driver's side glass went first and the guard reached in to unlock the door. Rakim looked on in terror.

Then, a terrible clamour of screaming and yelling and battle cries and automatic weapons fire filled the air as Stack and Dawson came running out of the woodland from both sides of the road, towards the SUV. It was a mad and fearless charge that relied on surprise and shock. The boy soldiers attitude turned from cocky, machine-gun wielding gangsters, to shocked and emasculated youths, their weapons hanging uselessly from their hands.

The older and more battle hardened of the three, recovered quickly, raised his AK-47. As he sprayed a deadly burst of 7.6 lead in Dawson's direction, a sudden gust of needle-sharp grit filled his eyes and spoiled his aim. Charlie threw himself to the ground and rolled over ready to fire as the hail of bullets skimmed just above his head and kicked up the dirt beside him.

Before he could let off a round, Stack, over at the tree line opposite, swivelled his MP7 a few degrees and sent a short burst in the direction of the shooter. The force of the impact threw the rebel back hard against the driver's door. He bounced off and fell forward into the arms of one of his young comrades.

Shocked, the boy soldier looked down into the eyes of the dying man he was holding. He struggled to support him, to keep him upright, as his comrade's life quickly ebbed away. Reluctantly, he let the dead weight to fall slowly to the ground.

He looked back up at Stack, his eyes filled with horror, and raised his bloodied hands above his head. The other rebel did the same. Charlie came over and took their weapons.

'What shall we do with them, Jim?'

Stack grabbed hold of one of the rebels, took his weapon and pushed him in the direction of the woodland.

'Go! Go!'

Stack indicated the boy should run as far away as possible into the trees and keep going.

Charlie got the message and sent the other youth running off in the opposite direction, into the forest and the desert beyond.

They dragged the dead rebel out of the road and left him out of sight amongst the nearby shrub. Then they each took hold of the barrier of trees and pulled them to the side of the road before returning to the Nissan.

There wasn't much to be said about what had just happened. The sudden, deadly violence. They remained in thoughtful silence as the SUV continued its journey along the dark, coastal highway. Half a mile later, the car turned into the forest road and down to the water's edge where the dhow was waiting.

The same seas that rocked the Ocean Trader as it sailed across the Mediterranean that night made conditions on the small dhow even more uncomfortable. Other than occasional seasickness, the crossing back to Tunisia was slow but uneventful.

***

Back in London, Maddy continued to debrief Bailey and Hedgeland.

'So, where are they? Where are Stack and the others?'

'They're chasing the container. It's probably in France by now,' Bailey said. 'Stack says he saw them drive a car inside it.'

'Why would they want to hide a car in a container and take it to France?' Cavanagh asked. 'Anyway, I'm more interested in the flightcase. You say they put it in the car?'

Still suffering from shock after her vicious mistreatment, Hedgeland struggled to remember things.

'I didn't see it, but Stack says so - he was watching,' Hedgeland's voice was quiet and hesitant as she spoke. 'He said Patterson got in the car too, with another person.'

'No, Patterson got into the *truck* with another person,' Bailey corrected her.

Hedgeland's state of mind worried Madeleine.

'Are you sure you want to continue? Do you want to take a break, major?'

'No, I'm fine. We haven't got time. Let's carry on.'

'I agree,' Madeleine said curtly. 'Time is critical.'

They were meeting in Major William Cavanagh's third floor office in the Secret Intelligence Service building – the wedding cake - on the Albert Embankment by Vauxhall Bridge. It was just past noon.

Cavanagh leaned across the table towards Bailey.

'Just so I'm clear, they put a car inside a container that's on a ship on the way to France, yes?'

'Yes, but that was three days ago. They must be in Marseille by now,' said Bailey.

Madeleine was busy lining things up on the desk; pen perfectly straight along the side of her writing pad, cell phone lined up next to it, the edges of a yellow post-it notepad in parallel. Each item a precise two-centimetre distance from the other. Others scribble random things on paper when they were deep in thought – Maddy was a liner-upper.

'You say Stack thought they may have a bomb on board. Why does he think that?' She asked.

Bailey shrugged.

'I don't know. He said he saw welding going on under the car. They're a terrorist group. Welding, plus car, equals bomb?'

'But you do that kind of thing locally. You don't need to transport it a thousand miles across the sea,' Madeleine said.

Cavanagh chipped in.

'But they have taken the trouble to secretly ship this car to France, hidden in a container. There is something important going on here, and we need to understand what it is.'

'Right now, I'm more concerned about Topaz,' Madeleine said abruptly.

'Why haven't we heard from Stack?' Cavanagh countered irritably.

Bailey had developed a deep respect for James Stack in the short time he had known him.

'You gave Stack, Charlie and Summer an ultimatum. Return with the flightcase and get your lives back. But you tricked them. You knew Breath of Allah had it. You'd sent them on a futile mission, with an extremely low likelihood of success.'

'Well, everything has changed,' Madeleine said, ignoring the rebuke. 'The device has been taken to France and as far as we know, it's still under the control of Breath of Allah.'

'Ah, no, that's not quite correct,' Hedgeland said. 'A group called, Sword of Liberation has it now. Breath of Allah sold it to them, along with Patterson to operate it.'

This news worried Cavanagh. 'Sword of Liberation? In Sirte?' he said. 'They're amongst the most deadly of them all.'

Maddy couldn't contain herself.

'Damn it! If that drone had hit the bloody target we wouldn't be having this conversation. Topaz would have been destroyed,' she said angrily, 'Along with half of the extremists on the worlds most wanted list.'

'As well as Stack, Dawson, Patterson and me,' Major Hedgeland chided, the stabbing pain behind her eyes suddenly increasing to a migraine-like intensity.

Bailey agreed. 'I believe we would have become what they euphemistically call, collateral damage,' he said sarcastically to the head of MI8.

Maddy ignored him.

'And by the way, the Americans are mightily pissed off too. Hellfire's don't come cheap,' Maddy countered before returning to her lining up.

The room became silent for a moment. Then Cavanagh spoke.

'Faruk has gone quiet. We need local eyes on the ground in Tripoli,' he said. 'Do you know where he is?'.

Silence descended again. No one had an answer to that.

'OK! Let's get back to what we do know,' Cavanagh said. 'We have to accept that the very thing we didn't want to happen has happened. The Topaz device has ended up in enemy hands. If it is the extremist group you claim it is, then it's as bad as it can get. For the moment, we are confident it's in France. Is France its final destination? Or is it on its way to somewhere else? And for Christ's sake, why haven't we heard from Stack?'

'From what I've seen, they're used to working on their own,' Bailey said. 'and they're probably still working under the rules you set for them.'

He turned to Madeleine.

'Remember, Maddy, I was in that room in Tunis. Shall I summarise what you said?'

Maddy didn't respond, so he carried on anyway. 'You told them you didn't want their activity to be traced back to London. You made it very clear that they were on their own. Expendable assets. You said something about a curse being lifted if they were successful and they would then be able to return to the UK. I recall you said, if questions were asked later you would deny everything. MI8 and MI6 will have no knowledge of the three of them, or their activities in Libya. Does that sound about right, Madeleine?'

With skin thickened by years at the very top of the civil service, and as resistant to criticism as a bullet proof vest, Madeleine ignored the rebuke.

'Maybe, but he still has a line of communication. He used it to delay the drone strike. He should use it again to tell us WHAT THE BLOODY HELL IS GOING ON.'

Maddy banged the pen hard on the writing pad to emphasise each of the last seven words. She slumped back in her chair and threw the pen on the table in frustration.

'OK,' Cavanagh said. 'If Stack is tracking the car, then maybe we should do the same. What do we know about it?'

'It's a white, early 2000 model Toyota Landcruiser, according to James Stack. He gave the licence plate number to Summer Peterson when he called her from Tripoli,' Bailey said.

'So, it sounds like he's sent her on ahead as a scout.'

'That would be my assessment. The container would arrive in Marseille before Stack could get there, so Summer would be well placed to spot it.'

Cavanagh gave that some thought.

'It seems to me there is some action we could take. We know the container number, and we know it has a white Toyota Landcruiser inside. Let's ask the Port of Marseille if they could check if such a container has arrived, or, if the car has been removed from the container, it might still be in the port.'

'I'll get on to that straight away.' Madeleine got up and left the office.

William Cavanagh turned to Susan Hedgeland.

'Look, major, you've done more than enough. Go home. Get some rest.'

Hedgeland just nodded wearily, and she too left the office.

'Stick around Bailey,' Cavanagh signalled. 'As one of the early members of the original MI8 team, your knowledge of Topaz is critical. The only person that knows more is Patterson and he's under the influence of a terrorist organisation. And worse than that, we have no idea where he or the Topaz device is.'

France

The sign said 'Clermont-Ferrand'. A small town west of Lyon, a short diversion from the A71 Autoroute. Mahmoud had chosen a longer route that didn't have tolls. One less opportunity for security cameras to record his journey. They drove a few kilometres down a road that passed to the east of the town. It was 8.30 in the evening by the time they'd checked into the Hotel 6 Star. Mahmoud paid for the room with cash.

'Hmm, nice,' Patterson said sarcastically as he entered the second-floor room carrying the flightcase.

'It's cheap and I'm paying, so get used to it,' Karim Mahmoud said. 'I'm knackered and I'm starving. Food first. There's a pizza place next door. We better get over there before they close.'

The pizza wasn't great, but after the nonstop drive from Marseille, it was hot and tasty. And Patterson was hungry. He'd eaten most of it before he got around to saying anything to Mahmoud.

'What about some wine to go with it, Chatterbox?'

'You'll have water, like me.'

'This is all part of your Islamic thing I suppose?'

'Why? Does that bother you?'

'Actually, no it doesn't. But your extreme ideology does.'

'Well, you'd better get used to it, mate. Times are changing and pretty soon our flag will be flying above number ten Downing Street.'

'In your dreams,' countered Patterson. 'That's what that radical hate preacher used to say from, what was it called?   Brilliant Light of Islamic

Dawn? Before they slung him into prison. I think he's still there.'

'That was a crime against Islam,' Mahmoud said, his mouth full of pizza. 'Asad Hassan is my friend. I'm a big supporter and there are many more like me. I promise you Patterson, after I'm done, he won't be in prison - he'll be running things.'

Patterson took a drink of water and tried to size up the man in front of him who was pushing another slice of pizza into his mouth. He was dangerous and highly motivated for sure. There was no doubt in Patterson's mind, his life and Hedgeland's were at risk if he didn't do as the maniac across the table demanded. But what was his game? Why had he brought the car all the way from Libya? And where were they heading? Paris, or maybe London?

These seemed like reasonable questions, so why not ask him, Patterson thought.

'Why did you bring that car all the way from Libya? What's so special about it?'

'Shut up and eat your pizza.'

Conversation ended.

Patterson shrugged and picked up the last slice. He was about to put it into his mouth when he looked up and noticed a woman sitting across the restaurant. She was stunningly beautiful, but most intriguingly, she was looking at him. He didn't think of himself as being much of a catch, so why would a beautiful woman take an interest in him?

She didn't look away as he looked up. Most people who are secretly checking out another person instinctively look away if they think they've been caught staring. She didn't. In fact, she remained looking at him and raised her finger to her lips as though passing a secret message to remain quiet – to not give her away. Perhaps he was reading too much into that gesture.

This all happened over Karim Mahmoud's shoulder as he stuffed the last morsel of pizza into his mouth. He looked up at Patterson and turned to see what he was staring at. He gave the woman a moment of his attention and turned back to Patterson.

'She's way out of your league, mate. Just another Christian whore. She should cover herself up like all western women should.'

***

Summer was irritated with herself for being caught out by the other guy. Had she looked away fast enough? Did Patterson get her message? She had put her finger to her lips and mimed a secret '*shooshing*' sound. Did he understand? Or did he think she was flirting with him?

***

Earlier, she had followed the Toyota as it turned into the hotel car park, grateful that its occupants had decided to take a break after the endless journey. She was exhausted and hungry. Nonetheless, she waited for a while before going in, hoping they had another room free. She was surprised at the cheap rates until she entered her room and discovered why. All three floors of the hotel were accessed by an external steel staircase and landing. Two stars would be a generous TripAdvisor review for Hotel 6 Stars. Snug, basic and uncluttered. It had a plastic feel about it, as though it had been pre-formed in a mould. A sink, but no bathroom. Guests had to share the facilities at each end of the external landing.

Before following the two men to the restaurant, she drove to a nearby gas station. She figured this may be her only chance to fill up before they hit the road again in the morning. While she was doing that, she grabbed her cell phone and speed dialed James.

Earlier, she had called to tell him about the unexpected departure of the Toyota Landcruiser from the port. That was the last time they'd spoken and that was several hours ago. As she had no idea where the Toyota was going, they had agreed she would call occasionally to update him. This would be the third call. The second had been at Lyon, just as the Toyota diverted away from a toll road.

'We've stopped. I'm at the Hotel 6 Star near Clermont-Ferrand.'

'Do you think they spotted you?'

'I don't think so.'

Summer gave James the address and told him she was going to the nearby pizza restaurant. She had seen Patterson and the other man going there earlier, and anyway, she was hungry.

***

The problem for Stack and Charlie had been what to do once they had arrived in Paris. Stack couldn't see any point in flying on to Marseille if the Toyota and Summer were already heading away from the port. So, they had hired a car from Hertz at Charles de Gaulle airport and driven south towards Marseille. They assumed that, as Summer was driving north, they would eventually come within a few kilometres of each other somewhere in the middle of France.

A four-hour drive south down the A71 had taken them close to Clermont-Ferrand. Stack had correctly guessed that the Toyota Landcruiser would attempt to avoid any toll roads. The last call from Summer at Lyon had confirmed it.

***

Patterson was still sitting at the table, stealing glances at the stunning blonde four tables away, when all his sordid fantasies about him and this exciting woman came crashing to an end as two men walked into the restaurant and sat at the table with her.

Mahmoud watched them too. He was immediately suspicious. He couldn't say precisely what it was about the arrival of these two men that put him on alert. They just didn't look like regular tourists or commercial travellers. Definitely not business men. Military came to mind for some reason. He decided to trust the prickly chill that crept across the nape of his neck and signalled the waitress for the check. A few minutes later she came over and placed the tab on the table. He told her to wait as he pulled some cash from his wallet and handed it to her. It included a small tip, which she thanked him for.

He tried to make it look as innocent as possible, taking his time and chatting amiably to Patterson as they walked casually out of the restaurant. He was certain they were being watched as they ambled past the big plate glass window, apparently in no hurry. It wasn't until he was sure they couldn't be seen that he picked up speed, urging Patterson to hurry with him back to the hotel.

Summer had nodded in the direction of the two men as soon as she saw Stack and Charlie entering the restaurant. Stack got the message and got a quick shot of the two diners as he and Charlie walked past them; one white European, the other Asian, maybe Indian or Pakistani.

Stack slid in beside Summer. Charlie sat opposite. She gave Stack an appreciative once over.

'The beard suits you, James. I kind'a like it. But Hollywood, that fluff just isn't working.'

Charlie was a little crestfallen but said nothing.

For Stack, the temptation to embrace and kiss Summer after such a long time apart was hard to resist. Instead he simply reached for her hand under the table and gave it an affectionate squeeze. Summer leaned closer and muttered under her breath.

'If you think you're going to get away with just squeezing my hand after all this time, James, you've spent too much time in the desert.'

Stack nodded back to her.

'Don't worry, I'll make it up to you later.'

'If the ardour-crushing ambience of the hotel room doesn't get in the way,' Summer teased.

James sniggered at the thought. But then he hadn't seen the hotel room.

'What news about our boys over there?' He lifted his chin slightly to indicate the table over by the window where the two men sat.

'To be honest, I don't have much to report. They arrived at the hotel earlier and have just had pizza. They talked together, but not much. It didn't look like Patterson was under much duress.'

'Have you seen the flightcase?' Charlie asked.

'I watched them take it into the hotel.'

'I had a quick look under their car to see if I could see anything we should be worried about,' Stack said. 'There were signs of welding. Some extra metalwork. Certainly not enough space to hold the quantity of explosives you'd need to blow up something big, like a building. It's an old car so perhaps they were fixing some rust problems. There's certainly nothing in the passenger compartment that looks remotely like a bomb, just seats, a bunch of sweet wrappers and a couple of empty plastic water bottles.'

'So why bring such an old car all the way to France?' Summer wondered. 'And onwards to who knows where?'

As she spoke the two men at the table across the room paid the check and wandered calmly out of the restaurant. They didn't seem in any hurry as they walked past the window, illuminated by the yellow tungsten light coming from inside the restaurant.

They watched until the two men were out of sight.

'So, it looks like this is our chance to grab the bloody device and rescue Patterson,' Stack said.

Charlie had another suggestion.

'Maybe, but I need some grub first.'

'No, Charlie. Follow them. Find out what room they're in. You can eat when you get back.'

'OK, order me a Margarita with ham and mushrooms and a beer while I'm gone.'

Three minutes later he was back.

'They're on the second floor. Far end. Room nine.'

'That's not far from me,' Summer said. 'I'm on the same floor, a few doors down.'

Their pizzas arrived. Summer had already eaten, so she watched while they ate.

Thirty minutes later they stepped out of the restaurant into the warm, summer evening. As they approached the hotel, Charlie said he needed something from their rental car.

Stack and Summer climbed the external staircase and were nearly at the second-floor landing when they heard the steel girder-work clanging tunelessly as someone pounded up the stairs behind them. They turned and saw Charlie just visible through the railings of the flight below.

'Guys, as they said in the movie, "Houston, I think we've got a problem".'

'Problem?' Stack asked.

'It's gone.'

'What's gone?' Both Summer and Stack said it together.

'The bad guys! The Toyota!'

All three rushed back down to the parking lot. Fresh oil had dripped on to the tarmac in the space where the old Toyota had been. Stack looked out into the darkness beyond the car park.

'We can't chase them with our car, it's nearly out of fuel.'

'Don't worry, I've got a full tank,' Summer said.

Charlie returned from wandering down the line of parked cars.

'Fuel is the least of our problems. Which one is yours Summer?'

'The Peugeot 308 further down.'

'Well that Ford Fusion over there is ours. All the cars along this row, including yours and our Ford have had their tyres slashed. We're not chasing anyone anytime soon.'

***

Patterson tried laying his head against the rock-hard headrest to get some sleep. The realisation he'd been close to being rescued back at the hotel, if Mahmoud was right about being tailed, raised his spirits. Someone knew where he was. At the same time, knowing that, with tyres slashed, they would be unable to follow sent him down into a spiral of gloom.

They were flying along the A71 autoroute north at over 120 kph. Mahmoud was confident he'd ended any chance they could catch up, so he'd stopped to refuel.

At the gas station he'd made a call. He wanted to ensure that the delay he'd created was permanent. To cut off any further interruption. The people he called were resourceful and fully committed to the extremist cause. They had connections all around France. The people they had in mind to carry out the work for Mahmoud were based nearby, in the city of Lyon, an hour and a half away.

They didn't know Karim Mahmoud's ultimate plan, very few people did, but, like Mahmoud, they were devoted warriors of Allah and eager to do anything that would advance the jihadi cause.

***

The stairs up to the second floor of Hotel 6 Star, were made of pressed steel with a raised diamond pattern embossed into the treads. As noisy as the autoroute that passed fifty yards away was during the day, in the evening the traffic began to thin out until it was reduced to just the occasional moan from a passing car, or rattle of a truck as its wheels beat against a join in the road surface.

The nearby restaurants and other businesses had closed long ago, their lights turned off and the staff gone home. Only a couple of street lamps at either end of the approach road cut pools of light out of the darkness. By twelve, even the noisy TV in one of the rooms on the first floor was turned off and a kind of stillness cloaked the night.

They had decided that it would be futile to try to get the tyres replaced at such a late hour. By the time they found a company prepared to do it, the Toyota Landcruiser would be beyond tracing. So, they settled down to spend the night where they were, Charlie in a room on his own, Summer and James together. All three on the same second-floor landing.

After James and Summer had exhausted themselves making up for time spent apart, they both fell into a deep and satisfying sleep, Summer's head resting lightly on James' shoulder.

Then came a barely audible, deep metallic note. It was the softest of musical tones. The kind of sound steel makes when it is lightly struck. The first sound roused Stack from sleep. The second made it certain.

***

The two men had driven their car slowly on to the slip road that led to the retail area and parked fifty yards or so from the hotel. They got out quietly and pushed the doors gently, not quite closing them. As they walked silently towards the hotel, they stuffed their semi-automatic pistols into the back of their jeans.

One had a Walther P38, the other a Glock 19. Both were old 9mm weapons that had changed hands repeatedly for a few hundred Euros in a long history of gangland shootings and bank robberies. Both were silenced.

The phone call had said where, but not much about who. It didn't matter. They were trained, they had surprise and they had Allah on their side.

External steel staircases don't take up valuable living space inside a building and they can build them wide enough to make it easy for people of all ages to get to the floors above. The external stairs at Hotel 6 Star included a halfway platform between each floor, where older folk could pause to catch their breath and allow others to pass at busy times. Including the platform, there were 17 steps leading up to the second floor. It represented a lot of steel under tension.

The first sturdy three or four steps benefitted from the deep concrete underpinnings of the main steel pillars. But, by the time the two men reached the platform, even the lightest step set off a vibration further up the structure that rattled loose ironwork.

The two men paused for a moment to let the vibration settle down. Listening, watching, waiting. The hotel seemed just as asleep as before. It was 3 am. Nothing stirred, and no lights came on. One man turned to the other and signalled for him to follow.

Slowly, quietly, they took the next seven steps until they reached the concrete floor that formed the open passageway to the second-floor bedrooms. They checked the numbers until they came to door number seven. This was the room where the receptionist had told Mahmoud, he would find the beautiful blonde woman. He was surprised how cheaply the receptionist could be bought with a few Euros and a story of a cheating wife.

Mahmoud had been certain that one of the two men at her table in the restaurant would be sharing her room. The other man had yet to check in, but he was confident the two thugs would have no difficulty persuading the woman to tell them which room he was in.

To knock? Or to kick the door in? Kicking the door open would be noisy. What's the point of suppressors on your guns if you've already woken everybody by smashing in a door?

They both brought their weapons up ready, then the lead shooter tapped twice, lightly, '*Tap, tap*'.

'Madame, s'il vous plaît.' The gentle tone of his voice sounded educated and reassuring.

He didn't want to alarm them. To raise their adrenaline level. Or warn them. He hoped they would think it was a visit from hotel management, or a guest in a nearby room who needed some help. Best if they answered the door still half asleep and unprepared.

Nothing.

One of the men eased the firing mechanism of his Glock 19 back as quietly as he could, but in the silence of the night, even the subtle sliding of the well-oiled chamber caused a muffled, metallic '*snick*' sound.

He tapped again, twice, '*Tap...*'

Before he could make the second tap, the door was pulled open violently and Stack rushed forward into the first man, grabbing his weapon and pushing it high, while at the same time throwing him back against the railings.

As the two men struggled, the silenced pistol fired twice into the air with a loud hissing pop. Shocked by the unexpected action, the second shooter took a moment to do a factory reset on the outcome he'd expected for their plan. He recovered and raised the Glock towards the two struggling men, waiting for a clear shot of the violent target.

He never took it, because his head suddenly exploded in pain as Charlie came up behind with his belt wrapped around his fist, buckle out, and threw the hardest punch of his life. The man's knees gave way, but he didn't quite go down. He clung on to the railings with one hand as he tried to recover. With the gun still in his fist, he pivoted around in a low crouch, bringing the weapon up as he turned, firing wildly, the compressed punch of silenced rounds ricocheting noisily off concrete and steel.

Charlie had retreated back to the open doorway of his room a few yards away. The second assailant followed unsteadily, rubbing his head, the Glock raised and ready.

The struggle between the first shooter and Stack became a monumental close combat fist fight, each man trying to throw a short punch that would disable his opponent. Stack was pushing the man hard against the railing, kneeing him between the legs, throwing left handers and head butting, while at the same time, trying to keep the assassin's gun hand as out of the way as possible. The shooter was doing the same, but trying to push himself away from the railings to get a clear shot of the man he'd come to kill.

Charlie had lost the benefit of surprise but expected the second shooter to follow him. He left the door to his room wide open and hid just inside, hoping to grab the gun as the shooter came around the corner. He'd wrenched a leg from a chair and raised it high above his head ready to smack down violently on the shooter's gun hand.

The sound of fighting on the second-floor landing wasn't loud, but neither was it silent. The muffled gunshots and ricochet sounds, the smashing of bodies against iron railings and the pummelling of fists into flesh created enough volume to wake light sleepers. One guest who was woken, ventured to his door to investigate the noise. He pulled it open and stepped out on to the landing just as the second shooter was about cross the threshold into Charlie's room, his gun hand already through the doorway. The sudden appearance of the hotel guest distracted the assailant for the smallest fraction of a second.

Charlie watched as the disembodied hand with the gun tentatively entered through the open door, just begging for attention. He smashed the chair leg down hard on to the shooter's wrist with bone-snapping force. The hand went limp and the Glock fell to the floor.

As the man yelled out in pain and grabbed his injured hand, Charlie dropped down and scooped up the weapon. He didn't give the shooter a chance to recover. He brought the handle of the gun up violently, smashing it into his face, forcing him to lift his hands up to nurse the new injury and freeing a vulnerable area between his legs, which Charlie took advantage of with a powerful kick. The man curled forward with pain.

A knee hard into the face was Charlie's next move but a sudden crash from the car park below made him pause and both men turned to see what had happened.

Stack had finally won the struggle. After a disorienting blow with his forehead that shattered the assailant's teeth, he tilted the man up and over the railings. Stack still had hold of the shooter's gun hand and, as he fell, he stripped the gun from the man's fingers.

The assailant landed on the roof of a Citroen parked directly beneath. It broke his fall, but he was badly winded. He slid painfully off and limped away into the shadows.

Looking on from the second-floor, Charlie dragged the other assailant towards the steel staircase and gave him a hard push with his foot. Both Stack and Charlie watched as the thug hobbled away following his friend into the shadows, one hand holding his face, the other nursing his crotch.

Three more guests were now out on the landing, woken by the noise, muttering to each other. One called out if everything was OK? Summer told them everything was fine. Just a couple of opportunist thieves. No need to call the police. It had been taken care of. Go back to your rooms.

'Bonne nuit.'

***

Back in Summer's room an urgent debrief was underway.

'Looks like they can call up help when they need it,' Charlie said. 'But we've scored two guns that might come in handy.'

Stack was rubbing his jaw.

'Maybe. But they'll only get us so far. What we need is our own back up.'

'Maddy?' Summer suggested.

'Possibly. They'll help because it's in their interest to help. But they won't do anything that could lead back to them.'

'Oh, the denial thing?' Summer said.

'Yes. They don't want our activities to pollute their own dirty water. This is all about recovering Topaz and the flightcase. But their overriding mission is to keep it secret. Remember, our lives and Patterson's life are way down the list of MI8 priorities.

'Let's leave it for them to choose how they want to handle the search for the Toyota. Should they leave it to us, or get the gendarmerie involved? I think I know what she'll say.'

'They can't leave it to us to find it,' Charlie said. 'France is a big country. The three of us can't search the place. And anyway, by now they could already be holed up at wherever it is they've been heading.'

'I'm not so sure. Think about it, Charlie. If I understand what the Topaz device can do, my guess is they're heading to a place where they can use it to cause the most damage. The UK. It has the most sophisticated spy centre in Europe at GCHQ.

'That's a great target if you want to screw around with information. But Britain also has one of the world's most important financial centres, think what they could do to the City of London. What fun they could have turning the UK economy into garbage and lining their own pockets at the same time.'

Summer was inspecting the damage to Stack's face. Nothing too bad: bruises from a head butt and a nose bleed that had already stopped leaking.

'So, you think they're heading for England, James?'

'I think so. Just a guess.'

Summer remained silent for a moment, recalling events earlier that evening.

'I think you may be right. Before you arrived at the restaurant, I paid a visit to the little girl's room. I had to walk past Patterson and the other guy. I could hear them talking, though it wasn't clear what they were saying.'

'And your point is?' Charlie asked.

'I'm sure the Asian guy spoke with a London accent.'

Exit France

In its simplest form, nuclear power should be the cheapest form of energy. Just bring two highly radioactive materials together in close proximity and the nuclear fission created between them will generate heat. Use that heat to boil water and the steam will drive turbines that will turn generators to create electricity. And all that by simply placing two particular flavours of radioactive material close together.

Before Mahmoud drove the Toyota Landcruiser into the container in Tripoli, the Topaz flightcase was placed on the rear seat. It stayed there until he and Patterson reached Clermont-Ferrand. The flightcase was then removed and taken to the hotel room. Later, when they rushed to leave the hotel, Mahmoud opened the tail gate and placed the flightcase inside on the floor. It was now much closer to the hidden, radioactive, plutonium-239.

***

The A71 is a four-lane highway known locally as L'Arverne. It runs north from Clermont-Ferrand to Orleans. From Orleans it's a further one-hour drive to Paris. The two most popular ferry services that cross the English Channel to the UK, sail from the French ports of Calais and Dunkirk, another hour or so north. However, both ferry service destinations are the same UK port: Dover.

***

It was just after nine am when Madeleine walked into Cavanagh's office further along the corridor on the third floor of the SIS building.

'We've just heard from French Sûreté about the Port of Marseille.'

'What did they say, any news?' Cavanagh asked with little apparent interest. He was at his desk, looking through some recent reports relating to other urgent business.

'Well, it seems they've found the Toyota. It was parked in one of the visitor car parks.'

Cavanagh looked up, surprised at the news.

'Parked at the port? What, do you mean abandoned?'

Madeleine sat down in one of the chairs facing Cavanagh's vast mahogany desk. She relaxed back into the leather seat, one hand resting on the desk, absent-mindedly nudging a yellow 'post-it' note pad until its edges lined up with the black plastic box-shaped pen holder next to it.

'Hard to tell,' she said. 'They're going to watch it to see if anyone tries to drive it away. The problem is, if someone does try to take it out of the port, they'd have difficulty getting it past gate security, unless they come up with some bulletproof paperwork.'

'Have they checked inside the car?'

'Yes. Inside and out. All the vehicle documents are missing. In fact, there's nothing inside apart from the seats and carpets. No rubbish, nothing.'

'Fingerprints?'

'Some. They said they'll get back to me on that.'

Cavanagh chewed on this new information for a moment as he turned his chair away from the desk and gazed out of the third-floor window to the River Thames below.

'Why bring a vehicle all the way from Libya, hidden in a container, only to leave it, apparently abandoned, at the destination port?' he wondered to himself.

He turned back to the desk.

'What if it was what was in the car that was important?'

Madeleine leaned forward.

'We know what was in the car, Major. The Topaz flightcase.'

'Come on, Madeleine, think about it. They didn't need to bring a car with them to get Topaz out of the country on a ship. A car, by the way, that was hidden in a container.'

Maddy picked up on Cavanagh's thread.

'*If*, the Topaz device wasn't the only high value item they were smuggling into Europe. What else might it have been, drugs?' Maddy ventured.

'Drugs – or guns perhaps – to hand out to local extremists.'

'They still had to get them out of the port,' Madeleine said.

Cavanagh nodded.

'True,' he conceded. 'What about port CCTV?'

'Again, they're going to check. We should hear something from them later today.'

The room became quiet as they considered their options. Only the rhythm of Cavanagh's pen tapping on the table to a tune only he could hear, broke the silence.

Madeleine spoke first. A simple. incontrovertible truth.

'But the flightcase and Patterson, and the other man have left the port. They must have.'

Cavanagh sniffed.

'Have they? What if they're still there, waiting to be taken out? Is the ship still in port? And what about the container, has anyone checked?'

Madeleine stood up eagerly.

'Good point sir. I'll get on to it straight away.'

As she reached the door, Cavanagh spoke again.

'You know, it was a risk bringing the French Sûreté into this. In a way, I'm glad the flightcase wasn't there. We don't want them getting their inquisitive little fingers on it, let alone opening up the bloody box to see what was inside. The unlicensed transportation of radioactive material would bring a whole mountain of international relationship problems the P.M. would have difficulty explaining. Under any circumstances, we have to be the first to recover it.'

'I agree.' Madeleine could say little else. She turned to leave again.

'Still nothing from James Stack?'

She shook her head.

'Not yet.'

***

The two rental cars were back on the road again by eight thirty the next morning. Charlie in the Ford, Stack and Summer in the Peugeot. The tyres had been fixed while they had breakfast.

They had managed to get some sleep, despite the pyjama party with the radical death squad in the middle of the night. Stack counted one small blessing; the driver of the Toyota won't have had any rest, so the resulting sleep deprivation and fatigue could work in their favour.

They figured that the Channel Tunnel was out of the question for any car turning up without a ticket. So, the sea crossing was the more likely. The last of the Channel ferries sailed at around eleven at night, which meant the Toyota would have had to wait until morning and because they'd arrive without a ticket, they'd have to wait until space on a ferry became available. They had no guarantee they'd catch an early morning sailing.

In the late summer, cross-channel ferries are packed with holiday makers returning from their vacations in continental Europe. Because of this, Stack reasoned, if they put their foot down, they might just have a chance to catch the same ferry or one soon after. It was an extremely long shot. Charlie didn't think it was a flyer, but couldn't come up with a better alternative.

They'd agreed that, with two Channel-crossing ports to choose from, they should split up. Charlie would head for Dunkirk, Stack and Summer to Calais.

It was as they approached Orleans when Summer had taken her turn to drive that Stack called Madeleine. He'd been putting it off; a stubborn streak of irritation with her that had finally been countered by the practical problems they faced.

Stack punched in the number and green-buttoned the phone. The call tone rang on and on for forty seconds or so. He'd dialled her cell phone, so maybe the signal had trouble penetrating the SIS HQ eavesdropping countermeasures.

'Come on Maddy, pick-up,' he said, just as the call was answered with a bleep. 'It's Stack. We're in France.'

'James Stack!' She attempted droll humour. 'So, the Hellfire missile didn't get you then.'

'Very funny. We're on our way to Calais, Dawson's going to Dunkirk. We're chasing the Toyota.'

There was silence at the other end that was filled with a background noise of digital hash and random clicks and buzzes, as though the connection was going through some kind of encryption software.

'Did you say you were following the Toyota? Wait a moment. I need to get Cavanagh in on this.'

There was a short pause as Madeleine rushed down the hallway to Cavanagh's office. She burst in without knocking. He was in deep conversation with a woman from GCHQ about other on-going business and seemed irritated at the interruption.

Maddy held the phone up for Cavanagh to see and mouthed silently, '*It's Stack.*' Cavanagh instantly ended his meeting and ushered the woman out.

She approached the desk and switched her phone to speaker so that Cavanagh could hear.

'OK, I'm with Major Cavanagh. Tell me again, where are you?'

Stack gave them a summary of the last twenty-four hours, ending with his best guess at the Toyota's likely destination.

'There's only one thing wrong with that,' Cavanagh said.

'Oh, what's that?'

'The Toyota is still in the port of Marseille. How can you explain that?'

Stack was shocked into silence by this apparent paradox.

'It can't be. Summer followed it out of the port all the way to Clermont-Ferrand. It was parked outside the Hotel 6 Star. It's now probably crossing the Channel by ferry. It is most definitely *not* in Marseille.'

'Do you have the registration number?' Madeleine asked.

Stack read it out. There was a pause and then Madeleine spoke to Cavanagh.

'A duplicate vehicle. Exact in all the important details,' Maddy said. 'Make, age, colour, plate.'

'Christ! The crafty bastards,' Cavanagh said, a note of respect in his voice. 'A driver enters the port legitimately in one car and leaves in the identical imported car. The first car is simply abandoned. I have to admit, it's bloody clever.'

Stack interrupted them.

'Why?'

'What do you mean, why?' Cavanagh asked.

'Why would someone go to such lengths. It's a crappy old car. Practically valueless.'

'Yes, we wondered about that,' Cavanagh said. 'We think they may be importing something. Probably drugs or guns.'

'But they have the most valuable thing on the planet with them right now, the Topaz device,' Stack said. 'Why get greedy and risk it all with drug smuggling, or guns? There's no synchronicity in the plan. Surely it has to be something Topaz related. Something that makes Topaz more useful or relevant in some way.'

'I don't know, Stack, these terrorist groups are extremely motivated. It's not about money unless it's raised for the cause. And, as for smuggling guns into Europe, well, the reasons speak for themselves,' said Cavanagh.

'Look, we have a more urgent issue,' Madeleine pressed. 'You think the Toyota and therefore the Topaz device is on its way to the UK, James?'

'That's what I think.'

'Then we have the making of a much more serious problem - security.'

Cavanagh jumped in.

'That's right. We cannot get any other law enforcement agency or security services involved in the search for this vehicle. It must be kept strictly within the confines of MI6 oversight, and even then, just those who are part of the Topaz Project.'

'That would include MI8,' Madeline said irritably, forever the civil servant defending her patch.

'But how on Earth can you hope to find the vehicle without help?'

There was a longer pause as Madeleine placed her hand over the cell phone microphone. Stack could hear muffled conversation from London. It lasted what seemed like a frustrating minute or so but was probably less. Eventually the hand was removed.

'We can't reveal that information,' Cavanagh said cryptically. 'Keep following the vehicle and report back when you have more news.'

Maddy signed off and the line went dead.

***

The drive had been long and boring, and tired as he was, Patterson merely dozed intermittently throughout the endless night. Mahmoud's preferred port had been Dunkirk, where there was more chance of a slot on a ferry, but fatigue made Calais, the closest port, their best hope. Any further and he was likely to nod off and total the car from exhaustion. He'd already noticed a couple of head drops that frightened him into opening the window and turning the radio up loud. He didn't care what channel, just so long as there was noise.

It took longer than he had hoped to get a slot when the ferry service resumed the following morning. But they were eventually squeezed onto one of P&O's fleet of giant transporters that shuttled endlessly between Calais and Dover.

They had been just one car in a line of fifty or so hopeful, standby travellers waiting for the call to drive forward on to a ship. Mahmoud looked over to Patterson, still asleep on the passenger seat next to him. His head had lolled forward, his chin practically on his chest. He, on the other hand, had worries that kept him awake despite his intense fatigue – or so he thought.

He woke with a jolt after a fleeting moment of deep, almost narcotic slumber, as though he'd fallen into a bottomless abyss. Heart racing and disoriented, a wave of panic washed over him as he turned to see if they had been followed.

He didn't know if the two gunmen he'd sent had solved the three problems back at the hotel, or whether the people tracking him had got their tyres fixed right away and sped off after him before the killers could do their work. It was the not knowing that rattled him. He'd dialled the number he'd called the night before but got no reply. He left a text saying to call him urgently.

***

He was still waiting to hear from them as he sat in a window booth with Patterson in the ferry's large cafeteria, three decks above sea-level, fifteen miles from Dover. They were eating a breakfast of eggs and baked beans on toast and coffee, watching other ferries cruise past a mile or so away, heading back to France.

Patterson was hungry, and the smell of food had him stuffing mouthfuls of egg and beans and gulping great swallows of coffee. On the floor by his feet he became aware again of the awkward bulkiness of the shiny aluminium flightcase. Now that his hunger had abated, he returned to the question that had bothered him since they'd parked three decks down, some thirty-five minutes ago.

Mahmoud didn't want the flightcase left behind in the Toyota. He used the remote fob to pop the rear tail gate open. As Patterson reached in to lift out the heavy box, he was surprised to find how warm it was. He swept his hands over the lid but noticed it wasn't a uniform heat. It was cooler at the edges, but warmer nearer the centre.

At first, he disregarded it, mentally shrugging it off as inconsequential and probably a result of the heat from the exhaust pipe underneath. He said nothing about it to Mahmoud, but his innate curiosity made him snap open the four locks and lift the lid. He ran his hand over the surface of the control panel, explaining to Mahmoud that he was just checking the device was OK.

There was no question, the temperature inside the box was noticeably warmer than the metal skin of the flightcase outside, and greater still near the door to the isotope chamber. It wasn't hot, but it was certainly very warm.

How can that be, he wondered?

The floor of the luggage space wasn't particularly warm, so he couldn't see how the tailpipe could have transferred so much heat to the box. And of course, the Topaz device wasn't switched on – it needed mains power anyway.

For the rest of the crossing to Dover, the question played on his mind; without power or any other apparent source of energy, how had the box and, more worryingly, the isotope chamber, become warm?

London Debrief

Calais: a little after 12.15 pm and the news from Charlie Dawson didn't come as a surprise. Stack and Summer had already been at the port for over an hour by the time Charlie arrived at Dunkirk and, much as he had expected, there was no sign of the Toyota. According to his text message, he'd got lucky and boarded a ferry without much delay. He expected to be in Dover by 4 pm. 'Look out for me' were his final words.

On board the Spirit of Britain, Stack and Summer had searched as much of the ship's extensive car decks as they could, before an officious crewman barked at them to get away from the area and up to the passenger decks. The colossal vessel held over a thousand cars and they were still being loaded. There had been no sign of the Toyota amongst the hundreds of cars lining up on the vast concrete loading area outside either. They tried to remain sanguine. It wasn't unexpected.

***

Two and a half hours earlier, in Dover, the Toyota pulled up passenger side to the passport booth. Mahmoud handed his passport over to Patterson so that he could pass both documents to the immigration officer in the booth. It was as the two passports were handed back to Patterson, that another part of Karim Mahmoud's secret life was revealed. It turned out that this South London Asian jihadist was as Home Counties as an Essex County Cricketer. Patterson had stolen a quick look at Mahmoud's passport as he handed it back to the person he now discovered was born, Karim Monroe – if the passport wasn't fake.

'So, who's this Karim Monroe guy then?' Patterson asked.

They were heading west towards London along the motorway section of the A2; the beige ribbon of concrete that cut through the rolling hills and valleys of the Kent countryside.

'That's me. OK?'

'OK. So, who *was* Karim Mahmoud, then?'

'He still exists. It's my jihadi name. My grandfather changed his name from Mahmoud to Monroe after he arrived in the UK in the sixties. I think there was a singer at the time called Matt Monro. My grandad got the spelling wrong. He confused it with Marilyn Monroe. I don't give a shit either way. I hate my Anglicised name, but it serves my purpose back here in England.'

'What purpose is that then, Karim - *Chatterbox* - Monroe?' Patterson goaded him.

'You will find out when I'm ready for you to find out. Now, shut up and let me drive.'

Patterson didn't know what to make of this new information, but it probably explained how they got through the security checks at the UK border so easily. What frustrated him was that salvation had been so close: police, customs, passport, security. They had all been within touching distance. A simple plea for help and the car would have been surrounded, Mahmoud, Monroe or whatever his name was, would have been arrested and he would have been home free at last – if it wasn't for that bloody hostage in Tripoli, Major Susan Hedgeland.

He'd begun to have misgivings. His sympathy for the woman less certain. She was after all a major in the British army. She knew what was at stake and she took her chances like the rest of them. For all he knew Hedgeland was already dead.

A strong sense of self-preservation rose in him as he followed the logic of his rationale. Hedgeland alive was his buffer against threats to his own life. If Hedgeland was dead, then the threats would be made directly against him if he didn't comply with their demands. Sure, they needed him alive to operate Topaz, but they could harm him, damage him, even cripple him and still leave him capable of working the device. Karim Mahmoud aka Chatterbox, aka Karim Monroe, had a gun and he seemed keen to use it. Call it cowardice, but Steve Patterson did not want to die. And if he could avoid it, he didn't want to get hurt either.

**

'Well, you wanted the flightcase brought back to England. It has been.'

'Very funny Stack,' Madeleine said. 'So, where is it?'

They had agreed to meet as soon as possible after Stack, Summer and Charlie arrived in London. They'd been back two days. The meeting was at their hotel, the Curzon Mews, Mayfair. A fashionable address located discretely behind the London Hilton.

'Is Major Cavanagh coming to this meeting?' Stack asked.

'He'll be along soon. He's bringing Chris Bailey with him.'

The rooms in the hotel, though luxurious, tended to be rather small. Stack and Summer had one of the larger rooms, which included just enough living space for a sofa and a couple of small mock Chippendale armchairs that surrounded a coffee table on three sides. The double bed occupied most of the rest of the space with a fitted wardrobe and sideboard along one wall, all painted in a distressed, pale cream eggshell, aged to give it an expensive, antique look.

Stack and Summer were sitting on the couch opposite Madeleine Clark who faced Charlie, in one of the fake Chippendale chairs. She opened her briefcase, pulled out a laptop and sat it on the coffee table. Within a few seconds it was connected to a high-speed network. She turned it so that Stack and Summer could see the screen. Charlie leaned in to get a view.

'You're the only people who have seen the driver of the Toyota. I want you to look at these images and tell me if you recognise anyone.'

She started to scroll through page after page of photographs. They varied in quality from clear full-face pictures, to grainy and ghost-like snapshots. One looked like an enlargement of a satellite image. The pixilation rendered it almost impossible to make out. All were taken covertly.

Stack leaned back when the beauty parade had come to an end and turned to Summer.

'Well, Summer, you spent the longest time with them in the restaurant, anything?'

'He had his back to me most of the time, but he did turn briefly once, and I got a shot of him another time as I returned from the bathroom. Go back a couple of pages.'

Madeleine swept her fingers slowly across the screen, working backwards through the mug-shots. Three pages back Summer told her to stop. A three-quarter shot of a bearded young man taken secretly from a distance. It was by no means a clear image. In truth it could be a blurry shot of any bearded Asian or middle eastern man.

'That's him, at least I think so.'

'I agree. That's our man,' Stack said. Though he had only seconds to scan the table in the restaurant, he had harnessed a natural ability to accurately recall essential details. His mind was already made up but wanted Summer to confirm it. Charlie had had his back to the man in the restaurant and only saw him from a distance in low light conditions as he followed him back to the hotel, so he was less certain.

Madeleine pursed her lips and nodded.

'We know this man. He was based in Sirte. He was the target for our MI8 team in Tripoli. Karim Monroe alias Karim Mahmoud. We called him 'Chatterbox.''

***

Now, Patterson was worried.

Sitting in the living room of the flat above the convenience store in Peckham for the last two days had given him time to think. Karim Mahmoud had spent most of the time since they'd arrived in London, away from the flat. He didn't tell Patterson what he was doing, he just came and went. Now though he had two accomplices. One, an angry Somalian called Ramaas, in his late twenties, seething with resentment and a willing soldier at the extreme edges of Islam. The other, an Iraqi, no more than eighteen, who called himself Youssef. He was perhaps the most dangerous of the three because his indoctrination into the cause had begun at birth. His hand was never far away from a heavily annotated and much thumbed Quran.

They were beginning to assemble weapons. First only knives, but Mahmoud had given his pistol to Ramaas, his second in command, and replaced it with an old Uzi submachine gun, which he enjoyed breaking apart and reassembling. They didn't seem short of 9mm ammunition. The sight of the Uzi caused the eighteen-year-old to complain that he should have one as well.

The weaponry gave them bullying rights. When they were together in the flat they spoke tough and radical words of revenge in the name of Allah. When they invoked their cause, '*death to the Kufir*', they turned to look at Patterson.

As frightening as those moments were, it was something else that chilled his blood. On the day they had arrived in Peckham, London, Mahmoud had parked temporarily in front of the store just off Rye Lane. Patterson reached in to the rear compartment to remove the flightcase. As he drew the heavy box towards him, his hand momentarily touched the aluminium surface of the lid. He was so surprised by the unexpected heat that he snatched his hand away as though it had been scolded. He reached in and tentatively touched it again. It wasn't exactly hot, but it was warmer than last time. The problem was, any kind of heat was wrong.

Mahmoud led Patterson up to the flat and told him to check the device to make sure it was still working. He was going to take the car to another location and would be away for twenty minutes or so. This information was accompanied by the inevitable threats to Major Hedgeland's life if he attempted to escape.

Patterson flipped the catches, removed the lid, and cast his hand across the control panel as before. Again, the surface was cool at the edges but, as he drew his hand across, the heat was still significantly warmer around the small isotope chamber access port.

As a quantum physicist he knew that without any source of power, only one thing could make the tiny quantity of radioactive material in the chamber react like that. But that was impossible. Ignoring hospital X-ray departments, there were no other radioisotopes within 50 miles of Peckham. Then he considered the Toyota and the question; why bring such an old car all the way from Tripoli to London? The answer, if he was correct, terrified him.

He pulled the laptop, cables and adapters out of the backpack and began connecting it to the sockets in the flightcase. Then he plugged the Topaz device into the mains and fired it up. The sound of the micro high-speed motors spinning up suggested the time shifting device appeared to be working.

The next question. Who could he trust to signal his status and his concerns without compromising his or Hedgeland's safety? He didn't trust Madeleine Clarke at MI8; she was a terrible risk taker - with other people's lives. There must be someone else.

He didn't have a cell phone, but he did have the laptop. It was purpose built to work in conjunction with the Topaz device but didn't have any of the conventional software and apps common to domestic computers. It was however fitted with a suite of GCHQ spyware that allowed covert connectivity with telecommunications devices such as cell phones. This was more than enough for Patterson's purpose.

**

'Hi Chris. You got back safely, then?' Stack said. Chris Bailey had just arrived with Cavanagh at the Curzon Mews Hotel. 'You remember Summer Peterson don't you, and Hollywood you already know.'

Bailey was pleased to see Stack and Dawson again and, like everyone who meets her, no matter how many times, he was happy to be in Summer Peterson's company again.

'I believe Madeleine has already gone through the family album with you,' Cavanagh said from his perch on the edge of the bed.

'Yes, it must get expensive at Christmas,' Stack joked sarcastically.

Cavanagh ignored the humour. He reached over and turned the laptop toward him and looked at the familiar image on the screen.

'Karim Mahmoud. He gets around. Iraq, Syria and lately, Libya.' Cavanagh sniffed his contempt and turned to Summer. 'So, you think he's here in London?'

'Well, I'm certain I detected a South London accent when I heard them talking in the restaurant back in France. Maybe he's coming home?'

Cavanagh turned to Madeleine.

'The London accent means nothing. He could be anywhere in the UK.'

Stack was astonished at the lack of intel on the man.

'You mean you have no idea who this man actually is, where he came from? No history whatsoever?'

'We're not entirely without assets, Stack. We've got his cyber fingerprints on his social media postings and under-the-wire, dark web communications,' Cavanagh said.

'This image was captured at considerable risk,' Madeleine added. 'We knew he was a Brit.'

'This grainy picture is the counterpart of another well-known irritant,' Cavanagh revealed. 'Until now, we hadn't taken much interest in him. But now we know he is one and the same person. We regarded him as just one of their backroom boys. One of Daesh's useful idiots. The problem is, he now appears to have been under the direct command of Ghazi Ibn Wali.'

Maddy shook her head slowly as she summarised the extremist leader's murderous CV.

'He and his *Sword of Liberation* are a nasty piece of work. There are no lives he is unwilling to take to advance his cause. Any Muslims caught in one of his atrocities are, in his view, either lost to western capitalism and therefore deserving victims, or unfortunate but inevitable martyrs to their cause.'

Cavanagh got off the bed and walked over to the window. Being in the shadow of the vast Hilton tower, there wasn't much to see. He turned and spoke with a sombre voice.

'Look, I'm afraid with Ghazi Ibn Wali involved, we must assume the worst. He's committed several high-profile atrocities across Europe and Africa that we know of. The total death toll is in excess of three thousand innocent men, women and children.' Cavanagh's tone became more serious. 'We've had it confirmed by UK Boarder Control in

Dover that Karim Monroe, alias Mahmoud, has entered the country. That much we do know. Which means Ghazi Ibn Wali has sent Mahmoud here on a mission. The Toyota has something to do with it, it isn't just for transport.'

'Jesus! And you let this man into the country without calling on other agencies for help?' Summer was furious.

'You forget, he also has Topaz with him,' Cavanagh replied irritably. 'Recovering it trumps everything.'

'And we also have you three mercenaries,' Madeleine said. 'Knowing that the device exists makes you a critical part of its recovery. And by the way, you're still operating under the Official Secrets Act.'

Stack, Charlie and Summer were shocked to hear the MI8 officer describe them in such derogatory terms.

'Mercenaries? I think you've confused us with your own lawless army of privateers over at Vauxhall Cross, Madeleine,' Stack was furious. 'And since when were we operating under the Official Secrets Act? You've got your own people. You don't need us anymore.' Stack started to get up to leave.

Cavanagh turned from the window.

'Well, consider yourselves deputised. You're now functioning as temporary operatives for the department. Welcome aboard.'

'I had no idea people could get on the MI6 payroll so easily,' Stack said sarcastically as he sat down again. He knew he was trapped.

Madeleine stepped in irritably.

'Not MI6. MI8. As I've already explained to you, we're a subsection of the intelligence service.

Nobody has heard of us. It's all very deniable,' she said, before adding a grim footnote. 'The rules haven't changed. You're all in the UK on borrowed time until the flightcase is recovered.'

***

With all the chairs in the room taken, Chris Bailey had braced himself against the sideboard. Not quite sitting or standing. He was taking particular interest in James Stack, a man he had come to know and respect. Of the people in the room, the least trustworthy in his opinion were Cavanagh and the duplicitous Madeleine Clarke. This was an important distinction, because he had that morning received a message from Patterson. Not a direct communication, but a curious reference to an old *Guardian* newspaper report from five years ago about abandoned research into faster than light neutrinos at CERN in Switzerland. The precursor to Topaz. It was a message from one quantum physicist to another. What made it personal was how it was delivered. The newspaper clip had been copied over a live web page sent to his smartphone. The web page showed a small clock face with a ticking second hand. Not just any clock, but International Atomic Time – the atomic clock. It gave the precise time measured using Caesium 133 and accurate to one second in a hundred million years.

It had taken a moment for the penny to drop. Bailey had looked at his watch. It was hard to tell; the old timepiece was always fast. He switched on the TV to Sky News. Again, the digital time it displayed was not precise enough. He went to his laptop and opened the browser to an atomic clock

URL that showed the same clock face as the one in the live video feed. He held his smartphone up to the laptop screen to compare the images. There was no mistake. The atomic clock on the smartphone that should have been showing the precise current time was five seconds ahead. It was future time and only possible using a faster than light device. There was only one such device. It was in Patterson's possession and it was called Topaz.

***

'So, Stack, you're Maddy's golden boy,' Cavanagh said as he walked over to the minibar, selected a miniature Gordon's, twisted off the cap and made himself a gin & tonic as he spoke. 'You managed to get Major Hedgeland out of Libya. I suppose I should thank you for that,' He raised his glass in a grudging toast to Stack.

'You're welcome. I'll send you a bill for the drink', Stack said dryly.

'Now, to business,' Cavanagh continued, ignoring Stack's sarcasm. 'As we are not prepared to broadcast to the world, news of our... how shall I call it? Our *Edge-of-science* device, all efforts to retrieve it will be handled by the people in this room only – and no one else.'

'But what about CCTV footage of the Toyota?' Charlie said. 'Have you asked to see any of it? There must be some images of it arriving at Dover. And other cameras will have seen it too, if it drove into London.'

'Fair enough,' Madeleine taunted, 'I'll arrange for you to review the recordings. There must be a thousand cameras both public and private to choose from. Where do you want to start?'

'Well, how about roadside CCTV at the London end of the A2?' Charlie said. 'Three locations in South East London: Eltham, the Blackwall Tunnel and New Cross. If we spot it at Eltham, the cameras at New Cross would give us a direction of travel to the south, *if* we manage to ID it of course. On the other hand, if we spot the Toyota at the Blackwall Tunnel, we'd know it was heading north of the river. It'll make it easier to choose the location of the next set of cameras to review.'

Maddy struggled to find a flaw in Charlie's impressive knowledge of south London or his logic.

'OK, I'll set it up for you now, but I want to add the M25 cameras at the A2 junction, in case they are heading north towards Birmingham or Manchester via the M25 orbital, instead of going into London.'

Stack agreed it was a good first step, but suggested that, as Summer had followed the Toyota through the French countryside for the best part of a day, she should check the footage with Charlie.

'Shouldn't be hard to spot, it's a vintage Toyota Landcruiser with French plates.'

Cavanagh looked at his watch, impatient to leave.

'Ok, how about you Stack? I'm told you're the brilliant strategist. It's time to impress me.'

Stack wasn't about to allow himself to be bullied by this ex-army officer desk jockey.

'I'll get back to you.' He pointed to the laptop. 'In the meantime, you should put an address to that face. You must have access to digital feature mapping or facial recognition software. Someone must know him. If the people in this room are the only team you have, then you and Madeleine are going to have to pull your weight and wear out some shoe leather.'

Cavanagh straightened his back fussily trying to regain some authority. Chris Bailey almost laughed out loud. He had just turned Stack's *respect* dial, up to twelve.

***

As they filed out of the hotel room, Bailey pulled Stack to one side.

'Meet me in the bar downstairs in five,' He whispered.

Stack closed the door and turned to his two friends.

'That was interesting. I suppose I'd better come up with a plan,' he said, as he sat back down on the couch.

'I don't know how. We've got nothing to go on,' said Charlie. 'Even if Summer and I come up with some useful CCTV footage, it's unlikely to pinpoint the address of this Mahmoud character.'

Summer nodded agreement.

'Well, a visual on the Toyota will confirm their likely heading. Then we have to answer the question, *why* he's bringing the Topaz device back to London – if that's where he's going?' She added. 'I don't think there's any question that it's here in the city somewhere.'

'I've been thinking the same thing, Summer,' Stack agreed. 'They obviously plan to do some serious mischief with it.'

'OK, boss,' Hollywood said. 'What kind of mischief?'

Stack leaned back into the sofa and closed his eyes as he considered the possibilities. He had a gift for clarity that served him well when planning covert operations as a captain in Special Forces. An ability to conjure intuitive insights from unpromising intel. It was a prodigious talent he now brought to bear in an attempt to answer his old army buddy's question.

'If I understand correctly how that Topaz device works, they might be able to undermine the UK's financial sector in the City of London. They could secretly change the offer price of share trades. As it's all done in cyberspace, using algorithms across multiple accounts in fractions of seconds. A sudden unexpected fall or rise in a share price would get an instant reaction from automated trading software.

They call it high frequency trading and by the time they've pulled the plug and closed it down, massive damage could have been done to the economy.'

'I've heard of it,' Summer said. 'The most recent crash was as a result of high-speed algorithm trading in the New York Stock Exchange back in 2010. They called it the *Flash Crash*. These things are barely under control.'

Stack looked at his watch.

'Look, Chris Bailey wants me to meet him in the bar downstairs. I think we should all go.'

***

Bailey was waiting when they arrived. Drinks were ordered at the bar and taken to a table further back in the lounge, where discrete, low-key lighting gave a sense of privacy. Stack summarised the conversation the three of them had just had about a possible City share trading scenario. Bailey instantly saw the danger.

'Topaz is the perfect weapon for that kind of sabotage. It works in the same world of quantum physics as automated trading. They wouldn't be able to tell it apart,' Bailey said. 'High Frequency Trading works at very near the speed of light. Topaz would push it beyond the speed of light. A saboteur could place fake trades that would appear as done deals by the time the automated software catches up. It only needs to be a nanosecond ahead of real time. The algorithms will go nuts trying to make sense of it. Then they'll do what they're designed to do – but it'll go off like a trade bomb.'

Stack lifted his glass and leaned back in his seat. He took a sip and considered Bailey's words, as the delicious oak and honey flavours of the twelve-year-old Glen Garioch whisky slipped smoothly down his throat.

'We have no evidence that Karim Mahmoud will do that, or that he has the skill to pull it off,' Stack said. 'You say it's possible, but do you think Patterson is capable of making the device do that?'

'Definitely,' Bailey countered. 'He knows the machine better than me – or anyone else for that matter.'

Stack nodded thoughtfully.

'Well, we have to consider all possibilities.' Summer brought up another concern.

'Patterson is still being held against his will. And I guess he believes Major Hedgeland is still a hostage in Tripoli. Under those circumstances I think he'll do whatever he's told.'

'That brings me to the reason I wanted to talk to you, James,' Bailey said. 'I had a contact from Patterson this morning.'

Charlie zeroed in on this.

'What? He called you?'

'Not exactly. It was an indirect, proof-of-life, kind of thing. He had time shifted it. Very clever. It couldn't have come from anyone else.'

'So, it proved he was still alive and he had the Topaz device with him. So what?' Summer quizzed.

It was Chris Bailey's turn to pause while he considered his response. He glanced around at the four or five customers sitting at tables further away in the lounge and the one lone drinker at the bar. Satisfied he couldn't be overheard, he leaned in towards the others around the table and spoke cautiously.

'The problem may be bigger than we thought.'

'Bigger? How so?' Stack queried.

Bailey paused again. It wasn't for effect. He was struggling to bring himself to say out loud what he believed Patterson had tried to convey in his message.

'I couldn't possibly say this to Madeleine or Cavanagh. They'd just laugh at me. They simply don't have the imagination to deal with it.'

'So?' Charlie asked. 'What is it?'

'Patterson's message contained two things that proved it was him.' Bailey took a sip of his beer, wiped his mouth and continued. 'But there was a third image. A schematic drawing of a nuclear reactor core.'

Silence descended around the table. Stack, Summer and Charlie all looked at each other in bewilderment.

'A nuclear reactor core?' Stack said. 'I don't get it.'

Bailey jumped in eagerly.

'Heat!' He said it out loud, and then realising others could hear, he lowered his voice.

'Heat!' he whispered, as though that explained everything.

'So? Heat? A reactor core?' Stack gave an uncomprehending shrug. 'I'm afraid that's gone right over our heads, Chris.'

'Sorry. Let me try to make it simple. The Topaz device has a small but highly radioactive isotope buried inside it. It's bloody dangerous stuff. You wouldn't want to touch it. But it's fine while it's inside the machine. It does nothing interesting until we excite it with another component. But, if a quantity of a particular type of radioactive material was placed near the flightcase, the two isotopes would have a fissile reaction.'

Bailey stopped, but quickly realised, as he looked at the others around the table, that they were still sitting in a thick London fog of incomprehension.

'They get warm!' he said. 'Patterson was telling me the Topaz isotope was getting warm. The only way that could happen would be if it had been near some other fissile radioactive material. Something like Uranium-235, or worse, Plutonium-239.'

This statement was greeted with the slow, nodding heads of gradual understanding.

'Wait a minute. Are you saying you believe these terrorists have got their hands on some uranium or plutonium?' Stack asked. 'And just because the device had got warm?'

'My God! That's a bit of a leap, Chris,' Summer said.

'It was the schematic of the reactor core, Summer. Nuclear reactors create heat when enough radioactive material is brought close together.'

Charlie was still struggling with this new information.

'You mean the stuff they make nuclear weapons with?'

'Could that be why they brought that old car all the way from Libya?' Summer suggested.

'A very good point,' Stack agreed. 'It would be almost impossible to bring it into the UK any other way. They must have buried it in the chassis under the car.'

He turned to Charlie. 'That's what they were doing back in the compound with the welding torch.'

'Yeah, we thought it might have been a bomb. But, you know, the conventional IED type,' Charlie added.

A renewed sense of urgency gripped them as they began to fully appreciate the implications of the new threat.

'So, which is it?' Stack wondered. 'A cyber-attack on the London Stock Exchange or some kind of nuclear threat?'

'Or both?' Summer added.

Bailey looked at the other three around the table and shook his head.

'Even if they had enough uranium or plutonium to make a viable nuclear bomb, there is no way they could actually build one. You need the kind of money and resources only governments can provide.'

Charlie looked relieved.

'Well that's alright then isn't it? They can't make a bomb.'

'No, they can't. At least, not the big crowd pleaser most people think of, with the mushroom cloud,' Bailey said. But they could easily make a dirty bomb. They'd just need to bury the radioactive material within some explosives and when it goes bang, it would contaminate everything within a few blocks. It'd take them years to clear it up, and who knows how many thousands of people would suffer radiation poisoning – *if*, they've got their hands on any radioactive material.'

Charlie's shoulders slumped forward.

'Jesus! It just gets worse.'

Stack looked around the table at each in turn. His eyes settled on Bailey.

'We can't keep this to ourselves, Chris. We've got to tell Cavanagh.'

High Frequency Low Down

It was raining. Not heavily, just the usual miserable drizzle for which London was famous. Early evening, about eight pm. Dark, but only in the way big modern cities are dark: car headlights, red tail lights, street lights and buses. Lights from taxis and tower blocks, houses and shop windows. An electronic brightness that shimmered off the wet road surface and the glossy rain-soaked paintwork of the endless lines of vehicles still struggling to get somewhere. The low cloud cover glowed so brightly from the intensity of the artificial light that it enveloped the metropolis below in a soft amber radiance.

Splashing along the sidewalk, a figure arrived at a doorway, soaked from the top of his white cotton hoodie to the bottom of his neoprene sneakers. He pressed the buzzer for the flat above the convenience store and was quickly let in.

Karim Mahmoud introduced the newcomer to his fellow gang members. He called himself 'Flash Harry'. He was a specialist in automated share trading. Although he was a Muslim himself, he was ambivalent about religion. But as a fervent socialist, he shared their grudge against capitalism.

In Libya, Ghazi Ibn Wali had instructed Karim Mahmoud to take the Jihad to London. There had been a few blows struck by extremist freelancers over recent years. Some deaths, many injured. It was all too slow. The fight needed to go up several gears. What was needed, Gahzi Ibn Wali believed, was a spectacular event. Now he had regained possession of the plutonium, he was less interested in what subtle mischief the strange time shifting device could do. He was much more eager to unleash the terror of radioactive poisoning. He had at last the means to make demands and threats and deliver human misery on a scale so massive that the British government would beg for mercy.

Mahmoud was fully committed to the plan, but he couldn't resist a little mayhem of his own. A little economic disaster on the side. Two for the price of one. After all, he'd brought the Topaz device to London. He was certain the extremist leader in Libya, Ghazi Ibn Wali, would be impressed.

Mahmoud, though a talented hacker, didn't have the skills to hack into the kind of algorithms share-trading outfits use on the Stock Exchange. He could get in, but he couldn't influence their activity. Quantum physicists are employed to devise ways to shorten the effective trading time. They had it down to nanoseconds, a fraction of time that was too small for Mahmoud to do his work. Only someone like Flash Harry, who understood how the algorithms worked could crack them. Once they'd done that, the time shifting property of the miraculous Topaz device could hold each trade frozen in time as they worked to change its offer from buy to sell.

Luckily, he had found Flash Harry through a friend who worked in the City of London; a tiny province of high value real estate that in world ranking was second only to New York in the financial services business.

Mahmoud was a cautious man. He agreed a meeting at a coffee house. Their conversation was informal and general: football, vacations, wives and girlfriends, TV programmes and, of course, the weather. Never the subject he was most interested in - that came later.

The problem was twofold. He didn't have much time and he didn't have much choice. Flash Harry was the only cow in the cattle auction. He would have to do.

Harry came highly recommended with a solid charge sheet of criminal activity in financial wrong doing, hidden under a veneer of respectable contract work. It took two days in all to go from introduction, to provisional gang member.

In the flat in Peckham that night, the three radical Islamists and Flash Harry talked about how they were going to carry out the fake flash trades. When Mahmoud thought the moment was right, he brought Patterson in from the bedroom next door and introduced him to Harry.

Harry had been told an extremely unusual technology could be utilised in their scheme. Mahmoud hadn't been able to explain how the Topaz device worked, but he assured Harry it would solve the speed problem when attempting to change a trade in full nanosecond flight. It was this miraculous device that intrigued Flash Harry. More than anything else, it was the reason he was there.

To Patterson, the new gang member looked Asian, possibly of Pakistani or Bangladeshi roots. His first reaction though, was to deny the machine existed. The idea of time shifting, he said, was absurd.

His attempt at denial was quickly undermined, when Mahmoud brought the flightcase in from the bedroom and opened the lid.

Harry eagerly reached over to play around with the controls. It wasn't plugged in, so nothing happened. It was when his fingers grabbed hold of the door to the containment chamber that Patterson leaped up and dragged the box across the floor away from him.

'Never, NEVER, touch that door.' He said. 'Don't touch it or open it. One man has already died from the effects of radiation poisoning.'

Mahmoud, recalling the fate of the leader of Breath of Allah, nodded his agreement.

'Actually, I can confirm that, so let's all agree that this machine is for Patterson to operate only, yes?'

That frightening bit of news had two consequences. The respect for the machine became total and it proved to Flash Harry that besides being deadly, a machine with some kind of radioactive substance buried in it must be special in some way. He was eager to see what it could do.

As trading on the London Stock Exchange had ended some hours earlier, making the tampering of share trades impossible, Mahmoud suggested Patterson played his party trick with someone's bank account, as he had with the late rebel leader's bitcoin account. To test the new gang member's allegiance, the account he chose was Flash Harry's.

This suggestion brought a long pause from Harry as he considered how he should respond. He didn't want his bank account details flashed around the room or to become part of the browser history on their laptop. He had another idea. He pulled his own laptop from his shoulder bag, placed it on the coffee table in front of him and turned it on.

'I'm not going to give you my bank account details but I have access to another account we can play with,' he said. 'One of my clients.' No one questioned the means by which he came by it.

The account didn't hold a vast amount, only a few thousand pounds.

Patterson already had the Topaz device and its laptop wired up and running. This was the first time Mahmoud's two henchmen had seen it operating. He'd told them about it, but they weren't ready for the whining sound from the spinning motors. Or the strange, unnerving static charge it emitted. Flash Harry was sitting closer and laughed as the hair on his forearms stood up. Patterson reached across and tapped his arm. The static gave the usual distinctive *snap* as it discharged.

As before, when he demonstrated it back in Tripoli, Patterson copied the URL into the address field of the Topaz laptop. With the password entered, the account and its balance were displayed on the screen. He turned to the Topaz control panel and made adjustments that caused the machine to give a low humming sound. He carefully slid one of the tube sliders slowly across and watched as the data on the small control panel screen swiftly changed. To Flash Harry, it was just scrambled digits and code. Patterson moved to the other slider and began shifting it slowly across in the opposite direction, again paying careful attention to the data display. Very quickly, the tiny high-torque electric motors started spinning up until they were screaming like banshees again.

He tapped more keys and the bank account emptied. A few more adjustments and the screen on Harry's laptop went slightly fuzzy for an instant. Harry stared. He was about to shrug a '*so what?*' when he noticed the line of zeroes in the credit column of the account.

Patterson reset the account on the Topaz laptop and told Flash Harry to wait for a moment.

The three fanatics squeezed around Flash Harry's laptop and watched. On the Topaz device's data screen, the clock counted down through time in a blur of digits until it reached zero.

On Harry's laptop, without even a hint that anything had changed, the balance instantly clicked back to the original amount.

'So, what just happened?' he asked.

Karim Mahmoud began to give his version of what the Topaz device had just done, but got confused and ended up letting Patterson finish the explanation.

'When your laptop showed that the account was empty, you were looking at the same account but a fraction of a second into the future. It was the future version of the account that had changed. Topaz had time shifted it and held it there until our time - real time - caught up with it. That's when the balance of the account changed back. It's the nature of time,' Patterson said, 'The present is always moving forward into the future.'

'And you want to use this box-of-tricks, this Topaz thing of yours, to hack into high frequency trades to change them?' Flash Harry asked.

The business of hacking put Mahmoud back on familiar ground.

'It's more complicated than that. We can't hack into high frequency trades; they happen too fast. But this machine will slow them down. That's when you go in and do your thing. You know – change the offer price from buy to sell.'

Harry sat back still staring at the laptop screen. He shook his head slowly in disbelief.

'This could do real damage if you picked the right trades. I'm talking about a major economic crash. They would never trust high frequency trading again,' Flash Harry declared in undisguised awe. 'Your Topaz could bring down the whole bloody system.'

This piece of good news had Mahmoud, Ramaas and Youssef jumping up and down in celebration at the inevitability of their forthcoming victory. They slapped high fives and threw their arms around each other, dancing and laughing. The collapse of the UK's democratic and capitalist system was coming, they shouted, repeating it until it turned into a chant.

Mahmoud had tears of joy in his eyes as he turned to Harry.

'This will really get their attention. The dawning of the new Islamic era begins tomorrow.'

***

Later, after Flash Harry had left and Patterson had been locked in the bedroom once more, the extremist cell set the living room up to make a video. One wall had a black flag pinned to it, much like the one used by Islamic State, but the slogan splashed across in florid script read, *Sword of Liberation.*

Youssef held the Samsung smartphone up and tapped the record button. Mahmoud was sitting in a chair in front of the flag, the Uzi submachine gun lying across his lap, his face hidden by a patterned cloth. It was standard terrorist theatre. He stared into the lens and calmly and very matter-of-factly, set out their demands.

The First Message

The rain had cleared up overnight and the new day brought with it the hazy mellow sunshine and gentle warmth of late summer. London was full of tourists looking the wrong way as they crossed the busy streets. Both traffic and pedestrians were noisy and bad tempered. By 11 am, the temperature had risen to hot and humid; the air so thick with exhaust fumes you could chew it.

Two things happened that morning.

Flash Harry had had a sleepless night. He knew only about Mahmoud's plan to cripple the City of London and the wider UK economy and nothing else. As much as he enjoyed the idea of bringing chaos to London's financial centre, Mahmoud's words about a new Islamic age had kept him awake. Like most Muslims, he was no extremist. He asked himself whether a new Islamic age would be in his interest? What he did know was that Islamic extremists could be pretty bloody extreme. There was another thing that worried him. He had a record for cybercrime. His fingerprints would be all over it. Self-preservation nagged at his thoughts as he lay there, weighing his options.

Perhaps there was another way. He couldn't pull out. Simply not turning up wasn't an option. They knew who he was and how to find him. They'd brought him on board because they didn't have a choice. He was one of a kind; a high frequency trade technology expert and a gun for hire, which meant he would be in control of the choice of trades.

In amongst the tide of stocks and shares that get traded are hidden a large number of hypothetical offers that fleetingly populate the daily trades like ghosts. Some people believe the fake trades are placed deliberately to clog up the system and slow things down, reducing the bandwidth for other players.

Flash Harry believed he could recognise these fake trades. Amending the share offer of such trades wouldn't have an effect because they would be pulled at the last second anyway. Importantly, it would still appear to the three co-conspirators that he was busy undermining the citadel of capitalism. He'd have to pick some genuine trades too, but the overall effect would be suppressed. There'd be no chaos. Just a nervous day on the stock market.

***

The second event happened at the offices of *The Guardian* newspaper, as a sub-editor nudged his laptop into life. He'd arrived late that morning and thrown himself into the familiar embrace of his threadbare swivel chair. He pushed the mess on his desk away to make space for his coffee cup and pulled a doughnut out of the jam-soaked paper bag on his lap. He carefully unclipped the lid of the cup, threw it in the bin under his desk, and took a swig. He was just pushing the doughnut into his mouth when the laptop came to life. It wasn't his usual screen saver that appeared.

His mouth remained open, the doughnut unchewed, as he watched the screen dissolve into an image of the Sword of Liberation flag. It had a caption superimposed over it that read "For the attention of the British government". Jam was slowly dripping down the side of the sub-editor's chin as the image dissolved again into moving footage of a masked man addressing the camera. He was talking but no sound was coming out. The sub snatched the doughnut out of his mouth and searched his laptop for the volume control. He found it after a couple of frustrating searches around the edges of the screen, clicked, and the sound suddenly blared out loudly. As the man in the video spoke, his aggressive ranting caught the attention of people sitting nearby. One by one, they started to get up from their desks and gather round.

The sub watched in fascination, never taking his eyes from the screen as he slowly reached for the doughnut again and planted it back in his mouth. The masked man was sitting in front of a Sword of Liberation flag, making a series of demands and threats. His finger jabbing skywards to emphasise Allah's authority.

When the video finished, the sub-editor sat for a moment staring at the blank screen before leaping up, barging his way through the circle of people, and rushing over to the editor's office far across the cluttered open-plan floor, shouting as he went, for someone to, 'find out who the bloody hell The Sword of Liberation are.'

***

Chris Bailey had contacted James Stack that morning to arrange a meeting. He had some interesting new information he wanted to show him. By the time they were seated together in the lounge bar in the basement of the Curzon Mews Hotel that afternoon, the story of the demands being made by a radical extremist group had already hit the online news media headlines. *The Guardian* had released it first, but very quickly other news titles had followed it up. Stack was reading about it in the *London Evening Standard*.

The later publication time meant it had the chance to print a revised headline: *Extremist Chaos Threat Downgraded.*'

Charlie and Summer were elsewhere in London reviewing CCTV recordings and weren't expected back until later, so Stack was on his own.

'Have you read this, Chris?' said Stack as he handed the paper to Bailey.

'No, but I heard about it on the radio.'

'Well, take a look while I get you a drink. I think it may be our boy.'

Flash Crash

By eight thirty that morning, the first fake trades were hitting the screens of buyers and sellers in trading houses and independent stockbroking businesses across the City. A safe bet had suddenly become a questionable risk. Brand Petroleum had been the golden boy of pension fund managers for decades. It was a speed-dial, go-to investment for every major financial institution. They loved it. Safe and secure - a steady earner.

Then, suddenly, someone wanted to sell. A large tranche of shares going far too cheaply. Someone knew something. The city jungle drums started beating out a rumour. It starts as a guess. Someone asks, '*Why?*'. Someone else gives an opinion. The opinion catches fire and now everyone is nervous. But flash trading, being the high frequency automatic trading algorithm that it was, had already done its job, long before anyone had the time to ask, '*Why?*'

The Brand Petroleum share price started to drop as thousands of shares were offered at below the opening price. Shareholders were quickly losing large sums of money. The nervous, smaller independent investors threw themselves over the cliff first. Old hands held firm – for the time being.

Then, another old favourite got hit with an unexpected drop in price. It made no sense. It was a solid earner with no hint of trouble on the horizon. Now, suddenly, whole tracts of shares were being offloaded. The yellow and green numbers crawling across the screens of trading floors across the City were turning into a panic inducing sea of red. Shouts of '*Sell!*' were screamed down telephones. Again, the flash boys with their nanosecond advantage steamed in, selling while the price was still high, keen to avoid being left with an unfixable position at the end of the day.

The same flash boys, who had been flooding the trading system with thousands of their own fake non-trades, were now getting stuck in their own swamp. They weren't just slowing everyone else down, they were getting hit too. It was like wading through digital treacle.

Back on the second floor above the store in Peckham, Flash Harry was putting on a show for Mahmoud and his henchmen. They had the TV turned on to Sky News and were practically hugging themselves as the news presenters kept re-running Mahmoud's dramatic video message. The opinions of commentators and politicians were sought and eagerly given. Then, in amongst the forensic examination of the terrorists' message, news of a semi meltdown at the London Stock Exchange was beginning to come through. It seemed that, just as the terrorists promised, the City of London and the British economy were starting to take a big hit.

What they didn't know was that Flash Harry had pulled back on the levers of economic Armageddon, allowing only a few carefully selected high value trades to go through with the altered price. For the benefit of those in the flat watching him, he appeared to be picking other valuable trades and marking them down too. In reality, he was making harmless alterations to the thousands of automated fake trades put out to gum up the works by flash boys who would have deleted them anyway if they hadn't already time-expired.

By lunch time, after 820 points had been knocked off the FTSE 100 trading index, things started to settle down on the London Stock Exchange. Panic over. Time to ask questions. Time to seek out someone to blame.

Flash Harry had gone long before Mahmoud and the gang realised they had been tricked. His next stop, an old university friend now working at GCHQ. He wondered whether he might be interested to know about the mysterious device in the flightcase. Harry figured it could be a useful bargaining chip if his involvement in the recent trading scare became known.

***

Stack was placing the drinks on the table as Bailey quoted from the newspaper.

'It says here that these extremists are demanding the release of that troublemaker, Asad Hassan. They've given the government 24 hours. "Failure to release him will result in extreme action and the Prime Minister will be to blame for the terrible consequences that follow". Sounds like the usual threats to me.'

'Yes, but if you read further down, they say they'll be issuing another message tomorrow, making further demands,' Stack said as he sat down. 'It seems to me, getting Hassan released is only part of their plan.'

Bailey gave that some thought as he raised his whisky glass in a gesture of thanks to Stack and took a sip.

'Well, it looks like the great financial crash didn't happen.'

Stack didn't agree.

'It happened, but not on the scale they had threatened. It wasn't a prediction, they did actually influence trading. How do you think they did that?' Stack wondered, already sure of the answer.

'Patterson,' said Bailey. 'I'm certain Topaz was their way in. But they'd need an expert in high frequency trading to drill into the share offers.'

'Well, it looks like the sky didn't fall in.'

'It's what they're planning to do next that worries me, Chris,' Stack said. 'You said something about uranium or plutonium the other day. I sincerely hope that's not what they've got in mind.'

'If my interpretation of Patterson's message is correct, then yes, Uranium-235, or worse, Plutonium-239. And worse still if it had been turned into a powder called Plutonium Oxide Dust. In that case, we could have a bigger problem on our hands.'

'Yes, I've heard of it. It's highly toxic. They say only a small amount can affect huge numbers of people. If it's breathed in, death comes slowly through cancers. Frightening stuff.'

Bailey reached for his glass again and nodded grimly.

'All they need is some kind of explosive device to scatter it over a large area,' he theorised. 'Any city centre would be particularly vulnerable.'

Stack lifted his whisky glass and they both downed the smooth peaty liquor in one. Bailey placed the empty tumbler on the table, reached into his inside jacket pocket and pulled out a thin envelope.

'I want to show you something. Not even Cavanagh or Clark have seen this yet.'

He slid out a glossy print of a world map. Not all of it, just the part that included the UK, Europe and North Africa. It had been overlaid with a number of white spots.

'What I'm going to reveal to you goes to the heart of the Topaz project,' Bailey said. 'Patterson and I were part of the development team. There were just a couple of others working on it. The Topaz machine is a prototype, a one-off. Its effectiveness was still being evaluated.

'We got the International Space Station to carry a small piece of research equipment for us. They were told it was a neutrino experiment for a university here in the UK. As you will probably gather, that wasn't quite the truth. Not the neutrino bit – the university bit. The ISS crew were asked to monitor it and send the results back every few days. Neutrinos are notoriously difficult to track, which is actually helpful to us because otherwise this printout would be covered in little white spots and streaks.

'Topaz uses super luminary neutrinos – the ones that go faster than light - which are just as difficult to track, but the particles they affect, the ones that create the Topaz stream, they can be tracked. Take a look at the picture, what do you see?'

The correlation between the white spots and the known locations of the Topaz device was immediately obvious to Stack.

'You mean you can follow the device?'

'Only when the stream is working.'

Bailey reached into the envelope and brought out another glossy image. It was a close up of Tripoli. The area to the north, near the harbour was covered in white dots.

'This is not the highest resolution, but you can easily see that every time the device was used a track was recorded.'

Stack was impressed.

'You mean a particle travelled two hundred and fifty miles out to space and got recorded by an instrument on the ISS?'

Bailey nodded.

'That's right. In any Topaz stream, one or two particles will scatter in several directions. I won't bore you with the science, but the important thing is, it creates a record.'

Then Bailey pulled a third sheet from the envelope. It showed a close-up view of London.

'This came in this morning. There are three occasions when Patterson used the device. As you can see, they all came from a single location.'

As he examined the image more closely, Stack zeroed in on the location.

'That's South East London, around Camberwell, Dulwich area.'

'I think it's closer to Peckham.'

Stack was astonished.

'That's it. If they haven't moved, we've got them. Tell me you've got a handheld version of that tracker.'

The Second Message

In a large complex of formidably secure buildings just south of the River Thames and east of London are housed some of the UK's most dangerous criminals. It's known as Her Majesty's Prison Belmarsh. Within its grounds is an even more secure prison that holds the really bad guys: gang bosses, drug barons, serial killers, psychopaths and religious extremists.

These inmates are clever, manipulative and lethal. An explosive cocktail if they were allowed to spend their lengthy sentences amongst the rest of the merely dangerous prison population. That's why they keep them apart, isolated in a prison-within-a-prison called the High Security Unit.

Asad Hassan's cell, painted glossy cream, was a paltry six feet wide and ten long. A stainless-steel toilet was fixed in one corner, and on the wall above, a small mesh-covered aperture allowed in the only natural light the occupant would see for twelve or more hours a day.

Hassan had already served three years of the twelve he'd been given. In normal circumstances, if he'd been a good boy, they'd let him out in another three. But as a volatile and remorseless radical preacher, who wanted nothing less than to overthrow the British government and install a brutal Islamic caliphate based on an extreme and medieval interpretation of sharia law, Hassan was considered a national security risk. He'd serve the full twelve.

For the last three days, he'd spent all his cell time with his eyes fixed to the screen of the small TV bolted to the plastic corner table. He'd had news a couple of days before via one of the screws who'd passed him a scrap of paper. It contained the cryptic message, '*Be ready – watch the news.*'

And that's what he did. And while he watched, he smirked arrogantly as he recalled the words shouted to him from the courtroom gallery after he was sentenced and taken down to the holding cells below: '*We will find a way. Judgement is coming, inshallah.*'

Two days ago, he watched as the capitalist system went into meltdown. Cheering loudly as the stock market dropped hundreds of points at a time. He laughed at the politicians who wrung their hands as they strained to provide a reassuring counter-narrative to Sword of Liberation's terrifying message.

But nobody had arrived at his cell to march him triumphantly to the gates of the jail. And the precipitous fall of the stock market had halted by mid-afternoon. By the evening, when the London Stock Exchange had closed, share prices had already started to recover.

Asad Hassan wasn't concerned. He knew it was only the overture to the main event. The appetising first course of the sumptuous banquet to come.

He was ready, and he was watching a news channel when they broadcast the second message. This time they wouldn't refuse. The cell door would be opened and he would step through the gates of the prison in spectacular triumph, cheered by thousands of his ecstatic followers. Prostrating themselves before him as the true and righteous leader of the new age of British Islam.

***

It was the *Daily Telegraph* that was honoured with the second message. The same masked man sitting in front of the flag. The same finger pointing skyward, the other hand resting on the semi-automatic weapon on his lap.

Now though, by the use of a single word, a new terror was threatened – plutonium. The population exposed to a toxic dust that would be expelled into the air. A terrible cancer-causing threat intended to spread horror and panic. Hundreds of thousands would succumb. Death was unavoidable.

The means to distribute the dust was already in place in a city somewhere in the UK.

But he offered hope that this terrible calamity could be avoided. His voice became calm and reassuring and filled with reason. He really didn't want people to die. He was a peaceful man, as was Asad Hassan, who must be released within ten hours. The deadline was five o'clock that evening, two hours had passed already.

The sting in the tail came when he ordered that Hassan's release should be celebrated with the lowering of the Union Flag currently flying above 10 Downing Street - the offices of the Prime Minister of Great Britain. In its place, he demanded, should be raised the Sword of Liberation's black flag, and, at the same time, sharia courts should dispense the new religious laws of the UK.

***

Flash Harry had every intention of contacting his GCHQ friend, but as the day wore on and the panic in the City subsided, he'd had seconds thoughts. Perhaps he should let things lie. Nothing too bad had happened. A few pension funds were a little light by the end of the day, but nobody died. No stock broker had thrown themselves out of a window. Normality had returned – more or less.

The second message, however, changed his mind.

***

'So, we completely wasted our time, Summer and me,' Charlie complained. 'The great CCTV in the sky was looking at it all the time. It would have been nice to have had that bit of intel a couple of days ago.'

Stack tried to calm Charlie down, but when he was on one of his disgruntled rants, it was best to just let him chuck everything out of the pram. Summer came to Stack's rescue.

'OK, Charlie. I was there too. Let's move on.' Summer's soft Canadian drawl had a soothing effect on Charlie. He was soon uttering embarrassed apologies, while his inner Labrador metaphorically lay with its legs in the air waiting for its tummy to be tickled.

They were in a taxi on their way to Vauxhall Cross, the Secret Intelligence Service building on the south side of the River Thames to meet Madeleine. They had crossed over Vauxhall Bridge and were just pulling up to the security barrier along Albert Embankment when Maddy stepped out and flagged them down.

This was unexpected. The meeting was supposed to be in her office. Stack got out of the cab, Summer and Charlie followed. Madeleine seemed edgy and in a hurry.

'Follow me.'

A black Jaguar XF was parked across the pavement, nose up to the road. Maddy got in the driver's side and indicated with a nod that the others should follow. Stack took the front passenger seat next to her.

She revved the engine impatiently waiting for a gap in the endless line of passing vehicles.

Once they were on their way, heading south east through heavy traffic, Maddy explained the change of plan.

'Got a head's-up from our people at GCHQ. Some ex-employee guy got in touch with them this morning with an address. That's where we're going.'

'Wait a minute,' Stack said. 'What ex-employee and address for what?'

'The guy was given an address by a friend...,' Madeleine paused as she negotiated a roundabout, then put her foot down again. '...we think it's the location of the cell that hacked into the Stock Exchange trading systems two days ago. The ones who are demanding the release of Asad Hassan.'

Charlie leaned forward.

'We're going to confront these guys empty handed? No weapons? I seem to remember in the video, at least one of them has an Uzi.'

They all held their breath as Maddy squeezed the saloon between a bus and a concrete traffic island. The pace dropped down to near walking speed as they passed into Camberwell High Street, with its endless sequence of traffic lights, suicidal mothers with pushchairs, delivery vans and road junctions.

'Armed police will be there. They'll have the area cordoned off,' she said eventually.

'Well, we don't have tin stars. How do we get in?'

'Check the glove box.'

Stack punched the little silver button, the door dropped open. He reached inside and pulled out three lanyards.

'Put those on. The badge is like a suit of armour as far as officials are concerned. The secret service impresses the hell out of them. And remember, they're temporary, OK?'

'Won't make us bulletproof by any chance, will they?' Charlie asked sarcastically.

It took another twenty minutes to get to the address in Peckham. They couldn't get closer than the end of the street. Tape had been run across both ends of the road. The convenience store was halfway down on the right. A couple of uniforms were standing outside.

As they were exiting the car, Stack's cell phone rang. He green-buttoned it and glanced at the screen as he handed it to Summer.

'I think this might be Chris Bailey. Can you take it while we go with Maddy?'

Summer followed them out of the car with the phone to her ear and was already in deep conversation as Stack and Charlie went with Maddy down to the store.

The badges worked for the coppers manning the police line tape, which was lifted to let them through. The same happened at the door to the flat next to the shop entrance. A policeman in full SWAT gear told Madeleine the place had been abandoned. The bad guys had gone. He nodded them through. Stack noticed the wooden door frame had been splintered around the lock where the SWAT team had smashed their way in.

They climbed the stairs and found more heavily armed police roaming around. One, presumably a higher-ranking officer, asked to see their ID's, then handed out white cotton gloves, explaining, 'Forensics' are on their way. We like to keep the place tidy.'

Stack stood in the doorway to the lounge and slowly scanned the room, sweeping it like radar, ceiling to floor, one side to the other. Then he walked to the middle of the room next to the coffee table and scanned it again, ignoring the uniforms that kept walking in and out. He turned to the senior officer.

'When do you think they left?'

'According to the owner of the convenience store downstairs, there's been no activity for a couple of days. They were always popping in to buy milk and newspapers.'

Madeleine overheard this and came over. She saw an opportunity to run the mug shot gallery past the owner.

'Is he in the shop now?'

'No, we've moved him and his family out of the area along with the other residents.'

Stack nodded and took another look around. There were two bedrooms, a small kitchen and a bathroom. Both the kitchen and bathroom were filthy. He checked the kitchen cupboards. The door to one of the three hanging cabinets was missing. Stack found it stashed between the cooker and the sink. Under the sink was a waste bin stuffed to overflowing. There was a strong smell of curry from old take away packaging. Laying loosely on top, unable to be wedged any further into the compacted refuse, was an empty Alesto Dates bag. He'd seen a couple of what he had assumed were skinny Brazil nuts in the ashtray on the coffee table. Now he realised they were most likely date seeds. The ashtray itself held no ash.

Madeleine came out of one of the bedrooms.

'At a guess, I'd say the flightcase had been in that room. There's a rectangular patch of compressed carpet that might just fit. It's very faint though.' Then her tone became sombre, 'There are a few small spots of what looks like blood on the wall and the duvet. Could be Patterson's.'

'Life threatening amount?' Stack asked.

Madeleine just shrugged her shoulders and pursed her lips, unwilling to hazard a guess.

Charlie had taken an interest in the walls of the flat. One in particular had his attention. He shouted across for someone to switch the light on. An officer near the door obliged, but with daylight streaming through the windows, apart from adding a slightly brighter yellow hue to the drab Magnolia emulsion, it wasn't much help.

'Come and take a look at this?'

Both Maddy and Stack went over to where Charlie was standing.

'Can you see it?' Charlie asked.

'What am I looking for, Charlie?' Stack said.

'Pin holes. I think this is the room where they shot the video messages.'

Maddy put her glasses on and went in closer. She followed Charlie's finger as he went from one pin prick to another.

'I don't know, Charlie,' she said shaking her head doubtfully. 'Could be.'

Stack took a step back.

'Point them out again, Hollywood.'

The shape was clearer from further back. Four pin holes that just might have held the Sword of Liberation's flag.

Stack had another question for the superintendent who had already started to leave.

The policeman's heavy shoes made a loud percussive clatter as he descended the uncarpeted wooden stairs. Stack followed him down.

'I'm surprised he and his family don't live above the shop,' Stack had to raise his voice against the noise.

The superintendent continued down as he replied.

'He does, but not this shop. They have another in Camberwell.'

They reached the bottom and exited into the street.

'You don't have an address by any chance?'

'Check the shop window here. It might mention their other place,' the officer said as he walked away, his mind already on other things.

Stack glanced down at the paving stones that butted against the entrance threshold. Blown into the corner next to a drain pipe were several cigarette butts. Scattered amongst them were half a dozen date pips. One, maybe two people had been standing here? A smoker and a date chewing friend? He crouched down, picked up one of the pips and put it in his pocket.

As Madeleine and Hollywood made their way out of the flat into the early afternoon sunlight, Stack checked the newsagent's large plate-glass window. The officer had guessed correctly, tucked away on the bottom left hand corner near the door was a notice that boasted: *Dear customer, if for some reason you find our delightful shop closed, please visit our other emporium in Camberwell.* An address was provided. Stack made a note.

In the Jag, on the way back to Vauxhall Bridge, Stack asked Summer about the phone call.

'Yup, it was Chris,' she said. 'He had news about recent Topaz activity. He wants to meet us, urgently.'

Madeleine's ear pricked up at this.

'Since when has Bailey been short circuiting the chain of command here?' she said frostily.

'Since you gave us the cornflake box 007 spy kit speech. We're deputised, remember?' Stack said. 'Anyway, Bailey trusts us.'

A taxi turned suddenly in front of the Jag causing Madeleine to brake sharply. She vented her frustration by hitting the horn hard and long.

'Listen, Stack. Don't cut me out. I want to know everything you're doing or plan to do, OK?'

'Copy that,' said Stack irritably.

***

After the damp squib of the stock market hack, MI5, the National Crime Agency and the Counter Terrorist Section of the Secret Intelligence Service all refused to believe the extremists had the capability of carrying out their plutonium threat.

There had been no murmurings on the intelligence grapevine of missing quantities, or clandestine transactions of radioactive substances. No whispers to connect any dots beyond the usual on-going tracking of returning ISIS supporters. Nor had there been any concerns flagged up of existential threats from radicals abroad. Nothing new had come up in the past week or so to make them unusually nervous.

During the COBRA emergency briefing at 10 Downing Street that morning, some hawks argued that the threat level should be jacked-up to '*critical – attack expected imminently*'. Others rationalised that London was an unlikely target. It made no sense, they argued, for the terrorists to crap on their own doorstep; why contaminate the very city you want to run your Islamic Caliphate from? Others were even more sanguine. Why worry the population unduly when the balance of expert opinion around the table suggested the threat was nothing more than a bluff? And anyway, they argued, what about the cost? It would be impossible to provide saturation police coverage for every city in the UK, even if they take London off the list of targets – a classic *Westminster Bubble* view of the world.

Despite the extremists' deadline being just six hours away, it was agreed that the threat level was left at '*moderate – an attack is possible but not likely*'.

To provide some cover against a bad call, the politicians insisted police forces in cities across the country were put on alert and SWAT teams placed on standby.

Then, just as the COBRA committee members were gathering their briefcases and coats as they prepared to leave, a voice that had, until that moment, remained silent, spoke to ask a simple question.

'Has anyone heard of MI8?'

***

Over at the top-secret micro department deep inside the SIS building on London's Embankment, they took a different view on the viability of the terrorist's plan. Having finally heard Chris Bailey's interpretation of Patterson's cryptic message which strongly suggested radioactive material had been brought into the country, they were certain something lethal was about to go down.

Nonetheless, Major William Cavanagh and Madeleine Clark refused to let the problem leave the MI8 domain. Topaz was their secret charge. Disclosure would not happen on their watch. Or so they hoped.

***

Madeleine entered Cavanagh's office with a sense of trepidation. The major had instructed her to get over to his office immediately. He didn't sound happy.

'Who else knows?' he bellowed. 'Who have you told?'

The accusation stung her.

'Told what? I don't understand.'

'There's a bloody leak.' Cavanagh was furious. 'I've just had Donaldson on the phone asking questions.'

'The Home Secretary?' Madeleine was astonished. He normally gets his underlings to do his dirty work. 'What did he want?' She asked the question, but she had already guessed the answer.

'They've just had a COBRA meeting. It turns out someone mentioned MI8.'

'So? MI8 is part of MI6. We don't shout about it, but there's no reason for it to come up during a Cabinet Office Briefing.'

Cavanagh sniffed.

'No, perhaps not. Unless Topaz becomes a topic.'

Madeleine was shocked. 'Are you telling me Topaz was mentioned during the meeting?'

'It came up, as a loose end. Something that needed clarifying. Donaldson seemed to imply that they didn't understand what it was about Topaz that made it, in his words, a "subject of interest", but the worrying thing is, whoever brought it up, had some knowledge of what Topaz was capable of.'

Madeleine though for a moment before answering.

'Do you know who it was that brought it up?'

'The Home Secretary didn't say, but he hinted at GCHQ as a source.'

'GCHQ? How the hell do they know anything about Topaz?'

It was Cavanagh's turn to ponder the implications of the unwelcome news. He turned and gazed out of the window at the Thames flowing below, before letting out a breathy sigh.

'As far as I can tell, they haven't put two and two together. I don't see how they could draw any hard conclusions.'

He turned back to Madeleine who, in deep thought, had absentmindedly begun aligning papers and pencils on the department head's desk.

'Donaldson didn't sound convinced such a machine existed, at least, one that could do what was claimed. I agreed with him and tried to put him off the scent.'

Madeleine looked relieved.

'So, we're in the clear?'

Cavanagh coughed, 'I am unwilling to lie to the head of a government department that oversees the country's national security. He wants to see it.'

'Jesus! But, we don't have it.'

'He doesn't know that – yet. He mustn't know.' Cavanagh's voice became grave, 'Getting Topaz back has just become even more urgent.'

***

After some skilful persuasion from Cavanagh, GCHQ admitted that they had some knowledge which had come via an external contact who had passed an intriguing and unsolicited morsel of information on to them. Even though they had spoken directly to the informant, they were as curious as Donaldson, the Home Secretary, to find out more about Topaz. Cavanagh quickly shut that avenue of enquiry down.

The information he did glean, however, helped MI8 locate the City hacker who had revealed the address of the extremist cell in Peckham. It turned out he was a known irritant, but inactive in recent years as far as they were aware. Even so, he'd been under *ad hoc* surveillance and they knew where to find him.

The Jaguar XF saloon was parked in the street outside his address. Madeleine was sitting in the back with her laptop open. Next to her sat Hari Reza, otherwise known as Flash Harry.

They spent twenty minutes going through the mug shot gallery. Harry recognised the one he knew as Ramaas. He was less confident when she showed him the shot of Mahmoud but agreed it could be him.

Then Madeleine moved on to the matter of Patterson. Had he seen him? What was his condition? Harry said he seemed OK, but a little nervous. He assumed he was a freelancer like him. She gave the impression of concern, but what she really wanted was news of Topaz. Did Flash Harry understand its significance? Without mentioning Topaz, she asked Harry how they had hacked into the high frequency trades.

It was clear from his reply that he'd been impressed with the technology Patterson had used, but was unconvinced about claims it could actually look into the future. In his view, messing around with time was for sci-fi geeks. He had his reputation to consider. Harry believed it did something clever but what, he couldn't be sure. Whatever it did, he said, it made the impossible – possible. Because of it, he was able to alter high frequency trade prices.

Madeleine was relieved at Harry's scepticism, and Harry was surprised that he wasn't arrested, but merely cautioned that he still might be called to account for his part in the stock market crime. He was unaware that his get-out-of-jail card was Topaz and Madeleine's need to keep knowledge of it to as few people as possible.

She let Harry go but told him to stick around, she may have other questions. They had his passport. He couldn't leave the country – not legitimately anyway.

***

During the afternoon of the City trading hack, it had become clear that the depraved capitalist system had survived, and for that the terror gang blamed Patterson. He had deliberately screwed around with the Topaz device. They had no way of knowing if that was true, but as Flash Harry wasn't around, they needed someone to take it out on.

It started with shouting at the TV during the newscasts, fists raised in frustration at the presenters as reports, 'live' from the City, gave more and more optimistic reports about 'the crash that wasn't'. It turned to angry accusations that

Patterson couldn't be trusted. They wanted revenge. To teach him a lesson. All this as they toyed with their guns, loading and reloading. Cocking the sliding mechanisms. It was loud and noisy and put the fear of God into Patterson, who could hear it all from the bedroom he'd been locked in since mid-afternoon.

It went on for an hour or so, some of it in English, some in Arabic. Then a murmured voice of authority, a gentle command that brought an unnerving quietness from the other room. It lasted just a few seconds.

Patterson sat on the bed staring at the bedroom door, his heart racing with fear. He heard a quiet metallic sound as the key gently turned. Then, with a sudden crash the door was kicked open, juddering to a stop against the wardrobe next to it.

Ramaas and his young acolyte, Youssef, stood in the doorway. A few paces further back in the living room, Mahmoud looked on impassively as the two men stepped into the bedroom and gently closed the door behind them.

The next ten minutes were filled with the sounds of violent punishment. The heavy thuds of fists on carcass. Slaps to the face. Gasps from punches to the stomach. But, as instructed by Mahmoud, there were no sounds of bones being broken. Mahmoud had not finished with Patterson's services yet.

It was dark when they abandoned the flat. Patterson had no idea what time it was. He knew only that he was in painful trouble. He recalled how Faruk had looked when they saw him standing in the doorway, back in the rooms on Souk al-Turk. He imagined that this must be how the poor bastard felt. They half-carried Patterson down the stairs, slowly, one painful step at a time. A pause at the street door, then a rush across the pavement to the open door of a car. He was thrown into the back seat and pushed against the far door as Youssef got in next to him.

In his confusion and hurt he'd lost track of time, but the slamming of the lid of the trunk told him the Topaz flightcase was probably travelling with them.

A short drive, no more than twenty minutes, and they did the whole thing again in reverse. He caught a glimpse of a block of flat-roofed houses, not town houses, smaller, with a prefabricated sixties look.

He was taken up to a first-floor bedroom. Curtains drawn, lights off. A final nose to nose threat to behave from Mahmoud, and he was pushed back on to the bed. His assailant slammed the door as he left.

Patterson couldn't sleep. He didn't attempt to remove his clothes or kick off his shoes; every movement brought pain. He just rolled over, curled up in a ball and planned his revenge. He'd heard them record the second message, not every word, but enough to confirm he had correctly guessed about the radioactive material. Now he knew it was not just plutonium, but the much more dangerous, plutonium oxide dust. Somehow, he had to find out how they intended to carry out their horrific plan and then alert Bailey.

The reality of the danger he was in at first chilled him, then, unexpectedly, calmed him. He had nothing to lose. He understood he was unlikely to survive the next twenty-four hours. A Zen-like peace settled over him and he fell asleep.

Park Up

'We've got just over two hours to find whatever it is they've done,' Stack said. 'The message said a city in the UK, suggesting it could be anywhere, but I'd bet my bank account it's right here in London, probably not too far from Camberwell.'

The three of them were back at the hotel in Mayfair. Chris Bailey was on his way and would be there shortly. The TV was showing a news channel that was buzzing with the emergency. At the bottom of the screen, breaking news banners counting down to the terrorists' deadline crawled from right to left. Urgent 'live' streams from locations around the UK breathlessly reported the latest guesswork from *experts* who knew no more than anyone else. One report came from the gate at Belmarsh prison. A camera crew placed there to catch the moment Asad Hassam walked free. The journalist reported that they'd heard nothing beyond the statement made earlier: "the British government does not bargain with terrorists". She went on to speculate that, if the terrorist plan succeeded and the British government capitulated, if Hassam was released, she guessed he would be driven away by one of his lieutenants to a location not yet revealed to the media, but she assumed the various intelligence agencies knew more than they were letting on. Let's hope so anyway. '*The clock is ticking*,' the reporter warned dramatically, before handing back to the studio.

Stack was lying on the bed, hands behind his head, staring at the ceiling.

'Why do you think it's in London?' Charlie asked.

'Control,' he said simply. 'Whichever method they use to spread the plutonium dust, leaving the thing lying around waiting to be found doesn't make sense. My guess is they haven't set it up yet. They'll do it soon though. That's why, wherever they put it, it won't be very far from South London.'

'And if the threat is real, they'll want to make as much impact as they can,' Summer said, adding ironically, 'let's face it, Camberwell, as lovely as it is, is not exactly the beating heart of civilisation. I still think they have their eye on the biggest jewel in the UK's economic crown – the City of London.'

'I agree,' said Stack. 'It's not just people the dust will contaminate. It's the entire financial district. It'll take years to decontaminate each building. The City will have to be abandoned.'

'Well, what are we waiting for?' Charlie was eager to do something. 'Shouldn't we go to the City and try to find the bloody thing?'

'We've only got two hours, Hollywood,' Summer reasoned. 'Where do we start?'

There was a quick, double knock on the door.

'And anyway, what the hell are we looking for?' Stack said as he swung his legs off the bed, got up and walked over to let Bailey in.

Without saying a word, he pushed past Stack, headed to the couch, sat down next to Summer and opened his tablet on the coffee table. Everyone waited while he found what he was looking for.

'I got this....' He glanced at his watch. '...twenty minutes ago. It's from Patterson.'

Summer leaned across to get a better view of the screen.

'What are we looking at?' she asked.

Charlie had walked around and leaned in from behind the couch. Stack was content to take a seat in one of the phoney Chippendale chairs and wait to hear what Bailey had to say.

'It's another message,' Bailey said.

'OK, what does it mean?' Charlie asked. 'It's just a picture of a road.'

Summer seemed to get it. She described what she saw.

'It looks like a security camera shot of a narrow street with cars parked along the right-hand side. It's very short. Space for maybe four or five cars and a handful of bikes. There are some cafés or bars on one side.'

Bailey agreed.

'Notice the line of traffic in the shot. Now, take a look at this,' he said as he swiped the screen to the left and another identical image appeared. He turned the tablet so that Stack could see.

'OK, what am I looking for?' Stack asked as he scanned the screen.

'Compare the two images.'

Stack swiped back and forth between the two pictures of the street.

Summer got it immediately.

'Jesus, James! We followed that car through France.'

In the first image, one of the vehicles driving down the road had a familiar profile and colour. It was the Toyota Landcruiser.

The second image had a very anaemic appearance. It seemed to have two or three versions of the same scene visible within it – like a ghostly triple exposure. In the second image, the Landcruiser had found a parking space, three cars down from the camera position. Stack noticed the time stamp in the top left corner: 3:40 pm. He checked his watch.

'Wait a minute, that's now. Is this a picture of the Toyota being parked, now, at this very moment? Stack asked. 'How did Patterson do that?'

Bailey said, 'he obviously managed to get an image from the CCTV camera that has a view of that road. He did this twenty minutes or so ago, so he must have accessed the server for that camera and used Topaz to move the data forward in time to get this grainy image of the car parking. As you say, Stack, it's an event that's happening now, somewhere in the City.'

Stack recalled their conversation on the dhow, as they were heading to Libya, when Bailey explained how the Topaz device worked.

'But this is different. I understood Topaz can see only a tiny slice of the future. A few nanoseconds, I think you said. The second image must be twenty minutes ahead of the first, how is that possible?'

Bailey sat back on the couch and thought for a moment.

'Nanoseconds ahead are not difficult for our infant technology. But we have to be careful not to overpower the networks we use to reach our targets. If the Topaz stream was any stronger, the networks themselves could fail, at least the parts the stream passes through,' Bailey said. 'It's like plugging a 20 volt power supply into a 5 volt gadget. Too much power and components start to fry. Patterson has taken a risk. He's upped the power of the stream. He's managed to reach much further into the digital future but, as you can see, the focus of the image is extremely poor. It's as though it's seeing more than one time-frame – like an old radio that's tuned into one station but gets interference from stations on either side of it.'

Bailey leaned forward towards Stack.

'And another thing. If the stream blew that section of the CCTV network, I'd be surprised if anyone could use that camera remotely again. It'll be off-line and useless now.'

This was all academic as far as Summer was concerned.

'That's all very interesting, but we have a bigger problem. We need to find that car, guys. Can you identify the street, Chris - anybody?'

***

It was late in the morning when Patterson finally woke up, still racked with pain. Every move, as he tried to ease himself off the bed, was agony. Cramp-like spasms seemed to affect every limb. He could take only shallow breaths, anything deeper and it was as though the muscles in his chest had been hammered through with nails.

The murmur of conversation in the room below filtered up through the floor. He made his way gently across to the door and cracked it open. Trying not to gasp with each unexpected pulse of pain, he quietly crossed the hallway and took the first step of the stairs. On the ground floor the door to the living room was open, but Patterson couldn't make out what they were saying. He needed to get closer.

The stairs were hidden behind a solid banister boxed in with drywall that ended at the bottom step. It gave Patterson cover as he descended further, crouching as he went. About half way down with his head just above the banister, he was able to make out more.

Hidden from view, the voice of a journalist struggling to breath excitement into an old script, was coming from a television somewhere in the room. Above the audio he could hear them gloating over the multiple rebroadcasting of their message on all the news channels. A laptop was open on a small table, its screen partially hidden by one of the fanatics who had his back to Patterson. He guessed it was Mahmoud. The screen was showing a still frame of a road. Patterson couldn't tell if it was a Google Map image or a frame from a CCTV camera.

From the crumbs of conversation that filtered up to him, Patterson gathered they intended to deliver the package later in the afternoon. It was already loaded and ready. A street in the City of London was the target. The way he heard it, it sounded like 'Creature Lane'. That was a weird one, but the City of London was full of streets named after long forgotten ancient places, the origins of which had long been lost in the passing of a thousand years.

There was a garbled moment partially hidden by laughter, but Patterson thought he heard something about 'fireworks'. A display of some kind. Then he heard his name and then a fragment to do with the Topaz device. This seemed to bring an angry reaction from one of the men in the room beyond his vision. The table was thumped angrily. Mahmoud was insistent, they would do it his way. He had his reasons. It went quiet for a while. Then he heard a grumbled murmur of an Arabic curse and Ramaas and Youssef suddenly walked through the doorway into the hall.

Patterson ducked down behind the banister, and tried to ease himself back up the stairs, but the men turned right, opened the front door and went outside, closing the door behind them.

They didn't go anywhere. They just hung around under the porch. Patterson could see through the rippled glass panel that the kid, Youssef, had lit a cigarette. He inhaled deeply to satisfy his nicotine addiction. Patterson couldn't see what Ramaas was up to. They both just stood there talking quietly.

Patterson was moving back up to the landing when Mahmoud walked out of the living room and began heading up the stairs. He had the Uzi in his hand. For the first couple of steps he was looking down at his feet, but then he glanced up and saw Patterson.

'Patterson! So, you're up and about,' he said without sympathy. 'Get back in your room, we're going to have a chat.'

***

By 3:10 pm, the Toyota had arrived in East Central 3, part of the district of London known as 'The City'. The City's hours of business matched the world's time zones, which meant that during the long working day, the streets were never free of traffic. Nothing moves fast. Nose to tail is normal.

Like the streets of most big cities, motorists just sat behind the wheels of their vehicles and submitted to the inevitable, occasionally growling in frustration, rarely using their horn. But these were the streets of London, where its reputation for tolerance and civility were tested almost to destruction on a daily basis.

The Toyota Landcruiser was one of several cars, nosing slowly down the short road, a distance, one end to the other, of no more than 60 yards. Like most vehicles navigating around London, they were looking for the rarest of things - a parking space.

Mahmoud had picked this road not just for its central location in the City, but for its bland anonymity. A mere conduit connecting one street to another. It had four parking bays and a zone with spaces for ten motorbikes. A handful of cafés and restaurants lined the pavement on one side. High up on a building facing the junction at the far end, a CCTV camera stared down with a clear view of the street.

The Toyota nosed its way down the length of the road and, failing to find a free space, turned into the adjoining intersection. It took them another twenty minutes to find their way back to the top of the road and try again. This time a patch of road just ahead of the bike zone was free, but a single yellow line road marking meant they couldn't leave the car, but they could sit inside and wait – though not for long.

By 3.30 pm, just ninety minutes from the deadline, the Landcruiser was still waiting. They were cutting it fine. It took another ten minutes before a space became available three cars down. A woman carrying an office chair fumbled for the key to pop open the tailgate to her Range Rover. This looked promising. They elbowed their way out into the passing traffic and stopped just ahead of her car, holding up a growing line of impatient vehicles behind them.

It took several frustrating minutes before the woman had finally stored the chair in the rear space to her fussy satisfaction, got into the car, faffed around with something on the passenger seat next to her, checked her make up and started the engine.

To the relief of the irritated drivers in the line of traffic behind them, the Range Rover finally eased out of the parking space and took off down the road. It was 3:40 by the time the Toyota had parked up with a parking ticket bought from a nearby machine.

Before they left the vehicle, Mahmoud reached for a second smartphone that had been hard wired into the device hidden in the rear of the car. He placed it on the centre arm rest, while he used his own cell phone to make a call to the house in Camberwell. It was show-time for Patterson.

***

Before the two men walked away from the vehicle, they gave it a final once over. It didn't look unusual in any way. The rear seats had been folded down into the floor and the space filled with three or four cardboard boxes. A smaller package that was sitting on top of a larger box seemed to have been jammed in hard against the roof. Other than that, all looked normal.

Mahmoud depressed the button on the key fob to activate the car's alarm system. The indicators flashed and beeped once. He turned and walked away, Ramaas beside him. Five steps later he stopped dead. Ramaas stopped a step ahead and turned to look back. Mahmoud was just standing there, frozen in thought.

'What's up?'

'I nearly screwed up,' Mahmoud said as he raised the key fob and disengaged the alarm again.

'We don't want the bloody alarm to go off by accident. It'll draw attention to the car.'

He walked back to the vehicle, slid the key into the door lock and turned it. The locks closed with a heavy electromechanical clunk, but the alarm remained inactive. Satisfied, he turned and rejoined Ramaas.

They headed for the nearest underground station, Bank, and took the Northern Line, south, back towards Camberwell.

***

Newscasts on every channel were buzzing with baleful predictions and contradictory stories; the terrorists' imminent toxic deadline that was about to arrive in an unidentified city in the UK in less than seventy minutes, and soothing Home Office opinion was that it was a bluff, and anyway, the Government doesn't do deals with terrorists.

Even so, there was a noticeable increase in police activity on the streets of most major cities. London inevitably got the lion's share.

Because of the dramatic scaling down of police levels through budget cuts, the extra officers came from cancelled holidays and extended shifts. The Metropolitan Police managed to find another three hundred beat officers this way. They put most in cars and vans and the rest on foot. Two walked past the Toyota without giving it a second look. Later, a traffic warden walked slowly past all four parked vehicles noting the validity of each parking ticket. She got to the end of the street and disappeared into the adjoining road. Her shift ended at four o'clock. She was already heading back to the police station to sign off.

***

Earlier, while Mahmoud and Ramaas were en route to the City in the Toyota, the terraced property back in Camberwell had become quiet and sombre. With the TV still showing a news channel but the audio turned down, Patterson spent the next twenty minutes trying to convince Youssef to change his mind; their plan could not possibly work, the government will not give in to their demands, people will die for nothing, now was Youssef's chance to get out of the house and save himself.

But Youssef was having none of it. Burning with religious fervour, this was his chance to serve Allah. Patterson's plea to him only fuelled his anger. Mahmoud had finally given him a battered semi-automatic weapon and he was eager to use it. He handled it threateningly, loading the chamber and pointing the stubby barrel at Patterson.

'I should shoot you now,' he said. 'One less Kufir in the world. No one will care. You are weak and corrupt.'

Speaking, as he reached across and thumbed the ragged pages of his beloved Quran, a book that was never far from him, he went through the full panoply of curses against the wretched nonbelievers.

'By this afternoon, if they don't release Asad Hassam, the world will be rid of millions more of you. Your precious City of London and the criminals that run it will be gone. I almost like that better.'

Patterson pointed out that if they set off their plutonium dust, nobody would die – not straight away.

'It could take years,' argued Patterson.

'I don't care. They will know what is coming. A living death.'

He put the gun down on the table next to the Quran and searched his pockets for cigarettes.

'You should suffer the same fate.'

'Many Muslims will die,' appealed Patterson.

Youssef had given up looking in his pockets and was searching around the room.

'They are not true Muslims. Not true believers. They have already been contaminated with western ideology. The dust can have them too.'

He had taken the search into the kitchen. Moments later Patterson heard him run up the stairs into the rooms above. While he was out of the room, Patterson eyed the Topaz device set up ready on the dining room table. It was up ended so that the control panel faced him. Cables ran between the special laptop and the flightcase and two more provided power and an internet service. Mahmoud's laptop was still operating over on the coffee table by the couch, though the screen had gone to sleep.

He knew what he had to do. He just needed a chance. He could feel the shape of Youssefs' cigarette packet in his trouser pocket. The young jihadist had a bad nicotine habit. He was constantly smoking. He couldn't go long without one. Patterson had taken a grave risk by hiding the packet, but it was about to pay off.

He heard the sound of feet hurrying down the stairs and Youssef came back into the room. He was as wired as a two-amp fuse in a thirteen-amp plug. He picked up his gun, turned and pushed his angry young, acne-pitted face into to Patterson's.

'Listen. You get up to your room – NOW!' He watched as Patterson walked up the stairs and entered the bedroom.

'The door. Close it. You stay there until I get back. You give me trouble and I shoot your legs.'

Patterson closed the door, stood with his back against it listening for the sound of the front door. As soon as he heard it shut, he opened the bedroom door again and crossed to one of the front bedrooms that looked down to the street. He watched as Youssef made his way up to the junction just a few houses away, turned right and walked out of sight. Patterson couldn't be sure how far away the nearest convenience store was, which posed an unanswerable question - how much time did he have?

What was certain, he didn't have time to waste. He ran painfully down the stairs and outside to the end of the street to look for a road sign. The answer to his first question was found high up on the front wall of a corner property. It was a cul-de-sac called Bakers Yard. A short road of no more than twenty houses. Ten on each side.

Back inside, he tapped the space bar on Mahmoud's laptop. It came alive still showing the same street as before. This was the City location towards which Mahmoud and Ramaas were heading. Ground Zero. It was a view from a live CCTV camera. Mahmoud was a clever man. A highly skilled hacker. Somehow, he had managed to get into the server for the camera that looked down to the road. It showed everything except its name.

He carried the laptop over to the dining table. He didn't have a cable to connect the two machines directly, so he copied the entire URL string by hand into the Topaz laptop. The image of the street didn't come up straight away. He checked the string again. It was long and complex. Calming himself, he slowly went through the chain of code, comparing it with the one on the Topaz laptop. He checked his watch. A meaningless waste of time. He had no idea how much time he had. On the second read through, he found a single error. He made the correction and the image of the street immediately flashed up.

His nerves jangling, he went over to the window and strained to see to the end of the road. There was no sign of Youssef. If there had been, he might have had just enough time to return Mahmoud's laptop to the coffee table and rush upstairs to the bedroom. But he had much more to do.

Now the Topaz laptop was connected to the CCTV camera, he could grab an image and send it to Chris Bailey. This was something he daren't do on Mahmoud's laptop. He would have instantly noticed his computer had been used and a message sent.

Even as he watched the screen, he saw the Toyota enter the picture, moving slowly down the road with the other traffic, away from the camera. He hit print-screen and saved the image. Time was his enemy. Given the slow-moving traffic, it was clear there wasn't time to see if the car would come back and park, but he was certain it would return because they had chosen this particular camera looking at this particular street.

He glanced at his watch. An automatic nervous reaction that offered no comfort or information beyond the current time of day. The Topaz device was on and humming. The prickle of static already present. His fingers danced over the controls as before and the image on the laptop began to move forward in time. He made more adjustments and, as the sound of the tiny high energy motors spinning up rose higher, the image shifted further forward into the future, becoming misty and less focussed. He kept increasing the energy of the stream until he found the moment he was hoping for, an image of the Toyota parked up several bays down. He grabbed that image and saved it. Just in time. The screen went black. The intense energy of the Topaz stream was the cause, he was certain. The network connection to the CCTV camera had burned out. He turned the device off.

He needed one more image. The GCHQ software installed in the Topaz laptop had access to Google maps to help the MI8 team locate the targets they wished to pre-delete. These were hi-res versions of the publicly available maps that could only be accessed through a unique search engine.

Patterson entered the name 'Bakers Yard - London' in the search field. An image instantly appeared. The same familiar tools were available to pan and zoom, but the Google camera van hadn't gone down the short street. The view was only from the top of the road. Patterson zoomed in as far as he could, but the frame was still too wide. Instead of the single view of the house in which he was held hostage, the image included three other properties. It would have to do. He was about to name the file 'Bakers Yard' when he realised he hadn't made a note of the house number. He got up and peered out of the window to see if the door and the house number was visible. It wasn't, but to his horror, at the top of the road, Yousef was just ambling into the close. Patterson sat down, hit save and put the file into the folder that held the other two images.

His heart beat like a marathon runner; the adrenalin made his hands shake uncontrollably. Like the last time, he used the specialist software to access Bailey's computer. Before he up-loaded the three images, he renamed one of the Toyota CCTV files - 'Creature Lane'. It was all he had to go on. He hoped it was enough for Bailey to do something with.

Time had run out. The sound of Yousef's lazy footsteps made a dull leathery scraping sound on the concrete path as he approached the front door.

As Patterson returned Mahmoud's laptop to the coffee table, he heard the scratching of a key being pushed into the brass door lock. But before the key was turned and the door pushed open, Yousef's cell phone rang. Patterson heard the gang member answer the call. It gave him just enough time to rush upstairs to the bedroom. He stood by the door and listened as Yousef finally entered the house.

Ground Zero

It was 4:01 pm. Back on the second floor of the Curzon Mews Hotel, they were running out of options. The terrorist's five o'clock endgame seemed to be approaching faster with every passing minute. Their frustration increased as once again, the screen on Bailey's tablet remained unyielding in its certainty: no such street existed in London.

Bailey and Summer had tried 'Creature Lane', the name Patterson had given to the CCTV image, Crettin Lane, Crematorium Lane, Creesy Lane and other variations of the word, but nothing appeared to exist in London under 'Creature', or anything similar they could think of. To be certain, they had also tried the same variations using: road, avenue, street, place and mews.

Earlier, they'd had more success with 'Bakers Yard'. Punching that name into Google maps got a direct hit on an estate in Camberwell. Once they'd zoomed in, the view was a match for the image sent by Patterson.

'Look, we're really at the short end of this,' Stack said. 'We have the one confirmed address in Camberwell. How about, instead of running around like headless chickens trying to find the Toyota, maybe we should cut our losses and go straight to the bad guys. If they plan to detonate the explosive by cell phone, maybe we can stop it from there.'

Charlie was up for it and keen to go, but Stack was cautious.

'If one of those four houses are where the bad guys are holed up, we need to be careful. We know for certain one of them has an old Uzi machine pistol,' Stack said. 'It looked beaten-up, but if it works, it can spit out six hundred rounds a minute.'

'So, where do we get weapons in a hurry?' Charlie asked, 'Guns-U-Like?'

Stack laughed.

'In the States there just might be a store with that name. I've got a better idea.'

He turned to Bailey.

'Get in touch with Cavanagh, now. Tell the Major we're on our way over. We need a couple of semi-automatic weapons. The make doesn't matter. Whatever he can lay his hands on. We'll meet him in the street outside the SIS building.'

Then he turned to the woman who meant more to him than life itself. 'Stay with Bailey and try to keep out of trouble.'

Summer knew he meant well, but she was her own woman. Smart and independent. As much as she loved James, sometimes his concern for her safety had the opposite effect.

'Same to you, James Stack, not a scratch. Capiche?' She countered with a smile. She knew he was running towards a very serious situation.

They held each other's gaze for several long seconds before he turned to go.

Stack and Charlie grabbed a taxi from the rank outside the hotel and headed for the Secret Intelligence Service building the other side of Vauxhall Bridge. On the way over, Hollywood had an idea. Black cab drivers have to pass 'The Knowledge' in order to ply for trade in London. If you don't have Google Maps handy, a black cab driver will know the name of every street in the city.

Charlie leaned forward and slid the partition window open.

'Driver, have you ever heard of Creature Lane? It's somewhere in London.'

The driver took a few seconds then shook his head.

'Do you mean Creechurch Lane, in the City?'

Charlie turned to Stack.

'Creechurch Lane. That's where the Toyota is!'

***

It was now 4:28 pm. It had taken Summer twenty-five minutes to get from Hyde Park tube station – the one nearest her hotel - to Bank station in the City, including a fast walk along Leadenhall Street, the road that T-bars Creechurch Lane. The first thing she had discovered, by glancing at a plaque fixed to a wall, was that the 'Cree' of Creechurch was Saint Katharine Cree, after whom the ancient Church on the corner of Creechurch Lane and Leadenhall Street was named. The original building dated back to the thirteenth century. It was old, but the history of the City of London goes back much further.

Creechurch Lane was a narrow thoroughfare with room for single file, one-way traffic only, if you didn't count the vehicles parked on the right.

Summer turned and looked up to the building behind her on Leadenhall Street. The CCTV camera that Patterson used to grab a shot of the vehicles along Creechurch Lane stared balefully down from its position thirty feet up. Except now it was blinded after Patterson zapped it with the high energy Topaz stream.

She wasn't sure what she hoped to achieve, but she carried on walking past the handful of cafés and restaurants towards the only white vehicle in a row of four just ahead of her. The Toyota seemed like an old familiar friend as she strode past, glancing through the vehicles windows in an attempt to see inside. Boxes were the one outstanding feature, stacked to the roof in the rear luggage space. It was obvious to her that they were hiding something. She found it weirdly exciting that in a city of millions, it was a secret Summer, alone, knew. The thought that she was standing close to one of the world's most dangerous radioactive materials made her shudder involuntarily.

She checked her watch. 4:30 pm. This was crazy. She asked herself what the hell she thought she was doing there? She should run! As far and as fast as she could. It was the only sane thing to do.

***

Earlier, when Charlie's call about the name of the street came through to her cell phone back at the hotel, Bailey was still on the phone to Cavanagh. It looked as though Cavanagh was playing tough. From Bailey's end of the conversation, it seemed the major didn't want two gun-happy players running loose in the streets of London armed with semi-automatic weapons. Summer guessed he was just covering himself in case it all turned into sewage.

MI8 were in a corner. James Stack and Charlie Dawson were their only hope of getting the Topaz machine back without the world getting to hear about it. He agreed to the guns, but he wanted

Bailey to go along as back up. *Get a cab,* he had said. *Meet me at the address in Camberwell.* Cavanagh told Bailey he'd take Stack and Dawson to the location in his own car.

Before Bailey had ended his call to Cavanagh, Summer had already punched Creechurch Lane into the Google Maps search field of Bailey's tablet.

'There it is,' she said. 'Bang in the centre of the City.'

Perhaps, *bang* is just a little too graphic,' Bailey said sardonically. 'At least we now know where the Toyota is. Let's hope we're not all going to the wrong party.'

As he grabbed his jacket and put the tablet in his shoulder bag, he told her what Cavanagh had said, apologised that he had to go, and gave her his cell phone number.

'Wish us luck' were his last words as he closed the door.

Summer grabbed her smartphone and used Firefox to reach Google Maps and the view of Creechurch Lane. The pictures Patterson sent had been from a 'live' CCTV camera, which showed the current view as of thirty minutes ago. The Google Map image she was looking at now was taken a couple of years ago. But everything except the traffic was essentially the same.

If the terrorists were to be believed, the deadline for the horror they were about to unleash was 17:00 hours, just fifty minutes away.

She sat down on the couch and looked around the empty room, like someone who was idly passing the time. Waiting like a good little girl for her boyfriend to return. Then she got up and went into the bathroom. She looked in the mirror and began fussing with her makeup. Leaning forward to make small adjustments with the tip of her little finger. She wasted another minute brushing her fingers through her blonde hair. It was perfect. Even when it wasn't, she looked great. But inevitably, her impulsive nature got the better of her.

'Summer Peterson, what the hell are you doing?' she asked her reflection rhetorically. 'I'll be damned if I'm going to keep out of trouble, James Stack. Why should you have all the fun?' She grabbed her phone, rushed out of the hotel and headed towards Hyde Park tube station.

***

Back in Camberwell, Youssef arrived back at the house after purchasing a couple of packs of Marlboro. He was just pushing the key into the lock after stamping out the stub of his last smoke, when his cell phone rang. It was Mahmoud calling from the Toyota parked in the City. Everything was in place and ready. They'd be on their way back soon. He wanted to speak to Patterson. Youssef entered the house and yelled for Patterson to come down.

Patterson hobbled down the stairs, took the phone into the living room and sat at the table. In front of him was the flightcase still warm from its recent use. He knew what Mahmoud wanted. They had gone through it earlier that day, when Mahmoud had forced him back into the bedroom with the Uzi. Patterson still wasn't sure whether he could do what Mahmoud had demanded. It was extremely technical, risky and possibly beyond the capabilities of the Topaz device.

'OK, turn it on,' Mahmoud commanded from the Toyota. He was watching the screen of the second smartphone - the one with the wire leading into the device hidden in the boxes behind him.

Back in Camberwell, Patterson used the Topaz laptop to call up the second smartphone. The signal travelled from the hardwired connection in the house and out into the 5G fibre optic cell phone network. Like all cell phone calls, the number carried a code that matched a particular interrogative signal that all cell phones ping out when they are switched on. It's a signal that says, *'here I am'*. There are hundreds of cell phone network transmission masts in London, but the one nearest the Toyota in Creechurch Lane had recognised the *'here I am'* signal from Mahmoud's second smartphone, matched it to the number sent from Patterson's laptop and connected the two devices.

The distance the signal travelled from the house in Camberwell to the smartphone at ground zero was fixed. The house wasn't going to move, and neither was the target in the City. This was important.

Patterson needed to be certain the distance was constant so that the Topaz time stream didn't vary. Because of the risky trick Mahmoud wanted to play, it was important that the point in time he had been told to reach using the Topaz device, didn't move forward or backwards. The setting was critical.

In the Toyota, Mahmoud watched as the smartphone screen came to life with a set of numbers. Slowly at first and then in a blur of speed, the numbers changed until they settled and stopped.

Mahmoud nodded with satisfaction. He held the other phone to his ear.

He asked, 'OK, is the number I'm looking at here, now fixed?'

Patterson replied that he believed it was.

'Tell me what number you're showing at your end?' Mahmoud demanded.

Patterson read out the number displayed on his laptop. It was in minutes and seconds.

'OK, we're on our way back to Camberwell. Set it running now.'

The numbers displayed at Patterson's end started to countdown. But at ground zero, on the smartphone screen in the Toyota, as planned, the numbers didn't change.

Bakers Yard

For most office workers in London, five o'clock was the end of the working day, but for some reason, the rush hour traffic always seemed to start building earlier. By four, roads were already slowing to a standstill.

Stack checked his watch for the third time. It was 4:14 pm. They were in Cavanagh's car, shouldering their way through the clogged roads of south London, but they weren't making much progress.

'Major, we have to pick it up a bit.' He kept his voice calm and steady. The same tone he had used when he led his elite squad into the bad-lands of Afghanistan.

He didn't need to tell Cavanagh why.

Stack was sitting in the passenger seat, checking the working parts of the semi-automatic pistol he had just been given. The car was full of the sound of steel sliding against steel and composite polymer as he loaded 9 mm brass-jacketed bullets into the fifteen-round magazine of the Glock 19. Charlie was doing the same in the back.

Cavanagh had a trick up his sleeve. He told Stack to open the glove box. The moment the door fell open, Stack understood what Cavanagh had in mind. He opened the window and positioned the blue police strobe as far across the roof as he could. The magnetic base made a clunk as it seized the metal of the Range Rover. Stack pulled the rest of the cable out and plugged it into the cigarette lighter. The effect was almost instantaneous. Those that saw the flashing emergency strobe did their best to make room, but in rush hour traffic, there was very little space for their vehicles to move into.

In the Range Rover they were now occasionally touching 20 mph. The satnav display showed their progress as they headed towards Camberwell, Bakers Yard and the confrontation with the terrorists.

Behind them, without the benefit of blue lights, Chris Bailey's taxi struggled through the choking traffic. Even so, the driver skilfully navigated back roads, doglegs and rat runs. Making up time. He was only ten minutes behind Stack.

***

After arriving back at the house in Bakers Yard, Karim Mahmoud had closed the drapes at every window. The living room stretched from the front of the house to the rear and was lit by two hanging ceiling lamps at each end. They were all that remained of a time when a wall divided the long room into two.

Patterson was seated at the Topaz device, his hands deliberately on his lap, away from the controls. He was watching the small screen on the Topaz control panel. There were three key lines of data he was interested in; one that clicked over steadily as it counted down the minutes and seconds. Another that displayed the state of the Topaz stream, and a third that showed the figure displayed on the screen of the smartphone in the Toyota.

Most of the data remained perfectly stable, but the data that displayed the condition of the Topaz stream waivered uncertainly, hovering between one set of numbers and another. Higher, then lower, then again higher. These were the figures that concerned him. He was sending a really strong

Topaz stream into the network. It had to hold until five o'clock. He looked at his watch: 4:35 pm. Then he looked around and noticed the three hard-core radicals watching him silently. Each had their weapons pointed directly at him. A threatening and deeply fanatical look on each of their faces. He had no doubt. They were going to take their threat all the way to its deadly conclusion, if their leader wasn't released from Belmarsh Prison.

The big screen television further down the room, in the corner of what was once the lounge, had remained on all day, albeit with the sound turned down low and almost impossible to hear under the high-pitched scream of Topaz's tiny, high velocity, electric motors.

TV news channels carried shots of journalists standing in front of the gates to Belmarsh Prison, repeating the same line that they had heard nothing new from government officials; their position remained unchanged – *the British government does not do deals with terrorists*.

It was clear that they, and the line of TV news crews out of shot, were hoping for a dramatic scoop. The journalist handed back to the studio where a news anchor spoke 'live' to a reporter at number 10 Downing Street. Once again, the camera was tilted up and zoomed in to the flag pole with the Union Flag hanging limply in the calm afternoon air. Another 'live' picture came from a helicopter showing the same flag pole from six-hundred feet above. There was no sign that it was about to be replaced by the flag of the Sword of Liberation.

Back in the studio the anchor reported ominously that the police and security services had made no progress on the location of the terrorists, but the deadline was less than half an hour away. *'What would happen',* the presenter asked, *'if the terrorists carried out their threat?'* He turned to yet another expert who, with deep gravitas, painted a picture of unrelenting horror and the eventual death of potentially tens of thousands of people in a city somewhere in the UK. The buildings themselves would be uninhabitable for years as they tried to decontaminate them. *'Remember,'* he said sombrely, *'the dead city of Chernobyl.'*

The news channel kept replaying earlier packages, one of which, using clever animated graphics, showed a number of ways Plutonium Oxide Dust could be delivered to achieve the maximum fatal dose.

Sitting at the table by the bay window at the other end of the room, Patterson continued to stare anxiously at the readouts. The one representing the figure displayed on the smartphone in the Toyota appeared to be holding – for the time being. But an active real-time graphic that showed the intensity of the Topaz stream had pushed further towards the red zone. This one bothered Patterson the most. If part of the network failed, or the distance shortened for some reason, the stream would feed back, and cause the Topaz device to become super-heated.

One of the terrorists got up and went over to the window. He pulled the curtain back a little to check the street outside. The road was empty except for someone delivering newspapers. Despite their macho bravado they were getting nervous.

It was late summer and though the sun was still well above the horizon, the light had dimmed noticeably. A portentous sense of menace filled the air. It wasn't just autumn that was on its way.

***

The Range Rover parked up in Bakers Walk, the street that led to Bakers Yard. The blue strobe light had been switched off and stashed back in the glove box.

Stack noticed a young girl moving from house to house delivering the local news free sheet.

'Wait here, I've got an idea.'

Charlie and Cavanagh watched as Stack walked over to her. She had left her two-wheeled canvas trolley by the gate of the house to which she had just posted a newspaper. It was still half full of undelivered papers. The girl, aged about fourteen and still in her school uniform, appeared cautious as Stack approached.

They talked together for no more than a minute. Stack handed something over. It looked like a five-pound note. She stood back as Stack walked off with the trolley. The girl followed him to the top of Bakers Yard and watched him from there as he disappeared around the corner, beyond the sight of the men in the Range Rover.

The picture Patterson had sent included four houses. One of which was the location of the extremist terror cell. He made a cursory effort to deliver the free sheet to the nearest couple of houses, then crossed the road and began pushing the newspaper through the letter boxes of the houses opposite. He skipped the first three properties at the very top of Bakers Yard and moved down to the next four – the ones in the photograph. They were numbered 8, 10, 14, and 16. One, with the drapes pulled closed seemed a likely candidate. As he pushed the free sheet through the letter box, he noticed the casually discarded cigarette butts on the ground. In amongst them were the same date seeds he'd found lying by the door next to the convenience store in Peckham. He had no doubt. Number 14 was their target.

As he continued delivering to the other houses, he caught the slight flickering of curtains back at number 14. Someone was taking an interest. He ignored it, posted to the last house and walked the trolley back to the girl.

'What was that all about?' Cavanagh asked as Stack got back in the car. Charlie had already guessed.

'So, which one is it?' he asked.

'Number 14, half way down. The drapes are closed, which could present a challenge,' Stack said. 'We have no idea what to expect when we go in. We think there are three of them, but that's only a guess.'

'Tricky. Patterson's the problem,' Cavanagh said. 'Otherwise you could just go in and take them out.'

Stack didn't bother to respond to Cavanagh's offhand summary of the ease with which an assault might be carried out.

'OK Hollywood, the clock's ticking. Let's do it.'

Stack opened the door and got out.

'Yeah, I was getting bored anyway,' Charlie said as he followed, stepping out on to the pavement.

They both checked their weapons were secure and tucked into the belts of their jeans. They wore their shirts loose, hanging over the Glocks. As they walked to the top of Bakers Yard, they talked over their options.

'We don't have a key, so the front door is a bust,' said Stack.

'Yeah, it'd be different if we were going in mob handed, we could just bust in and take them out. What about the back door?'

'Let's take a look,' Stack said.

They walked beyond the junction to where a narrow dirt alley led down past the backyards of the post war pre-fabs. It looked like it was being used as a dumping ground for old mattresses, sofas and general domestic waste that people couldn't be bothered to take to the tip. The path was lined each side with old shiplap fences that leaned drunkenly this way and that, and an old brick wall with huge gaps, like missing teeth, in the top course. On the other side of the fence, shabby gardens were split in two by crumbling concrete footpaths that led the few yards up to the glass panelled back doors of each property.

By the time they were half way down the alley, they could see the drapes to the rear of number 14. They too had been drawn closed. Whoever was in the property, they were just as blind to events outside the house as Stack and Charlie were to whatever was going on inside.

Stack took another look at his watch: 4:47 pm. It was now or never. If the back door was locked, it would be easy to break the window and reach in for the key – if it was in the lock.

At the boundary of the backyard, a wooden post propped up a rotting timber fence gate that scraped a muddy arc as Charlie forced it open. To keep their approach as silent as possible, rather than use the crumbling pathway, they walked on the weed covered dirt that had long ago replaced the patchy grass. They reached the door and Charlie took hold of the knob. He looked at Stack and gave a 'here-goes-nothing' shrug, the kind you might give if you were about to throw yourself off a mountain.

He slowly, silently, turned the handle. It rotated a full one hundred and eighty degrees. Charlie turned to Stack, raised his eyebrows hopefully, and pushed.

Time-less: Driving on Empty

Despite the news channels buzzing with the plutonium story, no one was buying the official government line: 'keep calm, nothing to worry about'. As the afternoon wore on, people were starting to get anxious. Already, the pavements and roads were filling with office workers choosing not to take the risk. Preferring to get out while they can.

Even in Creechurch Lane, it was beginning to get noticeably more crowded. Business in the two trendy cafés had thinned, as customers chose to spend their time heading home to safety rather than pointlessly nursing a large, three quarter decaf extra hot almond milk with two equals.

Summer was feeling lucky and gave the Toyota's door handle a try. Nothing doing. She went around into the road and tried the driver's door but got the same result. For a moment she was tempted to visit the construction site at the end of the road to find a half brick to smash the window. That idea was quickly abandoned. She wondered how people would react if they saw her breaking into a car. A video of her doing it would probably be up-loaded to Facebook or Instagram before the police arrived.

Then, Charlie came to mind. They didn't call him 'Hollywood' for nothing. There didn't seem to be an activity or comment that he couldn't find a suitable movie to associate it with. He knew them all. It was through Hollywood's passion for films that she'd found a way to escape from the clutches of the big east European henchman guarding her in a London hotel room during the Bank of England caper. That was over a year ago.

'OK, Hollywood,' she murmured to herself, 'What would you do?'

She didn't have to give it too much thought, because during one playful, time wasting day back on Grand Cayman, he had demonstrated a trick that Russell Crowe had used in a film called 'The Next Three Days' that they had just watched. She had argued that such a trick was simply a Hollywood movie gimmick and wouldn't possibly work in the real world. Charlie had promptly taken her across to the hotel's multi-storey where their rental was parked and very quickly popped the door open using that very same trick.

She had passed a sports shop along Leadenhall Street on the way to Creechurch Lane. Her watch warned it was 4:29 pm. She rushed back to it.

Two sales assistants, two customers. Summer queued. She was beginning to wonder whether she had in fact lost her mind. Doubt troubled her thoughts. She was about to turn and leave when a voice asked, 'Can I help you?'

Instead of leaving, she stepped forward to the counter.

'Tennis Balls?'

'We have all the usual brands: Slazenger: Dunlop, Penn, Wilson...'

Summer interrupted the young assistant before he went further.

'I just need one – any brand will do.'

He turned, walked along a row of shelves and came back with a six-pack.

'I'm sorry, we only sell them by the box. Smallest is a pack of six'.

She didn't have time to argue.

'OK, I'll buy the box. How much?'

He told her. She paid with a card. A simple tap on the card reader and the sale was done. She pulled one of the balls out of the pack.

'I need you to do something for me.'

'Certainly madam. How can I help?'

'Do you have a screwdriver, or a sharp blade, that will cut a hole here?' she said, pointing to a spot on the ball.

'Can I ask why you want to destroy a perfectly good tennis ball?'

The tone of Summer's voice changed from one of gentle enquiry to efficient business woman.

'I don't have time to explain. Can you do it?'

The salesman reached into a draw beneath the counter and pulled out a Stanley knife. He picked up the ball and began cutting.

'A small hole. No more than a centimetre,' she said.

Tennis balls are made of tough material and it took a full minute before he'd successfully cut the hole and handed the ruined ball back to her. Summer took it, thanked him and rushed out of the shop.

Another time-check, 4:41 pm. The Toyota was a left-hand drive vehicle, which meant Summer had to stand in the road to gain access to the driver's door. There were growing numbers of people moving quickly past on the sidewalk, eager to get out of the City. Most were either studying their smartphone screens or making urgent calls. Rarely, were pedestrians talking to each other. Summer was effectively 'not there' as far as the commuters escaping London were concerned.

Summer stood in the road facing the Toyota, the slow-moving, nose to tail traffic passing just inches behind her. She leaned in close to the door to shield what she was about to do. In one hand she held the tennis ball, its ragged hole pressed against the door lock. She glanced nonchalantly up and down the road, pulled her other arm back and punched the tennis ball with her fist as hard as she could. The impact caused a small but powerful volume of air to jet into the lock mechanism.

The noise of the passing vehicles almost hid the *clunk* as the door lock snapped up. Summer was so surprised that it took a couple of seconds before realising she had gained access. She was officially a carjacker. She got in, closed the door and found herself in a cocoon of silence.

The next problem was the one to which she had given no thought as a terrifying moment of fear rushed through her head. She was now sitting next to some kind of explosive device that contained radioactive plutonium dust. What the hell did she think she was doing? Was she completely out of her mind? she asked herself.

The cardboard boxes almost filled the space behind her. She looked for a corner or flap of cardboard that she could tear open. If she could look inside, maybe she could find the mechanism and stop it, or maybe pull some wires out somehow.

As she turned her body to face the boxes, her hand pressed down on the hand brake to support her. She was attempting to kneel on the seat to face the rear of the car; an easier position to deal with the boxes. As she did, her fingers touched against something loose that was wedged between the seats. She looked down and reached in between the narrow gap to retrieve it. As soon as she pulled it out, the smartphone's screen came to life. It was displaying a set of figures. If this was some kind of countdown it had already reached the last number in the sequence. By all reasonable expectations the bomb should have gone off, because the number she was looking at was 00:00.

***

Chris Bailey's taxi was just pulling up behind Cavanagh's Range Rover in Bakers Walk when his cell phone rang.

He answered it as he climbed out, lodging the phone against his shoulder in order to free his hands to pay the fare.

'Hello? Chris Bailey.'

'It's Summer. I need your help.'

Ordinarily, James would have been her first choice, but this was different. This particular problem was uniquely Bailey's area of expertise.

As Bailey walked over to the Range Rover, Summer told him where she was and about the inexplicable number that was showing on the cell phone screen.

'Jesus Christ, Summer!' was Bailey's horrified reaction as he opened the door and got in next to Cavanagh.

'In nineteen minutes that thing is going to blow. Get out. Run for your life!'

'But, Chris, if it was going to blow, surely it would have done so by now. Ask yourself, if it's a count-down, does it go 3 – 2 – 1 – Bang! Or does it go 3 – 2 – 1 – 0, *then* Bang? The zero always comes first doesn't it?'

Bailey started to get her point. He switched the phone to speaker, so that Cavanagh could hear.

'What? Are you saying you think it's stuck on zero?'

'Well, how long would you expect it stay on zero before it goes bang? It couldn't be more than a second. It's been forty seconds since I found the smartphone. Who knows how long it's been stuck on zero before then?'

Chris Bailey thought about it for a moment, as Cavanagh broke in to the conversation.

'Summer. You're wasting time. There *is* no more time. Get out. Now!'

'That's it!' Bailey said. 'Summer, the deadline is five o'clock. That's just over eighteen minutes from now. I don't think the screen is showing 'present' time. Patterson must be using the Topaz stream. The zero on the screen you are looking at is in fact eighteen minutes in the future. It will take eighteen minutes for our current time and that zero to meet. When that happens, the zero will click over and the device will go bang. Time itself is the countdown. The zero is just waiting in the future for present time to catch up.'

'That's a hell of a leap, Chris. Why the hell would they do that?' she asked.

'If Bailey is right, Summer,' Cavanagh cut in, 'I believe they want to trick anyone who discovers the vehicle into believing the countdown had failed and the bomb was safe. Bomb makers often add time wasting circuitry to delay the discovery of the genuine timing mechanism. This is just a subtler version of that. It's quite brilliant. You could see how it would slow everything down – take the emergency out of it. And then suddenly...bang.'

'OK. Time is the one thing we can't waste. What are you looking at, Summer?' Bailey asked. 'What's in the car?'

Summer had put her own cell phone on to speaker, so that she could use both hands to tear the cardboard boxes apart as she spoke.

'I'm looking at a long steel tube kind of thing, about six or seven inches in diameter and nearly a metre tall. It's sitting on a table fabricated out of angle iron and plate steel. The tube rises right up to the roof of the car. It's welded at the top. The whole thing is fixed solid. I can't move it.'

Cavanagh's long military experience gave him a possible answer.

'I think it's a mortar tube. It fires a shell high into the air over the enemy position.'

Bailey picked up the theme.

'That's it. I've been wondering how they intended to spread the plutonium dust. If you want to scatter it over a wide area, you need to get it into the air, as high as possible. A mortar would do that. There must be a hole in the roof to allow the shell to escape. It doesn't have to be a military weapon. A big firework could do the job. The kind that sends lots of starbursts high into the sky during a firework display. Add the plutonium dust to the starbursts and you have your weapon.'

'I don't think there's anything you can do, Summer,' Cavanagh said. 'Get out of there now. Run as far as you can and then get under cover.'

'Well, I don't know, major, maybe there is a way to prevent it...or at least slow things down,' Bailey said. 'Can you start the car, Summer?'

'Now, that's something I can do, I think'.

Summer remembered another useful little lesson Charlie had given her. Thankfully, the Toyota was so old it didn't have the sophisticated electronics of modern automobiles. She reached under the steering column, grabbed the edge of the plastic moulding and pulled with all her strength. One half broke away exposing the ignition assembly on the steering column. She pulled hard on the wires leading to it until they came free. She found a cloth in the glove box and used it to insulate her fingers as she wound the live copper ends of the red wires together. Then she simply touched the bare metal end of the single brown wire against the red live wires, causing a shower of sparks that snapped and fizzed alarmingly. The starter motor gave a couple of quick grudging whirs as it turned the heavy three litre engine over. After an initial struggle, the six cylinders suddenly coughed into smooth, reciprocating life.

'OK. The engine's running.'

'Good. I want you to drive out into the traffic and take the shortest route you can find to get you over Tower Bridge. You shouldn't be too far away,' Bailey said. He kept his voice calm and steady.

Summer put the car into gear and manoeuvred into the traffic.

'What have you got in mind, Chris?' She asked anxiously. 'Dump the car somewhere?'

'No time for that. This may sound crazy, but I'm going to use the Topaz stream against itself. I need to get the car as close to the Topaz device in Camberwell as I can. Patterson will have measured the stream to a very precise distance, that's how he can keep the 'zero' of the countdown fixed in time. But the countdown can be reversed. Believe it or not, the closer we can get you to Camberwell, the more time you will gain. The problem is, universal time – now time - will still be moving forward to consume it. It's like climbing up a down escalator.'

'Jesus! Are you kidding me? That sounds nuts!'

'Trust me, Summer. I'm a quantum physicist,' he said half-jokingly.

The flight of commuters from the City had started slowly at around midday. Just a few at first, but as time passed, more and more decided not to risk delaying. This included, not just commuters, but residents of the capital as well, adding to the already glacial speed of the home going traffic.

Bailey pulled his iPad out of the shoulder bag, turned it on and opened Google Maps to show an aerial view of Creechurch Lane and the roads around it.

'Head east along Leadenhall Street. Tell me when you're there.'

'Will do – if we ever get moving.'

Bailey put his hand over the cell phone and spoke to Cavanagh.

'There is another problem I didn't want to worry Summer with. The stream is going via the nearest cell phone mast. She may be moving away from it right now.'

'Why is that a problem?' Cavanagh asked. He was familiar with the capabilities of Topaz, but this was far beyond his understanding.

'Patterson would have measured the stream to the place the car was parked. It will be a very precise distance. Moving the car could mean moving further away from the mast, which will actually reduce the amount of time we have left. That's OK while we still have seventeen minutes left, but it'll become a real problem later.'

'I thought you said we could gain time if she drives towards the Topaz device?' Cavanagh said.

'That's right, but as you move around, the phone network uses the signal from your cell phone to choose the most suitable mast that will give the best reception. As Summer drives back to Camberwell, the signal will switch from one mast to another. The distance from each mast to the Topaz device will vary considerably because of the way the cables are laid. They don't go in a straight line, they often take very circuitous routes. We must make sure she drives towards masts that shorten the physical distance of the Topaz stream, not lengthen it. Remember, real-time is ticking away as well, so with every passing minute, the margin we gain by finding the shortest telephone signal route, gets smaller.'

'I'm on Leadenhall Street now.'

'OK, Summer. The second road coming up on your right is called Minories. Head down there. You'll come to a larger one-way system that will eventually take you to Tower Bridge. Follow the signs. Let me know when you're going over the bridge.'

Bailey opened another window on his tablet and found a site that showed all the cell phone masts in London. He zoomed in to include just the ones that headed south from the river, down to Camberwell. There were plenty of them.

If she wasn't at a standstill in traffic, frustratingly, as soon as it started moving again, the traffic signals would turn red. Despite that she had made some progress. Just ahead she saw the familiar steel lattice work that spanned the granite towers of Tower Bridge. Her watch gave the time as 4:41 pm. On the passenger seat next to her, the smartphone still showed 00:00, but even as she looked, the number clicked back to 00:09 and froze. She had gained nine seconds.

'Chris, I'm just about to cross Tower Bridge. An interesting thing just happened. The countdown just dialled back nine seconds.'

Bailey checked the cell phone tower map.

'OK, Summer, that will probably be because the smartphone has just picked up a local mast. One that you're just passing. The length of the Topaz stream has just been shortened a little.'

Summer looked out to the buildings on either side of the river.

'I can't see anything. Where are these masts?'

'Mostly on top of tall office blocks. It'll be difficult to spot them from the road,' Bailey explained.

'The traffic's started moving a little quicker. I'm on the other side of the bridge now.'

Summer noticed that the steering wheel felt sticky. She took her right hand away and examined it. Turning it over she saw blood smeared across the palm. The nail on her ring finger was broken, probably when she yanked the plastic moulding apart. She used the cloth still lying on the passenger seat to wipe the wheel clean and then wrapped it around her hand. Now she was aware of it, it had started to hurt with a sharp, stabbing pain.

Bailey checked his watch. 4:47 pm. He kept his voice calm.

'Try to pick up a bit of speed, Summer. You've only got just over two miles to go. Not far now.'

Cavanagh was even more edgy.

'That's two miles as the crow flies, Bailey. The road will take longer. Don't you think she should look for somewhere to abandon the car?'

Bailey ignored him.

'Summer, stay on the road you're on. In about half a mile, you'll come to a large junction. I want you to make a right hand turn on to the A201, towards the Elephant and Castle.'

'Copy that. Shit! We've come to a standstill again.'

Bailey and Cavanagh sat in silence in the Range Rover. The tension was starting to tell on the MI6 chief. He started to whistle a low, breathy, unrecognisable tune as he stared anxiously through the windscreen. His fingers tapped nervously on the steering wheel. He hadn't heard from Stack. This was all starting to feel bad.

'OK, I've made another two hundred yards. The countdown has just dialled back to 00:35. Looks like we've actually gained some more time.'

It was 4:51 pm.

Assault on Bakers Yard

Charlie pushed the door, but it was stuck fast. The damp wood had swollen and jammed against the door frame. He pressed his shoulder against it and heaved, forcing it to shudder open with a low rubbing sound. They waited a moment, then, quietly easing the steel slide back to cock the chambers of their semi-automatic weapons, Stack gave a nod and they stepped across the threshold.

There had been no reaction to the sound of their entry, but they could hear talking from somewhere inside. An announcement, quickly followed by a melodramatic jingle: the audio from a TV news channel at high volume. There was also a nerve-jangling whistling sound from somewhere in the house. This low background noise provided cover as Stack and Hollywood trod softly into a small kitchen. Before them was another door that opened to a hallway. As they moved forward it was clear that the arrangement of the first floor was a fairly conventional 1960s layout. Ahead, on the left, were some stairs that led up to the first floor. At the far end of the hall was the front door. On the right were two internal doors. Stack guessed the first gave access to the lounge at the back of the house. It was closed. The second opened into the front room. The door was ajar, and it was from this room that the unnerving whistling sound was coming. Now though, at a closer proximity, it had resolved into a sound not unlike two high-pitched dentist's drills droning slightly out of sync with each other. Not loud, but teeth jarring, nonetheless.

Stack crept forward past the first door, his back hard against the wall. He slowly eased round a little into the second doorway. The view through the narrow gap revealed, first, the drape-covered windows and then, as he changed his position, the back of a chair facing a table. He leaned in some more. Someone was sitting in the chair, his back to Stack. He was facing some equipment that had been set up on a table. He guessed it was Patterson and the equipment was the Topaz device. The shrill, whining sound seemed to be coming from it.

Stack pushed his luck and leaned a little further into the room. Sitting opposite Patterson was a man with a gun who might easily have spotted Stack if he had looked up. It wasn't just any gun he was holding. It was the Uzi. This, Stack realized, was Mahmoud, the man making the demands in the video.

Stack pulled back from the door and turned to Charlie.

'Two men,' he mouthed the words and held up two fingers. 'First man is Patterson. Second guy has an Uzi.' It was all said in a low whisper into Charlie's ear.

Charlie gave an upward nod of his head indicating he had something to say. Stack leaned in to hear.

'Do you think it's one big room or two rooms?'

Stack weighed the problem for a moment. His analysis was that they would be going into one long room. He reasoned that, if there were two separate rooms but everyone was in the front room, why close the curtains in the back room?

'Are you sure?' Charlie mouthed.

Stack shrugged, 'Let's find out,' he whispered. 'You take the first door.'

'OK. We go on, *Go*?' Charlie asked.

Stack gave a quick nod and raised his thumb.

Charlie moved the few steps back down the hall to the other door.

Their guns were raised and ready. Stack gave the order clear and deliberately noisy.

'Go!'

He went in hard and aggressive. Kicking the door open and rushing through, his arms outstretched holding the Glock in a two-fisted grip. He turned quickly, scanning the room to locate possible targets. He'd spotted one at the far end of the room, but kept his gun aimed at the man with the Uzi.

At the same time down the hallway, Charlie had grabbed the door knob, turned it and pushed hard. The door wouldn't open. It didn't seem to be locked because it opened a crack. He put his shoulder to it and heaved but it wouldn't open any further. Two shots rang out. He rushed back up the hallway, yelling loudly as he stormed through the other door into the front room, gun up and ready.

The first thing he noticed when he looked down to the other end of the room was that the sofa had been pushed up against the door. Presumably, they only used the door to the front end of the room.

The second thing he saw was a youth with a middle-eastern appearance sitting on the sofa, rocking back and forth, moaning loudly and clutching his leg. A gun lay on the carpet near his feet. There was blood oozing from a shoulder wound. Charlie rushed over and kicked the gun out of the way before quickly turning and dropping to his knee, his weapon raised to cover the scene at the other end of the room.

In Stack's earlier recce of the room, he had seen the man with the Uzi sitting across the table from Patterson. But by the time he'd kicked the door open and run into the room with his gun aimed at the target, the target had moved.

Mahmoud was peering through the curtains to the street outside when the sound of yelling and the door crashing open made him turn abruptly and bring the Uzi up.

Stack was already drawing his weapon round as the man turned from the window. Stack fell to a kneeling position and took aim. It was a Mexican stand-off. With Patterson in the line of fire he couldn't risk a shot.

There was no sign of Charlie storming through the other door, just a lot of banging coming from the hallway. He turned around for a quick second look at the target at the other end of the room.

Youssef had been half asleep watching the TV, but the noise of Stack bursting into the room and someone else trying to open the door behind the sofa shocked him awake.

It only took a second for Stack to read the scene. The young man was clumsily trying to pull the slide on his semi-automatic to load the weapon and bring it to bear on the assailant. In the next second, Stack sent two 9 mm rounds across the room in a double tap. One to the man's shoulder, the other into his leg. Then he spun back to deal with the Uzi guy.

The scene had changed dramatically. Mahmoud had twisted Patterson's collar with his fist and pulled him close in a choking grip. At the same time, he pressed the machine pistol hard against the hostage's head.

'Don't try it. I promise you. I'll spray this man's brains all over that wall.'

Patterson made a wide-eyed appeal to Stack, the palms of his hands held up defensively in case the demented stranger facing him decided to risk a shot.

Mahmoud looked at the time displayed on the Topaz laptop. Any moment now either Asad Hassam will be released from Belmarsh Prison or the plutonium dust will be blasted into the air above London to float down on to the buildings, streets and the general population like salt from a shaker. He had made a promise to the jihadi leader in Libya and he was determined not to fail now. When the digits click over to 5 pm, one way or another, the world would change.

***

4:49 pm. Summer shook her hand in an attempt to alleviate the stinging pain. The nail was still bleeding and soaking through the cloth. Progress was a lot slower as the congested road filled with even more traffic fleeing the approaching deadline.

On London's famously narrow thoroughfares, big red double-decker buses blocked the lane space, constantly stopping to pick up and drop off. Swarms of black cabs did the same. One moment she'd been making good progress, only to have to brake suddenly as a cab decided now would be a good time to do a U-turn into the unrelenting, fume-choked conveyer of pressed steel and vulcanised rubber that was the London rush hour.

The Toyota was heading towards the Elephant and Castle. A large junction that had recently been transformed from a roundabout into an omega shaped speedway track. But before she got there, the smartphone display went into reverse. Precious seconds were erased.

'Chris, something happened to the countdown. It just lost twenty-three seconds. It now reads twelve seconds. I'm getting a bit worried.'

Bailey tried to hide his concern.

'I was expecting that. You've just passed a tower to the north of you at Dickens Field. Don't worry, you're still ahead. It's 4:54 pm, plus the twelve seconds.'

'Jesus, Chris. I'm struggling to get a grip on this. Are you saying that when the clock hits five pm, I'll still have another twelve seconds before it goes bang?'

'That's right. Keep pushing it. As fast as you can. There's another mast at the Elephant and Castle.'

'Yeah, but do I gain or lose time? This is like some weird dystopian video game!' She tried to make a joke out of it, but she couldn't hide the fear in her voice.

In the rear-view mirror, further back in the traffic behind her, she noticed the occasional flash of blue light. And then a '*whoop*' of a distant siren.

Over in Camberwell, Cavanagh had his driver's window rolled halfway down. While Bailey and Summer were talking, there had been a distinct double pop of gunfire. Without interrupting his conversation with Summer, Bailey turned to see if Cavanagh had heard. The major gave the slightest of nods. Stack and Dawson had engaged the enemy.

'I hear you Summer. Don't worry about time, just keep making headway.' Bailey knew it sounded patronising. 'When you reach the Elephant and Castle keep going all the way round and take the A3 south. It's the road to Brighton you want.'

Though the traffic remained solid and unmoving in both directions, the blue light coming from behind had got closer. The siren more strident. It was just a few cars back. She noticed movement as cars attempted to steer out of the path of the on-coming strobe lights. She strained to see what kind of emergency vehicle was approaching and suddenly caught the distinctive green and yellow colours of an ambulance. It was three cars back now and manoeuvring along the middle of the road in the narrow space that had opened up. She drove as close as she could to the pavement, not making more than a couple of extra inches. Cars on the other side did better, shifting over just as the ambulance noisily squeezed past.

'Hang on Chris, I'm going to try something.'

Summer spun the wheel hard right, slammed her foot down on the accelerator and threw the Landcruiser into the space behind the ambulance. She kept tight up to the rear doors as she followed in its slipstream. Drivers in the stationary vehicles she passed sounded their horns angrily as the SUV stole an advantage over their hard-won position in the homegoing race.

Bailey said something that was buried under the wail of the siren. Summer was too distracted to answer anyway. Then, as quickly as it had come, the ambulance turned right and disappeared into a side street leaving the Toyota to force its way back into the line.

'Chris, I've just snuck in behind an ambulance and made a good two hundred and fifty yards or so. The junction is up ahead.'

'That won't make you popular. Keep pushing,' Bailey encouraged Summer.

The large green street sign coming up on the left showed a graphic of the Elephant & Castle junction. The thick white line she was driving along was joined by another four major roads. The graphic made it look simple, but during rush hour a driver unfamiliar with the layout could easily lose track and take the wrong exit.

At 4:56 pm the Toyota finally nosed into the junction. Summer found herself shuffling forward in intermittent bursts, traffic on all sides pushing into her lane or driving across it. Horns and the impatient revving of engines added to the pressure. Her hands trembled as a shockwave of adrenaline rushed through her body causing her heart to pound as she glanced at the quickly diminishing margin of time on the smartphone screen. She wiped beads of sweat from her forehead with the back of her hand and banged the steering wheel in frustration.

'Come on!' she shouted. It was a cry of utter desperation. 'Let's get a move on for Christ's sake.'

Now she was confused. Had she passed two or three exits? She couldn't look away from the vehicles pressing in around her to check the road signs. Summer wondered if she had remembered the sign correctly. Surely, she should be on the A3 by now. The road sign she had just passed said something about the A3, but in her panic, to avoid colliding with another vehicle, she couldn't recall if it had indicated to the south or the north. Then, by some miracle, the madness subsided and the traffic started behaving itself, all heading in the same direction in a two-lane road. She hoped it was the road she wanted.

She took a deep breath and tried to calm herself. Her watch warned there were just three minutes left. Then she checked the countdown read-out. An unexpected bit of good news. By some inexplicable law of impenetrable physics, the time on the smartphone screen had increased in her favour. It read 00:52 seconds.

***

'Your friend over there is in trouble. He'll bleed to death unless you get him to hospital.'

Stack knew he was wasting his breath on Uzi guy, but maybe the kid on the sofa would focus on the words 'bleed to death' and start to complain. So far all he'd done was moan with pain. Perhaps the idea of hospital treatment would start to appeal to him before he blacked out.

'He is a warrior of the Islamic revolution. Not a coward like you western Kufirs,' Mahmoud said.

'Well, pretty soon he's going to be a martyr of the revolution if you don't get him some help.'

Distraction had always played a part in Stack's many unconventional battle strategies. He was hoping Charlie, crouching further down the room, could use the time he was wasting to get a better position on Uzi guy – not that there were many choices in such a confined space.

The problem was, Uzi guy commanded the room from his position by the window, and he had Patterson in front as a shield.

Mahmoud's eyes kept flicking past Stack to check the TV at the other end of the room. With the end game now only seconds away, the news channel had chosen to stay with the news crew at Belmarsh Prison for the final moments of the story. A solemn reporter was once again chewing over the 'what-ifs' the 'might-have-beens' and of course, the 'who-to-blame' in the aftermath of a worst-case scenario. They had a moment of excitement when a police van drove through a few minutes earlier, the camera zooming in, hoping to catch a glimpse of something – anything. Then it all went quiet again.

A split screen on the right of the picture showed the view from Downing Street. The journalist's voice was drowned out by the sound of helicopters flying above, but the shaking of his head told the story just as eloquently – the government wouldn't budge.

'You're too late to stop us. Your government will have the deaths of tens of thousands on their hands if Asad Hassam doesn't walk through those gates in the next ninety seconds.'

Karim Mahmoud was a hardened jihadi, but Stack didn't buy his cocky bravado. There was doubt. The plan was falling apart.

For the first time Stack had a chance to assess the condition of Patterson. He didn't look good. He'd taken a beating recently.

'What about you, Patterson?' Stack asked. 'We've been looking for you and that bloody machine for days.'

'Have they still got Major Hedgeland?' was the scientist's first concern, his voice choked by the extremist's grip on his throat.

'No, we pulled her out of the compound in Tripoli the night they took you to the ship. She's safe here in London.'

Patterson just nodded. He was pleased for her, but it made no difference to his situation, and anyway, there was another problem. The shrill tone of the electric motors had risen noticeably.

'Something's happening to the Topaz stream. The data readouts have changed. Have you moved the car?' he asked Mahmoud.

This was the distraction Stack was waiting for. Worried by this unexpected development,

Mahmoud had turned to look at the laptop screen and then at the data read-out on the Topaz control panel. He couldn't hope to understand what any of it meant.

'Show me.' He flicked a quick look over to Stack waving the Uzi menacingly and then turned back to the screen.

Patterson pointed to one particular set of figures.

'This sequence here. It's measuring the distance to the smartphone in the car. It keeps changing, which means the time frame has moved. It's definitely not fixed on zero anymore.'

'Well, get it back on to zero again.'

'I can't. The target is moving. The time frame won't stay on zero even if I could find that point in time again, which I can't. But there's a bigger problem.'

The scientist pointed to another reading.

'The intensity of the stream is growing. It means the distance from here to the car is getting shorter. Can you hear that sound? The power of the stream is feeding back into the machine.'

Patterson put his hand on the control panel.

'You can feel it. It's definitely getting hotter.'

The screaming of the motors continued to climb. A howl, as though two miniature jet engines were being pushed beyond their operating tolerances.

As Mahmoud let go of Patterson's collar to put his hand on the control panel, Stack made his move. He dived to the left to reveal more of Mahmoud and get a cleaner target. He landed on his back with the Glock aimed and ready to shoot. Before he could squeeze the trigger, the explosive sound of two shots filled the room behind him. He turned just in time to see another man duck back into the hallway.

The double crack of gunfire sent the nerve shredded Patterson diving to the floor and crawling under the table. Mahmoud's Uzi sprayed bullets into the space Stack had just vacated. The trajectory of the lethal rounds sent them down the room towards Charlie, missed, and buried themselves in the far wall behind him. One penetrated the TV's LCD screen. Charlie had already thrown himself forward to take a shot at the new figure who had suddenly appeared at the door.

There was only one bathroom in the house. It was on the first floor. Ramaas had been busy relieving himself when Stack's two gunshots sounded from downstairs. He finished peeing, zipped himself up and gently opened the bathroom door. He expected to see the black, bulletproof vested uniforms of armed police swooping into the house but, as he slowly descended the staircase, it became clear this was not a SWAT team raid. The low murmur of conversation drifted up from the living room. One was Mahmoud, but he didn't recognise the other voice. He thought he could hear the sound of whimpering too.

He pulled the semi-automatic from the back of his pants, eased the slide back, and took the last few steps down to the hall. The door to the living room was open halfway. Ramaas did the same as Stack had done only a few minutes earlier and peered around the door frame to assess the situation in the room. Three people were in his field of view; Mahmoud, Patterson and a stranger. The gunshots had already warned Ramaas that something bad had happened. The scene inside the room confirmed it. Mahmoud was over by the window. The stranger was crouching on the floor.

Both had their weapons aimed at each other. In between was Patterson who Mahmoud was using as a shield. The assailant didn't have a clear shot. Ramaas couldn't understand why Mahmoud didn't just shoot the vulnerable attacker. He hadn't seen Charlie who was out of sight in the other half of the room.

Ramaas checked down the hallway to the kitchen. Nobody else seemed to be around, so there was just the one shooter on the floor. An easy shot. But just to make sure, he stepped into the room, raised his pistol and...

Charlie was waiting for a clean target. He knew that his former captain would go for a shot if he could. Most likely, he guessed, Stack would go to the left and try to get a clear line of fire around Patterson.

Something was agitating the man standing behind Patterson. With the rising sound of the electric motors, Charlie found it difficult to hear what was being said at the other end of the room. But he did notice that the extremist kept taking his eyes away from Stack to look at the strange equipment on the table. It was as the fanatic let go of Patterson and placed his hand on the flightcase that he saw Stack dive over to the left. As he did, a third gang member stepped into the room, his gun trying to follow Stack's unexpected move. He fired, missing Stack by no more than a centimetre. Charlie reacted instantly to the sudden change in dynamics. He rotated his aim a few degrees to the left and sent a round into the door where the late arrival to the party had been a split second before.

Ramaas was lucky to get out of the way. The shock of discovering there was another shooter in the room sent a sudden hit of adrenaline surging through his body, giving him a momentary rush of speed that saved his life as he leaped back into the hallway.

Charlie paused to consider his options. There didn't appear to be any. He did what Charlie always did – he rushed head first out of the room - towards the enemy.

***

4:58 pm plus 70 seconds and rising. The Toyota Landcruiser was making much better headway. The A3 traffic was flowing steadily, almost reaching 30 mph at times. Camberwell and the Topaz device was just over a mile away.

'Chris, what happens at five? Are you sure this thing won't go pop?'

Bailey and Cavanagh had just heard more gunfire. Eventually, someone would report it. Maybe they had. Police could already be on their way. He tried to ignore those problems for the moment.

'Nothing will happen. Let's just keep adding those seconds. You're not far now.'

Bailey was trying hard to sound reassuring, but Summer was no fool. She knew what was at stake. If she was a betting girl, she'd give herself no more than a ten percent chance of surviving her irrational stunt. She recalled what James had said: 'Don't get into trouble'. If only James knew. *James*! Suddenly she remembered, she wasn't the only one in danger.

'Have you heard from James, Chris? How are they doing? Any news?'

'James can take care of himself. I'll let you know when I know.'

Bailey didn't want to lie, but he didn't want to give Summer any more to worry about. Then, through the tiny cell phone speaker, he heard Summer's voice turn to ice.

'Chris. The countdown. Its spinning down. I've just lost thirty seconds.'

'Where are you Summer?'

Summer scanned the area she was driving through. Looking for landmarks.

'I'm just passing Kennington tube station.'

Valuable seconds passed as Bailey checked the map.

'Yes, there's a tower nearby. The signal must have switched to it. It's taking a much longer route now. We need to get you over to Camberwell Road to the east. Just down on the left is Cook's Road. Get there asap.'

Bailey didn't want to frighten Summer, but he needed her to take some bigger risks.

'Put your foot down. As quick as you can.' He attempted to keep his voice even. To edit out the tremor of panic that was rising in him.

Summer held her breath as the second hand on her watch ticked through the last second and landed on 5 pm, just as she turned into Cook's Road.

Nothing happened. No whirring of machinery, flashing lights or alarms ringing. And most importantly – nothing went bang. But Summer knew she had run out of real time. She was literally running on borrowed time - 'now time' plus whatever precious seconds she can steal from the future. Every second spent now was earned the hard way; beating a desperate path through the heavy traffic towards the mysterious Topaz device.

All around her she caught glimpses of drivers and their passengers listening intently to their radios. Leaning in and turning the volume up against the noise of the traffic. Everyone wanting to hear what had happened as they passed through the 5 o'clock deadline.

Summer noticed the worried tone in Bailey's voice and pushed her driving ability to the limit. The left hand driving position made overtaking even more hazardous as she leaned across to get a view of oncoming traffic. Flashing lights and car horns didn't stop her elbowing her way through. They'd just have to get out of her way. One van driving recklessly from the opposite direction didn't react when she pulled out. The driver had a cell phone pressed hard to his ear and paperwork laid out across the steering wheel. He hadn't seen the Toyota and only managed a tiny course-changing nudge of the wheel at the last second. The van skimmed passed, ripping the off-side door mirror from the Toyota. The broken remains of it hung from the control wires, banging noisily against the door panel with every violent swerve and sudden brake.

The rapid loss of extra seconds displayed on the smartphone screen began to slow as she headed east along Cook's Road. 12 seconds. 8 seconds. 5 seconds. Then 3 and slowly to 2. The countdown display stayed on 2 seconds for a short while, flicking between 2 and 1, then back to 2 seconds. It held for a moment before dropping back to 1 second again. Summer panicked when she saw the digital numbers flick over to 0.

Is it zero, then bang?

It stayed there for a fraction of a second before slowly starting to unwind, counting up - gaining precious time once more.

'That was close, Chris. It dropped to zero for a moment, but it's started to climb again. The display is showing 15 seconds.'

'Well, the good news is the thing didn't go bang at five o'clock,' Bailey said. 'But you're on borrowed time from now on. You've just passed between two masts that appear to be an identical distance from you as you drove past. But one must have had a longer ground distance to the Topaz device. The smartphone was flicking between them. That's why the seconds fluctuated.

'According to my map, you're heading towards a mast at the junction of Cook's Road and Camberwell Road. It's less than a mile from the location of Topaz. You may start to gain a little more time. It's not far now.'

The seconds kept being added, but every second she gained was quickly consumed by 'now time'.

Going up those down escalators.

Summer pushed herself harder to take even more chances. Grabbing opportunities to overtake that were less opportunities than they were reckless swerves into oncoming traffic. She forced cars to get out of her way, leaving blaring car horns and the shouts of angry drivers in her wake. Summer was doing little to improve intolerant male prejudices against female drivers. Tough!

The display on the smartphone continued to edge slowly away from the danger zone. But 'now time', the time experienced by everyone in the here and now, inexorably ticked forward, clawing back the stolen future seconds.

As the Toyota drew closer to the Topaz location, time was added ever more slowly until the display hovered at 86 seconds, stopped, then started going into reverse.

Gradually at first. Each reducing number seemingly reluctant to appear. But as 'now-time' flowed forward, the gap between the present and the future Topaz time began to close. Seconds that had passed with infinite slowness started to move more quickly.

Bailey knew that if the car made it to the destination, the length of the Topaz stream would be reduced to zero – and so would the ability to gain time. He still hadn't come up with a scheme to deal with that small problem – but, given time, as they say...

Until then, the speed of the countdown would continue to increase until, in the final seconds, when 'now time' met 'future time' – at the exact moment the Toyota arrived at the location of the Topaz device – the last second of the stolen 'future time' would be spent.

Zero...then bang.

Deadline

Under the table, shaking uncontrollably, Patterson curled into a ball of broken humanity, his nerves finally shot. On the table above him, the miniature jet engine sound of the high torque motors was screaming upwards at an ever-increasing pitch. He knew Topaz's quantum technology was reaching breaking point, but he couldn't be certain that by simply pulling the plug, the bomb wouldn't still explode and eject the plutonium dust – a much more lethal outcome than the localised problem of the Topaz machine catching fire.

Then, in a moment of frozen time, both Mahmoud and Stack turned to look at the television as the news channel announced the arrival of the extremist's deadline – five o'clock. Their weapons dropped a little as their attention was captured by the pictures from Belmarsh Prison. The stray round from Mahmoud's weapon had drilled a hole in the screen straight through the image of the huge steel prison gates.

The howling whine from the flightcase made it hard to hear what the journalist was saying, but her shaking head and lack of activity at the prison behind her told the story just as eloquently: Asad Hassan would be eating prison food again tonight.

The scene switched to a 'live' feed from a handheld camera in a nearby street where a group of placard-waving Sword of Liberation supporters had been awaiting the release of their leader. The group had grown in numbers and impatience during the afternoon and police struggled to keep them away from the prison entrance. Now, with the news that the release of Hassan had been denied, violence began to break out. Some managed to push through the police line and run towards the gates. More police were brought in. Agitators stoked the anger and frustration of the protestors, hurling incendiary claims and theories on an already explosive situation.

Mahmoud turned to the laptop screen. It confirmed what in his gut he already knew. At nearly two minutes past five, the mortar bomb should have already gone off and the skies above London filled with the deadly plutonium-oxide particles. But the news channel had reported nothing so far. It would have been a huge story, far bigger than the riot outside the prison. Why would they ignore it?

His disillusionment at the catastrophic failure of his plan put him off guard. It slowed him. He hadn't planned for defeat. The armed assailant crouching just feet away was part of it. He was the armed representative of a system he despised. It brought back into focus all the seething resentment and loathing that had given him burning purpose. It was why he'd joined the jihad against the hated western infidels. The non-believers who, even now, contaminated the lands of the Prophet.

Stack had already turned his attention away from the newscast and back to the extremist gang leader. He watched with detached curiosity as the man's expression changed from interest and anticipation, to dark clouds of bitter disappointment and murderous rage. Then, like someone suddenly aroused from a terrible dream, the jihadist's mind returned to the house in Bakers Yard...and the gunman watching him.

He spun round raising his weapon as he did, but Stack was ready. He fired a single shot into Mahmoud's gun hand. The shock threw him back against the window sill and the Uzi clattered noisily to the floor. Stack grabbed it and stood up.

Then he heard a voice, just audible against the tortured scream of the Topaz equipment. It was Patterson. Stack dropped down to listen. The scientist's hand reached out to Stack as he pleaded to him.

'Topaz. It's over-heating.' Patterson's voice shivered with fear. 'It's reaching criticality. The stream. You've got to stop it.'

Stack tried to help him out from under the table, but he wouldn't move. He just retreated even further back.

What, Stack wondered, could he do? He stood up again and stared at the strange machine with the unfathomable numbers flicking across the small screen. Nothing about the controls looked familiar. He touched the surface of the panel but snatched his hand away quickly. The machine was red hot. Even so, it appeared to be functioning - still doing whatever it was supposed to be doing. If it was possible, the screaming turbojet noise had grown louder. There were two wounded gunmen in the room. That was something he did understand. He turned just as Hollywood rushed back into the room.

'That other guy. He's blocked the bloody kitchen door.' He said as he rushed down to the other end and threw the curtains back.

***

In the Toyota, the time on the screen said 72 seconds. The countdown had started to gain speed. Bakers Yard and the Topaz device were only a few streets away now.

'I'm coming up to the corner of Camberwell Road. Which way?' Summer asked.

'Turn left and take the first on the right as you pass Camberwell Green.'

Summer drove as Bailey gave directions, her eyes constantly flicking to the smartphone. At first it seemed like she had plenty of time. But when she looked again, just a few seconds later, more than ten seconds had been lost.

These were shorter local roads. Bailey's directions took her past a row of shops and into the High Street.

'OK Summer, you're nearly here. A few blocks down on the left. Look out for Bakers Walk. We're in a black Range Rover.'

The numbers skipped faster. 47 seconds quickly dropped to 38. There now seemed to be a very definite correlation between the Toyota and the Topaz location. The closer she got, the quicker the seconds from the future were consumed.

'I'm in Bakers Walk. Is that you ahead on the left?'

Chris Bailey had stepped out of the Range Rover and walked a few steps towards the main road. He had his cell phone with him. But he waved anyway.

'Yes. Pull up behind us.'

Cavanagh also got out and walked over to join him.

As soon as she pulled up, Bailey opened what he thought was the passenger side door, forgetting it was left-hand drive. He didn't bother with welcomes or patronising statements of the obvious.

As Summer stepped out, he asked for the smartphone. The countdown had reached 29 seconds, but it was counting the numbers far too quickly. He handed the phone back and leaned into the car to see for himself. It was just as she had described it. A steel tube rising up to the roof. Uncomplicated, but effective.

He climbed up on to the seat, jacked his left knee over the windshield, hauled himself up onto the roof and immediately spotted the white sheet of paper that had been gaffer-taped there. He tore it away. It revealed a huge aperture about eight inches across that had been cut into the thin sheet metal. He peered through the gaping mouth into the throat of the tube, but it was too dark to see the mortar shell at the other end.

'Count the numbers for me Summer.'

'23 seconds,' she called back.

Lying flat on the roof, Bailey attempted to reach down into the pipe. His fingers touched something, but his arm wouldn't stretch any further. He pushed himself back up, threw his jacket off and tried again.

'18...'

He threaded his arm back down the hole. This time his whole hand could feel the curve of the mortar. It was a cannonball shape, but it had a small ring at the top that had probably been used to lower it into the pipe.

'14...'

He managed to squeeze it tentatively between his middle and index fingers. It wasn't much of a grip. He pulled his arm out slowly but the ring slipped, and it fell back down. Bailey guessed it must have weighed about ten pounds. He reached in, found the ring again, and pinched it between his fingers. harder this time.

'9...'

He gritted his teeth as he squeezed his fingers together awkwardly against the steel ring and began lifting the heavy shell once again. He figured the less time between his fingers, the less chance of it slipping. He raised it quickly in a smooth easy motion, but about halfway up, his elbow got stuck in the tube. He had to push himself away from the roof with his left arm, raising his chest a few inches before he was able to free his arm and lift the shell fully out, and away from the hole.

'4...'

Turning it around he saw that it wasn't simply a ball shape. At the bottom it had been reformed into a kind of box. He guessed this contained the lifting charge. A wire that snaked up from the other end of the tube fed into it. In a firework display, this wire would have been the means to ignite the charge and launch the mortar a thousand feet into the air.

'1...'

He yanked on it.

***

Outside, in the backyard of the house, Ramaas had crept up to the lounge window trying to find a gap in the curtain to see in. Charlie had run after him when he bolted down the hallway, but Ramaas had already reached the kitchen, slammed the door, dragged the refrigerator over to block it and bolted through the rear door into the garden. Charlie tried but couldn't break through.

He rushed back into the living room, past Youssef, still moaning weakly on the couch, and over to the window. He threw the drapes back, expecting to see Ramaas fleeing down the alleyway, but instead he came face to face with him. Only the glass separated them. Ramaas was quicker. He didn't bother to take aim, he just lifted his pistol and fired several random shots in quick succession that smashed through the glass, missing Charlie by millimetres as he leapt to one side. One round hit the wooden window frame, ricocheting noisily away, but two of the steel-sheathed, 9 mm missiles travelled unhindered towards the bay window at the other end of the room, skimming past Stack but penetrating Mahmoud's chest with a sickening double thud that threw him back hard against the glass, cracking the pane from top to bottom.

He bounced back from the window towards the table. It had been covered with a linen cloth which the Topaz device was sitting on. Inside the flightcase the intense heat had ignited the magnesium alloy components, which in turn had super-heated the aluminium framework causing it to combust in a searing arc-like plasma. Thick dark brown smoke had already started billowing ominously through the metal seams of the control panel. Beneath the burning machine, a black scorch mark on the table cloth was spreading quickly. As Mahmoud fell forward, the material suddenly burst into flames.

In his death throes, Mahmoud grabbed the cloth and sank slowly to the floor, dragging the burning material, and the furnace hot flightcase with it. Now burning out of control, the crippled machine dropped heavily on to his body, causing a sudden incandescent flare that reached up to lick the edge of the green velour drapes. The fabric quickly caught alight, erupting into a column of fire that spread rapidly, engulfing the entire window area. The heat of the inferno from the machine and the flaming curtains forced Stack to stagger back a few steps.

A gunshot from the other end of the room made him turn. Charlie had fired a wild round at Ramaas as he took off towards the alleyway at the back. It was his only chance to bring the man down. In an urban neighbourhood crammed with housing he was reluctant to risk any more shots.

'Charlie,' Stack shouted, 'Let him go. We've got to get out of here. Grab the kid. Take him with you.' Charlie took Youssef's arm, hooked it over his shoulder and walked him out of the burning room.

The flames were now licking along the ceiling, fanned by the breeze from the broken window. Stack looked for some kind of protection from the heat. He ran back to the rear windows and pulled on the drapes. It didn't take much for the whole lot to come down. Grabbing one of the curtains, he ran back to the raging fire. Black oily smoke was already filling the room. A billowing, toxic cloud that caused Stack to cough violently.

He threw the curtain over his head and tried to approach the flames. Even covered, the heat was formidable. He kept low and eased closer. The jet whine of Topaz's electric motors had long ceased and been replaced by the crackling roar of the flames.

***

Nearby, on Bakers Walk, a horrified, Summer watched Bailey up on the roof of the Toyota as he pulled on the cable. It came away from the mortar shell at the second tug.

Cavanagh, Summer and Bailey instinctively ducked away from the expected explosion. They gave it a few seconds before curiosity compelled Bailey to look up to confirm that the mortar shell in his hands was still intact.

Bailey wiped his forehead with his shirt sleeve. Then he looked over to Summer.

'So, was it zero then bang?' he called down to her.

She glanced down to the smartphone and back up to Bailey.

'We'll never know.' She had attempted cool bravado, but it came across with an anxious smirk. Relief mixed with slowly evaporating terror.

Bailey held the shell carefully as he climbed off the roof.

'This thing has to be taken apart very carefully, under strict anti-radiological conditions, to remove the Plutonium Oxide,' he said as he gingerly carried the mortar bomb over to the Range Rover. 'It's the only way to make the damn thing safe.'

Then came the sirens followed by blue flashing lights, as police cars and vans and two ambulances tore around the corner into Bakers Walk, tyres squealing on the warm asphalt.

They sped past without slowing and skidded into Bakers Yard. The ambulances followed but paused at the junction, waiting for a signal that it was safe to move forward.

'Wait here you two,' Cavanagh said.

'Where are you going?' Summer asked.

'To keep an eye on things. Just stay here until I get back.'

He took off, not waiting for a reply.

In the time between arriving in the Toyota and the disarming of the mortar bomb, Summer had heard the sound of gunfire from somewhere nearby. She knew it was James and Charlie. That they were well trained military specialists didn't make it any easier for her. They weren't bulletproof. They were confronting a bunch of desperate extremists armed with who knows what kind of lethal weaponry. James and Charlie knew what they're doing, she told herself. She needed to hold on to that thought.

Bailey had found a plastic bag in the back of the Range Rover and was placing the mortar shell safely inside it, when he looked up and spotted thickening smoke rising beyond the nearby houses. As he pointed it out to Summer, they could hear the sounds of sirens and claxon-like woops echoing across town a quarter of a mile away and getting closer.

'Sounds like someone has already called the fire brigade,' she said.

Then Summer noticed something on Baily's white shirt.

'What's that? It looks like some kind of brown stain.'

Bailey looked down anxiously. His first instinct was that the mortar shell had leaked the poisonous plutonium oxide. He cautiously touched the stained area with the tip of his fingers, then looked up with relief.

'It's sand!' His hand swept across the paintwork of the vehicle. 'The car is covered in dusty sand.'

***

'Patterson! Give me your hand,' Stack shouted as
he edged closer to the table, his hand reaching
through the thickening smoke for the scientist to
grab. He was hard to see, just a darker shape and
the whites of Patterson's eyes.

'Come on man! We've got to get out of here.'

He edged even closer. Finally, a hand appeared.
Stack grabbed it and pulled hard. It was like
hauling a dead mule out of a ditch. Stack put his
foot against the leg of the table and heaved. The
wooden leg cracked and collapsed, bringing the
table down on Patterson's head and Stack's leg.
Then the effort seemed to ease a little as Patterson
began to take part in his rescue. Maybe he had
started to notice the fierce heat. Stack dragged him
further away from the flames and into the middle
of the room.

They sat together coughing and spitting black
soot from their lungs. Stack looked around.
Through the cloying smoke he could see that, as
well as jetting along the ceiling, the flames were
now creeping along the walls on both sides. Soon
the door would become inaccessible. Convection
was drawing the smoke down, filling the room.
Only a half metre of barely breathable air remained
at floor level. Stack knew they had run out of time.
They had to get out now.

'Topaz! You have to get the machine,' Patterson
shouted.

Topaz! Stack thought. The whole point of the
mission in the first place had been to retrieve that
bloody machine. He looked across towards the
window. The wooden frame was well alight and
blackened pieces of curtain were dropping down on
to Mahmoud whose body was well ablaze. Stack
could do nothing for him. The carcass of the Topaz

laptop had melted and formed a grotesque puddle of plastic on the charred remains of his chest. Lying nearby was the blackened and heat warped hulk of the silver flightcase – the Topaz machine. Whatever it was that could ignite inside the case had turned it into a searing furnace. Soon it would be unrecognisable as anything more than melted aluminium, exotic metals, and glass.

'It's too late. It's gone. There's nothing to save,' Stack shouted across to Patterson above the roar of the flames, his voice rasping from smoke inhalation.

Patterson had stopped resisting. He had at last grasped the reality of their situation. Terror replaced torpor. Stack took his arm and pulled it over his shoulder. Half walking, half crawling, he carried Patterson towards the door and into the hallway.

The passage was already filling with smoke drifting down the staircase in swirling eddies from the burning rooms above. Stack couldn't believe how quickly the fire had taken hold. The last of the evening sun was shining through the glass panels of the front door, sending long smoky beams of light into the hall, like a lighthouse guiding the way to safety.

Heaving Patterson up, Stack shoulder walked him to the front door, turned the latch and stumbled out into the clear evening air.

Charlie was there. At his feet was the badly wounded young gang member. He wasn't alone. Tending him were members of the emergency services.

It was then that Stack noticed the blue flashing lights – and police fire arms officers, weapons up, the business end of a dozen Heckler and Koch G36 machine guns pointing at him.

***

Stack had tucked his Glock into his belt as he helped Patterson out of the house. He didn't need to be told. Using very clear movements, he used his finger and thumb to pull the gun out and away from his body. He lowered it gently to the ground and kicked it towards the armed officers.

He didn't resist as they rushed forward and pulled him to the ground, quickly binding his hands behind his back with plastic ties. They turned him back over and he sat in a squat position on the few square feet of dirt and weeds that passed as a front lawn to the property, the heat of the burning house scorching his back.

Charlie had already been restrained and was being walked over to one of the cars. An officer placed his hand on Charlie's head as he pushed him into the back seat and closed the door.

Two other officers manhandled Stack back on to his feet and were marching him over to another police vehicle, when Cavanagh intervened.

'Check his pockets,' he told the officers.

An officer tried one pocket then another. He pulled the temporary MI6 I.D. out and handed it to his superior. It had been removed from the lanyard, but it had the desired effect.

The superintendent ordered an officer to take the bindings off. As Stack was being freed, he told them about the other two gang members.

'There's one dead in the living room and another on foot somewhere nearby. I think he's wounded.'

The superintendent nodded that he understood.

'OK, the rest of you, check to see who else is running loose around here,' he turned to Cavanagh.

'Do you want to tell me what the hell's going on?'

It hadn't occurred to Cavanagh that the police arriving at the scene wouldn't immediately connect it to the current terrorist threat. Cavanagh took a breath. This wasn't going to be easy to explain.

'Walk with me,' he said to the superintendent.

They were only two or three paces into the conversation, when he heard a familiar voice of someone he knew, fighting their way through the growing crowd of onlookers, behind the line of police vehicles. It had a familiar, belligerent tone, and it was coming his way. The woman had finally reached the line of armed officers and was elbowing her way through, flashing her secret service card and parading her pushy self-importance in her usual irritating way. That's when Cavanagh spotted her.

'Ah, Madeleine,' he said, relief sounding in his voice. 'Just the person. I wonder if you'd care to fill the superintendent in on what's been happening here. Keep it relevant. Don't waste *time*.' He emphasised the word 'time.' They still had their secrets.

Maddy wasn't anywhere close to being up to speed at that point, but she told her version of events in a whispered, conspiratorial voice as she walked the superintendent away from the scene. She wanted him to feel part of her world of secrets. A finger touched knowingly to the nose. A wink of an eye. No questions asked.

Cavanagh turned back to find Stack. He was talking to Charlie, who had also been released from his plastic bindings.

They were standing on the road outside the burning house, when a sudden explosion, as part of the inner structure collapsed, forced them to retreat further back across the street. The fire engines had arrived and were making their way noisily towards them. Police officers pushed people back to allow the vehicles through. Others were moving from one house to the next, making sure all of the neighbours were safely away from the blaze. A couple of police officers had accompanied the wounded extremist, Youssef, as he was stretchered to an ambulance, which was already slowly nosing its way through the chaos of local eyewitnesses, past police vehicles and, at the top of the road, around the news crew trucks that had finally begun to arrive.

Patterson, sitting on the back step of another ambulance, was receiving treatment for smoke inhalation from first responders. His nervous breakdown would take longer to fix.

'OK, Stack,' Cavanagh said, 'what happened?'

Stack gave him the headlines. Charlie butted in occasionally, filling in the missing bits in his usual rambling way. The debrief took ten minutes. It covered almost everything.

'And Topaz?' Cavanagh's final and most urgent question.

'It's in there,' Stack said, nodding his head towards the burning building. 'It doesn't exist anymore. It's just a lump of molten metal.'

'Unrecognisable?'

'Scrap,' Stack said.

Patterson had made his way over by then and caught the last part of their conversation.

'For Christ's sake, don't let anybody near it for the time being, Major Cavanagh.' His voice was hoarse and he broke into a gasping coughing fit.

'Why's that?' Cavanagh asked.

When Patterson had brought his cough under control, he explained breathlessly.

'It may be scrap metal, but in amongst it, is some of the most lethal radioactive material known to man. The isotope at the heart of the machine. You'll need to warn everyone.'

'Jesus, Patterson! I'd forgotten.'

Stack turned to Patterson.

'Just how dangerous is it?'

'Deadly.'

The fire crew had finally got their hoses playing on to the flames, sending gallons of water jetting through the ground floor and upper windows.

Stack offered up a solution to Cavanagh that would deal with the danger quickly, safely and discreetly.

'You'd better warn those firemen not to go in there. Tell them there's specialist explosive material inside – it's safe for the moment, but it must be handled correctly. Tell them your people will deal with it.'

Cavanagh agreed.

'That should work. We have our own specialists.'

'Why am I not surprised?' Stack muttered to himself as the four of them turned to watch the fire crew as they fought to bring the blaze under control.

A moment passed, after which, Cavanagh checked his watch. He breathed a plaintive sigh. There was conclusion and finality in the sound. The unexpected melancholy of a journey that had ended. He turned to Stack and Charlie, his hand out stretched.

'You guys are done. I'll take those MI6 I.Ds.'

'That's a shame...,' Charlie said. He was about to say more when a familiar voice chimed in.

'What, no more playing secret agents, fellas?' Summer teased. She wrapped her arm around James' waist, pulling him towards her. He smiled and leaned in to kiss her. When he looked again, Cavanagh had gone.

'Looks like we've got our lives back,' Stack said.

'Well, let's not hang around waiting for them to change their minds,' Charlie said, already taking the first step through the chaos of police, fire crews and neighbourhood rubberneckers. Stack and Summer followed, heading up towards the top of Bakers Yard.

'There should be plenty of taxis on the High Street. If you get there first, flag one down,' Stack shouted to Charlie, who was now some way ahead of them. He turned to Summer and gave her one of those inquisitive looks only a puzzle can cause.

'I thought you were supposed to stay out of trouble back at the hotel. How did you get here? By taxi?'

'No, I drove,' she said enigmatically. Her smile, like the Mona Lisa, gave nothing away. It amused her to leave it at that. At least for the moment.

'Wait a minute. You drove? How? What car?'

Summer laughed.

'I'll explain later, when we have more time.'

A little way ahead, Hollywood had turned and walked backwards as he called out to them, his voice cheerful. The load lightened.

'OK, but where should I tell him to take us?'

'Who?' Both Stack and Summer shouted back.

'The taxi. Where are we going?'

Stack thought about that for moment. He turned to Summer.

'That's a good question. Where *do* you want to go, Summer?'

She didn't hesitate.

'The airport.'

A final word

The business of playing with time has been covered pretty thoroughly by many other authors and of course, in lots of wonderful films.

My interest in writing this novel came after reading a news story some years ago; the same one I refer to at the beginning of this book. When I first read the original report, which revealed that scientists had found what they believed were faster than light particles, the idea intrigued me. When later, their discovery was found to have been the result of equipment failure; a loose connection (yes, really!), and they had to retract their claim, I was hooked.

This, I thought, had the makings of a conspiracy. It took me quite a while to see how it could be made to work within the parameters of a James Stack novel. My first and most overriding concern was that it shouldn't be a science fiction tale.

I deliberately set out to make the Topaz device extremely limited, working only within the digital domain and within tiny temporal tolerances. It should be merely what the British film director, Alfred Hitchcock, referred to as a McGuffin: "An object or device in a film or book which serves merely as a trigger for the plot". Much more important are the adventures and dangers my protagonists encounter during the mission.

I sincerely hope you enjoyed the ride.

For my family and friends who, throughout the last twenty-three months or so, could always be relied upon to ask me for another *update on the new book*. You all deserve a medal.

A special mention to my friends and readers of the early drafts of the manuscript: Brian Cook, Barrie McKay, Jezz Leckenby and Bob Eastham. Every writer needs a few OCD friends to fussily pick holes in their work. You are all heroes.

I must also thank the many radio DJs and presenters who have been kind enough to invite me onto their shows to regale their listeners with tales about my former life as a DJ on Radio Luxembourg and of course, to talk about my novels. Thank you all so much.

Finally, I should mention a songstress that accompanied me throughout much of the writing. I am grateful for the cool jazz and mezzo-soprano voice of Stacey Kent. Nothing could provide a better counter-point while writing a scene of sudden violence than, 'Never Let Me Go'. To me, she is the voice of Summer Peterson. You should check her out.

ABOUT THE AUTHOR

After a lengthy broadcasting career, which included many happy years as a DJ on Radio Luxembourg, Mark Wesley enjoyed critical acclaim as a song writer and record producer.

Jingle composition and copy-writing for radio commercials followed, but his early love of film led him to launch the production company Mark Wesley Productions.

His first novel, BANGK! remains hugely popular, and was followed by FRACK! A tale of sabotage and greed. Like 'DEAD CITY EXIT', both feature his protagonist and allies; James Stack, Charlie 'Hollywood' Dawson and the beautiful Canadian, Summer Peterson.

Mark is married with two children and two grandchildren. He lives in the rolling countryside of north west Essex.

Printed in Great
Britain
by Amazon